The Ascension

The Lazarus Chronicles

The Awakened, Book One
The Ascension, Book Two

The Ascension
The Lazarus Chronicles
Book Two

By Richard Spillman

The Ascension
Published by Mountain Brook Ink
White Salmon, WA U.S.A.

The website addresses shown in this book are not intended in any way to be or imply an endorsement on the part of Mountain Brook Ink, nor do we vouch for their content.

This story is a work of fiction. All characters and events are the product of the author's imagination. Any resemblance to any person, living or dead, is coincidental.

The author is represented by and this book is published in association with Jim Hart of the Hartline Literary Agency, LLC. www.hartlineagency.com

Scripture quotations taken from the New King James Version®. © 1982 by Thomas Nelson. Used by permission. All rights reserved.

ISBN 978-1-943959-67-9
© 2019 Richard Spillman

The Team: Miralee Ferrell, Nikki Wright, Cindy Jackson
Cover Design: Indie Cover Design, Lynnette Bonner Designer

Mountain Brook Ink is an inspirational publisher offering fiction you can believe in.
Printed in the United States of America

To the Reader

This novel is a work of fiction. Names, characters, places, and incidents are either products of the author's imagination or used fictitiously. All characters are fictional, and any similarity to people living or dead is purely coincidental. In no way is the author claiming that Lazarus is still alive nor is he trying to rewrite Biblical history. His references to what Jesus told Lazarus are fictional and intended to create a 'what if' type question, correlating with the story premise as it is laid out. This is simply the author's take on what "might have been."

"And as it is appointed for men to die once…"
Hebrews 9:27

Dedication

Dedicated to my loving and supportive family. My wife, Bonnie, who, without her advice, suggestions, counsel and support this book would never have seen the light of day. My daughters, Annie and Kimberly, my son-in-law, Christian, my grandchildren Trevor, Hayden, Lilly, Rosie and Jacob who encouraged me every step of the way with their love.

Acknowledgments

No book is written by one person. This is certainly true for *The Ascension*. I had a lot of help during this process, and I want to thank everyone who played a role in getting this finished. Specifically I want to thank Mountain Brook Ink for taking me on in the first place. Miralee Ferrell, MBI's publisher, and Nikki Wright, MBI's marketing director and publicist, deserve a big thank you not only for all the work they put into helping me write this but also for the compassion and care they gave me not as an author but as a person as I struggled through some very dark and painful days while writing. I also want to thank the other MBI authors who were always there to pray for me and encourage me. MBI is far more than a publishing house, it really is a family, and I am so blessed to have been "adopted" into this family.

I also want to thank Jim Hart, my agent, for his continued support. He was the first to believe in me and he was there with encouragement when I needed it. Finally, I must thank Julee Schwarzburg who, once again, did a fantastic job on the initial edits and went far beyond the call of duty to help me through those difficult times when I felt so oppressed that I wanted to give it all up. She continues to amaze me with both her skill as an editor and her heart as a human being.

Chapter One

WE AWAKENS CALL THE DEMON-POSSESSED, REANIMATED creatures UDs or the UnDead. Some UDs even like it because the title contains the word *dead*. But UDs officially call themselves UVs, UnVeilers, because they view their job as unveiling the evil within mankind. It is the task of the Awakens to destroy UDs and bring out the image of God in mankind. —Awakened Incident Manual (AIM), Volume 2, Page 7

One-hundred years ago...April 2, 1918, Northern France

Lance Corporal Elliott Allen sat crouched in a muddy trench, huddled up against his Lee-Enfield rifle, shivering in the cold light rain. His stomach growled. His last meal, a single can of Maconochie, had been more than sixteen hours earlier, and that watery stew of turnips and carrots didn't fill him up much. He removed his helmet for a moment to scratch his lice-infested head and struggled to keep his eyes open as he waited for the order to climb out of the trench and attack.

He stared into his helmet at the faded, scratched photo of his wife, sitting on the beach, her bare feet buried in the sand. For a moment he was able to focus on her lovely face and leave this canyon of mud behind, her smile a reminder of better days. Her best feature was her eyes, eyes that sparkled with a bright...a bright... The color of her eyes suddenly eluded him. His chin trembled.

Why can't I remember the color of Anna's eyes? What's wrong with me? He stared at the black-and-white picture, searching for some sign of color.

His second lieutenant signaled the attack. Elliott's body shuddered as if coming out of a trance. He donned his helmet. No longer afraid, he had long ago become numb to the thought of his own death in this land cursed by God.

Elliott turned to the other eleven men in his section. "Lads, it's time to hop over the bags. Let's get those Huns."

A low roar made its way down the trench as men stood, some for the last time. Elliott knew what lay ahead. A larger force dug in and armed with MG 08 machine guns. He led the way up the ladder. Keeping his head down, he waved his men up and over the sandbags that lined the trench. As the last man came over the bag, Elliott glanced at the battlefield ahead to map out his path, but a thin covering of fog blanketed the area. Barren and desolate—a sea of mud, barbed wire, and populated by the occasional body, he could make out the shadowy figures of men as they crept toward the Huns. All color had drained from this world, and like the picture in his helmet, everything was shades of gray. No one lived here; they only died here. Died by the thousands.

If only I could remember the color of Anna's eyes.

Crouched over, Elliott wove his way around burned-out stumps and red-tinted, water-filled craters trying to find his footing in the ankle-deep mud. He passed the rotting carcass of a horse, its large, black vacant eye staring up at him.

The place smelled of decaying flesh and cordite, yet it was strangely quiet. A white butterfly perched on a burned-out stump briefly caught his attention, it's delicate beauty totally out of place in this desert of death.

He glanced behind to see his men making their way toward the enemy's trenches. His focus returned to the path ahead. He took a deep breath sucking in air heavy with the thick burning residue of war. He coughed. His eyes watered. He rubbed them.

At that moment Lance Corporal Elliott Allen froze. Now he knew why it was quiet. A dirty yellow cloud drifted toward his lines like a fog bank rolling in from the sea. It was HS, Hun Stuff. Mustard gas.

He reached for his gas mask. Gone. In a sudden panic he patted himself down. Nothing. A tremor raced through his body. It must have fallen off when he crawled out of the trench.

He turned to run back to get it but slipped and dropped face down in the mud. He struggled to get up, but before he could stand, he was engulfed by the toxic cloud. He tried not to breathe it in. His face flamed as if he had been dipped in fire.

He couldn't hold his breath any longer. His blazing lungs forced him to gulp in air. It tasted sweet but his throat burned. His eyes watered, and he turned his head to vomit in the mud.

His men's screams sliced through to his very soul. He cried out to God. The gas was too thick to see anything…until…a dark form walked, almost glided, toward him like a black phantom against the yellow wall of gas.

His arm shook as he raised his hand. *God, thank you for rescuing me.*

When the form got closer, he saw it was a man without a gas mask but seemingly unaffected by the poisonous cloud that surrounded them.

Elliott tried to focus on the man through stinging eyes. He struggled to his knees and raised both hands. "Help…me."

The phantom stood over Elliott and smirked. "I'm not here to help you." The phantom leaned down and glared at Elliott. A chill rolled down Elliott's spine. The creature's eyes were dark, like shiny black pearls. It shook its head and spoke with a deeper, hollow sounding voice. "Your God will not help you either. If He had any sense, He would wipe all of you off the face of the earth like He almost did in the time of Noah."

It looked up and scanned the battlefield. "Maybe He doesn't have to. You seem to be doing a fine job on your own."

Elliott could no longer see. He rubbed his eyes, a scream building in his throat, begging to be released.

The phantom took a deep breath. "Ah, mustard gas…it has kind of a sweet taste to it, don't you think?"

As he heard it walk away, he dropped his head back into the mud. He knew who the phantom was. He'd heard stories from men who had taken days to die from the vile gas. Stories of a "yellow devil" who prowled around in the poisonous fog.

Elliott threw up again as the phantom stopped. "By the way, your wife's eye color is green. She'll be oh so saddened to know you forgot that." With a sardonic smile it turned and left.

Someone with a gas mask found him and pulled him back into the trench. He was evacuated to a field hospital behind the lines. A week later he died, but not before he whispered the story of his strange encounter to a thin man with a slight middle eastern accent who seemed to believe him.

Awakened Incident Manual (AIM) Report #1120. The Dusting of Aharon, the self-proclaimed exalted one, entered by Lazarus, A.D. 1918

Having confirmed from Lance Corporal Allen before he died that an UnDead, a UD, was stalking the battlefields around Somme in the gas clouds, I determined to hunt him down and dust him.

I couldn't pass up any opportunity to take out a UD, even if it meant I would have to search the battlefield it seemed to inhabit. Having already died, I hate looking at so much death. I waited near the front lines until a report came through of another gas attack.

My eyes burned to the point of anguish, but my Awakened body fought off the deadly effects of the mustard gas. The real pain came from the realization that Naturals could commit this atrocity on each other. As thick as the gas was, it couldn't cover the stench of death, of lost dreams, of abandoned humanity that permeated this place.

I must have wandered the field for over an hour when I first caught sight of it. The UD was standing over a fallen soldier much like Corporal Allen had described. As I approached, the UD looked up and sneered at me.

This was no ordinary UD.

"Ah, Lazarus, boker tov. I wondered when our paths would cross." It scanned the battlefield, dark delight dancing across its face. "Don't you love what mankind has accomplished here?"

It knew my name. "Who are you?"

"That's a good question. I go by so many names." It stroked its chin, a smirk riding its lips. "But you can call me Aharon." It stared me straight in the eye, something no UD had ever been able to do. Dressed in a black suit, complete with a black shirt and gray bow tie, it seemed out of place yet at home in this wilderness of death.

Its dark, venomous eyes sickened me. I had to turn away. I glanced at the soldier lying at Aharon's feet. He was breathing so I sat down in the mud and rested the dying soldier's head on my lap. Watching a Natural die ripped at my heart.

Aharon looked down with a snort. "How touching. You do know that this man has killed." I ignored him, having learned long ago that you do not argue with evil.

"I suppose you've come to dust me." It shrugged. "I'm tired of this decaying body anyway, so let me save you the trouble." It swung its arms out wide in a broad gesture, as if preparing to hug the desolation. "Look around you. This field alone is full of fresh real estate for me to inhabit, and more will become available tomorrow. By seeking out a new home, I'll be sharing my blessing with the newly dead."

I looked up, silent, struggling to maintain some semblance of eye contact. *Who is this creature? Could it be a new breed of the UnDead?*

"When we cross paths again, I will be in a form you cannot touch." It paused as its smile grew wider. "Our meeting like this today is oh, so significant." It nodded. "I'm sure you think it's something that *carpenter* arranged. You give Him too much power." It spat on the ground, then suddenly dissolved into dust without contact from me.

I sucked in a deep breath, something that was quite painful in the gas-filled air.

Somehow Aharon had dusted itself.

In almost two thousand years of hunting UDs, I'd never

encountered one like this. Certainly the most enigmatic Level 1 UD I've ever dealt with. Could it have been *The UD*? If so, why did it dust itself?

I stepped forward to collect the reddish-brown dust when someone behind me said, "Don't."

I turned and saw the two men I had first seen thousands of years ago in the plaza where Jesus was beaten. Since then the Gatherers have reappeared many times, often to help the Awakened, especially new ones. Over the centuries they have been assigned various names, in part because they never stopped long enough to introduce themselves. I believe the current names were Holmes and Watson. Both were thin but very muscular. Both were dark skinned as if they had spent all their lives on the desert. Holmes was the taller of the two by a good six inches. Watson had light brown hair while Holmes had brilliant red hair.

"We will take that dust." It was Watson who spoke up.

"Why?"

They only smiled. They never were big talkers. I walked away leaving the dust to them.

Chapter Two

ONE OF OUR ROLES IN THIS world is to be a source of peace. This can only be achieved by guiding Naturals to follow the desires of their heart that are from their spirit rather than their flesh. — Awakened Incident Manual (AIM), Volume 2, Page 7

August 29, present day, 10:34 am, Secret place in Korea

Somewhere near the border shared by South Korea and North Korea, Renaud Christian Yount entered the conference room first as had been agreed upon by the parties in the negotiations. He took his place at the head of the large oak-stained table that filled the center of the rectangular room. It had no windows—perfect for such a secret meeting. An over-sized map of Korea adorned the wall behind Renaud. The wall to his right had the South Korean flag, to his left the North Korean flag.

From the doors on either side, the South Korean delegation and the North Korean delegation marched in and took their seats beside Renaud, to the right and to the left respectively, though the North Korean delegation delayed their entrance by a second or two.

Renaud glanced at both parties. "Messieurs, now that the ground rules for this negotiation have been set, it's time to—"

"Except the North has already violated the agreement." The South Korean leader interrupted. "They delayed their entrance so they could sit last, not simultaneously as we had agreed."

The North Korean leader's nostrils flared in a scowl. "Perhaps you entered too fast."

Renaud was careful to maintain a serious expression, instead of the laugh fighting to burst out. He loved to see such silly, selfish squabbling among humans. It spoke a lot about the image of God they were supposed to carry. But he had to successfully conclude these negotiations by October 10.

He held up his hands. "Messieurs, this is not the way to start these historic proceedings. I have duly noted the complaint and will see to it that the agreement will be strictly adhered to next time." Renaud leaned back in his chair. *Des imbeciles.*

So it begins. No one thought this could be done. That's why the foreign minister handed the hopeless task to him. *But it will happen. I will see to it. No one knows the ace I have.* Warmth radiated throughout his body.

This would end in a way no one expected.

September 1, 1:15 pm, Hidden Location in Lebanon

Miraj Barak Qudir ran a quaint little antiquities shop in Syria, which brought in millions to ISIS by selling stolen goods on the black market. He worked hard to project a grandfatherly image. His wide-set bright eyes, thin, silvery beard framing his round face, and inviting smile all served to reinforce it. But it was a look that belied his lethal nature. People around him had a habit of dying, especially if they crossed him in any way.

Today he sat at a table in a small, moldy-smelling room in a little-used ISIS safe house. He tried to relax but to no avail.

When would that North Korean Seong-Jin get here?

A lightness radiated in his chest as his pulse raced. He got up from the table and paced the room, stirring up dust with each footstep. When Seong-Jin did arrive, Miraj would complete the deal for a weapon of mass destruction that would cause the world to fear ISIS.

Jalal Bashir entered the room. He was young but skilled beyond his age. He had quickly risen in the ISIS ranks to become Miraj's heir apparent.

Miraj stopped pacing and stared out a grimy window. "What time is it?"

Jalal glanced at his watch. "It's only 1:18. We don't expect him until 1:30. Why don't you sit back down? It won't be long now."

He raised his hand to stroke the slightly raised, dagger-shaped birthmark on his right cheek.

Miraj turned. He watched Jalal rub his distinctive birthmark. It was Jalal's tell. *So, he's not as confident as he makes out.* Miraj knew the history of that birthmark. He used what he knew to manipulate Jalal when necessary. He'd watched him grow up. He'd seen the ridicule Jalal had endured as a child. He sensed the heartache it caused. Miraj exploited that mark along with the emotional stress it caused to shape Jalal into the ruthless killer he was today. Now Jalal wore it with a certain amount of pride because it symbolized his favorite method of killing.

Miraj used his index finger to wipe a line of dirt off the window. He rubbed the grime between his thumb and forefinger. "You know, in this dark, dank place the fate of Israel will be sealed. What Islam has been trying to do for centuries, what Nazi Germany couldn't do, I will accomplish. By the time I'm done, there will not be a Jew left alive on this earth."

He walked back to the table, sat down, and opened the suitcase to once again examine its contents. He thought of his brother who was killed by Israeli soldiers during a raid in Palestine twelve years ago. *This will buy your revenge, Faheem.*

Miraj ran his hand across the stacked bills. "Two and half million US dollars is not much, though I could buy a nuclear weapon for that price." He leaned back and stroked his beard. "When I took this post, that was the expectation—that I would find a bomb for ISIS to use. But that is far too shortsighted. A nuclear weapon can only be used once. When we acquire this weapon and unleash it, it will spread on its own. Everyone in its path will die, but I'm only interested in the Jews it will kill. The other deaths are collateral damage and of no interest to me. What excites me is that one infected Jew will pass it on to several Jews. It will spread death exponentially. But..." he scowled at Jalal. "News of our plan is already beginning to filter down the ranks, generating too many rumors."

Someone tapped on the door. Jalal raised a muscular arm to

look at his watch. "It's only 1:25. He's early."

Miraj pursed his lips. "That's a good sign. The deal must be important to him as well. Let him in."

As Seong-Jin entered, Miraj rose to shake his hand. Seong-Jin was a short man with an oval face and sharp cheekbones. He had a short military haircut that complemented his assured military bearing.

"Please, sit down." Miraj motioned to the chair opposite him.

Seong-Jin focused on the suitcase as he sat. "I assume that is the down payment."

"Yes…yes, it is. What is the progress on the weapon?"

Seong-Jin reached out to take hold of the suitcase. Jalal grabbed his wrist. "Not yet." Seong-Jin winced as Jalal squeezed. "Answer the question."

Seong-Jin pulled away. With a playful grin at Jalal, he said, "All right." He faced Miraj. "It's good news. Our doctors are sure they have a usable strain. They have one or two more tests to conduct. Our Great Leader has assured me it will be shipped in time to arrive by October 9 as we agreed."

Miraj twisted a ring on his finger. "Good news…very good news. We need to stick to that schedule because it is getting more difficult to keep Operation Blood Red quiet. Certain high-ranking members of ISIS are showing too much excitement."

Seong-Jin grabbed the suitcase as he stood. He gave a small nod to Miraj. "Then our business today is complete. We will expect the remaining twenty million dollars when we hand you the vials. It is important to our country that you launch it on October 10."

Miraj, still twisting his ring, nodded back. "We are also committed to that date. On October 10 Israel will be no more."

Seong-Jin's face grew into a malevolent smile much like the Cheshire cat. "The world will change on that day in more ways than you can imagine."

Chapter Three

LIFE LIES ON BOTH SIDES OF death, but death contains two doors: one leading to the fragrance of eternal joy, the other to the stench of eternal loneliness. —Awakened Incident Manual (AIM), Volume 2, Page 4

September 5, 4:12 p.m., Paris

Renaud.

It's a name that had troubled Lazarus, or L, as he liked to be called, ever since the dusting of Abdul Ba'ith in Cairo almost five months ago. A name that first appeared on a UD message to a terrorist leader.

Renaud.

Who was he? Where was he? What was he? Most importantly, was he The UD, the prophesied leader of the UnDead and, as a result, untouchable?

L shook his head.

If so, he may very well be the source of the darkness I've seen coming.

Renaud.

The name sat in his mind as if it had been branded into his brain.

One thing was certain, he was more than just a name on the bottom of an encrypted telegram. It was a name that had sent L to Paris on his first UD hunt since…well, since Berlin in 1938. It hadn't been profitable. Blind UD hunts rarely were. But he had to come. Had to at least try something. To have a UD rise to such a pinnacle of power undetected was…well it was a failure of his leadership within, the Society of the Awakened and Restored, the organization that L had led for centuries.

The message that had introduced the name Renaud had originated in Paris. So L roamed the streets looking for a UD, any UD. Chavvah Shain, the UD prophet, second only to The UD, was here, though no Awakened had ever seen her. It made sense that if this Renaud was The UD leader, the leader that was prophesied to appear at the end times, as L suspected, he would be where she was.

Now he found himself strolling along the Seine near the Ministry of Foreign Affairs. The river's peaceful flow allowed his mind to drift with the water. The unusually warm September sun reflected off the rippling current. He took a deep breath as he passed vacationers taking pictures and Paris natives enjoying the day. The air had the distant smell of baking baguettes and croissants as well as the faint odor of burnt paper that always reminded L of Paris.

As he watched the boats float by, a chill spidered up his spine as the hairs on the back of his neck bristled. He turned and scanned the area. Across the street and through the traffic, he caught a glimpse of a short man with a cane staring at him. The man wore an expensive gray silk suit with a brilliant white shirt and light-blue tie, clearly a high-level government official or a successful businessman. Nothing about the man seemed out of place.

That was, until the man flashed a sly smile, then turned and strolled away from the Ministry building. Something about the man was unsettling but at the same time familiar, especially that smile. He had seen it before, but where?

L watched the man until he faded into the crowd. He shook his head as a tenseness coiled in his stomach. Could he be…? Still, the man was clearly a Natural, not a UD.

September 5, 4:17 p.m., Paris

Lazarus is in Paris. Renaud glanced back as he walked away. Lazarus was staring at him with a puzzled look. Lazarus must be looking for him. *It's begun.* For now, let him stew on what he saw or thought he saw in Paris. The encounter had made his day.

The last time Renaud had seen him was... He guessed it was in France a long time ago, in that beautiful gas cloud. *I miss that war, but another, even larger one, will break out soon.* The look of confusion on Lazarus's face validated all of his planning. *Lazarus never expected that I would return as a Natural.*

Renaud picked up the pace, his cane clicking on the sidewalk in a rhythmic, playful motion. The thought of all the death that was coming energized him.

Half an hour later, he walked into Chavvah's office. "I have to give you credit. He's here exactly as you predicted."

She looked up from the desk. A cocky smirk formed on her face. "I told you I would get stronger. Did he see you? Did he recognize you?"

"He saw me for a moment. I must admit he did appear puzzled. I could tell it was driving him crazy, but no, he didn't recognize me. As I suspected that short sighted Awakened never imagined that I would arrive as a Natural." His eyes glowed as he looked up at the bright blue sky shining through Chavvah's skylight. "Did you get that, God?" He shook his fist in the air. "Your errand boy dropped the ball. I can manipulate him as easily as any Natural."

"You should be careful. He may presume your identity."

Renaud shrugged. "It won't be long before it's obvious to him. Which brings me to the real reason I stopped by. How are things going in North Korea?"

"Good news and bad news, I am afraid. The *une bonne nouvelle* is that Sok Kang Ju has reported that the virus is nearly ready, and it will exceed our expectations."

"And the bad news?" Renaud clenched his jaw.

"Ah, the *de mauvaises nouvelles*... It seems Sok Kang Ju no longer wants to sell the weapon to ISIS first. Instead, he wants to use it on South Korea, then sell it to ISIS."

Renaud's nostrils flared, his right hand squeezing into a tight fist. "That pompous, egotistical piece of real estate. He's beginning to believe his own press. He got them to worship him like a god.

Look at what that idiot calls himself: Eternal General Secretary of the Party, Father of the Nation. He even calls himself the savior.

"No one questions my orders, ever. Using that on South Korea would destroy my plans. It would wreck everything. You tell him..." He stopped. A slow smile drifted across his face as he loosened his fist. "Wait. I may be able to turn this around in my favor."

He sat on a padded leather, russet-colored armchair and rubbed his cheek. "He's decaying real estate anyway. It's time we condemn the property and tear it down." He nodded as he grinned. "Of course, I can't be seen doing it."

Renaud stared up at the late-afternoon sun shining through the skylight. After a short pause, he pointed at Chavvah. "Tell Kang Ju he can use it on South Korea, but only after he turns some over to ISIS. They will strike first on October 10. Then Kang Ju is free to use it on South Korea as early as October 11. Sign the message with my name. Then send it in a cipher that's strong but one the Awakens can break—like the one we sent to Abdul Ba'ith." He glared at Chavvah. "The one they were able to break because you had Monsieur Kruger, that mousie little codebreaker killed and then he woke up." His mouth curled in sadistic pleasure at Chavvah's cringe. "Might as well get some mileage out of your screwup."

"But then won't Lazarus learn about the virus?"

"Yes, but too late to stop it from being shipped to ISIS. Lazarus will only be able to stop it from being used on South Korea by dusting Kang Ju."

Chavvah had been quiet during his tirade. "I will do that but what, if I may ask, are you planning?"

"Kang Ju's son, Sok Park Kye, is a newer UnVeiled and more under our control. Once Kang Ju is out of the way and Park Kye takes over, I will play a larger, more secure role in North Korea, which is vital for the first stage of my ascension."

"You speak of your ascension like you know how it will be achieved, events in Korea may be the first stage but I have not yet seen the final stage."

"Oh, but I'm beginning to get a glimpse. Do not worry. I'm confident it will all start on October 10, and that will be the beginning of the end of mankind."

And what a majestic tsunami of death that would be. Renaud laughed. *Oh, Lazarus, if you only knew how I'm going to play you.*

Chapter Four

WE ARE HERE TO TEACH NATURALS how to live like Jesus, how to do what Jesus did, how to declare that the limitations of the natural world do not apply to them. We show them how to live in the supernatural and truly believe in the most literal sense that nothing, absolutely nothing is impossible with God. —Awakened Incident Manual (AIM), Volume 2, Page 37

September 6, 9:30 a.m., Tel Aviv

Declan Walsh sat in his spartan office in the US Embassy in Tel Aviv. By its nearly empty bookshelf, clear but dusty desktop, and a computer that was rarely even turned on, it was obvious this was not his favorite place to be. He was and always had been a field man. Besides, he couldn't smoke in his own office, though sometimes he'd sneak a cig.

Today he was reading the summary report he'd received from Langley of the blood sample taken from the bullet he'd retrieved in Cairo after Abdul Ba'ith was killed. Somehow, given the events of five months ago, the startling nature of the report didn't surprise him.

Report on Sample 211

The DNA was of a human female, but the other findings suggest an error in our equipment. It appeared to differ from standard human DNA by 2 percent, ten times the typical variation. In addition, all the bonds appeared to be stable, without any sequence errors. Suspecting our lab equipment was at fault, we shut down the lab, tested, and recalibrated all our equipment. Since our testing destroyed the sample, we need an additional sample in order to provide a new, more reliable analysis.

A handwritten note was attached to the bottom of the report.

THE ASCENSION | 17

Declan, where did you get that sample? I was sure there was a mistake in our equipment, but the recalibration tests indicated everything was operating well within standards. It was flat-out perfect DNA, like something out of the Garden of Eden. Where did it come from? Was it the result of some secret Russian experiment that went wrong, or something out of Area 51? Seriously, where did you run across it?

Roger

Declan's hand shook as he set the report down on the desk. He'd talked to a dead man who later dissolved into dust when hit by a bullet that contained perfect DNA. That about summed it up, so what was going on here?

He turned to stare out his window at the embassy courtyard three stories below. He had to light up. Forget the rules. He had to blow a few perfect smoke rings to clear his mind of the bitter taste of…of what? The absurdity? The impossibility of recent events?

His friend Roger's reference to the Garden of Eden also unnerved him. It brought back memories of his childhood. Declan's mother had always called him Dec in private, but one Sunday as she dropped him off for Sunday school, the kids heard his nickname. From that time on, all the kids in church called him Dec the Wreck. It caught on and spread throughout the school. He no longer cared much for "church people."

Then he was assigned a partner who was a committed believer. She never pushed him, but she did acknowledge God. Ten years ago, she was tortured and killed. Where was her God then?

And though he might believe in God, He was impersonal to Declan. At best He was an elusive, uncaring God. At worst, He didn't exist at all. Besides, how could Declan believe in a loving God after all the hate and death he had seen in his years serving in the Middle East?

There had to be some explanation other than the supernatural for Abdul Ba'ith, for the events in Cairo, for the perfect DNA.

Otherwise, Declan would be trapped in a real-life episode of *The X-Files*. He blew a couple of smoke rings to calm his mind as he leaned back in his office chair.

The truth, as puzzling as it might be, was out there, and it lay with the woman who collected the red dust in Cairo. He was sure he'd seen her before. She had something to do with Israel's intelligence agency.

He would start poking around Mossad to find her. She'd better have answers. He would not stop until this all made some kind of sense.

Declan sat up in his office chair and blew another perfect smoke ring. This is a nasty habit. *I'll have to stop before it kills me...but not today.*

September 8, 7:43 a.m., Seattle

L was in his office after flying in from Paris with a short stop in Washington, DC, to pick up Ricki. She had spent the last week with Odette. On his way to his desk he stopped to stare at the Space Needle. He rubbed the back of his neck in a slow circular motion. Once at his desk he leaned back in his chair and stared at the ceiling. *What a waste of a week. No Renaud and an uncomfortable return flight with Ricki.* He had pretended to be asleep for most of the flight.

He closed his eyes and thought about how their paths had crossed a short five months ago and how much his life had changed since then. Her entrance into his world was... He leaned back in his seat...*it was...I guess the best way to describe it is...convoluted...so much so that it could only be an act of Providence.*

How else could anyone characterize her sudden appearance at this crucial time in history? In five months, she went from being just another Natural to someone at the center of world events holding the key to a 2000-year-old secret.

L took a deep breath. *Not only that. She also pried open a crack in*

my heart allowing a thin beam of light into that dusty, closed off place.
He brushed off a solitary tear rolling down his right cheek.

I have centuries of experience working with Naturals, studing the subtle clues to what is going on in their mind. He took another deep breath. *I usually can read a Natural so why can't I read her? I have no idea what's going through her mind. Yet she seems to understand me. She saw how lost I felt when we talked in Washington D.C. sitting in front of Treebeard. Her pep talk during the critical moments of bringing down Abdul Ba'ith gave me the strength to make the right decision.* He shook his head. *Still she's a mystery to me. Why did Jesus choose her to discover the secret in my journal? Why am I more concerned over my uncomfortable feelings about her on the flight home then I am in not finding Renaud?*

L opened his eyes and resumed staring at the ceiling for a moment. Then he sat up and unlocked the drawer in his desk. He reached in and pulled out the drawing of a woman. "It's been 2000 years, but I still love you as much as I did on the first day I saw you. And I see so much of you in Ricki. Do I have your blessing to get closer to her?" L paused listening to the faint sound of air circulating in his office. Nothing. He frowned as he put the picture back in the drawer and locked it.

L wasn't sure how long he had been staring at the ceiling when his assistant burst into the room with a handful of files. It was Matthew, L's right hand man. At 363 years old he was much younger than L, but they both looked like they were in their early 30's as Awakens never age past that point. "Boss, I'm so glad you're back. There's a problem. I guess you could call it fallout from the Abdul Ba'ith dusting."

"Just what I want to hear after the Paris flop."

"Paris was a long shot." Matthew plopped the files down on L's desk. "Blind hunts are always problematic. You win a few but you lose a lot. Besides, 'Success consists of going from failure to failure without loss of enthusiasm.'"

L smiled. "I actually met Winston Churchill once. It's a great story. Remind me to tell you about it sometime. And I haven't lost my enthusiasm. I'm not giving up."

"Good for you, and I do want to hear that story. Look, there's a CIA officer stationed in Tel Aviv who's asking around Mossad about a female agent."

"So?"

"The description he's giving appears to be Shiri and here's the kicker—he's asking about Cairo five months ago."

L was silent for a moment. He began to gently rock in his office chair. As quickly as it started the rocking stopped. He leaned out over his desk letting out a slow but thoughtful sigh. "I'm not surprised that Shiri is involved in some way. Ever since she woke up on the day Jesus died she has managed to find her way to the center of what ever was happening." L shook his head as a subdued smile inched its way across his face. "Shiri, Shiri, Shiri, what am I going to do with you?"

Matthew held up his right hand. "Hold on a moment. This isn't her fault."

"Of course not, it never is...you know...you know she was the first to dust a UD?"

Matthew nodded. "I've read your journal, remember ...more than once, I might add."

L rewarded Matthew with a growing smile. "I can still see that moment in my mind running in slow motion. It was our first encounter with a UD and neither of us knew what we were doing. I remember the shocked look on her face when that thing grabbed her. I can see the wheels turning in her head as she realized that she had become a hostage. Then it happened. She bit that thing! Took a big hunk right out of its arm and then it was gone in a puff of reddish brown dust and everything changed." L shook his head as he drew in a deep breath. "She was a dragon then, she's a dragon now and I can't think of a better agent to get into the middle of this whole Abdul Ba'ith thing than her. L paused for a moment then looked Matthew straight in his eyes. "So do we know this guy?"

"We do now. Declan Walsh. I checked up on him. It turns out

he's considered somewhat of a rogue over there, but he gets results so they give him a lot of leeway to operate. He has a reputation for being determined and unrelenting when he thinks he's on to something, and I guess he thinks he's on to something here."

"Do you think he might be a UD?" L asked.

"Don't know for sure, but what UD would hunt an Awakened?"

"Perhaps you've noticed, UDs have been doing strange things lately. Besides, if he *is* a UD, he may not know Shiri is an Awakened. Anyway, he's in for a big surprise if and when he finds her. Shiri can handle it herself. Warn her and tell her to take any action she deems necessary and keep us informed."

"Will do, Boss, I'll get right on it."

As Matthew rushed out of the office, L checked his watch. A little after eight in the morning Seattle time. *With Paris nine hours ahead of Seattle, my body thinks it's already five in the afternoon. I guess I'll be tried earlier than normal, but it will not be as bad as when I lost those nine hours flying east.*

He turned to look at the Seattle skyline. He found it relaxing, especially on a warm morning like this. His thoughts drifted to Paris a few days ago. The image of the strange little man with a cane along the banks of the Seine who stopped to stare at him haunted him like a song stuck in his head. What about him was so familiar? He seemed to know L. Who was he?

Chapter Five

TRUTH IS TRUTH, RIGID AND UNADAPTABLE. The attraction of lies is that they can be molded to satisfy the darkest of hearts. — *Awakened Incident Manual, Volume 2, Page 17*

September 12, 4:07 a.m., North Korea

Yong Joon had lived in Camp 14 for twenty-five years, ever since his family had been arrested for hiding a Bible in their home. They were lucky not to have been executed, though some would say otherwise.

This morning, like every morning since his arrest, he was on his way to the fields to do whatever the guards told him to do. For the last couple of years, he'd been plowing, planting, and harvesting wheat. It was hard work especially for something he would never get to eat. The prisoners were fed a gruel of corn and cabbage in portions barely enough to sustain life. Joon, like every prisoner that survived longer than a year, supplemented his diet by eating bugs and rats.

Joon was twelve when he was arrested. Life, for him, kind of dragged on. He missed his friends, but he made new ones. He was hungry all the time, but that was not much different than life before the arrest. He kind of missed the Bible that had gotten them into trouble, but now he understood why his parents had insisted he memorize parts of it. They started with Psalms when he was only six. By twelve he could recite almost all the Psalms from memory. They were a comfort in his new dark world.

His work group was made up of twelve prisoners marching in two columns of six. He recognized the man on his left but didn't know his name. Names were not useful because talking was not allowed within a work group, a rule that was difficult for Joon to follow. Besides, once you got used to someone's name, they would disappear.

Nevertheless, Joon liked to make up names for prisoners he worked with. Names that reflected something about the person. He studied the man to his left and noticed that he was favoring his right arm letting it hang down and not move as they walked. He tried to hide it but Joon saw it. He hoped a guard didn't or only eleven men may return this evening. He thought for a moment then decided to call him Apeun Pal, Korean for sore arm. Along with the name, Joon made up a story about him.

Apeun Pal was thirty years old. He was arrested because he was smuggling contraband from China...no, he was arrested because he was a spy for the Americans. He was planning an escape with the help of the CIA. He injured his arm last night when he killed a guard and hid the body. Joon smiled. He liked Apeun Pal.

As they got close to the main gate, Joon looked ahead. Two guards were waiting there. Joon could feel the blood drain out of his face as his shoulders tensed. It was the two most merciless guards—Bong Jun-Ho and Woojin Gunwoo.

Woojin Gunwoo was skinny with a short haircut and narrow face. He appeared to be a five and a half kg weakling, but anyone who assumed that was in for trouble. He was the camp sadist. He lived for fear, for pain, for death, for torture. They were like food for his soul and the camp was his buffet table. He held the record among the guards for the most kills. Joon had watched him kill. While torturing some poor victim his eyes would sparkle, he would hum, tell jokes, laugh. When it came time to kill the victim, he would get serious and inventive. The rumor around the camp was that he never killed in the same way twice. That wasn't quite true because Joon had seen him using the same method multiple times. Still he could be quite creative. In spite of all that, Joon feared his partner, Bong Jun-Ho the most.

Bong Jun-Ho was short and stocky with long dark hair. His arms and legs were thick with muscle. Overall, he looked like a Korean that time had forgotten. In other words, he had an ancient Korean look, a warrior built for hand to hand combat. He was strong and menacing. But the most unsettling thing were his eyes. They were jet black. When he stared at you with those eyes, it felt like they burned through you. He'd killed his fair share of prisoners but not nearly as many as Woojin Gunwoo. In fact, it appeared he enjoyed watching his friend torture and kill indiscriminately more than he enjoyed killing on his own.

Now those two guards were standing by the main gate that lead to the fields. As his group got closer, it appeared they were waiting for them. Joon whispered loud enough so that only Apeun Pal could hear him...he hoped. "You better do something about that arm. I think those two guards up ahead are interested in our work group."

When they reached the gate. Jun-Ho stepped out in front blocking the way while Gunwoo walked down the rows. Gunwoo's eyes were focused on the last row. Jun-Ho announced, "We need to talk to ..." He glanced down at the sheet of paper in his hand. "Yong Joon. The rest of you can go on to your work station."

By this time Gunwoo was standing beside Joon, but his attention quickly switched to Apeun Pal. Gunwoo turned and yelled back to his friend. "It appears we have an injured one here as well." Jun-Ho signaled an okay as he watched the other twenty-two members of the work group walk through the gate on their way to ten hours of back breaking work with little water and no food.

Gunwoo's face lit up with a cruel smile as he pointed to Apeun Pal. "You will have to stay here with your friend."

It seemed like it took hours for the workgroup to get through the gate. They finished just as Jun-Ho arrived. Joon shivered as beads of sweat dripped down his forehead. It never was a good thing when a guard called you out by name. The only way to survive in the camp was to be invisible.

Joon's hands were clammy. He rubbed them on his dirty grey pants. *I'm no longer invisible.* He shook his head and closed his eyes. *I wish I could say goodbye to my family. They'll not know what happened to me and asking questions could lead to their disappearance as well.*

Gunwoo took out his wooden baton. Joon cringed expecting it to be used on him. It wouldn't be the first time a guard hit him with one. But, instead, Gunwoo threw it on the ground in front of Apeun Pal. "I want you to bend down and pick that up with your right hand."

Apeun Pal glanced down at the baton. He looked over at Gunwoo, his face ashen.

"Yeong-yeloun gfadeu, honorable guard, I... I can't."

Gunwoo seemed to radiate joy like a kid sitting by the tree on Christmas morning. "What do you mean, you can't? Bend over and pick it up immediately!"

Apeun Pal bit his lip, took a deep breath and slowly extended his right arm as he bent over. They all heard a crack followed by a scream as brittle bones from malnourishment broke. Apeun Pal straightened up holding his right arm, tears flowing down his face, his breathing shallow and rapid.

"So you've broken your arm. You know we put horses out of their misery when they break a leg." Gunwoo reached out to grab the arm, "Let's see if I can move it around to a place that's less painful."

Apeun Pal stepped back.

Jun-Ho tapped Gunwoo on the shoulder. "Ordinarily, I would love nothing more than to sit here and watch you manipulate his arm, but we have to deliver Yong Joon."

Gunwoo nodded. "What a waste of a good time." He pulled his pistol out and shot Apeun Pal between the eyes. His body fell backwards on to the ground. Joon knew it would stay there untouched for a couple of days as a reminder of who was in charge.

Jun-Ho turned to Joon. "We have orders to take you to the base hospital."

Joon looked down at the body laying at his feet. "Why? I'm not sick."

Joon looked into Jun-Ho's eyes. They looked like dark pools of death. He shivered and looked away.

"Let's see." Jun-Ho paused for a moment. "Before we go, why don't you recite the Ten Laws?"

Joon knew that if he couldn't recite them, he would be beaten or outright killed. He closed his eyes. *Lord, help me.* He struggled to remember the first one. "Anyone who...who...tries to escape will be shot immediately." *Thank you, Lord. One down and nine to go.*

He closed his eyes again. "Anyone... Anyone..." He clamped down on his eyelids and wiped the sweat off his brow. All at once words started to dance across the blackness. He had to race to say them before they disappeared. "Anyone who enters another zone without permission will be shot immediately. Anyone who steals a weapon will be shot immediately. Anyone who disobeys an order will be shot immediately. Anyone who protects an outsider will be shot immediately. Anyone who does not report suspicious activity when they see it will be shot immediately. Anyone who neglects or fails to carry out the work allotted to him will be shot immediately. Anyone who has unauthorized contact with another prisoner will be shot immediately. Anyone who doesn't admit to or confess his wrongdoings will be shot immediately. Anyone who disregards the camp rules and regulations will be shot immediately."

Joon stopped, opened his eyes, and took a deep breath. "There..."

Jun-Ho grinned. "Very good job. I'll bet you got some help didn't you? Let's get you to the hospital."

They started off. Under his breath Joon started to recite one of his favorite Psalms, "The Lord also will be a refuge for the oppressed..."

At that moment Jun-Ho leaned down and whispered in Joon's ear. "...a refuge in times of trouble. Psalm 9:9. We know our scripture too."

Joon's eyes widened. His mouth fell open. *What kind of prison guard knows scripture?*

At the end of the day, he'd been placed in a sealed room with a dead body. He only spent five minutes in the room, and he was told to stay as far away from the body as he could—one of the rare commands he was happy to obey.

Since then he'd lived in a locked room with a glass wall opposite the door. At first he was scared, but as time went on, he got used to it. It was a far cry from the crowded, dirty barracks he had lived in for years. This room was light beige, antiseptic, and even had a real mattress and toilet as well as clean hot and cold running water.

Food was served once a day through a panel below the door. Each meal was a banquet compared to the standard concentration camp fare. But most of all, the room didn't smell. That actually took some getting used to. Strangely, he sometimes missed the foul but familiar smell of the camp.

Twice a day someone dressed in a full-body protective yellow suit came in, measured his temperature and blood pressure, then took a small sample of blood. He didn't know why because he had felt fine except for a slight sore throat and minor temperature three days after his encounter with the dead body. And that had lasted less than a day, a far cry from his sick days in the camp.

The surprising thing was no one punished him or even tried to stop him when he knelt to pray. Sure, he lived like an animal in a zoo, but he'd never felt so good in his life. *I could get used to this. If only I could see my family.*

Of course, he had no privacy. Daily, men and women in white coats stared at him through the glass wall taking notes, but he quickly adjusted to it. Growing up in a concentration camp, he had not developed a sense of modesty or an overwhelming need for privacy. Still, the serious looks on their faces and the cold, clinical nature of their long, white coats gave him an empty feeling in the pit of his stomach.

On day two of his stay the doctors, or whoever they were, lined up in front of the window wall. One spoke into a microphone, and Joon heard a command over a loudspeaker on the ceiling. "Move to the back corner by this wall. Stand facing into the room and do not move until we tell you to."

Joon did as he was told. After standing there for a few seconds, the door to his room opened. A prisoner stepped in and moved to the corner opposite Joon. From the man's wasted look Joon could tell that he had just come from the camp.

"Hi. My name is Yong Joon." Joon refused to be called by a number.

The prisoner looked down and didn't say anything.

Another command blared over the loudspeaker. "Do not speak. Remain quiet and take deep breaths."

Once again Joon obeyed. He stood there for what seemed like an hour, but he knew it was much shorter than that.

"Subject 71, you may leave the room now." The prisoner nodded and walked out. Joon heard the lock click behind him. "Subject 43, you may leave the corner now."

Joon walked back to the bed and sat down. He must be Subject 43.

This event was repeated about every two or three days. Sometimes the prisoner who came in was a woman, sometimes it was a man. Joon no longer paid any attention, though he noticed the subject numbers steadily increased, the last one being Subject 173.

This morning he woke up shivering, but he was also covered in sweat. He pulled up the blanket. Without warning he was struck with an intense headache, as if someone had hit his forehead with a hammer. He heard food slide under the door. He tried to stand to get it, but that made him dizzy. He swayed on his feet, then fell back on the bed.

He covered his face with his hands for a moment to stop the room from spinning. When he removed his hands, they were covered with blood. He felt his nose and around his eyes. Blood was seeping out of them.

He looked to the glass wall. A group of men in white coats

was studying him. He tried to stand again but couldn't. This time he fell to the floor and vomited. He grabbed the mattress. It took all his energy to rise to his knees. He tried to stand but didn't have the strength.

He crawled on his hands and knees toward the window. Every few steps he had to pause to suck in air. He coughed up blood. It left a coppery taste in his mouth and he grimaced. Blood was seeping out of his ears. He tried to rub it off his face.

He made it to the wall at the feet of a short, chubby man behind the glass, the only one with some kind of medal adorning his bright-white coat. The man looked down at him with a blank stare.

Joon silently prayed Psalm 41:3: *"The LORD sustains them on their sickbed and restores them from their bed of illness."* His last action was to slap his hand on the glass. With his last breath he heard it squeak as his hand slid down, leaving a streak of bright-red blood on the glass.

September 12, 4:43 a.m., North Korea

Dr. Hak Seong was the director of the Democratic People's Republic of Korea's bioweapon development program. It didn't bother him in the least that he was creating a weapon that would silently, painfully, indiscriminately kill millions. It only bothered him that his work went unnoticed by the world. The DPRK's nuclear program got all the press. That may be how the Glorious Leader wanted it for now, but the day would come when Seong would be acknowledged for all his hard work.

At least for now he could wear the Hero of the Republic ribbon with the gold star of Korea, given to him by the Glorious Leader himself in a small, secret ceremony. But he could only wear it while at work in the camp.

He touched the red-and-gold medal hanging above the left pocket of his white coat. The day would come when he would be able to wear it in public. *Then my genius will be known. Then I will be feared.*

He stood with his team studying Subject 43, who had been problematic. He had outlived most of the other recent test subjects. But today, he watched with a smile as Subject 43 crawled to the glass. How pitiful, but he was surprised the subject had the strength to move that much. He glanced at his notes. So Subject 43 was in for possessing a Bible. *Subject 43, where is your God now?*

Seconds later, when the subject died at his feet, Seong turned to his colleagues. "I believe this proves that we have a virulent strain of airborne Ebola. We have completed the task our Glorious Leader asked of us. You should all be proud of what we have accomplished here. We have created an incurable virus that will cause a victim to bleed out of every orifice. Someday all of you will have a medal like this." He pointed to his medal hanging off his scrubs, as he often did. "We must keep this secret for now, but soon the world will fear us."

Someday soon the world will tremble at the mention of my name.

Seong's gaze scanned the group. "What we do here has a time-honored past. The Mongol Empire conquered China by throwing plague-infested corpses and excrement over city walls. They killed almost twenty-five million Chinese. But their greatest accomplishment was spreading the Black Death throughout Europe, killing one-third of the Western population. Now it's our turn. We will kill most of the Western world and do it quicker and more efficiently than any time in history." Seong puffed out his chest and raised his chin.

One of the interns gestured to the body on the other side of the glass. "This one seems to have lived longer than the others. Three of the subjects exposed to him died days ago."

"That's a relevant observation." Seong nodded. "All of you should take note of that. Does anyone have a theory to explain that?"

A tentative hand went up in the back.

Seong pointed at him. "Yes."

"Subject 43 was exposed to the virus on a dead body and the others were exposed to the virus on a live subject."

"Excellent. Does anyone have a theory about why the virus on a dead subject is less potent?" Seong regarded the group. No one had an answer. "All right. I want a written explanation from each of you before the end of the day. Now let's move on to..." He glanced at his notebook. "Subject 87. I wouldn't be surprised to find her near death too."

As the interns made their way down the hallway, Seong signaled a nearby orderly. "Have Subject 43's body taken to the camp crematorium. We are done with it."

"Yes, Doctor."

Seong took one more glance at Yong Joon lying on the floor in a fetal position, blood oozing out his eyes, ears, and mouth. *Your God couldn't save you and He's powerless to stop the Glorious Leader.*

Chapter Six

THERE IS NOTHING WRONG WITH ASKING to know God but *know* is such a passive word. Perhaps what we should ask for more is to experience God. It's the difference between knowing the dance moves and actually going on the dance floor and immersing yourself in the music and the movement—Awakened Incident Manual, Volume 2, Page 117

September 12, 7:41 a.m., North Korea

Joon gasped as he filled his lungs with air and opened his eyes. It was dark. He was cold. He was covered with something. He struggled to move it off him. No, he was in a bag, a plastic bag. How did he get here?

In a panic he started to push and tear at the plastic as he yelled for help.

He heard the sound of a zipper followed by a whispered command in a peaceful, soothing voice, "Quiet or they'll hear you."

Joon calmed down. Light made its way in. He squinted as his eyes adjusted. A man's face appeared. "What's...what's going on? Where am I? Who...who are you?"

The man bent down next to Joon's ear and whispered, "I said be quiet. I'll explain as soon as we're safe. Right now, I want you to roll out of the body bag and onto this cart. Then don't move a muscle, keep your eyes closed, and try to hold your breath as long as possible. Take shallow breaths when you need air."

Body bag? What? Joon did as he was told. The cart started to roll. There was a sudden blast of heat. It took all his willpower not to move.

The man whispered again. "You're doing good. Don't move until I can get to a safe place."

Joon fought the urge to nod and stayed motionless as the cart rolled down a hallway and then turned to the left. He heard a door close.

"Okay, you can open your eyes but keep quiet."

Joon opened his eyes. The room was small and cluttered and smelled of cleaning fluid. On the right, shelves were packed with cleaning supplies, paper, and tools. Hung on the left were several of the special uniforms worn by prisoners who'd gained a level of trust.

The man standing over him appeared almost normal. He wore the pale-blue uniform of a trusted prisoner, but he either hadn't been here long or had access to better food and working conditions. Joon assumed it was the latter. He guessed the man was in his mid-twenties. He had short, dark hair and what looked like a couple of days' growth of beard. A sense of peace emanated from his soft, hazel-brown eyes. He had the biggest smile Joon had ever seen on a prisoner.

The man was shaking his head and whispered, "I can't believe it." He fell to his knees with his arms raised. "Praise God. Praise God."

Joon sat up on the cart. "What's going on? Who are you? Where am I?"

The man looked up. "Keep quiet or they'll hear you. My name is Dong Hwan. I've been a prisoner here for six years. I'm a pastor…at least…I was a pastor. I was arrested when my undercover home church was betrayed. But I haven't given up on God. He has me here for a reason."

He paused for a second. "Maybe you are the reason. Where you are is in the crematorium not far from the camp hospital. As for what's going on…a miracle." Hwan shook his head. "You're a miracle. An amazing miracle of God."

"What are you talking about? Why am I in the— Wait, you were going to burn me!" Joon stood up at the sudden realization.

"Yes, that's my job. At least, one of my jobs." Hwan got to his feet.

"But, I wasn't dead." Joon stepped away from Hwan. What

was his game?

"What's your last memory before you woke up here?" Hwan asked.

Joon rubbed his eyes. His last memory? He concentrated. "I was in that strange room, the one with all the glass along one side. I felt sick. I was bleeding..." Joon rubbed his face again, then checked his hands. No blood. Was that a dream? "I couldn't stand. I crawled to the glass wall to get help. Not one of the doctors cared. They just stared at me. I remembered Psalm 41:3 about how the Lord restores. Then everything went black until...well, until I woke up here."

"You were dead. The bodies that come here inside those heavy plastic bags are all dead. We're supposed to burn them immediately, but I pray over every one before I put them in the furnace. When I prayed over you, you started to move. It was all I could do not to scream."

Joon struggled to take all this in. *I was dead? God raised me?*

Yet as he thought about it, it somehow felt right. Only a few hours earlier he had been sick, bleeding out his eyes, ears, mouth. Now he felt better than any time in his life. "Is there a mirror?"

"There's one by the uniforms."

Joon walked over and stared at himself in the mirror, rubbing his face. "This can't be me. I look...I look...well fed, healthy even." *Either I'm in heaven or God raised me.* He glanced around. This was definitely not heaven.

"Why did God bring me back to life? I don't deserve this." Joon wiped a tear from his eye. "I've done nothing for God. I haven't even gone to church or read the Bible since it was taken away. Why me?"

"I don't know why, but I know for sure that you don't have to earn God's favor. Anyway, you couldn't if you tried. Besides, if God does it, you deserve it. Whatever the reason, I'm sure it doesn't involve you staying in this hell. We have to get you out."

"If I escape, they will kill my younger sister, her husband, and my two nieces. I've already lost my parents, I couldn't bear losing anyone else. I can't leave."

"Don't you see? You have already escaped. As far as the camp is concerned, you're dead. All that's left of you is a pile of ashes mixed in with the ashes of the last three people I burned in that furnace. They won't look for you, so they have no reason to hurt the rest of your family." A sharp crash like the sound of breaking glass filled the room. Hwan's head popped up and he froze. He signaled Joon to be quiet while he took soft delicate steps towards the door. Once there he leaned over, his right ear flat to the door. After what seemed like hours to Joon, he watched Hwan smile and reach down to twist the door lock.

Hwan walked back "This can be a busy place. Should have locked the door in the first place. If anyone knocks, you're going to have to play dead. Now where were we…oh yes, about your family. If they find you alive, they'll think you deceived them in some way. Then they will kill you again, if they can, and your whole family. You have no choice; you have to get out of here as soon as possible."

"But how?"

Hwan fell to his knees again. "Father, you raised…" He looked up at Joon. "What's your name?"

"Yong Joon."

"Father, you raised Joon for a purpose. Give us the wisdom to carry out your plan." Hwan stopped and surveyed the room. He stood and set his hand on Joon's shoulder. "I know how to get you out of the camp. After that, it's up to you."

"How?"

"There are over fifteen thousand prisoners in this camp. Dozens die every day. We only burn the bodies of those who die from some unknown illness. The rest we ship to a mass grave about two kilometers outside the camp. Every morning we pile those bodies on a truck." Hwan eyed the clock on the wall above the uniforms. "The next one leaves in thirty minutes. I can put you on it near the top. After you are out of camp, you can slip off the back. The drivers don't pay any attention. They only carry dead bodies. What could possibly happen?" He suddenly smiled. "It's not like any of them have walked away...until now."

Joon thought about it for a moment. It was his only option. He didn't want to risk his family by being caught in the camp alive. Then he realized he was naked. Modesty was not an issue in camp, but he could hardly walk through the countryside naked. "I don't have any clothes."

Hwan pointed to the uniforms. "Pick out one that fits. You can't wear it when I lay you in the truck, so you'll have to hide it between you and the real bodies."

"I can do that." Joon found a uniform that was a little big, but it fit well enough. He lay down on the cart, playing dead once again as Hwan wheeled him out to the loading dock.

When they arrived, Hwan whispered, "You're in luck. This truck is almost full. The driver is off smoking. None of them want to be around when we're loading. Keep your eyes closed and try not to panic."

As gently as he could without giving anything away, Hwan put Joon on a pile of bodies near the rear of the truck. It had the faint odor of decay. Flies were already buzzing around him. The bodies were cold and in spots covered by a thin layer of sticky fluid. Joon closed his eyes. Every muscle in his is body tensed up as he tried to make himself as small as possible. His thoughts became consumed by Psalm 94:19, In the multitude of my anxieties within me, your comforts delight my soul. As he meditated on the scripture, he took Hwan's hand and squeezed it. Hwan lightly squeezed back.

"God be with you." Hwan whispered.

Within seconds another worker brought several bodies and threw them on top of Joon. At first, he cringed but then decided it was actually easier and safer when no one could see him.

When the truck started, Joon opened his eyes to see a little light peeking through between the arm and torso of the body on top of him. This was going to be a macabre ride.

September 12, 8:52 a.m., North Korea

Joon sensed the truck stop at the gate. He heard the guard walk around the truck doing a cursory inspection. Then the truck started again. Once through the gate, he took his first breath of free air since he was twelve. Even filtered through the bodies on top of him, it was sweet. He could feel the sun shining on him. It was the same sun, the same air as in the camp but still, it was different. He was free.

From that point on, the ride was bumpy. Dust from the dirt road formed a cloud over him and stung his eyes. The truck's diesel fumes seeped into his nose. He tried to lay still but with each bump he was poked in the back or the side by a foot or a hand. He cringed at the thought of being buried under all these bodies.

He had to get off the truck. He didn't want to do it too close to the camp, but he didn't want to do it at the mass grave either.

Hwan had said it was about two kilometers to the grave site. Joon estimated that the truck couldn't be going much faster than fifteen kilometers per hour. He decided to count out, as best he could, about six to seven minutes. That should put him near the halfway point.

After what seemed to be about six minutes, Joon grabbed the uniform hidden beneath him and waited. As soon as the truck hit a bump, he pushed the body on top of him off and to the side. Keeping low, he shimmied to the back, carefully pushing bodies to the side, not wanting any to fall off.

Finally, at the edge of the truck, he pushed himself off. His leg caught on a piece of broken metal on the railing, and it dug into his calf. He bit back a cry.

He hit the ground on his stomach and lay flat until the sound of the engine faded. Not knowing where he was and who might be nearby, he rolled into a ditch on the side of the road.

He lay there a moment, then decided it was time to put on the uniform, but first he used it to wipe the blood off the wound. It no longer hurt, but it had to be a deep cut.

He sat up and bent his leg to examine it. His mouth dropped open. He ran his hand up and down his bare leg. *What?* He couldn't find a cut of any size or any blood. Both his calves were smooth and intact. It sure felt like he cut it open.

Joon slipped on the uniform then stood. *Where do I go now?*

Surrounded by a forest of white birch trees, every direction looked the same. To his left the dirt road led back to camp. To his right it led past the mass graves. Into the forest it led...where?

He decided to stay on the road and head toward the mass graves in the hope that the road went beyond the grave site to a village. He walked on the forest line so he could hide if he heard the truck. The day was clear. Only a few clouds dotted the sky. It was quiet, even peaceful.

It wasn't long before the stench of decaying flesh assaulted his nose like a punch in the face. He stopped and covered his mouth and nose with his hand. He must be near the grave site. Should he continue to go in this direction? Any village would have to be far away to avoid this smell.

For a moment his attention was drawn to a lone white butterfly resting by the side of the road on a blade of green grass. It seemed out of place so close to this fetid place of death.

He glanced in both directions. Nothing but dusty, empty road. *Lord, where do you want me to go and what do you want me to do?*

He'd only taken two or three steps to his right when he heard from behind, "Joon, Yong Joon."

Joon stopped and turned around. Had he been caught? Two men stood a few yards behind him. How did they get there? They weren't there when he just looked. And how did they know his name?

His first reaction was to run into the forest, but as the men moved closer, a sense of peace washed over him. They were

THE ASCENSION | 39

Korean, but they didn't wear uniforms. They were casually dressed in western clothes. They were as out of place as that butterfly.

Joon stood still until the men were next to him. "Who are you? How do you know my name?"

One of the men put his hand on Joon's shoulder. "We're here to help you. You need to leave this country right now. You are needed in the United States."

"What?" This was some kind of trick.

"God raised you because He needs you in the United States."

"How did you know He raised me?"

"Trust me."

Somehow, I do, but... "How can I get there? What does God want me to do? I can't speak English. I've been in prison since I was a child. I don't even know how to live in Korea, so how could I survive in the United States?"

"Trust God. He already knows. He'll fix it. Everything will work out."

"How?"

"You'll see. Hold my hand."

As soon as Joon grabbed the man's hand everything went blurry.

Chapter Seven

THE PROBLEM WITH SIN IS THAT you get far more than what you see and none of it is good.
  —Awakened Incident Manual, Volume 2, Page 51

September 12, 11:09 a.m., Pyongyang

Sok Kang Ju sat in his favorite throne-like stuffed chair at the far end of his receiving room, right off his office where he often met with dignitaries. The room could best be described as a garish statement of tasteless wealth. Criminal in a country where most of the population was starving. It was as if the Italian Renaissance design had been mixed with classic French baroque in a high-speed blender and then poured out over the room.

The entrance from the main hallway consisted of twelve-foot-high, extra-wide double doors. The door from his office, through which he would often make a dramatic entrance, was bordered on both sides by thick marble columns. On one side of the room was a marble table with twelve chairs arranged around it. The other side of the room was lined with uncomfortable chairs. On the wall behind his "throne" was a large picture of himself waving to an imaginary crowd, flashing an insincere smile that only hinted at the loathing behind it.

Today he leaned back on his throne, smiling at the six generals and nine aides who tried not to squirm in the chairs that lined both walls.

Kang Ju glanced at his watch as his smile melted. "It appears our guest is a little late." He turned to the general sitting against the wall to his right. "General Sunghoon, do you know where Dr. Hak is?"

A slight, almost-imperceptible tremor ran up the general's body. Kang Ju loved this.

Before the general could answer, a knock sounded on the

door. The aide nearest the door opened it. A short, round-faced man in a white lab coat adorned with the Hero of the Republic medal took a few tentative steps into the receiving room. His head was bowed, and his soft voice trembled. "Great Leader, Superior Person, forgive my tardiness. The guards at the front gate took more time than necessary to check my credentials."

Kang Ju stood, walked over, and gave Dr. Hak a bear hug. "Do not be afraid, Doctor. I'll see to it they are suitably punished. Now come over and sit by me." He motioned to the chair immediately to his left. The general who occupied the chair bounced out as if it had burst into flames and moved down to the end of the line.

Once both men sat, Kang Ju turned to Dr. Hak. "I've been told the weapon is ready."

Dr Hak nodded. "Wise Leader, it has been perfected, and the first batch is already loaded to be shipped out this afternoon."

"And how deadly is it?"

"We can expect eighty percent fatalities if the victims don't get treatment. Even if treatment is available, the disease will spread so fast the fatalities will drop no lower than sixty percent."

"Excellent." Kang Ju rubbed his hands together. "Dr. Hak, you have done the Democratic People's Republic of Korea a great service. You will be rewarded. Now, I want one new batch produced as quickly as possible. How long will that take?"

"No more than two days."

"Excellent. I'll expect to hear from you in two days." Kang Ju dismissively waved Dr. Hak out.

As soon as Dr. Hak had left, Kang Ju frowned. He addressed General Joon-Ho. "As soon as Dr. Hak completes this task, execute him and his entire team. Destroy all records. I don't want any hint of this bioweapon to get out, and I never want it to be traced back to us." Kang Ju paused, then smiled. "At least until we are ready for the world to know the true extent of our power. For now, let the West continue to worry about our nuclear capability while we prepare for their total destruction." *Then we can say good-*

bye to the wretched plague of Naturals. I'll succeed where even Renaud can't.

General Sunghoon nodded. "Yes, Great Leader."

"All right. We are done here. I want everyone to leave. Send in my son."

Kang Ju didn't have to wait long for his son to walk in.

"Father," Sok Park Kye said. "Are we ready to wipe Naturals from the face of the earth?"

"We'll come close. We'd do better if Renaud stayed out of it." At the mention of Renaud's name, Kang Ju's face burned, and his nostrils flared.

Park Key crossed his arms and narrowed his eyes. "What is he up to?"

"He's coming here in a few days to lead the peace talks on the 'Korea Problem.'" Kang Ju made a fist with his left hand. "I've been instructed to lighten my position and, eventually, accept his proposal and timetable for reunification. He says that will put him on the world's stage and lead to his ultimate ascension."

Kang Ju rhythmically pounded his left fist on the arm of his chair. "I say we use our bioweapon on the South and then march in and take what is mine. Then the world will fear me."

"But Father, it's Renaud. He is the Anointed One. We can't go against him."

Kang Ju sneered. "Renaud, Renaud. He's a Natural. He's weak. If we don't do something bold, it will be like Noah all over again."

Park Kye bit his lower lip. "Sure, he's a Natural for the moment, but Chavvah Shain supports him. Mind you, I'm not afraid of her but we do have to be careful, dealing with her."

Kang Ju grinned and ever so slightly thrust out his chest. *The best thing I ever did was killing my son and finding a strong demon to step in.* "Chavvah is a two-bit prophet. We need someone like me to show God what he can do with His creation. We need to move from a position of strength, which is exactly why I wanted to talk with you today."

"About what?"

Kang Ju smiled. "Of course, Renaud will be at the presentation. As a Natural he's vulnerable. As soon as he's out of the way, we move on the South."

Park Kye shook his head. "Father, that's risky. Besides, no UnVeiler would dare harm Renaud."

"You need to learn that risk is the fuel for great leadership." Kang Ju opened his fist. He leaned back. "Besides, I've already set up a surprise for Renaud."

Park Kye's brows drew close as his face tightened. "What are you planning to do?"

Kang Ju stood, walked over to Park Kye, and set his hand on his son's shoulder. "I don't want you involved in the 'accident,' but be ready to move on the South as soon as Renaud is out of the picture."

Park Kye looked down and rubbed the back of his neck. "Okay, Father."

"He will die on October 10. That is the day that the world, as the Naturals know it, will end." Kang Ju stared up at the ceiling. "Did you hear that God? Your precious little jewels are going to disappoint you and then they will all die."

September 11, 8:11 p.m. Seattle

Lord, have I missed something? Five months ago you warned me that something was coming. A great darkness was impending on this world. I don't know where it is. I don't know how to stop it. I don't even know if you want me to stop it. L sat alone in his office lost in thought while he stared out at the dark Seattle sky. He listened to the gentle beat of rain against the window. Occasionally a gust of wind would blow across the building and the once gentle beat would erupt into drumming.

He found the rain soothing, almost hypnotic. *You sent Ricki to us. You said she had the ability to discover our role, to deliver your plan for us and to...to heal...me. Yet five months later and none of that has been accomplished. How much longer do we have to wait?*

A flash of lightning lit the sky followed by a distant clap of thunder. L smiled. *Was that for me, Lord?*

There was a knock on his office door. He didn't want company. "Go away."

Another knock followed. "It's important boss."

Matthew. L took a deep breath and rubbed his eyes. "All right, come in."

Matthew opened the door, walked in, and took the seat by L's desk. "Are you okay?"

"Feeling a little lost today."

"I understand but isolating yourself will not help. Thomas Carlyle wrote that 'Isolation is the sum total of wretchedness to a man.'"

L shrugged. "He was that Scottish philosopher wasn't he? I never met him but I may have read some of his stuff." L shrugged. "You...*he* may have a point."

"Have a point? He also wrote that 'Adversity is the diamond dust Heaven polishes its jewels with.'"

"So, I'm being polished am I?"

Matthew smiled. "I think at the moment we all are. Which is why we have to stick together through this."

L leaned back in his office chair. "In the spirit of sticking together, what brought you here?"

Matthew handed over a few files he had brought to the office. "These are the updated reports on activities in the Middle East. Something is going on there that we haven't seen before."

"I thought we've seen everything. I've been following events there for the last 2000 years after all."

"Not this one."

"What has you spooked?"

"It's quiet."

L reached out and grabbed the first of the files Matthew brought in. "You say that like it's a bad thing. Hasn't that always been our goal?"

"Yes, but not this way. Read over those files. One day ISIS is beheading people, posting vile stuff on the web, making threats, sending out teams to terrorize the area, and the next day, nothing."

"What do you mean by nothing?"

"Exactly what the word means. ISIS seems to have melted away. It's like they picked up all their marbles and went home."

"And you think it means…"

Matthew leaned forward on the desk. "I think it means something big is in the works. I think they are laying low while they prepare for an attack that will make 9/11 look like a training exercise."

September 12, 2:17 p.m., Haeju, North Korea

Gyeong Kwang served as a colonel in the North Korean intelligence service, better known as the Reconnaissance General Bureau. He was also the sole UV on the *Blue Mist*, a large cargo ship flying the Tanzania flag to avoid unfair U.N. sanctions against North Korean ships.

When he had been alive, his slender body was a disappointment to him. He died from illness at the age of twenty-nine, just after the failure of the second Japanese invasion of Korea in 1599. He had wanted to fight the Japanese, but he was too short. When he was reanimated, his body remained small, but his UV status gave him an unusual amount of strength. The name he chose for himself meant "respected and powerful." Respected as a North Korean spy. Powerful as a UV.

He wanted to kill a Natural or two during this long voyage at sea, but he had to hold that urge in check. His task was to insure the safe delivery of a small crate to ISIS. He was accompanied by Young Ki, a clueless Natural and a lieutenant in the Reconnaissance General Bureau who would come in handy as a hostage should they run into an Awakened.

He felt the ocean breeze on his face, smelled the salt in the air, and watched the ship churn the sea as the *Blue Mist* left Haeju harbor. It was on its way south through the Indian Ocean and the Suez Canal to Lebanon and its place in history. The trip would take twenty-one long, boring days.

He took a deep breath of fresh sea air before leaving for his cabin. As he walked away, he stole a glance at the rolling hills slowly passing by. This would be a place of real beauty if it wasn't crawling with these human parasites.

Kwang's cabin was small by Western standards. Having traveled around the world on Korean business, he'd experienced Western luxury, and this wasn't it. But it would have to do. The mission was far too important to be seduced by decadent Western practices. The cabin had two beds, a small desk, a closet, and a porthole. The bathroom was down the hall, and much to Kwang's chagrin, he had to share it with a shipload of dirty Naturals.

He found Young Ki lying on his bed reading some story about how the Great Leader single-handedly saved the country from an invasion of large beasts set loose by Japan. He smiled. These Naturals were so easy to manipulate. What did God see in them?

Kwang walked over and slapped Ki on the legs. "You will stand at attention when I enter."

"Sorry, sir." Ki struggled to get up as he offered the North Korean salute, left palm down by the side of his head between the eye and the ear. "I thought our mission was secret and we were to travel as civilians. I didn't want to expose us."

"*Dwaeji*, pig, do you see anyone else in this room?"

"No...sir."

"Then when we are alone, you will treat me in accordance with my rank. Is that clear?" And once they delivered the goods, Ki was going to have a little accident.

"Yes, sir." Ki visibly trembled, which made Kwang enjoy this encounter all the more.

"Okay, now we understand each other. How is our package doing?"

"I have it secured under my bed. It's not going anywhere, no matter how rough the seas get."

"Good. One of us must be with it at all times. You understand?"

"Yes, sir. Ah…sir, can I know what's in the crate?"

"No, you *jogjebi*." The weasel. "No, you may not."

Chapter Eight

DEATH HAUNTS US LIKE A DARK shroud. It's the ultimate fear that controls our existence. Imagine a world not without death but without the fear of death, because that is a world of life. — Awakened Incident Manual, Volume 2, Page 21

September 12, 3:21 p.m., Aleppo, Northern Syria

Miraj Barak Qudir, now safely back in his headquarters in Aleppo, shut and locked the door to his antiquities shop. He checked the time: 3:21 p.m. *At least I can be thankful Syria is in the same time zone as Lebanon.* He glanced at his desktop. It was the same as he left it. *Good. No new work. Besides, Jalal should be here soon.*

His nine-year-old American bulldog brushed against his right leg followed by a short-lived whimper. He looked down and smiled. "I haven't forgotten you, Adara. You'll get your dinner as soon as my meeting is over." At the word *dinner*, Adara gazed up at him with large eyes, her small tail wagging.

He chuckled as he scratched Adara between her ears. "I know what we can do while we are waiting." Miraj looked at the lines of shelves to his right. "We are lucky to have so much history here. Let's visit another time, another place. And this time you can pick it."

Her ears perked up as she sat facing the shelves. Miraj pointed toward the rear of the shop. "Adara, go for it." She leaped and with a chorus of barks she ran between shelves two and three and stopped near the end. With one last bark she sat facing shelf three.

"That's a good girl." Miraj walked back to her, then reached up and pulled a dog treat out of a small bowl. "Here you go, old girl, you earned it." He glanced back to the shelf. "I see you have taste."

Miraj gingerly picked up one of his prized items, a Sumerian cuneiform tablet from Mesopotamia dated 3000 BCE. He held it like a piece of spun glass. He sniffed it, trying to breathe in the ancient dust he wished was still on it. He imagined the sweet yet tart fragrance of a pomegranate the author may have been eating at the time. It carried him back to a less complicated world, a world of mighty empires and honorable wars.

He looked down at his dog sitting peacefully at his feet. "We were born in the wrong century. We would have had such great times back then."

Adara gazed up at him with adoring eyes, as if he had announced dinnertime. Miraj put the cuneiform tablet back on the shelf and laughed. He reached down and stroked the dog behind her ears. In a wistful tone he said, "My only beef with ISIS is that they want to destroy these beautiful timeless objects." He stared off into space. "It's why I wanted this job, to kill the notion of nuclear weapons. What mindless destruction they would bring. No, a bioweapon is perfect for our needs."

He pulled out a letter and reread the message one more time. He gave it a thumbs-up right before he used his lighter to set it on fire. He watched the flames dance before he dropped it in the nearby wastebasket. Miraj Barak Qudir was about to unleash carnage on the world. The right kind of carnage. Carnage that would kill, not destroy. He felt warm all over.

He turned as the doorbell announced a visitor. Jalal Bashir, his second in command and most trusted field operative, entered the shop.

"It's done." Miraj smiled. "The North Koreans have come through, and the weapon is on its way. It should arrive by ship late on October 9, and I want it deployed as soon as it is in our hands. We can't leave this kind of volatile material sitting around. The North Koreans are right to insist this attack be launched on the tenth, and I'm more than happy to oblige them."

Jalal nodded. "Especially since some buzz is going around that we are on to something big. We can't keep the lid on this much longer. The sooner we use it the better."

His nostrils flaring, Miraj simmered with anger. "I suspected as much. We have to close those leaks immediately." He had been double-crossed and those involved must pay. "Keeping this under wraps will be your job for the next few weeks. You have my full authority to silence anyone you suspect of sharing any kind of information about Operation Blood Red. As far as the world is concerned, ISIS must be, at the moment, quiet."

"Operation Blood Red will come as a surprise. I'll make sure of that, sir."

They walked into his office at the back of the store. Miraj sat behind his desk. Jalal stood, rubbing his dagger birthmark. "I know some had their doubts that you could accomplish anything of this magnitude, but I always knew you would succeed."

Miraj leaned back in his chair, satisfaction filling his chest. "You're right, I was told this couldn't be done. Of course, everyone at the time expected me to get my hands on nuclear material. But in spite of the fact there is a lot of it hanging around, it's more difficult to acquire than you might imagine. It's true Abbud Abbas got hold of a little, but that turned out to be a fiasco in Dubai. This won't be a repeat of their failure. I was right to go after a chemical or a bioweapon from the start."

"And you were right to seek North Korea's help." Jalal paused for a second. "But are they giving you a cure or some kind of antidote so our people will be protected?"

"There is no antidote. No cure. We will stay out of the infected area, and Allah will protect us. In less than a month, Israel will be no more, and its destruction will not trace back to us." Miraj laughed. "At least until we want it to. We will be the hammer of Allah that disappears as quickly as it appears. October 10 will be a day the world will never forget."

September 12, 11:04 a.m. Tel Aviv

Declan Walsh walked into his third-floor apartment with a

swagger like he was the cat that just ate the canary. It was wasted because nobody was here to admire his victory walk. In fact, the apartment had an unlived-in look. The living room was populated with a single couch that sometimes doubled as a bed when he didn't bother to move to the bedroom, a table with a few piles of paper next to a computer, and suitcases stacked against the wall. His work was his life and his life was his work.

This visit to his apartment was a short break in a typical day filled with...well, anything other than sitting in his apartment alone.

He'd returned from a brief meeting with one of his Mossad contacts who told him that there wasn't a beautiful field agent with streaks of blue interspersed in her long jet-black hair, high cheekbones, and killer curves, but there was an analyst. That was enough to remind him of a meeting a couple of years ago.

Of course, Shiri, Shiri Liora. He knew that woman in Cairo looked familiar. Declan pumped his fist in the air. He finally had a name to go with the image of the woman picking up the dust that moments earlier had been Abdul Ba'ith. His instincts were right. They were always right. He leaned back on the couch. But what was an analyst doing out in the field?

Declan put down his notes on the Abdul Ba'ith incident he had taken with him to the meeting and walked to his apartment window. He pulled back the curtain and surveyed the street in front. That black Ford SUV was still there. He seemed to have picked up a tail the last few days. Did it have anything to do with his snooping around Mossad?

He dropped the curtain with a smirk. If it was Mossad, they were losing their touch. He grabbed his cell phone and dialed Terivel Adelman, Mossad's operations chief.

After a short conversation, Terivel agreed to set up a meeting with Shiri.

Dead men turning to dust, hollow point bullets filled with blood, and not just any blood but blood with perfect DNA... Now, he'd get some answers.

Declan glanced out the window again. The black SUV still hadn't left. He planned to stay in and catch up on some paperwork for the rest of the day. *Guess they'll get bored sitting out there.*

Declan, always a light sleeper, woke to the faint sound of rattling at his door. He sat up and listened, focused on picking up any sound. He heard it again. It was the unmistakable sound of someone trying to pick his lock. Whoever it was, he wasn't very good at it.

Given the obvious hazards of his job, Declan was prepared. Grateful he was wearing pajamas so he didn't have to waste time putting something on, he jumped up, grabbed the Glock 19 on the nightstand, and put it in his emergency go bag. He positioned the footstool next to the bed under the ceiling entrance to the attic, opened the trapdoor, slid in, closed and locked it. This was why he'd asked for an apartment on the top floor.

He crouched in the small attic, making his way to the main air vent. A large rat scampered by. He paused and grimaced. *Rats.* He hated them.

He opened the air vent and stuck his head out, looking up at the roof. He squeezed partway through the vent, reached up and grabbed the edge of the flat roof. He pulled himself out and, using his feet on the air vent ledge, pushed up and yanked himself onto the roof.

He ran across the light gravel on the rooftop to the access door. Locked. He could bust it down, but the noise might alert the idiots breaking into his apartment. Instead he fished a lock-pick tool out of his go bag. It only took a few seconds to get the door open. He listened for a moment. Silence.

He stepped onto the top landing of the stairs and eased the door closed. He inched down the stairs one step at a time toward his apartment, his Glock in hand. He hoped to come in behind whoever was breaking in. Given their level of skill, they might

THE ASCENSION | 53

still be poking around outside the door.

When he reached the middle landing, he could see his front door was open. The fools must be inside.

He made it to his door and set down the bag. While holding the gun with both hands, arms extended, Declan swung in with one motion, scanning the living room. It was empty, but sounds were coming from the bedroom. Two men were arguing. *Idiots.*

Declan made his way to the bedroom door. Two tangos were there with their backs to him. The short one was on the footstool trying to open the trapdoor. He had an H & K MP5 strapped to his back. The other was bald with a full beard. He was looking up offering advice.

"Come on, hurry up," Baldy said. "He's getting away."

The small man pounded on the trapdoor. "Look, if you don't like the way I'm doing this, let's switch." He pounded on the door again. Nothing moved. "I think he locked it."

"Then shoot it out."

These guys were not professionals by any means. He moved closer. "Boys, if you had called ahead, I would have ordered a pizza."

Baldy spun around at the sound, his pistol pointed at Declan. Declan tapped him in the head before the guy could get a shot off. The tango fell backward onto the bed.

The one on the stepladder turned, grabbing for the semiautomatic on his back. Declan raised his gun, squeezed the trigger, and tapped him twice in the chest. He fell to the floor. Declan made his way forward and checked both bodies. Both men were dead. He checked their pockets. Nothing.

They made a fine mess of things. Good thing he didn't sleep here very often, or he'd be really mad.

He grabbed the phone and called the CIA station chief. "Boss, I need a cleaning crew over here tonight. I have two tangos permanently down in my apartment." He went on to explain what had happened.

Once that was set up, Declan took his always-packed suitcase from the hallway and left for the nearest safe house for the night.

As he walked out, he saw the nearest streetlight was shot out. He walked over to the tangos' car and searched it. Again nothing.

They certainly were not Mossad who occasionally checked up on "friendly" operatives. What did they want with him?

Chapter Nine

SOMETIMES THINGS HAPPEN IN OUR LIVES that defy explanation. No matter how hard we try we just can't make any sense out of the things God puts in our path. Yet, if we remain faithful and patient, God often puts all the pieces together and reveals His purpose. He truly works in mysterious ways.—Awakened Incident Manual, Volume 2, Page 71

September 12, 4:12 p.m., Seattle

Joon shook his head in an effort to force his vision to stabilize. When it did, he let out a gasp. The trees, dirt road, and sky were all gone. He was standing in the lobby of a large building, still holding on to one of the men. Only the men no longer looked Korean, they looked Middle Eastern. But Joon was certain they were the same two men.

He glanced up. The lobby atrium rose four stories high. His legs almost buckled. He'd never seen a place so large. "What…happened? Where am I? What is this place? How…?"

The man holding his hand grinned. "It's okay. You're where God wants you to be. In a moment you'll meet someone named L. Trust him, listen to him, do what he says. Be sure to tell him what happened to you."

Before Joon could respond, the two men were gone. Vanished as mysteriously as they had appeared. His heart raced. He wanted to run somewhere—anywhere—to hide, but his legs didn't seem to work.

He looked around. A man stood behind a counter speaking into a phone. Several people were sitting in a small carpeted area to his right staring at him. None of them were Korean.

Someone walked up behind him and tapped him on his shoulder. "Sir, I can help you. Will you come with me?"

Joon jumped, then turned around. The man was wearing a

dark suit, white shirt, and blue tie. He was definitely American, of medium height with a muscular build. Something about him seemed...calming? Safe? Exactly like the two men who somehow brought him here.

The man held out his hand. "Welcome. My name is Ray Springer. I'm head of security here at SOAR, the Society of the Awakened and Restored. You must have a lot of questions. We'll answer them as best we can. Come with me, please."

"You speak perfect Korean." He didn't have a gun? All security agents were armed in North Korea. Joon scanned the area again. This wasn't Korea.

"Actually, I don't speak Korean at all. I'm speaking English. I know this is confusing for you, but don't worry. Come with me."

Joon nodded and followed Ray. *I understand him. He must be speaking Korean. Why does he deny it?*

Joon was led into a bright, colorful room with a spongy, pale-blue carpet. Up ahead was a large cross. He stared at it. He'd never seen a cross that size before. This must be a church. Joon slowly formed a smile. He'd never been in a church before, though as a child he imagined what it would be like. This was much better.

The room was filled with the sound of falling water. He turned to his right. An indoor waterfall! He walked over and plunged his hands into the water. In the concentration camp, dirty, foul-tasting water had been a valuable commodity. In this room it was fresh and clean and pure and plentiful and...and beautiful. *I must be in heaven.*

He looked back at the cross and saw the words written above it. *Life lies on both sides of death.* It was clearly not written in Korean, yet he could read it. What was going on? He could read English? How could this be? Was Ray telling the truth when he said he was speaking English?

Ray tapped Joon on the shoulder. As he turned, Ray said, "Yong Joon, I'd like you to meet Matthew Hansen and L."

Joon held out a hand. "Those two men told me I would meet

an L. They said I'm supposed to listen to you. Am I really speaking English?"

L took Joon's hand. "Yes, you are. We call those two men the Gatherers. You must have a lot of questions. Where do you want to start?"

Where do I want to start? Joon's head started to spin. His knees buckled.

L took his arm and led him to a chair. "I know this can be overwhelming. Here...take a seat and we'll start over."

Joon sat and tears began to form in his eyes. "In the last twenty-four hours, I died, woke up right before I was to be cremated, escaped the camp on a pile of dead bodies, met the two most extraordinary men, and suddenly found myself in a new country. And to top it all off, now I can speak and understand English. I have no idea where to start."

L nodded. "I fully understand. It will take time to come to terms with all that has happened to you. Right now, we have urgent business to discuss. I'll let Matthew explain things to you. Over the years he has gotten far better at it than me."

Matthew sat next to Joon as L made his way out of the chapel. "It's interesting that you would use the expression 'woke up.' All of us here are like you. We died and God raised us. We call ourselves the Awakened. L was one of the first. His real name is Lazarus..."

Joon held up his hand. "You mean the Lazarus from the Bible?"

"Yes, that Lazarus. But there's more. Lots more."

Joon listened as Matthew explained the Awakened the UnDead, Naturals, and the fact that he would never die again. Before long, Joon became very tired. His head began to nod.

Matthew put his hand on Joon's shoulder. "I'm sorry. I can easily get a little carried away talking about all this. You're clearly exhausted. I'll get Ray to take you to one of our guest rooms. You can get some sleep and we'll answer more questions as well as get your story in the morning. Oh, and there will be a fresh change of clothes for you."

A few minutes later, Joon paused at the doorway to the guest room. His eyes widened, and he turned to Ray. "I'm going to stay *here?*"

Ray nodded. "It's all yours while you're with us. I hope you find it acceptable."

Joon let his gaze scan the room. "It's...it's...beautiful."

The room was light green with a matching couch and two stuffed chairs in the middle of the room. Fresh flowers sat on a small table in front of the couch. Between the two chairs was another small table with a phone sitting on it. A large window was beyond that.

A small refrigerator sat to the left of the front door. Joon pointed to the door on the right wall. "Where does that lead?"

"That's your bedroom. You'll find a closet and a bathroom inside there as well."

Joon walked over to the couch. "Can I sit down?"

"Sure, this is your room. Do what you want with it." Ray pointed to the phone. "If you need anything or have any questions, hit 0 on the phone and someone will help you." He glanced at his watch. "I'll leave you here for the night." Ray waved as he closed the door behind him.

Joon looked at the device Ray had pointed to. *Phone?* He walked over to the window. One glance and he stepped back. He'd never been up so high in his life. He felt dizzy and his heart pounded. *It will be okay.*

He stepped forward again. The sky was a light blue with a few clouds floating above. The setting sun sparkled on a large body of water. He stood mesmerized for a few moments.

He walked into the bedroom. Ahead was a double bed with a beautiful pale-blue blanket on top. He looked to his right and his mouth froze open. The door to the bathroom was open. He put his hand over his mouth. There was a door to the bathroom? He peeked in and saw a sink, a toilet, and... What was that big white thing? What was he supposed to do with it?

He walked over to the bed and plopped down. The pillow looked big and inviting. He rested his head on it and within seconds was asleep.

September 13, 9:01 a.m., Seattle

As L walked down the hallway to his office he glanced at Ricki's door. It was closed. *I wonder where she is?* L shrugged, unlocked his door and walked in toward his desk.

A knock sounded on his door. He turned. It was Matthew, a little out of breath as if he'd run down the long hallway. "Boss, we have a potentially big problem."

L waved Matthew in. "Come on in and sit down. Did Joon tell you something?"

"Yes. He said he died in a North Korean concentration camp from what he assumed was an experimental disease. I ran his symptoms by Dr. Meakin. Linda says her best guess is some kind of new Ebola strain. But Ebola is not and never has been reported in Korea. I guess it's possible that someone from North Korea harvested the virus from, say, Africa. And here's the worst part. The fact that Joon never had any direct physical contact with anyone with Ebola tells her it might be an airborne strain."

"Airborne?"

"Yes. What makes Ebola less of a threat is that it requires transfer by contact with bodily fluids. If it's airborne it could spread everywhere, and fatalities may run at eighty percent or more. But even worse, this morning we decoded a UD message in Zag that confirms what Joon said, and it was from Renaud."

L sat up straight. "Renaud?"

"Uh-huh. To Sok Kang Ju telling him that once he sold the virus to ISIS, he'd be free to use it as he wants. This is while Kang Ju is talking about peace."

L's stomach suddenly felt…light? Empty? He wrinkled his brow. "All right." He leaned back in his overstuffed chair and paused for a second. "This answers so many questions. It appears that this Renaud has some level of authority over Kang Ju, which means what we have always suspected—North Korea is ruled by a UD. Renaud must be The UD, meaning we have to keep our hands off him. But Kang Ju is another matter. We need a team to go in and dust him quickly before he can use this virus. Ariella's our best, especially on such short notice. Call her and put her on it."

"But it won't be easy getting a team into North Korea undetected and then finding Kang Ju out in the open. That's been impossible up till now because he surrounds himself with Naturals. Besides, doing that while these peace talks are going on may not be the best political move. It may sabotage any chance of peace."

"We have to try. Maybe Joon will be able to help sneak them in. As far as the peace talks are concerned, like you said, this Ebola development is more evidence of what we already knew. No UD, especially a UD like Kang Ju, would seriously be interested in peace."

"Okay. I'll get Ariella on Kang Ju. Anything else?"

L thought for a moment. "I want to brief Ricki on this."

"Why?"

"Why not?" L paused again and swung around to look out the window. "Actually, Matthew, I'm not sure why. I have a feeling. Ricki's making progress in finding the secret in my journal, but she still hasn't cracked it. The nature of that secret might depend on the events of today. Even though I wrote the journal, Jesus said I would not be able to recognize the secret. We need Ricki's input, and we need it soon."

"Earl Nightingale once said, 'All you need is the plan, the road map, and the courage to press on to your destination.'"

"Never met him. But he was right, and in our case, the journal may be our road map."

"Okay. I saw Dr. Spenser in her office. I'll send her over."

L rested his elbows on his desk and steepled his fingers as

Matthew walked out. L wanted to see Ricki for more than the reason he told Matthew. He constantly marveled at the way she had come into his life. And, as he had so many times, his mind rehashed the series of incidents that added up to a miracle. It began when she accidently fell onto UD radar. She was kidnapped, threatened, and released with the promise that they would be watching her. *I…we, took her in to protect her.* At which point she uttered the words he had been waiting to hear for two thousand years. Words that identified her as the one who would unlock the secret in his journal.

But she had become more than that. Over the last few months, she had brought a kind of peace to his world he hadn't experienced for centuries. He needed that now, especially as he thought about the kind of carnage the UDs were threatening to unleash.

He opened the locked drawer in his desk and pulled out a drawing of a man with a beard. *Is this how you planned it to end?*

Chapter Ten

THE DARK EVIL THAT HAS INVADED God's creation is not here for us to endure; it is here for us to overcome. —Awakened Incident Manual, Volume 2, Page 13

September 13, 9:05 a.m., Seattle

Ricki came arrived at the office early. She spent the last half hour staring out her window down at CenturyLink Field. It had the makings of a bright sunny day. Something that was actually common in Seattle in mid-September, one of its hidden secrets because most people believe it always rains in Seattle. She wished the Seahawks were playing today so she could watch through the telescope Matthew had given her. She made a mental note to look up their schedule. Maybe SOAR could get her a ticket for one of the home games.

She picked up L's journal to resume reading it. It was her second time through the early events because she wanted to make sure she didn't miss anything.

Odette had walked in on her during her last week in DC while Ricki was reading the journal and said, "I think it's good you're reading that. It will help you better understand L." Then Odette paused. "I think the times when Jesus was around were the most significant."

Ricki hadn't asked her what she meant by "significant," but it made her want to go back and start over at the beginning. After all, the woman she knew as Odette today was with Lazarus and Jesus, only under the name Sapphira. It would make sense that if Jesus knew there was a secret in the journal it meant that He planted it. So much depended on her getting this right. Of finding the right secret.

Matthew knocked on her open door. "Welcome back, Ricki. Did you have a good time with Odette?"

"She's wonderful. We had some great girl time together. Next to Mary, she's becoming my best friend."

"I'm glad. We all need friends." Matthew rubbed the back of his neck. "Especially in these times… L wants to see you."

"Now? What about?"

"I'll let him tell you."

Ricki closed her computer and went next door. He briefed her about North Korea and his fears. She was quiet for a moment, trying to take it all in.

Her shoulders sagged as bile bubbled up from her stomach. "Why would one human being want to do something like that to another human being?" Ricki shook her head. "I don't think I'll ever understand the depths of evil. What leads man to even contemplate something like that?"

"In this case Kang Ju had help."

"So he's a UD?"

"Yes, and we strongly suspect his son is one too."

"The leaders of North Korea are UDs? Does that happen very often? I mean UDs running nations?"

"It has from time to time. Germany and Russia during World War II, for example, and, of course, Cambodia. Almost any country where government-sponsored mass killings occur. It's what UDs like to do."

Ricki shook her head. "What do you think I can do?"

"I was hoping that the secret in my journal might give me some guidance. Have you found anything? Any clue at all?"

Ricki stared down at her lap. "Not so far. I don't even know what I'm searching for." She looked at L as she grabbed a strand of chestnut hair and twirled it around her finger. "Actually, I went back to the beginning of your journal. I have a feeling the answer lies, or at least begins, in the early stuff."

"Interesting. Don't let me stop you."

Ricki returned to her office, fired up her computer, and advanced to where she had left off, at Lazarus's discovery that Jesus had returned from the dead.

I found Josias and Sapphira, Jairus's daughter, in the compound. I could not contain my joy as I told them what Mary Magdalene had told me. "I just got the most wonderful news," Mary shouted to anyone who would listen. "He's alive. Jesus is alive!"

Josias's eyes widened. "Are you sure?"

I shrugged. "His body wasn't there, and an angel told Mary and her friends he was alive."

Sapphira started to cry. "He came back, just like us. He came back." She wiped her eyes as the tears turned to a smile. "I knew he would." Her eyes twinkled.

Josias asked, "Then where is he? When can we see him?"

"I don't know. He seems to appear, then disappear. I've heard an unconfirmed rumor that two men saw him somewhere between here and Emmaus. I'm sure he'll want to talk with us, but we will have to wait on his timing."

Word quickly spread throughout the compound. Some of the Awakened had, like me, actually been around Jesus, but many had not. It didn't make any difference. Everyone was excited to hear he was alive. Some wanted to go out and look for him, but I convinced everyone the best strategy was to wait here until Jesus came to us.

That wasn't to happen for two more weeks. In the meantime, the day-to-day business of organizing the Awakened consumed my attention. We had food to arrange, questions to answer, and Miriam and I had those creatures to worry about.

Stories about Jesus began to circulate. We heard about his first appearing to the disciples and how he let Thomas inspect his wounds. That was not only comforting to Thomas, but several Awakened had their doubts, which were put to rest by the story of Thomas. The stories made us more eager to see him. I even began to wonder if my strategy of waiting until Jesus appeared to us had been the right one. Maybe I should have searched for him myself. After all, I needed to see Jesus too.

The day eventually came when Jesus appeared in our compound. By then we had swelled to about five-hundred

Awakens and family.

I had called a meeting that morning and barely began to speak when I heard a commotion at the rear of the crowd. I looked out and saw Jesus. Before I could say anything, he appeared beside me. He gave me a comforting smile and proceeded to talk to the group. He told us more about who we were and what we had been called to do. He taught us about his role in Scripture and ended with instructions for us to do nothing until the Spirit of God was poured out on us. I think that was his message wherever he went. I don't think anyone really understood what that meant until it happened a few weeks later.

He dismissed the group, and as they broke up, he turned to me and put his arm around my shoulder. I immediately sucked in my breath. My whole body tingled. I had forgotten the power his touch carried.

He told me I had done well. Then said he had to leave, but that he wanted me to join him on the Mount of Olives in three weeks. He said he would explain more to me then.

I started to say, "Lord," but before I could get the word out of my mouth, he was gone. Tears formed in my eyes, and I yearned for Jesus' touch once again.

Ricki put the journal down. For the briefest of moments, she felt Jesus's touch. Unlike the ugly touch of her uncle, this was intoxicating and peaceful at the same time. She closed her eyes and leaned back. It was gone as quickly as it came, but she knew what it was. *Thank you, Lord.* For a few minutes she felt warm, safe, and loved. Her mind wandered back to the hug Lazarus gave her while celebrating the dusting of Abdul Baith. *Maybe I pulled back too soon. Maybe I should have let myself feel the truth of that moment.*

September 13, 9:21 a.m., Seattle

Matthew needed to contact both Shiri and Ariella to get the ball rolling. Since he was only warning Shiri, that call came first.

Shiri answered on the first ring. "Hello, Matthew, what's up? Got a job for me?"

"Hi. No job, but congratulations on the Abdul Ba'ith dusting."

"Thanks. I hadn't been on a UD hunt for a long time. I was hoping you might have another one for me."

"Not today, but I need to alert you to a development that resulted from that hunt. Do you know a Declan Walsh?"

There was a short pause. "I assume you're talking about someone from this century."

Matthew could imagine the smile on Shiri's face.

Shiri continued. "Seriously, that name does sound familiar. Is he CIA? I think I heard that name at a briefing last year. Why do you ask?"

"You're right; he's CIA. He's asking around Mossad about a woman who fits your description."

"What makes you think it's related to Abdul Ba'ith?"

"The word is that he mentions an event in the City of the Dead. He wants to know if you were there five months ago."

More silence on Shiri's end for a second. "I don't remember seeing him there, but a lot happened very quickly. Do you have the video of the dusting?"

"We do."

"Then could you email me a copy? I'll study the scene and see if I recognize anyone from the CIA."

"You'll get it within the hour. Let us know what you find."

Matthew hung up. What was he going to say to Ariella? Dusting the "supreme leader" of North Korea while keeping to the three laws of UD hunting would be a difficult task. And L told him he planned to join her along with Joon. After a few minutes of thought, he picked up the phone and called Ariella on a secure line.

"Hi, Matthew. Is this a social call or business?"

"As much as I'd love to call you just to chat someday, this

isn't it. I have a job for you."

"Great. I'm beginning to love your calls."

"Are you sitting down?"

"Let's say I am. Who are we dusting today?"

"Sok Kang Ju."

Ariella whistled. "It's about time. And L is okay with this?"

"Not only is he okay with it, he is going to join you and bring along a new Awakened from North Korea. Yong Joon."

"This must be urgent to take on a target like that."

"It is. It appears that Sok Kang Ju's nuclear project has been a ruse all along. What he really developed was a bioweapon. If we don't get to him soon, he will deploy that weapon."

September 13, 10:00 a.m., Tel Aviv

Ariella Blick looked to the mantel on the fireplace. "Alexa, stop play list." The room went quiet. She'd been listening to the songs of her new favorite musical, *Matilda*. She needed to listen to musicals more often since Matthew seemed to call with the most challenging assignments when she did. And this time was the most challenging of all.

She sat for a moment to gather her thoughts. Aside from The UD, L was sending them after one of the most dangerous UDs in history.

She swept a wavy strand of dark hair behind her ears as a dark tingling sensation skittered down her back. *What's wrong with me?*

She leaned back, looked up at the ceiling, and realized she had started taking quick, short breaths. *All right, Ariella. What's going on? Why am I so nervous about this hunt?*

She took another deep breath and let her mind wander in search of an answer. She smelled the faint odor of peppermint coming from the essential oil diffuser she always had running in her apartment. The fragrance had a calming effect.

She listened to the silence that seemed to engulf the room. It was peaceful but not long lasting. She found herself humming her favorite song from *Matilda, When I Grow Up*.

She opened her eyes and sat up straight. "That's it. It's that song." *Matilda is facing the greatest challenge in her young life and she sings about being strong enough to carry the weight of a grown up and brave enough to fight the creatures that live under her bed. Am I grown up enough, am I strong enough, am I brave enough to take on this evil when the lives of millions are at stake?* She let that thought wander through her mind for a moment. *The answer is yes. I am strong enough and I am brave enough,*

Finally being given a shot at the most notorious UD of them all besides The UD, whoever that might be, she knew the team she wanted, starting once again with Agam. She called him and Shiri and set up a meeting at her apartment in an hour. *Time to once again save the world.*

This was going to be quite a hunt.

Chapter Eleven

JUST AS PARENTS PROVIDE A ROOM, paint it, and fill it in anticipation of a new baby, God prepared a home for us but that home would be empty and meaningless if the sixth day never happened. Everything thing that God did in the first five days of creation had one purpose—it was His gift to us.—Awakened Incident Manual, Volume 2, Page 86

September 13, 9:17 p.m., Tel Aviv

Ariella, Shiri, and Agam gathered in Ariella's apartment to plan their next UD hunt. Shiri came in first and gave Ariella a big hug. Agam walked in next with a wide grin, rubbing his hands together. "All right, who's the target this time?"

Shiri turned to him with a sly smile. "Don't you want to admire Ariella's flowers first?"

"What? Oh...it's that flower thing again like at our first meeting. No, I'll leave flowers to the women. Now let's get down to business." Agam didn't take the bait this time.

Ariella pointed to the couch. "You'll have to sit down for this one."

Agam sat next to Shiri, his broad, muscular frame taking up over half the couch. "It's a big one. I can feel it."

"You're right." Ariella sat on the chair across from them. "Try Sok Kang Ju."

Agam let out a high-pitched whistle. "L authorized this?"

"Yes, he did."

Agam shook his head. "But I thought Sok Kang Ju was off-limits. He is always surrounded by Naturals. If we tried anything, someone might die."

"Apparently, he has control of a weapon of indiscriminate mass destruction. A bioweapon. And he plans to use it. Soon. Possibly against South Korea or in the Middle East. We can't afford not to act."

Agam was tapping his foot. "How do we know this? I mean, are we sure?"

Ariella nodded. "SOAR intercepted a coded message that talked about it."

Agam stopped tapping.

Ariella turned to Shiri. "You've been quiet. What's up?"

Shiri collapsed back into the couch. "I'm afraid there's blowback from our last operation together. A CIA agent, Declan Walsh, has been asking around Mossad about a field agent in Cairo who fits my description. I looked him up and compared his picture to that of the man standing beside Abdul Ba'ith on a video of the dusting. It's a match. He must have seen me when I collected the living dust."

"So," Ariella narrowed her eyes, "how much does he know?"

Shiri shrugged. "I don't know. From the video it's clear he's a Natural. A Natural who witnessed a dusting. The problem is, he's not just any Natural. He has a reputation as a pit bull. When he's on a case, he does not let go of it until he gets answers. And now, given what he's seen, he has a doozy of a case."

Agam sighed and cross his arms. "So what does L want you to do?"

Shiri rubbed her cheek. "He wants me to handle it. I need to meet Walsh and assess what he knows and what he wants. If it comes to it and if I think it's safe, I'm authorized to tell him the truth. At least, part of the truth."

"Hold it!" Agam started tapping his foot again. "We already let Ricki in, now you want to let in another Natural?"

Ariella held up her hand. "We might not have gotten L to okay the dusting of Abdul Ba'ith if it wasn't for Ricki. She's been a good addition. Who knows? Things are heating up. This CIA agent could be an asset."

Agam shook his head. "He won't believe it anyway."

"Ricki did," Shiri said. "If God wants him in, he'll believe it. At any rate, I've got to stay here. I can help, but only from a distance. I'm scheduled to meet with him at a coffee shop tomorrow evening."

"This may work out. L is going to join us on this hunt, along with a new Awakened," Ariella said. "It seems Yong Joon is from North Korea. He's the one who tipped us off to the bioweapon, so he should be a big help getting us into the country. Where we really need your help, Shiri, is formulating a workable plan."

"Yeah." Agam turned to Shiri. "Do you have any ideas to get us started?"

Shiri looked up at the ceiling. She was in full analyst mode. After a few seconds, her mouth started to move but no sound came out.

Agam smiled and tapped Shiri on the shoulder. "We can't hear you."

"Sorry." Shiri's attention shifted to Agam. "I was talking to myself. The curse of the analyst, I guess. As I see it, we have four problems. First, getting into North Korea without alerting Kang Ju. Second, getting close enough to him so we can verify it's the real Kang Ju and not one of his Natural doubles. Three, dusting him. And four, getting out of North Korea without harming a Natural."

Ariella nodded. "Guess we have our work cut out for us."

For the next five hours, the three discussed possible solutions to all four problems. Eventually, Ariella checked her watch. "Guys, it's almost two thirty in the morning. I think we have a good start, but it's time to quit and get some rest. Tomorrow I'll run our ideas by Matthew and see if he can give us more information. Let's meet here on the sixteenth when L and Yong Joon can join us. In the meantime, give some thought to what we discussed tonight."

Once Agam and Shiri left, Ariella stood by the window looking out at the dark Tel Aviv sky. "God, this is a tough one. We really need your help."

September 13, 10:23 p.m., Tel Aviv

Declan paced in the small safe house, unable to return to his apartment until it was clean. It'd had been over twenty-four hours since his apartment had been invaded, and he was getting antsy.

He kept checking his watch until the phone finally rang. Declan took the call. It was Tom Johnson, the CIA station chief. He heaved a sigh.

"Declan, I'm glad I caught you. Your apartment is now spotless. All traces of the other night have been removed."

Declan suddenly felt lighter. "Thank you, I'll head over and pick up my stuff, but I don't think I'll move back until I know why they came after me."

"I may be able to help you on that one. We identified one of them as a Jabir Sadik. We have him on a list of suspected Abbud Abbas members, and he is a known associate of Abd al Hakim, also in Abbud Abbas. He could very well be one of the links between them and ISIS."

Abbud Abbas was a fast-growing terrorist group, but they always suspected it could only grow that fast if it had roots in a more established organization. "I don't know. I didn't recognize either tango. If this Jabir was close to the Abbud Abbas organization and/or their leader Abdul Ba'ith, I never ran into him."

"Still the opinion here is that these guys came after you because of something related to your work with Abdul Ba'ith."

"Perhaps. I did get close to him. He seemed to trust me. But it didn't last long."

"Too bad you had to pop them. If there was a connection between these two and Abbud Abbas, they might have been able to fill us in on what happened to the organization. Maybe even tell us where Abdul Ba'ith is." A short pause followed.

He wants something from me. Well, he wasn't going to get it.

Tom continued. "That reminds me. He disappeared after you left him in the City of the Dead, and no one has been able to pick up his trail since then. You may very well be the last person to see him. Do you know what happened to him?"

Declan sighed. "I don't understand what happened at all." That was the truth. No need to elaborate and say Abdul Ba'ith turned into dust in front of him. But soon he would get answers.

Chapter Twelve

As you serve God, you need to understand that at times you will be rejected and you will even make mistakes, get over it. — *Awakened Incident Manual, Volume 2, Page 60*

September 13, 9:45 p.m., Paris

Renaud walked with an uncharacteristic spring to his step. When he reached the Ministry of Foreign Affairs, he stopped and sat down on the steps leading up to the main entrance. He scanned the area around the Ministry, watched the moonlight reflect off the lazy ripple of the Seine, listened to the music from a local nightclub as it wafted across the grassy park in front of the Ministry. He took in a deep breath and slowly allowed it to escape his lungs as he took in the sweet aroma of Paris on a clear night. *Less than a month and this will all belong to me. The next time I return to Paris crowds will line the road cheering me on.* He smiled. *And I'll be in a limo not on the back of some filthy donkey.* He looked up at the sky. *Well God, I'm afraid this centuries-long chess game is about to end in my favor. If you weren't blinded by these Naturals you would kick over your king and resign now, because in a month, Naturals all around the world will abandon you. I will be their savior.*

He got up and entered the Ministry. He walked up to Chavvah's office and seeing the door wide open, he stepped in. Chavvah was sitting back in her chair, staring at the Paris moon shining through the skylight.

He cleared his throat.

Chavvah swung around in her chair to face him. "It's late. Did you need something?"

"Yes. I'm leaving for the DMZ in Korea tomorrow morning to inspect the area and then heading on to Pyongyang for the peace talks. As I planned, Minister Pinay has given what he thinks is a hopeless mission to his newest assistant secretary for Asia. He has no idea what I'll accomplish." Renaud paused for a moment, then grinned. "The truth is, he has no idea what I'm capable of, but first we have to get Kang Ju and his foolish plan to infect South Korea out of the picture. I assume you sent him that coded email?"

"Of course."

"Then Lazarus has certainly broken it by now and knows all about our little bioweapon. It's too late for him to do anything to save Israel because it's already on its way to ISIS, but he can put a stop to Kang Ju and any use of the weapon on South Korea."

"And how do you know that?"

"Actually, I'm not sure yet. But I think we might call on your prophetic powers." Renaud lips twisted in a mockery of a smile.

"You still doubt them, don't you?"

"Let's say you've had your successes and your failures."

"I hope you noticed UVs are getting stronger and my powers are as well. If I foresee any problems in their little quest, I'll do what I can to help them."

"See to it that you do, a lot rides on preventing Kang Ju from attacking South Korea."

Renaud stood up and started to leave when he stopped and looked back at Chavvah. "One more thing"

Chavvah looked up at him, "Yes?"

"With my accession coming soon, we need to clean house a bit."

"How?"

"I still hear among the rank and file the term 'UD' or UnDead being bounced around. I want that to stop. We are the UnVeilers, we are UV's. I know a lot of them like it because it uses the word dead but, as we stand on the edge of victory, that term makes us seem like ghouls. It's vulgar."

"I'll see what I can do."

September 15, 6:21 a.m., Pyongyang

Sok Kang Ju usually liked to sleep in, but today he was in his office early waiting for Pong Pak Ju to arrive. He needed him for an important but highly secret step in his plan to take control of the UnVeilers. Pak Ju was a UV loyal to Kang Ju who had taken on several sensitive tasks in the past.

Kang Ju leaned back in his chair beneath a life-size painting of himself sitting on his "throne," much like the one in his receiving room. He often remarked that the only thing the painting was missing was a crown. He twisted around to admire it. It wouldn't be long now. That crown was on its way.

A moment later Pak Ju, Kang Ju's son, was ushered in. He stood maybe four-feet-nine-inches tall. What he lacked in height he more than made up for in muscles. He was barrel chested and bulky. His bald head was shiny, almost as if he waxed it.

Pak Ju walked up to the desk, bowed his head, and remained standing. No one sat in the presence of Sok Kang Ju unless ordered to do so.

"Pak, I have a very important task for you, one that will require all your skills."

Pak Ju tipped his head in a slight nod.

"There's this Natural called Ricki Spenser. Though she is closely associated with the Awakens, Renaud has declared her off-limits. He says she is the key to his ascension, but I think he's just gone soft. I want you to go to Seattle in the United States, find her, and kill her at the first opportunity. But it must be before October 10. I want Renaud to be alive when he hears about it. Do you understand?"

"I do, Glorious Leader."

"Good. No one must know of your mission. You will leave immediately and fly to Beijing. There you will meet your contact. He'll have a South Korean passport for you. From there you will take the next flight to Seattle, where you'll be met by the UV office chief, a Lucas Endre. He is an idiot, but he's sympathetic to our cause. He will fill you in on all you need to know about Ms. Spenser. He does not know the goal of your mission, and you will not tell him unless you deem him useful. Can I trust you with this?"

"You can."

Kang Ju waved him out. "Then be on your way. Remember this must be done before October 10."

Pak snapped to attention, nodded, and walked out.

Kang Ju leaned back in his chair once again and smiled. Everything was going smoothly. In a month he'd have the Awakens on their heels, Renaud out of the picture, South Korea under his thumb, and the UnVeilers in his pocket.

September 14, 7:34 p.m., Tel Aviv

Abd al Hakim had been following Declan for the last two days off and on, ever since Jabir and Fadel vanished without a trace. He'd been waiting for the perfect opportunity to strike. He watched Declan pace back and forth in front of the coffee shop. This would be it. Tonight Declan would die. He licked his lips like a predator ready to pounce on its prey. *I will have my revenge.*

Abd hated all Naturals, but there was a special place in his UD heart for this one. Abd had been a lieutenant in Abbud Abbas and a loyal follower of Abdul Ba'ith. As one of the strategically placed UnVeilers in the organization, he had been there when Abdul was dusted, while this Declan, this scum of a Natural, stood beside him in Cairo.

He has to die. He has to die now. And he has to die painfully.

Abd squinted as the fire within flared. He suspected the Natural got to Jabir and Fadel somehow, but he would not escape him on this night.

Through steely eyes, he continued to watch Declan standing outside the coffee shop. It wasn't long before the Natural was joined by a woman. Something about the woman was unnerving, but he was too far away to discern what. Though his eyesight had been improving lately, for some unexplained reason, the streetlights were too dim at this distance to pin down exactly what bothered him. It didn't help that her back was to him and he couldn't see her eyes.

Declan and the woman talked for a few minutes, then turned and walked into the dimly lit park nearby. Keeping his distance, Abd followed them.

Shiri took a deep breath as they found a bench in the park. She had to satisfy Declan's curiosity tonight without giving anything away.

It was a pleasant September evening with a slight breeze that made it comfortable to talk outside as well as being more private since at this time of night the park is empty. The park was getting dark, but the full moon hung in the sky like a large luminous pearl. The few wisps of clouds did nothing to obscure the light.

"I understand you've been looking for me. What can I do for you?"

"You can help me understand what happened a few months ago in the City of the Dead."

"Go ahead." Shiri could sense the uncertainty in Declan. From what she heard he was not accustomed to feeling this way.

"Were you there when Abdul Ba'ith was taken out?"

"I was." Shiri wasn't going to volunteer anything more than she had to until she knew the extent of Declan's knowledge. He had seen her there, so she couldn't deny it.

"I saw him turn to dust, dust that you collected."

"That's right."

His eyes narrowed and a frown crossed his face. He was irritated by her uncooperative answers.

She stared him in the eye and let him see the honesty in her face and voice as only an Awakened could do. "Mr. Walsh, why don't you tell me what's bothering you, and I will attempt to explain what happened as best I can."

Declan rubbed his chin then took a deep breath and slowly

released it. "Okay. To start with, I saw a man turned to dust. When I checked into his background, I discovered he had been dead for two years. Finally, I retrieved a hollow bullet from the scene that contained blood instead of gunpowder. I sent the blood out for DNA analysis. The results showed it differed from human DNA by more than 2 percent. The report called it perfect DNA. I usually hate mysteries, but when not one but three impossible things happen in front of me, I won't rest until I have answers. And here is my dilemma. Sherlock Holmes said, 'Once you eliminate the impossible, whatever remains, no matter how improbable, must be the truth.' But in this case, all I'm facing are impossibilities."

Shiri hated lying, but if she told the truth, he wouldn't believe it. Besides, if he continued this investigation, he might get hurt or be led to a UD, who would kill him without giving it a second thought. She couldn't allow that. She had to divert him for his own safety.

"I don't know if I can be much help, I'm afraid, but I can tell you this. I too, was puzzled by the dust. That's why I collected it — so I could bring it back and have it analyzed. The best we can determine right now is that he was poisoned by some new fast-acting substance that completely breaks down cellular structure. The lab told me they couldn't analyze its structure. It was an unknown enzyme." Shiri gave herself an internal thumbs-up because in a way that was close to the truth. On a chemical level, this must be what happened when a UD was dusted.

Declan didn't seem convinced, but he appeared to soften. He reached up and rubbed the back of his neck. "Okay, I'll have to think about that. Now what about the other two?"

"As far as Abdul Ba'ith is concerned, I'm afraid I can't help you much there, either. We were able to trace his movements back two years, then we hit the same wall you did. He seemed to suddenly come out of nowhere. If you traced him back to a dead man... I'm sure you can understand why I find that difficult to accept. The DNA?" Shiri shrugged. "I'm at a loss." She really was.

Of course this was Ariella's DNA since it came from the hollow point shell that missed. First time she'd heard their DNA was perfect. Did L know? As far as she knew, this was the first time an Awakened's DNA had ever been analyzed. "Could it have been a lab error?"

Declan shook his head. "They thought that too, so they shut down the lab and checked everything. The equipment was well within standards."

"Then I can't help you."

"Understand, one way or another, I'm going to discover the truth. So if you're holding back on me, you're only delaying things. I don't care how long it takes—I will get answers. You can count on it."

Shiri reached out and set her hand on Declan's arm. She allowed her genuine compassion to shine through, something that was easy for an Awakened, because they could see a Natural through the eyes of Jesus. "I understand, and I wish you success. I'll ask around Mossad, and if I learn anything, I'll get back to you. But to be honest, I don't think there is an answer, at least not a reasonable one." She glanced at her watch and stood. "Now I have to leave."

Declan watched Shiri walk away. He needed a moment to think about their discussion. He lit a cigarette and blew a few smoke rings. They danced in the light evening breeze, shimmering in the reflected moonlight like a waltz of ephemeral fairies. He got essentially no information from her, yet somehow, he felt at peace about it. She was a remarkable woman.

He stood and started to walk back to the coffee shop for his car when a tall, thin Arab approached him from the shadows. "Declan Walsh."

Declan stopped. After the events of the other night, he was extra cautious. The man stood under a streetlight. The light glowed off his white thawb, giving him an almost angelic look, a look that was betrayed by the deep well of evil in his eyes.

Declan froze. The man had a scar on the forehead of his dark, weather-beaten face. He had that tense, prepared-to-kill stance that signaled a battle to the death was about to happen.

Declan stared right into his eyes. He had seen cold, inhuman eyes like that only one other time, when he'd first met Abdul Ba'ith. The breeze suddenly felt frigid as a shiver traveled down his spine. "Do I know you?"

"I am Abd al Hakim."

He did look familiar. Someone who worked for Abdul Ba'ith, perhaps?

His heart rate accelerated; his muscles tensed. He reached behind his waist and put his right hand on the grip of his Glock 19. "What do you want?"

"You betrayed my leader, Abdul Ba'ith, the Servant of the Resurrector, to the Awakened. You must pay."

Declan raised his left hand. "Now hold on a minute. I don't know who you're talking about, and I certainly don't know anything about, what did you call them? The Awakened."

The Arab smiled. "When he was dusted you were by his side, like Judas was by that *Carpenter's* side." He spit on the ground.

Declan, not wanting a confrontation, took a step back. "Look, sir, you've made some kind of mistake. I have no idea what you're talking abo—"

Before he could finish, faster than he could pull out his Glock, Abd's hands were on Declan's neck. His grip was freakishly strong for such a thin man.

Abd growled, "You're going to die...slowly." His eyes seemed to glow red in the darkness.

Declan struggled to breathe. He grabbed Abd's wrists and tried to break his chokehold, but the man was too strong. Declan reached out and clutched both elbows, then pulled down with as much force as he could muster. But the man's grip on his neck didn't move.

His lungs were about to burst. He slid his hands along Abd's arms and reached up to grab his face. Declan dug his thumbs into the man's eyes, gouging as deep as he could.

The man screamed, released his grip, moved back, and covered his eyes.

Declan bent over and sucked in air. He moved his hand to the small of his back and drew his Glock right as the man recovered. Abd stepped forward, grabbed Declan by the neck, and started squeezing the life out of him again. Declan pressed the Glock's barrel to Abd's forehead and pulled the trigger. The man fell backward onto the ground.

Declan dropped to his knees and tried to breathe. He looked at the body, expecting to see a gruesome, bloody mess. A shot from a Glock 19 at that close range could do a lot of damage. Instead, he watched in disbelief and horror as Abd's eyes opened. There was no head wound. Declan stared down at the gun in his hand.

What was going on? Declan had that gun right on the man's forehead when he fired. He heard it discharge. There should be nothing left of his head.

Abd stood up and grinned. "That stung." He laughed. "Foolish Natural, you can't kill me. I am Death, and now you're going to feel the full force of my wrath."

Declan froze as his whole world collapsed around him. This had to be some sort of nightmare.

Abd rushed him, knocking him to the ground. Instantly on top of Declan, the man once again squeezed Declan's neck. Declan struggled hopelessly. *This can't be the way I'm going to die.* Then a long-buried thought came to mind. *Lord, don't let this happen.*

As soon as that strange thought raced through his waning consciousness, a figure ran up beside him, grabbed Abd's arm, and ripped him off Declan. It was Shiri.

Abd looked at her and his hands trembled. Fear whipped across the monster's face and he snarled, "Awakened."

Shiri looked down at Declan. "I'm sorry you have to see this...again." She pulled back Abd's sleeve and bit him on the arm. Instantly, the man dissolved into reddish-brown dust.

It covered Declan. He let out a gasp. Another one turned to dust. *Am I in the Twilight Zone?* A shiver traveled down his body. He wanted to get up. He wanted to run. He wanted to hide. He didn't want any part of a world where monsters could be turned to dust. This was Abdul Ba'ith all over again only worse. Far worse because he was covered in that dust.

He tried to breathe, only sucking in a mouthful of dust. Turning to his side, he coughed up the foul-tasting gunk and then looked back up at Shiri. *What did she do?*

Shiri made a face like she had sucked a lemon and spit out dust. "I hate that."

"What is—going—on?" Declan rasped out the words between coughs. "Are you some—kind of—vampire?"

Shiri reached out to help him stand. "I'm so sorry, Mr. Walsh." She sported a sheepish smile. "No, I'm not a vampire, but you're not the first to ask that question of us." She paused as a serious look washed over her face. "I haven't been entirely truthful with you."

He raised an eyebrow. "You think?"

Shiri pulled a plastic bag out of her coat pocket. "Help me gather this dust, and we'll go to my apartment. I'll tell you the whole truth, but I warn you—you won't believe it."

"I just shot a man point blank in the head, who then proceeded to strangle me right before he turned into dust after you bit him. I might be more open to believing what you have to say than you think."

Chapter Thirteen

OUR SAVIOR SEES HOW GOD DESIGNED us and loves the Awakened for it. Our adversary sees our potential and hates us for it, but even more important, it's the reason he fears us. —Awakened Incident Manual, Volume 2, Page 11

September 14, 9:17 p.m., Tel Aviv

Shiri stood in the elevator of her apartment complex next to Declan as it made its way up to the seventh floor. She silently sized him up, something Awakens could do far better than Naturals. He was a strong man and that was important to him.

Yet she noted the almost imperceptible tremor in his right leg, the way his face seemed frozen, and the way he kept his gaze focused on the floor indicator lights rather than look at her.

He was trying hard to maintain his image, but that was difficult given what he'd seen in the last few months. The world as he knew it had slowly morphed from something familiar to something foreign. Tonight, she would deliver the final blow. Nothing would be the same for him ever again.

Neither spoke on the ride up. Shiri drew her eyebrows together and glanced at the floor indicator. What was wrong with this elevator? It had never been this slow before.

The elevator stopped and the door opened. "This is my floor, and my apartment is 725. To the right and three doors down."

Declan nodded and followed her out. Shiri paused in front of her apartment door. She briefly closed her eyes. Her stomach felt like it was suddenly filled with helium and was floating away. She was stepping way out of line here, not talking to L. Letting Declan in like this was skirting all the rules. When Matthew told her to take whatever action she deemed necessary, she was sure he didn't count on bringing another Natural in. But after all Declan had seen, what else could she do?

Shiri exhaled as she opened the door and stepped inside. *Lord, guide me on this.*

She loved her apartment. It was a warm place that reminded her of God's love for her. She took a moment to soak it in. The west wall that spanned the living, dining, and kitchen area was almost all glass. During the day, the apartment was always bathed in light. Having been born blind, she had an aversion to darkness in any form. Even centuries after she had gained her sight, she still remembered that world of total darkness. The world that Jesus had delivered her from.

She set her jaw. *All right, God. I'm ready.*

She motioned Declan to the plush blue chair by the window while she took the light-green one opposite him. For the same reason the apartment was bathed in light, it was also a rainbow of colors. Her rule of decorating was a different color in every direction. The word *clash* was not in her vocabulary.

She took a moment to admire his physique: tall with short black hair, muscular arms, a firm square jaw, and a look of confidence—his most appealing feature.

Shiri, get down to business. "Mr. Walsh…"

"Call me Declan."

"Okay, Declan. I'm not sure where to start."

He smiled. "Why don't you start at the beginning?"

Shiri smiled back. "You don't know what you're asking." She looked out the window at the night sky bathed in the moonlight. "Okay. Do you believe in Jesus?"

His smile quickly slid into a frown as he shifted his weight in the chair. "You're not going to tell me Jesus is responsible for everything I saw?"

Shiri shook her head. "No…uh…yes, in a way." She held up her hand like a crossing guard signaling stop. "Just answer the question, then you'll see what I'm getting at."

Declan leaned back and crossed his legs. "I did once." He looked down at his feet, stalling, like this was the last thing he wanted to talk about. Then he shrugged. "A decade or so ago, I got close to someone. She was a committed believer. She always told me that God loved her and even me. Then her God allowed her to die in a horrible way and far too young. That didn't look like love to me."

Shiri watched as Declan's face morphed into a paradox of emotion. His jaw tightened as his mouth formed a frown. But his eyes softened as a thin film of water formed over them. This was a complex man.

"Now all I see is evil, death, and darkness in this world. A far cry from a world governed by a loving, forgiving God." He swung his arm out. "I guess you could say I've soured on the whole idea of Jesus, God, what have you. Don't get me wrong, I think there's a higher power. But I don't think He's very interested in us. You could put me in the agnostic camp."

"Okay, I can work with that." Shiri nodded. "Let's begin with my name. It's not Shiri, or at least Shiri is not the name my parents gave me. My parents named me Merriam when I was born more than two thousand years ago." She paused to give Declan time to soak up that little *pelia*—that little miracle of God.

Declan crossed his legs again as he leaned back in the chair, back in control of his face, hiding his emotions. "That's a surprise. You don't look a day over a thousand." A slight, forced grin appeared on his face.

"Why thank you." Shiri tipped her head, appreciating his sense of humor.

Declan was silent for a second. "So you're telling me you're immortal like...like the Highlander in those movies? What do you do, go around killing each other until only one remains? And worse, you think I'm gullible enough to believe it?"

Shiri wrinkled her brow. "I don't know that reference, but no, I wasn't born immortal. In fact, I died at a relatively young age."

"Hold on." Declan clasped his hands behind his head. "From immortal to dead in one sentence. This is too much..."

Shiri shook her head. "Mr. Walsh." She had to get him to pay attention. She let her natural Awakened believability take over.

She stared him in the eyes, baring her soul through them. Uncharacteristically, she found herself getting lost in his deep-blue eyes. *Shiri, get in control. You have to do this right.* She took a deep breath. "I'm not dead. I'm clearly alive. You see, Jesus raised me, and anyone Jesus raises never dies again. It's in the Bible, Hebrews 9:27: 'It is appointed for men to die once,' and I reached my limit of one death." She continued to search his eyes. "Look, you've seen a lot of impossible things and, unlike Sherlock Holmes, you won't be able to eliminate any of them. You've seen two men turn to dust right in front of you. One of them had been dead for two years. You found a sample of perfect DNA. Those are all facts."

Declan slowly shook his head. "All right, I've seen a lot of strange, unexplainable things. Still, I hope you appreciate how difficult this is to believe. You mean to tell me that nothing can kill you?"

"Nothing." It was a condition that had helped her more than once over the centuries. "You saw that man in the park. Remember, you put a bullet point blank between his eyes, and yet..." Suddenly Shiri had an idea. "I'll give you a little demonstration."

"Don't think for a moment I'm going to shoot you."

"No, something simpler than that." She motioned for him to follow her into the kitchen where she turned on the largest burner on her stove. They stood silent for a second until the burner was bright red. Then she slapped her left palm down on top of it. She bit down on her lower lip, forcing back a whimper.

Declan let out a gasp. "Doesn't it hurt?"

"It does...not as much as it might hurt you, but it's not fun." She slowly counted to ten, then lifted her hand off the burner. She held it up for him to examine. The skin was bright red, even a little charred in places. They both watched as it healed in a matter of seconds. "See, not a mark, and it's not even warm."

He examined her hand. His touch seemed to linger a little longer than necessary, and to her surprise, she liked it. She gazed into Declan's eyes. There was something about this tall man standing in front of her. Something that tapped into feelings that had lain dormant for centuries.

"Is your skin made of soft Kevlar?" he asked with a sheepish grin.

She laughed. "No, it's the hand cream I use that makes it so soft yet burn proof. Satisfied?"

They walked back to the living room. Declan sat down, tilted his head to the side, and studied her for a second. "So...are you like my opponent this evening? Can someone bite you and turn you to dust?"

"No. He was what we call the UnDead, a demon-possessed dead body."

He lifted his hands in the air and plopped them back onto his legs. "Oh, now you tell me there are zombies in this picture."

"No, well...kind of, I guess, but I'm not at all like that. We call ourselves the Awakened. We have all been raised at one time or another by Jesus, and we've banded together to help Naturals."

"Naturals?"

"Oh, that's people like you, people with normal lifetimes who are not aware of the true nature of the world in which they live."

"So, I'm the only Natural who knows about this?"

"No, at the moment there is one other. Her name is Dr. Ricki Spenser. You should meet her. You'd like her. And there have been a few others throughout the centuries, but not many."

"I would like to meet her. We could compare notes and all you..." He twirled his right hand in a small circle while he was searching for words. "What did you call yourselves? Awakened?"

"Yes."

"All you Awakeneds have been raised from the dead by Jesus and will not die again?"

"You got it."

"Then..." Shiri could see the wheels turning in Declan's head. "Then that person, you know the famous one that Jesus raised, ah...Lazarus. Is he an Awakened too?"

"Yes. In fact, he is our leader."

Declan shook his head. "I'm having a hard time swallowing this, but I guess I've got a lot to learn." *What's going on here? Things are not making sense.*

"That you do."

Declan rubbed his chin. "Do you mind if I smoke?"

She bit her lip. "Usually, I do, but if it will relax you, go ahead this once."

"Thanks, it will." Declan lit up, and while he smoked four cigarettes, she filled him in on some basic background. By the time she was done with the fundamentals, Declan was starting to fall asleep in the chair.

She covered him with a blanket. "Here, you need some rest."

She stood over him for a few minutes, watching him drift off to sleep, as an unfamiliar warmth washed over her body.

As she walked to her bedroom, she suddenly stopped as a slightly outrageous idea popped into her head. She smiled. *It just might work.* She grabbed her phone and talked with Ariella for almost forty-five minutes and then went to bed. It had been a very good day.

Shiri woke up early the next morning. Ever since she had awakened, she'd never required more than four or five hours of sleep. Before she was done fixing breakfast, Declan woke up.

"Well, good morning. You fell asleep on me last night."

"I guess zombie wrestling takes a lot out of you." Declan sported a big grin.

Shiri ignored Declan's humor. "So how do you feel about what I told you last night?"

He was quiet for a second. He ran his fingers through his hair. "If I hadn't seen two men turn to dust and everything else, I would have said you were flat-out crazy. But as it is, I kind of have to accept it, though I'm still a little shaky on the Jesus stuff."

"You still don't think God is behind all this? Do you have a better explanation?"

He shrugged. "I don't know. Maybe you're a race of aliens."

Shiri laughed. "And you'd believe that over believing Jesus is involved?"

"Not necessarily. I told you I'm an agnostic. There's still room for doubt here. Just don't push Him on me, okay?"

"We don't push Jesus on anyone." *He'll come around.* "Tell me, how did you get so close to Abdul Ba'ith so quickly?"

"I've been working the intelligence game in the Middle East a long time. No one has been working off the books here longer than I have."

She raised her hand. "Not true. I have."

"Okay. Two thousand years is hard to beat, I'll give you that. But I do have lots of trustworthy contacts."

"Even in ISIS?"

Declan nodded. "Even in ISIS."

"I hoped that was the case, because while you were sleeping, I was working on a project, a project in which we could use your help without directly involving the CIA. As you say, off the books. Interested?"

"Might be. What's going on?"

"We have information that North Korea has developed an airborne strain of Ebola. Sometime in the next three weeks or so, they are delivering it to ISIS. We are sure ISIS plans to unleash it on Israel before the end of next month. We have to intercept it before that can happen. Game?"

"Will I be working with you?"

"You'll be working with me."

"In that case, I'm in."

"Okay, we're partners." Shiri smiled. *Partners, she liked that.*

For the next three hours, Shiri answered questions as she told Declan about UDs, dusting, UD hunting, SOAR, the truth behind a few major historical events, and threw in a little about Jesus as well.

Chapter Fourteen

Jesus came to show us how to live in the shadow of death, to be constantly tempted by sin, yet never to fear evil. So it follows that it is our responsibility both to accept his gift of salvation and to live by the model He set. We are called to continue the work He began on earth. We are called to live like Jesus in every respect because the purpose of His life was to teach us how to do just that until He returns. —Awakened Incident Manual, Volume 2, Page 11

September 15, 11:21 a.m., Seattle

Lucas Endre waited in baggage claim at the Sea-Tac Airport for Pong Pak Ju to arrive. He had never met him, but odds were, he was the only UV on the plane. UVs could always recognize other UVs.

He was more than happy to do a favor for Sok Kang Ju. He was a take-charge UV, unlike Chavvah. Lucas frowned. He'd discovered The Journal, the journal that was the UDs version of the holy grail. And she didn't even thank him. Kang Ju would have promoted him. He recognized talent when he saw it.

Lucas continued to brood for another five minutes when he saw a short, bald UV walking in his direction. Korean. Must be Pong.

Lucas walked up with his hand out. "Welcome to Seattle, Mr. …er…Mr. Pak Ju."

"Mr. Pong."

The strange little Korean looked down at Lucas's outstretched hand and wrinkled his forehead. "Ricki where?"

So much for pleasantries. Lucas checked his watch. "Most likely at SOAR headquarters. Why?"

"So, home is empty."

Lucas shrugged. "She hasn't lived in Tacoma for months."

Pak Ju smiled. "Take me."

"What for? I told you, she hasn't been there since this all started."

Pak Ju's smile morphed back into his usual frown. "Take me."

Lucas held up his hands. "All right, but it's in the opposite direction we were supposed to go." He knew he should have brought something to drink.

Pak Ju just grunted.

A little over an hour later, they arrived at Ricki's house.

Lucas led Pak Ju up the steps to the door. "You're in luck. She's pretty much abandoned the place. A while ago, we had one of our locksmiths come late at night to make a key for us so we could search for the rest of the journal. We came up empty, but we still have the key."

As soon as they stepped in, Pak Ju motioned with his hand. "Bedroom?"

"All the way upstairs, but there's nothing—"

Pak Ju didn't wait for Lucas to finish his thought before he headed up the stairs.

Not very friendly, Lucas thought as he followed him up.

There were two bedrooms upstairs. The one directly across from the stairs was clearly empty, but the one to the left had a bed, a few items of clothing strewn on the floor, and a couple of drawers hanging open. It looked as if someone had left in a hurry.

Lucas stood in the doorway and watched Pak Ju's strange behaviors. First, he flopped on the bed and stared at the ceiling. Next, he peeked under the bed. Strangest of all, he picked up a shirt from the floor and buried his head in it. Then he turned to Lucas.

"Office?"

"What was that all about?"

"Learning."

Lucas nodded even though he had no idea what that meant. "Oh."

"Office."

"Downstairs, across from the kitchen." Lucas's neck tensed with his frustration. "What are you going to do? Eat some of her papers?"

If Pak Ju heard, he didn't react. He brushed by Lucas and hustled down the steps. Lucas followed him to her office. Once again, he watched from the doorway as Pak Ju touched the bookshelf, got down on the floor and sniffed the rug, then sat at her desk, running his hands across the desktop as if it had been covered in mink. Finally, he smiled as he leaned back in the chair and closed his eyes.

What? Was he falling asleep? Where did Kang Ju find this guy? Lucas was about to walk over to wake him up when Pak Ju, eyes still closed, pointed to the wall. "Twelve? Strange bird."

Lucas looked in the direction Pak Ju pointed. "What?"

"Why twelve?"

"Oh, that means she's a big Seahawks fan, our local football team. Er, it's American football."

"Playing now?" Pak Ju opened his eyes and stared straight at Lucas.

A shiver went up Lucas's back as he looked away. "Yeah, the season is just starting."

Pak Ju shook his right hand with the index finger pointing down. "Playing here, now?"

"As a matter of fact, they are playing a home game later this week. It's against my team, the Patriots. But that game is sold out."

Pak Ju shut his eyes and leaned back in the chair. After a few seconds, he opened his eyes again and held up his right hand with two fingers extended. "Need tickets."

"I told you, the game is sold out. I was lucky to get two tickets for myself."

Pak Ju pointed at Lucas. "Your tickets."

Now Lucas was really irritated. "These are the hottest and, I mean, the hottest, most expensive tickets in town. I had to call in some special favors to get them. I'm not giving them to you. Besides, you know nothing about the game. You won't enjoy it."

The light in the room dimmed. Pak Ju stood, walked up to Lucas, and poked his index finger in Lucas's chest. "Not enjoy game, but have fun... Your tickets."

UVs had little to fear, with the exception of Awakens and Chavvah, but Lucas felt real fear at that moment. Pak Ju's eyes were suddenly dark, like black pearls, his face twisted and distorted. Lucas was dizzy. "All right, all right, calm down. I'll get them to you tomorrow."

The room lit up again. Pak Ju's eyes returned to their normal hazel. He smiled. "We're done. Have plan."

September 15, 1:11 p.m., Seattle

L glanced in Ricki's office and saw that she seemed to be concentrating on something at her computer. *Must be his journal. Had she found any clue yet?* He stood in the open doorway for a few seconds watching her work. *She was a remarkable woman. He could see why God chose her for this task. L could see the strength in her. A strength he was sure she was unaware of.*

He shook his head. *But why couldn't he see more? What was it about Ricki he couldn't access? What remained hidden below the surface? What is it that draws me to her? Is this God's doing?*

His heartbeat sped up. *Draws me to her? Where did that come from?* He looked down for a moment, then cleared his throat and tapped the door frame.

Ricki didn't budge. Still staring at the computer screen, she waved him off. "Don't bother me, I'm close to something. Come back later."

L struggled not to laugh. "Sure, my time isn't very important."

She took the red Tootsie Pop out of her mouth and smiled. "To what do I owe the honor of your presence, O Great UD

Duster?"

L smiled back. "Knock it off, O Great Pattern…ah…Locator."

Ricki chuckled. "You really spit that one out, didn't you?"

He held up his hand. "Okay, I'll grant you, you're better at this banter than I am. So how is the search going?"

"Slow. But then I don't know what I'm looking for. I had an idea that made me start over, but it hasn't worked out. At least not yet. Now I'm on to new stuff—when Jesus was raised from the dead."

The thought of that time brought a warm feeling to L. "An amazing time." *Jesus, I sure could use you here in the flesh now.*

Ricki nodded. "But that's not why you stopped by, is it?"

"Actually, no. I was on my way to Matthew's office when I saw your door open and thought you might want to know where I'm going."

"Sure, I appreciate you keeping me in the loop. Where are you going?"

"On my first UD hunt since Berlin, if you don't count my recent visit to Paris, and I have you to thank for it. Your pep talk during the Abdul Ba'ith incident snapped me back into reality."

"I didn't do anything." Ricki shrugged and looked down. "So, is it anybody I know?"

"Sok Kang Ju. I've decided to join the team going after him."

"You're going to North Korea?"

"Yes."

"How long will you be gone?"

"A week…maybe two."

A few moments of silence descended as Ricki's face turned a little white. *I wish I could hug her, if only to reassure her.*

Ricki broke the silence. "Be careful. You know you're walking into a hornets' nest."

"You know I can't be hurt. I've already died." As soon as he said it, he regretted the reference to his death. It made him feel different from her. "Besides, I will not be alone. I'm going with part of the Abdul Ba'ith team and Yong Joon."

"Still…" Ricki said in almost a whisper.

"Well, I'll be on my way. Matthew will be in charge while I'm gone. He'll let you know what's going on, if you're interested." L turned and quickly walked out.

Ricki watched L leave, staring at the open door. She couldn't believe how much her life had changed in the last few months since meeting him. But North Korea? She hoped he took care of himself. She wished she could've given him…well, a hug good-bye.

As she turned back to reading L's journal, she put the Tootsie Pop back in her mouth and let the cherry flavor roll over her tongue.

For the next couple of days, not much work got done in the compound. It would take time to process everything Jesus had said. Not to mention the fact that he appeared to us at all. We got to see Jesus! The risen Savior! He wanted to be with us! That's all anyone wanted to talk about.

People walked around the compound with a certain smile, a kind of glow. Maybe it was something like the way Moses looked when he came down from Mount Sinai after meeting with God. Besides, we were still unsure of our new role. What were we supposed to do? Part of that depended on what Jesus did. Was he going to stay? Take control? Was this his and our victory? No one knew. It was a happy time but very confusing as well.

On the morning of the third day after Jesus appeared to us, I was walking across the compound when I heard my name from behind me.

"Lazarus."

I turned. Merriam was bent over, hands on her thighs, sucking in gulps of air. "Are you all right?"

She held up one hand, palm facing me. "Yes…I will…I will be. Give me…a second."

I studied her face as she caught her breath. Her brow

wrinkled. She bit her lower lip.

"What's going on?"

She straightened. "I went into town, you know, just to see what others are saying about Jesus."

"And?"

She took a deep breath. "There's lots of talk. It is kind of fun watching the people who tried to kill him—"

I shook my head. "Not tried, succeeded."

Her forehead wrinkled. "Right, well you should see them try to make sense of the fact that he is alive after all they did to him."

"That is a good thing, is it not?"

"Yes…well, actually no. That is what I ran here to warn you about."

"Hold on. Warn me? About what?"

"I'm getting to it. The Pharisees and especially the Sanhedrin are upset. It's almost amusing the way they are promenading around the city, trying to pretend that nothing has happened while at the same time lashing out at everyone. And, of course, the Romans are angry. After all, they were supposed to be guarding the tomb. There is a general fear among them that Jesus just might declare himself king and take over. How can they stop someone they've already killed? So everyone is saying it's a lie. No surprise there. But there is someone else, someone far more dangerous…" She paused and started to shake.

"Who?"

"He calls himself Eli."

"Eli? He calls himself the ascension, huh? That might be significant. What's he doing?"

"He is saying it's a lie that will bring the Romans down on us. If the lie continues, the Romans will shut down synagogues. He is very persuasive. He says anyone who spreads the lie should be killed. He specifically mentioned Peter and John. And…" She bit her lower lip.

"Peter and John? Really? Is anyone taking him seriously? Are people listening to him?"

"Yes, at least, I think so. But that is not the biggest problem."

"And what is the biggest problem?"

"I think he's one of those creatures. You know, like that one who turned to dust."

I nodded, so she continued. "A crowd built up while I was there. They listened and I could sense the rising support for the speaker. And who's going to stop that person," her nose turned up. "That thing? The Pharisees and the Romans will not. He plays into their hands."

I formed my hands into fists. "Peter and John…you mean one of those creatures wants them dead?" I shook my head. "Then we have to stop it before someone gets hurt."

Merriam smiled. "I was hoping you would say that. I saw him in the marketplace. He's probably still there, but we should leave now."

It was normally about an hour walk from our compound to the marketplace. We made it in less than forty minutes. Our new bodies didn't tire as fast as they used to.

Merriam pointed at a gathering to our right. A tall, burly man, who must have been standing on a platform, was speaking to the crowd. I tried to listen to what he was saying.

The best I could make out was something like, "How many of you have seen this so-called resurrected Jesus?" No hand went up. His face lit with a manic grin. "I thought so. It's all lies, lies that will bring the Romans down on us. Lies that we have to stop. You know what God says about lies. Do I have to read the Ninth Commandment to you? His followers must all die."

The crowd cheered.

I looked closely up into his face. Merriam was right. His eyes were deep wells of evil. My stomach churned. This was one of those creatures, and it was misusing Scripture for its own purposes.

I turned to Merriam. "We have to stop this now."

Thus began our first UD hunt. It was a hunt without a plan, but we had no choice. Peter's and John's lives, plus the lives of other followers, were at stake.

I thought for a moment, then told Merriam, "All right. We have to get close enough to it to…I guess…to bite it." I cringed at the thought. "We can't let it see us until it's too late. Luckily, its attention seems to be focused on the crowd. I suggest we split up and approach it from both sides. Keep your head down and try to keep people in front of you until you get to the edge. The first one who is within reach has to…bite it."

Bite someone so they would turn to dust. He didn't think he'd ever get used to that.

Merriam nodded and made her way to the left while I inched up from the right. She got there first. I was in place a second or two later. Just as she was set to reach out and grab its foot, the beast saw her. For a brief moment, it froze. Then it jumped from the platform and grabbed the nearest person in the crowd. It flashed a knife in front of the man's neck.

The people in front of us tried to run, but it was difficult. They had to push through those in the back who didn't know what was going on. Panic broke out.

In the midst of the growing confusion, some people in the crowd screamed, "His disciples are here!"

"They're armed!"

"It's the Romans coming to arrest us!"

The creature glanced over and saw me. It slowly backed away about five or six steps from us and faced Merriam. "Move away, or I slit this worthless being's throat." It nodded my way. "That goes for your friend too."

Merriam and I stood our ground. I held up my hand. "Okay, we will back away. But let him go."

It smiled as I took a step backward.

While its eyes were focused on the two of us, the hostage reached down, grabbed a knife out of his belt, and thrust it behind him into the beast's belly.

The creature let out another snarl, then chuckled. "It will take more than that to stop me."

The hostage's face turned ashen. He started to tremble and looked right at Merriam with pleading eyes.

A couple of men, most likely the hostage's friends, approached from my side. They got within a few feet when the beast turned and snarled at them. Its face contorted into something unearthly. The friends froze.

Merriam held out her hand. "Give me the knife, and we will let you go." Her muscles tensed.

I yelled, "Merriam! No!" But it was too late. She leaped at the beast. With one powerful motion, the beast slid the knife deep across the hostage's throat, dropped him, and leaped out of the way, grabbing one of the friends who had come to the hostage's aid.

"I warned you," it said in a deep, guttural voice. "Now move back, or this one dies too."

Merriam was no longer looking at the beast. Instead, her eyes were focused on the body at her feet, one hand covering her mouth. Tears forming in her eyes. "I'm sorry. I'm so sorry."

I held my hands out again. "You win. We will leave. Don't hurt him."

It sported a malicious grin. Before it could say a word, someone leaped on it from behind and dug her teeth into the beast's neck. Instantly the beast turned to dust. The new hostage and his friend ran.

I looked down at the dust, then back up. Sapphira stood in front of the pile of dust, shaking her head and trying to spit it out of her mouth. "That is foul-tasting stuff."

Ricki flicked off the computer and walked over to the window. How could she find a pattern in this? She had no idea where to start. Maybe she could come up with an encoding system and then run a cluster analysis? She wrinkled her brow and shook her head. *I don't want to fail L.*

Ricki stared out the window at CenturyLink Field. And what was this about going after Sok Kang Ju? She hoped he was careful. So much could go wrong, and what if Naturals got caught up in this like she'd just read?

She rested her hands on the window like a kid looking at her favorite toy in a store at Christmastime. She wished there were a game today that she could get lost in. She'd ask Matthew if he could get her tickets to the next home game.

Chapter Fifteen

LIES ARE THE FUEL FOR SIN. The more you believe the lies of the enemy, the deeper you fall into the fire. —Awakened Incident Manual, Volume 2, Page 41

September 16, 3:00 a.m., Seattle

Pong Pak Ju sat in a car with Lucas, two blocks up the hill from the main entrance to SOAR. It was dark, but a few dim streetlights pierced the blackness.

Lucas rubbed the back of his neck as his gaze scanned the area. He pointed to a dark alley to the right. "Go up that alley. There's a locked parking area. Climb over the chain. To the left you'll see a fire escape that extends all the way up the side of the building to the top. Dr. Spenser arrives around six thirty every morning. I'll return shortly after that to pick you up."

Pak Ju stared at the alley, then turned to Lucas. "No, you come."

Lucas glanced out the window, rubbed his neck again, and faced Pak Ju. "I don't do this kind of thing. At least not this close to Awakened headquarters. Besides, you don't need me."

Pak Ju frowned. "Need you to look for me. You come."

"No, you look. We have a rule—stay at least four blocks from SOAR. I don't know about you, but I don't want to end up as a pile of dust."

Suddenly the air in the car felt oppressive and hot. Lucas struggled to breathe. He grabbed his throat as if he could open an airway. Pak Ju's nostrils flared. He jabbed his index finger on Lucas's chest. "You come."

Lucas held up his hands and struggled to speak. "Okay...okay I'll come. But if we succeed here, you'll return my tickets, won't you?"

As suddenly as it had changed, the air thinned and Lucas

could breathe easily. *How does he do that?*

Pak Ju smiled. "Glad." He got out of the car, walked around to the rear, opened the trunk, and pulled out a small suitcase.

Lucas checked the rearview mirror and glanced at the side mirrors. Safe. No Awakens. He stepped out of the car. *I need a drink. Why didn't I bring a bottle of Dark Horse with me? You'd think I'd learn.*

Pak Ju motioned to the alley. "Go."

Lucas had walked around the car to follow Pak Ju when he suddenly froze at the sound of movement. He whipped his gaze to the right and saw two figures moving his way. The streetlights were dim and flickering so their faces were hidden by the night shadows.

Awakens? Thoughts of becoming a pile of dust raced through his mind. After what seemed like an eternity, the faces of the two men were exposed in the nearest streetlight. Lucas took a deep breath, not realizing that he had held it. *Naturals.*

They looked like they were in their early twenties. One was short and thin, the other slightly taller and overweight. They reminded him of Laurel and Hardy. That reference dated him.

As they approached, Hardy asked, "What's in the suitcase, old man?"

Pak Ju answered, "Gun, big expensive gun."

Why did he say that? It was asking for trouble. Not that Naturals were a threat, but any incident might attract an Awakened.

Laurel's thin lips curled into a sneer. "Ain't that a coincidence? We happen to collect guns, and it just so happens that we need a big, expensive gun to complete our collection." Laurel reached behind his back and pulled out a Kel-Tec P-32 semiautomatic pistol. "I want to thank you for contributing to our collection." He signaled to his friend to grab the suitcase. "While we're at it, why don't you contribute to our other growing collection? Hand over your wallets."

Lucas noticed that the air had a metallic taste to it, like

lightning was about to strike. He looked over at Pak Ju. What was he up to? Lucas didn't want to risk Awakened involvement, so he raised his right hand. "Guys, you don't want to do this. Put the gun away. Walk on, and nothing will happen to you."

Hardy laughed. "We're the ones with the gun."

At that moment Pak Ju stepped in front of Laurel and positioned the barrel over his own heart. "Shoot, Chicken. Shoot."

Laurel glared at Pak Ju. "You must have a death wish. I could pull this trigger and walk away whistling."

"Do it. I dare you. Scared?"

Laurel's face turned red, and he bared his teeth. "Old man, you get your wish."

A loud bang reverberated in the night as the gun went off. Pak Ju rocked back but didn't fall down.

That had to hurt. How did he not flinch? Lucas looked around to see if an Awakened might have responded to the disturbance, but the area still seemed quiet.

His face turning red again, Laurel wrinkled his brow as he gaped at the gun. He jammed the firearm on Pak Ju's chest and fired three more times.

Pak Ju stood his ground, jerking back a little with each shot. He looked Laurel in the eye with a big grin.

Hardy was shaking. He grabbed Laurel's shoulder. "Let's get out of here."

But Laurel was frozen. "Who...are...you?"

Pak Ju's face turned dark and contorted into a twisted ugly form. "Death. Your death." Pak Ju grabbed Laurel's head and twisted it in one powerful motion. With a crack Laurel hit the ground.

Hardy backed away mumbling, "Don't...don't." He turned and ran back the way the two of them had come.

Pak Ju bent down and picked up the gun. He pointed it at the fleeing man. "Three...two...one." He fired and Hardy went down.

Pak Ju turned to Lucas with a big smile. "Fun."

Lucas hid the bodies and climbed to the rooftop to join Pak

Ju. Disposing of bodies was something he was good at and reminded him of his work as a bootlegger in the twenties before he died. Maybe this Pak Ju wasn't so bad, after all. Lucas couldn't remember when he'd had so much fun. He only wished Pak Ju didn't do this so close to SOAR.

Now why didn't Chavvah let him do things like this more often? She let Lucas plan the death of that Bobby fellow. It wasn't his fault it backfired.

He walked over to the makeshift sniper's nest Pak Ju had set up. Pak Ju finished the assembly of the Barrett M90 sniper rifle fitted with a laser sight. He nodded toward the weapon. "Rifle special."

Lucas shrugged. "It was the best I could do on such short notice. I don't know how much good it will be. You haven't had any practice with it."

Pak Ju pointed to the front entrance of SOAR. "Not far." Then he pointed to his head. "Success in here."

"I hope so. Then you'll return my tickets. They were hard to get. It's an important game…" Lucas scanned the area. "Ah…so…ah…what do you need me for?"

Pak Ju reached into his bag and pulled out binoculars. "Here." He pointed at SOAR again. "Spot for me."

Lucas took the binoculars and checked his watch: 4:17. He rolled his eyes. *Great, I have to wait for over an hour with Mr. Talkative.*

Ricki woke with a start and bolted upright, sucking in air. She forced herself to slow her breathing and, eventually, settled down. It was dark. Quiet. She looked around but only saw faint shadows cast by the starlight through her bedroom window. Still, something was wrong. She sat there afraid to move, like a statue frozen for all time. Then out of the corner of her eye, the shadow moved.

It spoke in a whisper. "Little Ricki, I love you…"

It was her uncle.

Ricki screamed, "No, you're dead!"

She buried her head in her hands and wept.

A knock sounded at her door. "Dr. Spenser, are you all right?" It was her Awakened bodyguard, Ralph.

She gasped, then wiped her eyes. "Yes, it was only a nightmare." She hadn't had one of those for months. Why now?

She glanced at her clock: 4:20 a.m. *Hope I can get some more sleep.*

September 16, 6:00 a.m. Seattle

"Dr. Spenser, the car is ready." Ralph again. He was a large burly man at six-foot-six and 325 pounds of pure muscle. Affectionately known as Wreck-It Ralph, he was one of the gentlest men Ricki had ever met. He had died in 1811 when he was hit by a stray bullet on the streets of New Orleans. The shooter was a drunk out celebrating something.

Ricki had been a little slow getting ready this morning, still reeling from this morning's nightmare. "I'll be there in a minute, and call me Ricki."

"Yes, ma'am."

True to her word, a minute later Ricki got in the car and Ralph followed her into the backseat. The driver took off for the fifteen-minute drive to SOAR. Ricki usually spent the time asking Ralph what it was like growing up in the late 1700s and early 1800s, but today she preferred to ride in silence, something Ralph always respected on the rare days it happened.

The driver stopped to the right of the SOAR main entrance. Ralph got out first, followed by Ricki. As they walked to the main doors, the driver left to park the car. They had taken no more than three steps when Ricki heard a whispered, *"Little Ricki."* It was like the voice from the nightmare only softer, more compassionate.

She started to shake and dropped her briefcase.

"You need to pick that up right —now!"

She did as the voice told her. As she bent down to pick it up, she heard a *whoosh* and something struck the wall behind her. It was followed immediately by a second *whoosh*. She stood and saw a red dot move up her side.

"No!" Ralph jumped between Ricki and the red dot. There was a *crack* as a bullet hit Ralph in the back, pushing him into Ricki.

She fell backward leaning against the wall and hit her head. Her eyes glazed over as she struggled to remain conscious. What happened? Why was it so quiet? Slowly, everything went dark.

Like a rag doll, Ricki slid down to a sitting position with Ralph looming over her. A faint blood trail marked the movement of her head down the off-white marble wall of SOAR headquarters.

There was another loud *crack* as Ralph was hit in the back of the head, dropping him down over Ricki. Momentarily frozen and disoriented while his wounds healed, Ralph lay on top of Ricki, his massive frame swallowing her petite body.

He shook his head and lifted himself off her. The sight of the blood trail on the wall jerked him back into awareness. He gently cupped the back of her head and felt the warm flow of blood. He stared down at Ricki. She looked like she was sleeping, like she was at peace, like she was alive.

His face burned as a primitive yell burst out his mouth like a wolf baying at the full moon. For the first time since he had died on the streets of New Orleans, anger rose within him.

Two SOAR security guards ran out the front door. Ralph pointed to the south and yelled, "Behind me, two blocks up, top of the building."

Both guards fired a couple of quick shots in that direction, then sprinted towards the building Ralph pointed too.

Ralph, keeping himself between Ricki and the sniper, scooped her into his arms and carried her limp body into the safety of the SOAR lobby where he laid her out on a couch.

Lucas lowered the binoculars. "Those Awakened guards are on their way. We have to go."

Pak Ju stood and shrugged. "Guess plan B."

Relieved, Lucas picked up the M90 rifle. Pak Ju shook his head. "Don't need. Leave everything here."

Lucas dropped the rifle. "Okay, then let's get going. If we're still here when those Awakens arrive, we'll end up as dust."

"Worry too much." Pak Ju pointed to his chest. "Never be dust."

Lucas glanced toward the SOAR building and started to pant. "I don't know about you, but I'm leaving now."

"No, not now." Pak Ju pulled a slip of paper out of his shirt pocket. He reached out to Lucas. "Pen, now."

"What, you're going to write them a note?" Lucas's voice cracked when he yelled.

"Pen, now."

Lucas grabbed a pen and handed it to Pak Ju. He glanced back down the street, and his knees started to shake. He turned to Pak Ju to say something right as the man dropped the paper by the rifle. "Okay, go now."

Lucas ran to the fire escape. "You're crazy, you know that?"

Pak Ju only smiled as he followed Lucas down. "Like say in America, crazy like a fox."

They made it down the back of the building and into the car, leaving everything behind. Then they melted into the Seattle streets.

Chapter Sixteen

THE TRUTH IS YOU CAN'T CLAIM you believe God exists and then go on with your life as if He doesn't exist. True belief changes your life. It puts a demand on you that comes not from God, but from the natural state of belief itself. Just as repentance, which we so often associate with a change in behavior, actually means changing your mind—belief, which we so often associate with a state of mind, actually produces an observable change in behavior. —Awakened Incident Manual, Volume 2, Page 131

September 16, 6:31 am, Seattle

Ralph took his gaze off Ricki lying on the couch long enough to find the building receptionist. "Get a doctor down here *now!*" He knelt by her side and held her right wrist as a few tears made their way down his face. He gently rocked back and forth.

After a few moments he took a deep breath as a smile crawled onto his face when she woke. He stood and stooped over her, sliding his hand up to her shoulder. "Dr. Spenser, are you all right?"

She blinked several times and focused on Ralph. "I think I'm okay. And call me Ricki."

"Yes, ma'am." He bowed his head. Thank God she was okay.

"What happened?" Ricki rubbed her head.

"Someone shot at you."

"But why would anyone want to shoot me?" Ricki tried to sit up, but Ralph gently held her in place.

"Please don't move. A doctor is on his way down to check you out. Ray is on his way as well. We'll find out what's going on."

The doctor got there first and examined the wound on the back of her head. The bleeding had, for the most part, stopped. Next, he ran her through the concussion protocol. "You're going to be fine. The cut on the back of your head is too small to require stitches. Keep the area clean and it will heal by itself. Other than that, you appear to have suffered a mild concussion. Take it easy for a day or two, and if you get any headaches or anything else changes, let me know. But I don't expect you'll have any problems."

Ricki sat up, then started to sway with her hand on her forehead. Ralph reached out to steady her. "Thanks, Doctor. I think I got a little dizzy."

"That will happen for a couple of days. Avoid any sudden moves and you'll be okay." He patted her on the shoulder. "And you're quite welcome. I'm glad I could help. There's not much use for me as a former physician around SOAR. It's like I'm a calculator in a room full of computers."

Ray Springer, the head of SOAR security, had arrived right after the doctor but remained silent until the examination was done. He looked at Ricki. "Do you feel like you can come up to my office?"

She stood and nodded.

"Good." He turned to Ralph. "Ralph, I'd like you to join us."

Ray's office was smaller than L's, but it had the same wall of TVs. These TVs cycled through scenes inside and outside SOAR. Ricki glanced at them as she walked in but quickly turned away. The full impact of what had happened pummeled her.

Someone tried to kill me. I should be dead.

She started to tremble. She wasn't ready to see the video of her attack. She deliberately chose a chair with its back to the screens. Ralph sat next to her. Ray sat opposite them.

Ray leaned forward. "I've seen the video. Now I want to hear in your own words what happened."

Ricki shivered. "I...I can't right now." She wiped a tear from her eye.

Ralph put his hand on Ricki's shoulder. "I can describe it." He proceeded to fill Ray in on the events of the morning.

When Ralph finished, Ray looked at Ricki. "Do you feel up to answering one question?"

Ricki ran her fingers through her hair. She took a deep breath and released the air slowly. "I...I can try."

"Good. Why did you drop your briefcase at that moment?"

Ricki stared at him for a second. "W-what?"

"You bent over to pick up your briefcase at the exact moment the bullet would have hit you. What caused you to drop it?"

She rubbed her forehead. "I'm not sure." She closed her eyes and tried to visualize that moment. "Wait." She pointed at Ray. "I heard a sound, a whisper really. Someone called me 'little Ricki.' It startled me...then the voice said something like 'bend down...bend down now.'"

She wrinkled her brow. "It was like my nightmare last night. My uncle...he used to call me Little Ricki...right before he..." Her eyes welled up. "Well, just before he...you know." Her cheeks warmed and she knew she was saying way too much.

Ralph patted her arm. "That's okay, you don't have to say any more."

Ray looked at Ralph. "Did you hear anything or see anybody nearby?"

"No, sir."

"I'm not sure what's going on here," Ray shook his head, "but that whisper saved your life today."

Ricki sat silent. Did God intervene to save her? Did He use her past to insure she had a future? *I don't understand Him.* Could a memory that knew no time have been the instrument of her salvation today?

Ray continued. "We have to find out who's behind this. Ricki, do you have any enemies who might want to see you dead?"

"I don't even have to think about that. The answer is no, none. Hey, until I was kidnapped and run out of my home, I never met anyone who would wish me harm."

Ray nodded. "Thought as much. The fact is, only the UDs and

we even know you're here, so it has to be a UD operation. But they let you go after the kidnapping so I thought they wanted you alive."

Ralph added, "That means something's changed and now they want her dead. It also means we have to be more diligent in protecting her. Does L know?"

"Matthew knows. L is in the air on his way to Tel Aviv. l sent him a text, but that was less than an hour ago. I don't expect him to respond until his plane lands in Israel in," Ray glanced at his watch, "about five more hours." Ray's gaze locked with Ricki's. "Do you want him to come back?"

Yes, yes I want him back. He understands me, I think I understand him. She felt safe around him, and after that shooting in Cairo, she thought they were closer. But he had seemed more distant ever since his trip to France.

Ricki shook her head and spoke in a low voice. "No. I'm safe here with you."

"Do you want to go back to the safe house and rest there?" Ray asked.

Ricki shook her head again. "I have work to do here, and it will help me to think about something other than this morning. Besides, I don't want to step outside now."

Ray shared a sympathetic smile. "I don't blame you. Let me know when you want to leave so my security team can arrange your protection detail, all right?"

She nodded.

"Good, then I'll let you get back to your office. Call me anytime if you need my help." Ray turned to Ralph. "Will you stay so we can discuss the protection strategy?"

"Sure."

Ricki stood. "Thank you both. I'm beginning to feel safe." *Not.*

As soon as Ricki left, Ray frowned. "One of our agents found a note the sniper left at the scene." He pulled a piece of paper out of his pocket and unfolded it. "It says 'SHE'S MINE."

Ralph took the paper and studied it. His nostrils flared and his face reddened. He handed it back to Ray. "Sir, I want permission to immediately start a UD hunt. I want to find this thing and personally dust it."

Ray shook his head. "I need you by her side to oversee her protection. In fact, from now on I want four Awakens with her whenever she's outside this building and exposed. I want them surrounding her so there's no line-of-sight access to her. When she's en route, I want a second car following her at a discreet distance."

"I'll get right on it, sir. Sorry about today."

"Don't worry, it's not your fault. You saved her. But I don't understand this attack in broad daylight on our doorstep. It's madness on their part. Why Dr. Spenser? Why now?" Ray narrowed his eyes as he shook his head. "I'll bring this up with L and see what he might know."

Ralph started to leave when Ray stopped him. "Oh, and let's not tell her about the note. It'll only scare her."

Chapter Seventeen

FEAR IS A POWERFUL MOTIVATOR. WHEN it keeps us out of physically dangerous situations it serves a positive purpose. When it prevents us from serving God to the fullest, it is a negative. All too often, the reason we fail to live like Christ is that we fear man's disapproval. We fear either rejection or making a mistake. --Awakened Incident Manual, Volume 2, Page 103

September 16, 7:38 am, Seattle

Ricki walked into her office and made a beeline to her window. She stared down at CenturyLink Field. Through the open roof she saw figures moving. Something was going on. She grabbed the telescope Matthew had given her. The ground crew was working on the grass. Must be a game coming up. It'd been a long time since she'd attended a game. It had been a long time since she'd done anything normal.

She watched awhile, her mind only halfway tracking events on the field. More than anything she wanted to escape this crazy world and go back to her world of academia. After a few minutes she sat down but could only stare at the window in a daze.

A knock sounded on her open door. Ricki jerked up in her seat and let out a little gasp. She turned to see who it was. *Oh, Matthew.*

"I'm sorry. I didn't mean to scare you."

"You didn't. I was lost in my thoughts. I guess I'm still a little jumpy."

"I'm so sorry for what happened. Ray assures me it won't happen again. Are you okay?"

"I think so. Does L know yet?"

"When he lands and checks his text messages, he'll know. I wouldn't be surprised if he called you immediately."

"Oh yeah, I guess Ray did say something about that. So, if

you talk to L before I do, tell him I'm okay and not to worry."

"Will do." Matthew smiled. "I'll tell him that Martin Luther said, 'Pray, and let God worry.'"

"Did L know him?"

"I don't know. I'll guess we'll find out." Matthew turned to leave.

Before he got to the door, Ricki drew in a deep breath. "Oh, Matthew..."

He stopped and turned back. "Yes?"

"I was wondering if you can do me, ah, a favor."

"Sure, I can try. What is it?"

"Ever since my kidnapping, I've had my whole view of the world turned upside down, and I haven't been alone since. So I was thinking ... the Seahawks have a game coming up with the Patriots. Could SOAR get me a ticket so I could go by myself and escape all this for a while and, you know, clear my head?"

"After today you want to go out by yourself?"

"Especially after today. I'm a little scared but I also need a break. I have to do something...normal. Besides, at this point I might be safer without Awakened bodyguards hanging around, making me stand out to the UDs. Look, I'll wear a disguise. Someone can follow me as I walk from here to CenturyLink Field. Once there I'll be hidden among sixty thousand other fans."

Matthew shrugged. "I'm not sure about this, but I'll talk to Ray."

"Thanks."

I really need a break. Ricki sat at her desk, her head in her hands.

She stood and walked to the window. This time her gaze focused on the clear blue sky dotted with a few wisps of clouds. *I wish L were here. I feel safe with him.*

She returned to her desk and sat down, then switched her computer on and started reading. *Maybe I can escape into this for a while.*

During this time the air seemed charged with energy. All we could do was talk about Jesus. Where was he? What would he do? Would he become king? Should the Romans be afraid? What about the Pharisees? What would life be like with Jesus ruling?

Things were peaceful. After the incident in the public square, the UDs went into hiding. The few we saw would immediately duck out of sight. They no longer had death in their eyes; instead we saw only fear. Which was a nice change for us.

Merriam ran up to me, something that was quickly becoming a daily event, as I was eating my lunch under a beautiful olive tree in the middle of the compound.

"Lazarus."

I set down the fig I was about to eat. "Yes."

"A Pharisee is at the gate. He is asking to come in and talk with you."

"Then let him in and bring him to me."

Merriam's eyes widened. "Are you sure? He is a Pharisee, after all. Maybe it is a trap."

"Even if it is a trap, he cannot hurt us."

"Oh, of course, but what if the Pharisees are working with those creatures? We know we can hurt them, but what if that means they could hurt us in some way?"

I had to admit that up until that time, I had never considered the possibility that we might be vulnerable to those creatures. "As long as he is alone, there should be no problem. I will walk with you to the gate and see what he wants."

I glanced down at my lunch with a longing look. Since this all started, I don't think I had been able to finish a single meal. Could we possibly starve to death? (Note: I discovered later that we cannot, though going hungry for long periods is not a pleasant experience.)

It was a short journey to the gate of the compound, which stood open. Right beyond it was a tall man with an aristocratic bearing. He wore a white robe with a mantle adorned with long blue fringes. He had a phylactery strapped to his left arm.

Merriam pointed. "There he is."

I walked up to him. "My name is Lazarus. You wanted to talk to me?"

"Yes, my name is Arioch." He looked around as if he did not want to be seen with me. "Can we go somewhere private?"

I led Arioch to a small room on the first floor of a nearby building. As soon as I shut the door behind us, he turned to face me. His face held a slight tint of red. He had a pained, watery gaze as if he had been crying recently. "Is Jesus here?"

I shook my head. "No."

"Has he been here? Do you know when he is coming back?" Desperation filled his voice. The fingers of his right hand were twitching as if he had lost control of them.

A Pharisee quizzing me about the location of Jesus days after they so cruelly murdered him bothered me, but I sensed something about this man. He wasn't here to hurt Jesus; he was broken. (Note: This was the first time I became aware of our ability to sense the heart of Naturals.)

"He spent some time here, but I do not know if Jesus is coming back. Why?"

Arioch looked down. "I helped kill him. I need to ask for his forgiveness."

I stepped forward and put a hand on his shoulder. "I was there when he died. I heard him asking God to forgive everyone involved."

Arioch's eyes filled with tears. "I was there, too. I heard him say that and I laughed." He looked me in the eyes. "I didn't know who he was at the time. I have to find him and beg for forgiveness."

I searched for the words to comfort him. "You never have to beg for his forgiveness. He wants to give it freely."

Arioch shook his head. "Still, I need to talk to him. I need to lie on the ground before him and tell him how sorry, how misguided, how sinful I am."

"If I learn anything about his plans, I'll send someone to find you. Will you be all right?"

He nodded, and I hugged him for a few moments. When he was ready, he stepped back, lifted his head, and wiped his tears.

"Thank you, Lazarus. I will wait for your message."

I walked him back to the main gate in silence. Once there I embraced him again. "Jesus already knows you want forgiveness, and he feels your pain."

"Oh, how I want to believe you, but how do you know that?"

It was more of a plea than a challenge, and the question caught me by surprise. My mind raced, searching for an answer. I did not say that as a platitude, as an acknowledgment that Jesus always felt this way about everyone. No, Somehow, I knew, at that moment, Jesus felt that way about Arioch.

It was the first of many moments I would have a feeling like that.

"Because I know Jesus."

Ricki stopped reading. Did that mean L was somehow connected to Jesus? Like the voice she'd heard this morning? She'd have to ask L. Ricki returned to the journal.

"Still I have to hear that from him." Clearly Arioch was unconvinced. I watched him walk out of the compound.

I turned and headed back to the main building. I didn't get far when Merriam yelled, "Get away from him."

I ran back to the main gate in time to see her run out into the street. Arioch lay on the ground up ahead. Motionless.

When I reached him, Merriam knelt beside him crying. He had a gaping neck wound and blood pooled around his head. He was dead.

"What happened?"

"I saw one of those creatures come out of the shadow of that alley over there." She pointed up ahead. "It said something and then pounced on him. I yelled as the thing bit Arioch in the neck. Arioch dropped to the ground and the creature ran back down the alley." Tears shimmered in her eyes.

I looked down the alleyway for a glimpse of the beast that had done this. But nothing was there.

"Why would it do this?"

I shared her disgust for these creatures. I wrinkled my noise as if I smelled something foul at the very thought of one of them. "I don't know. Maybe they are targeting anyone who visits us but who isn't one of us."

"Then we need some of our people out here to stop them."

A crazy idea hit me. "You are right, but first, I have a plan. I'll grab his shoulders, you grab his feet, and let's take him inside."

We brought Arioch's body in and started to pray over him. I noticed it first. His hand twitched a little. His neck wound closed and his eyes opened. Confusion lined his face. His mouth moved but nothing came out. Finally, he said, "What...where...where am I?"

Merriam stroked his forehead. "You are safe now. You're back with us in the compound."

With a glazed expression, he looked around the room. "H-how?"

It was my turn. "Will you tell us what happened? Then we'll explain everything."

Arioch sat up, his brow furrowed. "I remember I...I walked a short distance. Someone approached me from the shadow of a narrow alley. At first I didn't pay any attention, but as he got closer a chill went up my back. I halted. That was when I saw his eyes. They were dark pools of death. This was not human. Before I could run, it pounced." He looked me in the eyes, pleading, "What was that thing? Do you know?"

I nodded. "What did it do?"

"It hissed in my ear, 'So you want to see Jesus?'" Arioch paused. "How did it know that?"

"I don't know. What happened next?"

Arioch looked down. "It gripped my throat and said it could arrange that for me. It said something like, 'One less of his followers will improve this world.' Then it...it bit me in the neck."

Arioch reached up to feel his neck, then looked puzzled. "What happened? My neck is fine, but I'm sure it bit me. I could feel the blood flowing down my chest. That is the last thing I remember until I woke up here. Lazarus, what is going on?"

How in the world did L explain that to Arioch? Ricki turned off her computer and grabbed a cherry Tootsie Pop from her desk drawer. She was done reading for a while. She unwrapped it and popped it in her mouth, then relaxed in her chair. How great it would be to get away from all this for a few hours and watch a Seahawks home game.

Then her phone rang.

September 16, 10:12 p.m., Tel Aviv

"Are you sure you're all right?" L was glad this discussion was over the phone so Ricki wouldn't see the tension that blazed through his body at the news of the assassination attempt. "I'm so sorry I wasn't there. If you need me, I'll fly home on the next available flight."

"No, don't worry. I'm fine."

She was not. It was one of those rare moments when he could sense Ricki's real feelings by the slight tremor in her voice. He wished he could be there when she needed him. He tightened his grip on the phone. *I need to protect her. She holds the key to so much.*

"I'm not entirely comfortable…"

"You're sweet, L, but Matthew's here, Ray's here, and I'm surrounded by Awakens. I'll be all right. Though I was wondering…" Ricki's voice trailed off.

"Is there something you want to ask me?"

"Well, I guess. Yes. I really need to step out of this world back into my own if only for a few hours. There's a football game next door tomorrow. Could SOAR get me a ticket? It would really help me calm down."

"I don't know. I'll tell you what. I'll talk to Matthew and see what he thinks. Deal?"

"Deal."

"Okay, if anything changes let me know."

"I will. Take care of yourself." Ricki hung up.

Not entirely confident, L hung up. *I'm sweet?* He didn't think he'd ever been called that before. He smiled.

Joon, Ariella, and Agam sat at the dining room table patiently while L made another flurry of phone calls. When finished he faced them. "I suppose you're wondering what's going on."

Ariella laced her fingers together on the tabletop. "Not at all. You're a man of many secrets. You don't have to share anything with us."

Agam grinned and looked up at L. "Don't listen to her. She may not be curious, but I want to know what's so important that you'd drop everything and rush back to Seattle."

L smiled. "It's not a secret. Someone took a shot at Ricki outside SOAR headquarters."

"Someone or something?"

L nodded at Ariella. "Undoubtedly a UD."

Agam made a fist. "We should dust that one back to hell."

"I'd love to be the one to do that, but it doesn't make any sense. Unless somehow the UDs know what she's up to." He shuddered. *I should fly back. She needs me.*

Ariella asked, "How's she doing? Why would Dr. Spenser be a target?"

"Apparently fine, and I have no idea."

Agam stood, walked over to L, and clasped L's shoulder. "She'll be okay. She's surrounded by Awakens."

L looked down. "That's what she said."

"Agam's right. She's right." Ariella stood. "Perhaps the best thing we can do for her is to take down a high-ranking UD like Sok Kang Ju. I know he doesn't have anything to do with the attack on Dr. Spenser, but dusting him will send a message. You don't mess with the Awakened."

"Now you're talking." Agam rubbed his hands together. "That's my kind of message. Let's plan how we are going to do this." Agam turned to L. "And by the way, it's about time that tyrant is dusted back to hell."

"I know." L looked down.

As the three sat around Ariella's dining room table, she rolled out a map of Korea. "Our two problems, as I see it, are first, getting into North Korea without having to take drastic action against a Natural, and second, making sure we hit the real Sok Kang Ju and not one of his Natural doubles."

"Those are the problems we've always had. Especially the second one." L pointed to Ariella, "It's exactly like your roadblock in getting close to Hitler."

She nodded. "Only this time we may get lucky. It turns out on October 10, to coincide with one of North Korea's holidays, Sok Kang Ju will be giving a major address on developments in the reunification talks. It's the kind of thing he will want to deliver himself. Besides, he'll be with the South Korean representative and the French chair Renaud Christian Yount."

Renaud? L's mind suddenly went in another direction. "Exactly who is this Yount fellow?"

Agam answered, "Apparently, he's a rising star in the French Ministry of Foreign Affairs. He must have stepped on some toes during his rise because this assignment is a guaranteed loser."

L nodded. Could he be the Renaud L was hunting? "So where will this address be given?"

"In Pyongyang and this is the best part." Ariella sported a wide grin. "He's arranged it to be given at Kim Il-Sung Square. It's surrounded by buildings that could hide a sniper's nest, and two hundred yards away is the Juche Tower, which also may be a good site for a nest." She turned to Joon. "Do you know anything about this area?"

Joon nodded. "I've never been there myself, but because both are monuments to our Glorious," his neck tensed at the word, "Leader, we had to study both in school. Of course, the concentration camp school was not about education; it was all about politics, so I suspect we spent more time on things like this than other schools.

"The square is named after the founder of North Korea, and it's the thirty-seventh largest square in the world. There is enough room to hold a big crowd. The Tower was built to commemorate Kim Il-Sung's seventieth birthday. It's taller than the Washington Monument, something my teachers liked to consistently remind us." He snorted. "But only by less than a meter. The observation deck at the Tower is 560 feet above the square. That's about all I can remember or care to remember."

"Thanks," Ariella said. "To pick up where Joon left off, my thought is that for security reasons, the square will be closely guarded, but we may be able to get to the roof of one of buildings on the perimeter. As far as the Tower is concerned, the observation deck should be cleared during the presentation and the base guarded, most likely by UDs because no Natural could get by them. So if the Tower works out, our best plan is to dust the UDs at the base, set up position on the observation deck, and dust Kung Ju when he starts his speech. Of course, I'll have to be there to scope things out before we select a final site."

Agam whistled. "The square, huh? Sounds like it couldn't be better if they handed us the opportunity on a silver platter."

L nodded. "It sounds like the only feasible plan. We have to check the area first, then work out the details for getting to a roof or that observation deck undetected. That leaves us getting into North Korea as our biggest problem, and that's where Joon comes in." L gestured with a wave of his hand to Joon. "We'll need your input on how best to get into North Korea."

Joon rubbed his hands on his thighs. "I'll do what I can."

"Problem two solved." Agam patted Joon on the back.

L was a little bothered by this. *It's too easy…*

They spent the rest of the night poring over maps, consulting reports, and discussing alternatives before they finally came up with a plan.

L glanced at his watch: 7:21 a.m. "So we are all agreed?"

Joon, Ariella, and Agam all nodded.

"Then let's get some rest and tomorrow we can start gathering supplies."

Agam left. Joon and L were staying with Ariella. As L lay down on the couch, something Agam had said bothered him. *"Couldn't be better if they handed us the opportunity on a silver platter."* *He was right, and that makes it too easy.*

Chapter Eighteen

HOPE HAS NEVER BEEN FREE. IT was purchased by the blood of Jesus. –Awakened Incident Manual, Volume 2, Page 213

September 16, 5:32 p.m., Paris

Chavvah checked her watch: 5:32. That would make it 1:02 a.m. in Korea. She had to call him. Renaud would never *pardonner* her if she did not drop everything and tell him what she'd learned. Chavvah fired up Skype on her computer.

It didn't take long for Renaud's image to appear on her screen. "Hello, Chavvah. Do you know what time it is here?"

"Of course, but you need to hear this. Someone took a shot at Ricki, and Lazarus has gone missing."

Renaud looked straight into the screen. There was no reaction.

"Did you hear me?"

Renaud rubbed the back of his neck. "Sorry, I'm just waking up. Something about Dr. Spenser wasn't it?" He shook his head.

"Yes, someone tried to kill Ricki and Lazarus is missing."

"I don't think we have to worry about Lazarus for the moment. I can handle him."

Chavvah watched as Renaud's eyes appeared to sparkle above the grin that formed on his face. *That's something you don't see very often.*

"Is Dr. Spenser okay?"

"The shooter missed, so she is fine."

"Good, because she's the key to everything, I feel it in my gut. Let me guess. It was a UV that shot at her."

"Not sure yet, but who else would do something like that?"

"Kang Ju must be behind this. That idiot!" The sparkle and grin melted away.

Chavvah shivered at the fury in Renaud's voice. "He's not

going to be a problem for long. He failed and it's going to cost him. The sooner Kang Ju is a pile of dust, the better."

"By the way, things here are going exactly as you predicted. That fool selected Central Square to make the reunification announcement. Juche Tower is right across the river from it. So all we need to do is make sure Kang Ju uses a couple of UDs to guard it during the speech and no Naturals." The smile started to ease back onto his face. "Take care of it."

Chavvah nodded. *"Absolument."*

"As for the rest of our plans, you've lined up the UVs we can trust and given them my instructions?"

"I'm working on it."

"Good. Put the word out that if anyone so much as breathes on Dr. Spenser, they will feel the full force of my wrath."

"I'll get it done."

Renaud's smile became a full-on grin. "Lazarus thought he got the best of us with that debacle in Cairo, but that will be nothing compared to what I have planned for October 10. I only wish I could see his face when this all comes down."

"I might be able to arrange that for you."

"Okay, if you can, please do. Thank you for calling." Renaud hung up.

Renaud thanked me…and used please *as well.*

September 17, 11:41 a.m., Seattle

After a good night's sleep, Ricki was in her office trying to read more of the Journal but found herself unable to concentrate. After she had read the same paragraph four times, she turned the computer off and walked to the window.

She really needed to get away by herself if only for a few hours.

She glanced down and over to CenturyLink Field where a crowd funneled in to watch the big game. That's where she needed to be today, not in this fairy tale where people died, only they didn't, where demons roamed freely, where Lazarus still lived after two thousand years. A world where she got kidnapped and shot at—Ricki cupped her face in her hands and rubbed her eyes, brushing away the tears.

She glanced to her right at the telescope Matthew had given her. *Was that really only a few months ago?* She slowly shook her head. *No, that was a lifetime ago.*

She focused her attention on the telescope. It looked like a three-foot-long bright-red flashlight mounted on a tripod with an eyepiece on the narrow end. She twisted a strand of her hair between her fingers as a small smile formed.

I bet I could see part of the game through the open ceiling of the stadium.

She adjusted the telescope so it pointed down to the field, then bent over to peek through the eyepiece. Once again a smile broke out on her face. Looked like she'd be able to watch most of the game from here. Maybe this day would end on a high note.

Ricki had been scanning the field for almost ten minutes when the loudspeaker embedded in her office ceiling crackled. "Dr. Spenser…are you there?"

"I'm here."

A loud sigh floated down from the ceiling. "Oh, great. I'm Roger at the front desk. A messenger left an envelope for you. I could either put it in an interoffice mail envelope, or you can come down and sign for it yourself. Sorry I can't bring it up to you, but I'm the only one on the desk today."

"Oh, don't apologize. I'll be right down to grab it."

"All right, Dr. Spenser. It'll be here."

What could that be? She wasn't expecting anything.

Fifteen minutes later she was back at her desk with a medium-size yellow envelope. She tore it open and pulled out a Seahawks ticket for today's game along with a note with a single word: enjoy. She raised her arms and let out a yelp. *He understood, L understood. I could just kiss him.*

Ricki checked her watch. She could walk over and maybe only miss the kickoff. She gathered her purse and coat only to stop at the door. Ray said she had to contact him when she was ready to leave. She looked at her watch again. She didn't know where he was, and it might take time to find him.

She reached for the door, then stopped, pressing her lips together. Ray might not be happy about her going to the game. He might even try to stop her. But L made it possible for Ricki to attend. And besides, she'd be one out of sixty-eight thousand people, a needle in a haystack.

I need this escape, if only for my sanity.

She looked at the ticket in her hand. L wouldn't have given her this if it wasn't safe. With half a shrug she opened the door, stepped out, put a Do Not Disturb sign up, and headed for the stairway and down to the side entrance.

What could possibly happen hidden in a big crowd like that? *I'll be safe.*

Pak Ju arrived at the arena early. He wanted to be sure he took his seat before Dr. Spenser got here. He double-checked the hard plastic, seven-inch knife he had smuggled in. The edge was razor sharp.

With a playful grin, he rubbed his hand on the back of the empty seat beside him. It had the feel of death. *Soon my target will be sitting next to me.* He wanted to see her eyes as life left them. He pictured her slouched over with his knife stuck in her heart.

He looked around the stadium. It was filling with Naturals. They made his skin crawl. He'd get this done and leave this place with one less of these foul-smelling vermin. *How fun.*

Ray stood outside Ricki's office. She hadn't answered her phone for the last twenty minutes. Her door was locked with a Do Not Disturb sign on it. He knocked on the door. "Ricki, are you in there?"

Nothing.

"I need to talk to you. Open the door, please." He wrinkled his brow. "Okay Ricki, I'm coming in." He reached into his jacket pocket for the master keys and used one to open the door. The room was empty. He was somewhat relieved because he'd feared she might be unconscious in her office from yesterday's concussion. *Where is she?*

He glanced at her desk. There was a torn yellow envelope next to a blank piece of paper. He glanced at the other side of the paper. A single word was printed in large black type.

Enjoy.

What? He called down to the lobby desk. "Did Ricki leave today?"

"No, but about an hour ago she came down to pick up an envelope addressed to her that was delivered by messenger."

Ray rushed down to his office and called up the security footage from each of the exits. He went through it all, one on each screen, at three times normal speed until he saw her at the south exit. He froze that screen and zoomed in on her hand.

"She's carrying a..." He quickly called Ralph.

Chapter Nineteen

THERE ARE NO SMALL VICTORIES. ANYTIME we resist, even if all we do is say we no longer want to walk the path of rebellion, is enormous because God will use it. If we say it enough, eventually we will find ourselves walking the path of righteousness. — Awakened Incident Manual, Volume 2, Page 116

September 17, 12:01 pm, Seattle

Ricki made it to the North Plaza entrance in record time. She ran up the steps and walked in under the Hawks Nest, site of the least comfortable but most coveted seats in the vast stadium. She looked at her ticket: Section 109, Row S, Seat 25. There was a sign inside the entrance that announced section 109 was off to her left. She wove through the crowd along the curved path to her left. She had never been to a Seahawks game before, so everything was new.

She stopped for a moment. So this was CenturyLink Field from the inside. The smell of fresh popcorn, the energy of the hometown crowd. She stood for a second, mesmerized by everything. She wanted to soak this all in.

She shrugged. See, she got here safely, and nothing would happen to her in this crowd. Besides, only L knew she was here. About ready to burst, she resumed her search for Section 109. A few hours with no Awakens, no UnDead, no secrets, no surprises—this was exactly what she needed.

She stopped at the head of the stairs for Section 109 leading down to her seat. Puzzled, she examined the ticket in her hand. L got her a ticket on the fifty-yard line down near the action. *Wow, Lazarus, I owe you a big thank-you.*

She kissed her ticket and started to bounce down to find Row S. In just a few steps she dodged traffic and saw her seat three rows ahead. The man she would be sitting by turned and looked straight at her as if he had sensed her presence. He was almost too small for the seat. She might have mistaken him for a child if it wasn't for the fact he was bald. But there was something disturbing about him.

A whispered voice said, "Run, Ricki, run. Run now."

Time seemed to slow. She looked around to see who said that, but the stairs were empty. Strange. The stadium seemed quiet. Her head jerked back to glance at the man in her row.

Now his eyes were dark, empty, and evil.

"Run," the voice whispered again. "Turn and run...*now!*"

It was a UD!

With their gazes locked, she slowly backed up a step. *He must be the one that tried to kill me. He's here to kill me now. How did he know?*

She backed up another step as she glanced down at her ticket. *L didn't send these.*

Ricki turned and, in a panic, rushed up the steps. At the top she veered to the right and collided with a man carrying a cup of beer. It sloshed on him and her.

"Hey! Watch where you're going!"

"Sorry." She bounced off him and continued running, afraid to look back. The man she ran into hollered, "You owe me a beer!"

She wanted to ask for help, but what could she say? The UnDead were chasing her? A zombie was loose in the stadium?

She ducked behind a tall blue pillar. Her back to the pillar, she slid to the floor to catch her breath. *Easy...take it easy.*

She scanned the crowd. *What? No security? No police?*

Ricki clenched her jaw and brushed the sweat off her brow. Maybe she should scream at the top of her lungs. She shook her head as tears pooled in her eyes. No help there.

She massaged her forehead with her right hand. Why? Why did she come here? *Stupid.*

Stupid.

Stupid.

She stopped mentally hitting herself and wiped the tears from her eyes.

Ricki, get yourself together.

She slowly filled her lungs with air and exhaled counting to three.

She had to get herself out of this mess.

She was alone.

At that moment she heard a calm, deep voice. "No, you're not."

She gasped. Her gaze darted from one side to another. She whispered, "Who said that?"

"Me." It was that same voice again.

Ricki looked around but no one seemed to notice her.

Her legs tingled as a warmth flowed through her. With it came a feeling of power. She felt stronger than she'd ever felt.

God is that you? There was no voice this time, but she knew the answer as soon as she asked the question.

So now you decide to help me? She'd take it, but she was still angry over what God didn't do all those years ago.

She stood using the post to support her back. Where was the UD? Did she lose it while she sat behind the pillar?

She glanced up at the digital clock hanging on the wall between two TV screens. Only fifteen seconds had passed, not minutes?

She chanced a look behind. The UD had stopped about twenty feet away. It was searching faces in the crowd, clearly looking for her.

Ricki scanned the area for an escape route. To her left there were restrooms and to her right was a wall. With a glance back, she saw the crowd around the UD was dwindling, and the UD had moved a few feet closer. All that lay between them was the ever-thinning crowd.

A tremor rippled through her body as she wiped the sweat off her forehead. *Lord, I need your help. Show me the way out of this one.*

She looked up and saw a large group making its way toward

her and the UD. Like a tall wave on the ocean, this group threatened to push everyone out of their way. She knew what she had to do.

Ricki waited for the group to pass between her and the UD. *Three…two…one.* She made a dash for the restrooms. There was a line at the women's but no one at the men's. That made the decision easy. She darted into the men's room. Two men were inside. They both gave her a playful smile.

Ricki raked her fingers through her hair. "I'm sorry, but I couldn't wait in the line for the women's restroom." The nearest man nodded as they both left. She looked under each of the four stalls. Empty. She fished a beer cup out of the garbage and filled it with water. She poured the water onto the floor in front of the third stall, then entered and stood on the toilet. She tried to slow her breathing and relax.

It wasn't long before Ricki heard someone enter the room. Her heart pounded and her chest tightened. She could sense it was the UD.

"Dr. Spenser…I know you're here…"

She could feel its smile. She froze like a lion waiting to pounce on its prey. *Quiet…quiet*

"You…die."

She heard it open the first stall, then the second. She took a moment to center herself. Time slowed as it stepped in front of the third. Its feet on the now-wet floor.

"It's…fun."

"Now!" She screamed and hit the stall door with all her weight. The UD slipped on the wet floor and hit the ground with a *thud* and a yell.

Ricki ran out. She spotted the ramp up to the next level ahead and to the left. She darted for the ramp. It wasn't that steep, but by the time she got to the second level, she was out of breath.

She leaned against the wall, took a couple of deep breaths, and glanced down the ramp. The UD stood at the bottom staring up at her with a smirk. It started up in no hurry, taking one slow, determined step at a time. Its dark eyes remained focused on her. Ricki slid along the wall as if it alone held her up, unable to tear her eyes away from the UD. After a few sideways shuffles, her left shoulder hit something hanging on the wall. A fire extinguisher. She froze there powerless to move, watching the UD weave up the ramp around football fans, seeming to enjoy her fear.

Suddenly there was a deafening roar. Something had happened on the field. People stopped to look at the TV monitors hanging everywhere. The renewed energy in the stadium broke the spell that held her frozen.

Ricki broke open the glass panel beside her and yanked out the fire extinguisher. She pulled out the lock pin and pointed it at the UD, now eight feet in front of her. She squeezed the handle, spraying the UD in the face with foam.

It screamed and covered its face with its hands. Then she pointed it at the UDs feet. It tried to rush her but fell back as soon as it stepped on the slippery foam, letting out another scream. People in the immediate vicinity panicked and started to flee.

Ricki ran in the direction of the field, down the steps between sections 214 and 215. At the end of the rows, there were three empty seats on the edge overlooking the field over two stories below. She darted down the steps, taking them two at a time.

Hunched down, she slid along the last row to the three empty seats at the end. She sat in the corner seat and bent over, hoping the UD would not find her. She struggled to catch her breath. If she didn't calm down, she'd hyperventilate and pass out. *Breathe...deep breath.*

The loudspeaker summoned security to the southeast corner of Level Two. She lifted her head and looked back in the hope of seeing security, though she had no idea what she'd tell them. She wished Ray or Ralph or Lazarus—especially Lazarus—were with her. Once again she wiped the sweat off her forehead as she continued to beat up on herself.

What was I thinking? In this strange new world, there was no safe way to escape even for a moment.

Instead of security, to her horror the UD, still covered in foam, was running down the steps toward her. The sick smile replaced by pure hate. Ricki stood and backed into the corner. She looked over the edge. Could she jump?

Before she could decide it was in front of her. With a knife in its hand. "I'm going to enjoy this."

A burly man in a seat behind her stood. "Is he bothering you, ma'am?"

It turned and waved the knife at him. "You're next, Natural."

Shock suffusing his face, the man took a step back and fell over his seat. Others in the row panicked and tried to get out. Ricki realized she was still holding the fire extinguisher. While the UD was threatening the man, she swung the extinguisher as hard as she could at its head. With an expression of disbelief, the UD plummeted over the edge to the concrete below.

Ricki dropped the extinguisher and looked at the startled man behind her. "Thank you."

She walked past him and started up the steps. She was about halfway up when Ralph ran down to her, accompanied by two other Awakens. She collapsed into his arms as the other Awakens continued down to look over the edge for the UD.

Chapter Twenty

WHEN LIES GO UNDETECTED, THEY APPEAR to have immense—almost overwhelming—power. But when they are exposed to the light of truth, they melt away like a block of ice in the noonday sun. –Awakened Incident Manual, Volume 2, Page 23

September 23, 2:21 p.m., Seattle

Ricki had been dreading this phone call ever since she got back to SOAR. Now she sat in Matthew's office listening to him as he described to L the events at CenturyLink Field.

"She's sitting right here." Matthew looked up at Ricki. "He wants to talk to you on speakerphone."

Ricki nodded. He must be angry with her. She didn't blame him.

Matthew pushed a button and hung up the phone. "Go ahead, L."

"Ricki, are you all right?" L's voice sounded muffled.

Or maybe that's him holding his anger back.

"Ricki?"

She wiped her eyes. "Yes… I mean, yes, I'm all right. And I'm so very sorry. I thought you had sent me the ticket. I thought I'd be safe…lost in the crowd."

"Ricki, slow down. Don't worry," L said. "You're not responsible."

She took a deep breath. "Are you sure?"

"Of course, you were set up. Somehow the UDs discovered that you're a football fan and sent you the ticket to lure you out. It so happened they were lucky that you desperately wanted out for a few hours. But I am concerned about the risks you're taking."

Matthew nodded. "General Patton said, 'Take calculated risks. That is quite different from being rash.'"

"That's good." L smiled. "Never met the general, but

Matthew's absolutely right. Ricki, it's time that you only take calculated risks. The enemy who has crossed your path is ruthless and powerful. That's why Odette's flying out to stay with you."

Ricki's flushed hot. *I'm not worth all this.* "L, thanks, but I've learned my lesson. There's no need to fuss over me this way."

"I'm not fussing. I care about you...your safety. While I'm gone, I would feel a lot better knowing Odette is with you."

Of course, he's right. "All right, it could be fun spending more time with her."

"Good. Now my main concern is why do they want to kill you now? They could have done that when they kidnapped you. They couldn't possibly know what you're doing for us so in their minds, what's changed?"

Ricki shrugged. "I don't know."

"Right. Matthew, could you get hold of the security footage from the CenturyLink incident and see if we have any record of the UD that was after her?"

"I'll get right on it."

"And could you pick up Odette at the airport and take her to the safe house?"

"Done, Boss."

Ricki brushed the hair out of her face. "Can I go with him?"

There was a short pause, then L said, "Now is not a good time for you to be out in public, especially with that UD after you. At least until we know what's going on."

She rolled her shoulders to loosen her tense muscles. "Forget I asked."

"I have a meeting in a few minutes so keep me posted on anything important. And Ricki?"

"Yes?"

"Take care of yourself."

"I will."

They hung up and Ricki looked at Matthew. "I'll be up in my office until it's time to go back to the safe house. Okay?"

"And no more Do Not Disturb signs?"

"No more anything without checking with Ray or you first."

"That's great. Let me know if you need anything."

Ricki left Matthew's office. She couldn't hold back a smile. *So he cares about me.*

September 17, 11:33 p.m., Tel Aviv

Shiri and Declan arrived at Arielle's together. L waved at them and put down the phone. So this was the CIA officer on Shiri's trail.

Shiri introduced Declan to the rest of the team. When she got to L, Declan said, "I assume the L stands for Lazarus?"

"It does." L nodded.

"You're telling me you are the two-thousand-year-old man mentioned in the Bible and who knew Jesus personally?" He massaged the back of his neck. "Can you understand how difficult that is for me to believe?"

"It must be terribly difficult for you. Nevertheless, it's true."

"Was the perfect DNA I found in the bullet yours?"

Ariella raised her hand. "That would be mine."

Shiri cuffed Declan on the shoulder. "Ariella was the sniper that day."

Declan turned to Ariella. "Are you a two-thousand-year-old sniper?"

Ariella chuckled, her eyes sparkling with mirth. "I'm afraid I'm less than two hundred years old."

Agam patted Ariella on the back. "And I'm just a few years older than her."

Joon cleared his throat. "I'm the baby in this group, having been born a little over thirty-seven years ago, I can appreciate your struggle with all this because I still struggle with it, and I'm an Awakened. Granted, a new Awakened in the last few days." Joon grimaced. "I died in a North Korean prison camp as a result of exposure to a new strain of Ebola. I woke up in the morgue, then was smuggled out of the camp. On the outside I met two unusual men who seemed to know me. They grabbed my arms and the next thing I knew, I was in the SOAR lobby understanding English."

Declan shook his head. "Teleportation too? What have I gotten myself into?"

Agam said, "You are here because—" Before he finished, he glanced at Shiri standing behind Declan shaking her head and mouthing *no*. Agam started over. "What I mean to say is that God has put you in the middle of this for a reason."

Declan frowned. "As far as I'm concerned, the jury is still out on this God business."

This was getting off topic. L stepped up and put his hand on Declan's shoulder. "We have work to do. Welcome to our little group, Declan. We need someone with your connections, so why don't we move to the dining room and make plans to save the world?"

They all took their seats around the table. L remained standing. "North Korea has a weapon of mass destruction that's never been seen before. A weapon that is small, easily delivered, difficult to trace back to an aggressor, and kills without destroying the infrastructure. It's controlled by a UD and may already be on its way to ISIS. As I see it, we have two tasks. Shiri and Declan need to stay here and either prevent ISIS from getting their hands on this weapon or stop them from using it. The rest of us need to slip into North Korea and dust the UD behind all this."

Agam burst out, "It's about time we dust that *dran,* that devil, back to hell."

Ariella patted Agam on the back. "We all feel that way."

Joon stood. "Sometimes I think this is all a dream, but right now I pray it is not. I have feared Sok Kang Ju all my life. I have seen his lies, I have felt the carnage he has brought on my people, I have tasted his evil. I am ready to do whatever I can to bring him to justice."

L scanned the assembled group, smiled, and said a prayer.

They spent the rest of the night planning a workable strategy. In the early morning hours, they reached a consensus and called it a night.

As L left he thanked God. *This group can succeed.*

September 18, 9:47 a.m., Paris

Chavvah had been dreading this phone call ever since she got the news, but now that Renaud was on the line, she could no longer delay. "There was another attempt on Dr. Spenser's life."

"By attempt, I assume you mean she survived." Renaud's voice had a flat tone Chavvah had never heard from him before. Did he already know? Was he playing some kind of game? "Yes, she appears to be fine. And you'll be happy to know we've identified the UV involved."

"How?"

"Of all things, he was caught on surveillance. His name is Pong Pak Ju."

A long silence passed. He was clearly not happy.

"So Kang Ju *was* behind this. I'm not surprised. *Imbécile!* First, he plans to attack South Korea against my explicit orders, then he goes after Dr. Spenser because he knows she is important to me. I just had a meeting with his son, Park Kye. Even he has reached the end of his tolerance with his father. He told me Kang Ju plans to have me killed sometime during these talks. That idiot. He's going to ruin everything I've so carefully planned."

"What do you want me to do?" *You planned? How about* we've *planned?*

"You can start by making it perfectly clear that the full weight of my wrath will fall on anyone who goes after Dr. Spenser. And I want to make an example out of this Pong Pak Ju. Find him but don't approach him. I want reports on his every move. When this is all over, I will personally take care of both Kang Ju and Pak Ju."

"Should we take measures to protect you?"

"I already have. He won't succeed, and soon Kang Ju will be a pile of dust."

She hung up. What was he hiding from her? Why was she—? Chavvah's head jolted back so she was staring up at the skylight in her office. *What the…?* She couldn't move as a slight tremor migrated down her body from her shoulders to her knees.

She focused her eyes on the light-blue Paris sky as a few cottony wisps of clouds morphed into a thick, tar-like blackness. Something played out over that blackness like a grainy old black-and-white movie. As she watched it, an involuntary smile grew on her face.

Then as suddenly as it hit, it was gone. She could move and the Paris sky was once again shining though her skylight. She almost fell out of the chair as she gulped in air. She cupped her head in her hands and rubbed her eyes.

How long was she out? Chavvah glanced at the digital clock on her desk. Her eyes widened. Only a few seconds? The vision seemed to last at least ten minutes.

She was getting stronger. She'd never had an otherworldly experience like that. She closed her eyes and replayed the scene in her mind. *"Enfin!"* She slammed her fist on the desk. *"Enfin! Enfin!"* Finally.

She slowly rocked back and forth, her fingers steepled beneath her chin. She wouldn't share this prophecy with him. *I can have my secrets too.*

She stopped rocking, took another deep breath, and stood. Now she knew why Dr. Spenser was so important.

He's right. She is the key to everything.

Chapter Twenty-One

THE MEASURE OF WISDOM IS THE degree one understands how little one actually knows. Wisdom is a combination of knowledge and humility.–Awakened Incident Manual, Volume 2, Page 116

September 18, 11:33 a.m., Pyongyang

Kang Ju was not happy with the news that Dr. Spenser was still alive, but he was also in a surprisingly forgiving mood. His time was coming and coming soon. Nothing could stop him now, not even her survival. Her death was not integral to the success of his plan, but that didn't lessen his anger. He'd wanted to torment Renaud before the pretender was assassinated. He had been looking forward to Renaud's reaction to the death of Dr. Spenser. Over the years he'd become less tolerant of being denied something he wanted. He turned on his intercom. "Show Pak Ju in."

As the assassin was ushered in, Kang Ju motioned for him to take the seat in front of his desk. Boiling with fury, he speared him with a venomous look. "What went wrong?"

Pak Ju shivered under Kang Ju's glare. "I don't know. Something is protecting her. She seemed to know right when I was ready to pounce."

"You mean something like Renaud?"

Pak Ju shook his head. "Far stronger."

"Don't tell me God is protecting her or I will vomit."

Pak Ju shrugged but remained silent. After a few moments of Kang Ju's unrelenting gaze, he bowed his head.

"What should I do with you, Pak Ju?" He rubbed his chin. "I could turn you over to Chavvah, or I can see to it you never have a chance to kill another Natural…"

As Kang Ju's voice trailed off, Pak Ju looked up, displaying the level of panic Kang Ju loved to see. He reveled in watching

Pak Ju's face turn ashen and his lips tremble. It was almost as good as terrifying a Natural.

"Great Leader, I have served you faithfully. This was not my fault. I tried, but as I said, she is protected."

"You have tried, I'll give you that. You have nothing to fear. I'm feeling generous today. Besides, I have a job only you can accomplish. Succeed, and all will be forgiven."

Pak Ju's face brightened. "My savior, I will not let you down. I'm sure I will succeed at whatever job you have for me, and it will be fun."

"Good. I have a problem. The South Korean wants to back out. He doesn't want to kill Renaud." Kang Ju frowned. "A Natural with a budding conscience—now that makes me sick. So I need you to kill him ASAP. Then we'll outfit you with a South Korean military uniform. I want you to shoot Renaud from the position we planned for the Natural-with-a-conscience on the announcement day."

"Great Leader, I will get it done."

"Of course, I need you to be arrested so the South will clearly take the blame. It will prove that they have always opposed reunification and will justify our attack with our new weapon. But don't worry, I'll see to it that you escape. Any questions?"

Pak Ju stood at attention and bowed. "Your Excellency, I will do your will."

Kang Ju waved him out and leaned back in his chair. It wouldn't be long now. The plans for the "celebration" that Renaud would not survive were taking form, and the "medicine" was already on its way to ISIS. Then Kang Ju would rule this earth and hunt down every Natural. He put his hands behind his head and closed his eyes. No more coddling them either.

September 18, 4:17 p.m., Tel Aviv

Declan hung up his office phone and looked over at Shiri. "It's begun."

"How has it begun?"

"We're going to a party tonight at the Chinese embassy in Tel Aviv."

"A party in a party city. Hardly a novel concept. What's so special about this one?"

"An informant of mine will be there. On matters of ISIS, he's where I always start."

"And I'm invited?"

"Of course, if it's not too short notice for you. We only have a couple of hours to get ready. After all, we're a team now. Besides, what if we come up against one of those things?"

"A UD?"

"Yup, one of those." Declan found it difficult to actually call them UDs. "I can't believe I'm talking about zombies, real zombies."

"They are not zombies. They are demon-possessed bodies."

"Yeah, and that's supposed to make me feel better..."

Shiri shrugged. "It will. Give it time."

"By the way, it's black tie. Do you have something to wear?"

"Of course, I have just the thing. A dress that was only worn once by the Queen of Sheba. She gave it to me herself, and I've been saving it for such an occasion."

Declan looked puzzled. "Wouldn't that be...ah...dated? Don't you have something a little more modern? The point is to fit in, not stand out."

Shiri smacked him on the shoulder. "I was only teasing. The Queen of Sheba was way before my time. How old do you think I am?"

"My understanding is when a woman asks that question, it's best to change the subject. In your case, especially since my Bible knowledge is spotty at best, that goes double."

Amusement twinkled in Shiri's eyes. "I do have a dress I got a few months ago that I haven't had a chance to wear. It will work fine. I'll go home to get ready, and you can pick me up later."

"I'll be there at seven."

"It's a date."

Declan smiled as she left, *A date, huh.*

Declan arrived fifteen minutes early to find that Shiri was ready. As soon as he saw her at the doorway, he froze. She wore a pale-blue silk dress that flowed down to her ankles. It had a scooped back and a modest front. She whirled around like a model, her long, blue-streaked jet-black hair swinging out. Declan's lips parted but there was no sound. He was too stunned to speak.

"Something wrong? Is this dress too old-fashioned for you?"

Declan shook his head. "Not at all. It's beautiful."

Shiri smiled. "Why thank you."

He stared for a moment longer, then Shiri tapped him on the shoulder. "Declan, we should leave. We have spy work to do."

He nodded. "I'm sorry. Of course we should get going. But that dress will attract a lot of attention."

She smiled again. "And it will make you invisible. That's the idea."

"Oh, I see you've done this before."

"Only for a thousand or so years."

Declan shrugged. "Guess you could teach me some old tricks." He'd never get used to this age difference. He grinned inside. What would his mother say?

Half an hour later, they arrived at the People's Republic of China embassy. He quickly scanned the crowd—there must be fifty to seventy-five guests milling about in the main ballroom, and perhaps another twenty were in the adjacent room listening to live piano music.

Declan searched the crowd to find his contact. He turned to Shiri. "About twenty percent of the guests here are spies of one form or another. The man we're looking for is short, with dark hair, olive-colored skin, and large brown eyes. He's the naval attaché to the Cyprus embassy. He usually wears the Cyprus flag as a lapel pin. It's white with two olive branches under the map of the island. If you see him, let me know."

"He sounds handsome."

"I guess…to some. He's half Greek, half Arab. He presently goes by Artem Bahadir."

"His spy name, I presume?"

"A lot of the people here are known by 'spy names.'"

"So is your real name Declan Walsh?"

He waggled his eyebrows at her. "Wouldn't you like to know? Besides, Shiri isn't your real name."

She gestured off to her right. "Who's that tall, thin man waving to you over there?"

Declan glanced that direction. "Oh no, that's Bob Hoskins, the deputy chief of mission at the US embassy. He's a bit of a pain. He doesn't like the fact that I'm given free range throughout the Middle East. He thinks he should be in charge of my assignments in Israel, even though he's never been a field agent with the Company."

As Bob walked up to them, Declan could hear his booming voice. "Well, I'll be. Declan is here with a date. Wrap me up and send me to heaven. I've seen it all now."

They shook hands. Bob was the poster boy for two-faced. Though the lower half of his face sported a smile as big as a house, his eyes glared. "Dec, you just have to introduce me to this gorgeous young lady."

He hated being called Dec. If only he could say she was his two-thousand-year-old girlfriend and they were here to clean up the zombie problem in Tel Aviv. That would keep Bob's revolting attention away from her. But he knew better. "Bob, this is Shiri Liora. She's a chief analyst for the Israeli government. We met a few months ago when she provided the Company with some critical information."

Bob checked Shiri out from top to bottom. "Didn't know they had girls in a senior position over there. I guess it's about time."

"Oh, you'd be surprised. I've been very good at my job for a very long time. Isn't that right, Declan?"

Shiri can hold her own. "Yup. In fact, Bob, you have no idea. This woman knows more about the Middle East and its history than anyone I've ever met. It's like she's lived through it all."

Bob smiled at Shiri. "Maybe you can come over sometime and teach me a little history." His attention was diverted to Shiri's right. "Ah, my counterpart at the French embassy is here. If you'll excuse me, I need to go talk with her." Without waiting for a response, Bob walked off.

Declan leaned in close to Shiri's ear. "You'll have to excuse him. He is a pig."

She chuckled. "Maybe, but he is a child of God. There must be something good in him."

He shook his head. "There's where I have a hard time understanding God."

"Yeah, He can be difficult to comprehend sometimes, but if God were totally understandable, He wouldn't be God, now would He?"

"I guess." Declan shrugged. "Oh, there's my contact." Declan tilted his head to the left.

Shiri glanced over. "Where?"

"He just poked his head around. He's talking to that woman in the white dress."

Shiri looked again and suddenly turned so she faced Declan with her back to the contact. She stroked her fancy silver necklace.

"What's up?"

"That man in the Chinese uniform walking up to your contact, do you know who he is?"

He glanced around Shiri's shoulder. "I don't know his name, but he has been pointed out to me. That's one of those spies I told you about, and we have trouble. He's not Chinese. In fact, he's North Korean. The Chinese are letting him serve as the number-two military attaché to their embassy. What does he want with my contact?"

"We've got more trouble than you realize. That spy is a UD."

"Like the one who attacked me? Could you work your magic and turn it to dust?"

"Yes, but not here. Not in front of everyone. It would violate the second law of UD hunting. More important, we can't let him see me. I have to leave now. Quietly."

"You mean run from it?"

"Yes. If it sees me, it's liable to panic and take a hostage. Maybe even your contact. And when it's done, it'll kill the hostage."

"Surely you could step up and dust it, couldn't you?"

"Not really. The first law of UD hunting, the law that cannot be broken, is no Natural can be harmed. If it had a hostage, most of the time I'd have to back down."

"Okay. Granted, if you step in the hostage may be harmed, but if it's allowed to roam free, it's one hostage versus a potential of many more deaths. Doesn't the greater good call for you to act now rather than later?"

Shiri's shoulders dropped. "A lot of damage has been done in the name of the greater good. Say it took your informant. What would be the greater good for him, his family, his friends? Part of having faith in God is letting Him take care of the 'greater good' His way. Our responsibility is simply to do what is right in the immediate present."

Declan started to say something, but Shiri pressed her finger to his lips. "I know. This is another issue that's difficult to understand, but if you let God speak to you, you will come to accept it."

Declan stared at the UD. "I guess I have to take what you say at face value, given the amazing things I've witnessed over the last few days, but it's still difficult."

She smiled. "Good. Now you know why Jesus performed miracles. They serve as witness to the truth of who He is. I have to leave now. I'll wait in the car while you make contact. Be careful around it."

"All right. As soon as I'm done, I'll come out and join you.

Our first date and we run into a zombie. I hope you won't hold this against me."

Shiri hit him on his arm. "It's not a zombie."

Chapter Twenty-Two

HOPE EXISTS BECAUSE GRACE ABOUNDS. –AWAKENED Incident Manual, Volume 2, Page 310

Seong-Jin had just started talking with Artem Bahadir when Declan Walsh walked up. He had a difficult time hiding his surprise, given that Declan should have been dead.

First, Abd al Hakim sent Fadel and Jabir to kidnap him, but they failed. Then Abd had taken it on himself to kill Declan, a task for which he'd shown extreme enthusiasm. Abd held Declan responsible for the Abdul Ba'ith dusting.

Seong-Jin thought that unlikely because that would mean Declan was associated with Awakens. *The Awakens bring in a Natural? Never. They want to remain in the shadows.*

Seong-Jin thought about the last time he'd seen Abd. It'd been several days ago, at least. Perhaps he was still out there hunting for Declan. And here came his target waltzing in to this party.

I could take Declan out right now, but Abd would not take kindly to my stepping in on his little revenge. He'd get intel from Declan instead and pass it on to Abd.

Declan strolled up to the pair and slapped Artem on the back. "It's been a while since we've attended the same party. I hope tonight will be more fun than the last time."

Artem smiled. "I hope so too. You saved my *future* when you ushered me out early. Who knew that Middle Eastern drink … you know, *arak* packed such a punch?"

"Just about everybody in Israel, but you were new here and didn't know the power of a glass of *arak*. I hope you've learned your lesson."

"Oh, I have. Declan, this is Seong-Jin, a military attaché assigned to our host's embassy."

Declan shook hands with him. Seong-Jin…it meant "planet shaker." These UDs came with quite an ego.

Seong-Jin gave Declan a decidedly unfriendly look. "I heard you'd been out of town. Did you recently return?"

Shock flashed across Artem's face. It was an unwritten rule that military attachés did not pry into each other's business uninvited—while at a party or anywhere else, for that matter—unless it was official business.

Declan decided not to take offense. Instead, he would lie. "Got back yesterday."

"Going to be here long?"

"At least a month, probably more."

Seong-Jin nodded, then turned to Artem. "I have to make the rounds." He shrugged. "It's the cost of representing the host. I hope you will give some thought to what we discussed. And Declan, a pleasure meeting you. Since you'll be around for a while, maybe we will run into each other again."

Declan dipped his head in a quick nod. "I think you can count on it."

They both watched as Seong-Jin walked away. When he was halfway across the room, Declan tapped Artem on the shoulder. "I need help. Could we meet outside in, say, half an hour?"

Artem glanced at his watch. "I should be done with what I came here for in about an hour. Would that do?"

"Sure. I'll be in the parking lot in an hour."

Exactly one hour later, Declan saw Artem step out of the embassy and head toward the parking lot. Shiri had decided it was still best for her to stay out of sight and watch for any UD interference, especially from the North Korean. Besides, there was no need for Artem to know of Mossad's involvement.

When Artem got to the prearranged spot, Declan didn't waste any time. "I need to know if you've heard any talk about a new ISIS weapon, or an upcoming offensive action, or even an increased level of excitement."

Artem took his time answering. "It's been pretty quiet up until tonight, at least with my contacts."

"What happened tonight?"

"Besides you asking me that loaded question?"

Declan narrowed his eyes and growled. "Don't make me dig it out of you."

Artem smiled. "I don't think I'd like that, not the way you work. That Korean I was talking to when you walked up. Do you know him?"

"I've seen him before, but we've never been formally introduced. He's a typical military attaché, but he's new to this post in Israel. It's out of character for the Chinese to send him to this embassy. Off the top of my head I can think of at least five Chinese embassies where a military diplomat poking around would be more useful to North Korea than Israel."

"Me too. Though he has talked to me a few times since he got here. At first it was the typical back and forth we attachés engage in. Then there was tonight."

Declan crossed his arms over his chest. "What did he want tonight?"

"I didn't think much about it until right now. He asked me about shipping in the Mediterranean. He had been contacted by a company with interests in the Democratic People's Republic of Korea, and they wanted to know if it would be difficult for a ship with even small DPRK connections to travel in these waters without interference. I told him it should be okay as long as tensions are low in the region. Do you think North Korea is planning to ship weapons to ISIS?"

Declan shrugged. "I don't know for sure. I hear things from time to time that worry me, but that's the nature of the world we live in, especially in this region. Besides if The Company thought it would be useful for you to know what they suspect, then you would know by now."

"Sorry I couldn't be more help. I'll ask around discreetly, and if I hear anything, I'll let you know.

September 18, 10:02 p.m., Tel Aviv

Declan walked over at a slightly quicker pace than usual. Shiri could see the excitement in his eyes. She knew he had discovered something important. "What have you learned?"

"What have I learned? How about I know it's coming in by boat." Declan puffed out his chest as he told Shiri the news.

"Are you sure? I would have guessed it would be shipped by private plane. That would be faster and more secure."

"A plane from North Korea coming into ISIS-controlled Syria or Iraq could be targeted by US fighters. We basically control the air over ISIS' head. Travel by truck or rail is out of the question, too many borders to cross. Besides, Artem told me your UD friend—"

"I am no friend to any UD." Shiri narrowed her eyes.

"Right. That UD dude asked Artem questions about safe passage through the Mediterranean on a ship originating from North Korea. That has to be where the vials are located and how they're coming to the Middle East."

"When will the North Korean ship leave North Korea?"

"I'm not sure. My best guess is either it's already left or will leave soon, say, a day or two at most. But at the moment, that's only my gut feeling."

"Headed for a port in the Mediterranean. Which one?"

"Ah, that is another unknown question. I think we can rule out a port in Israel—too much security. That leaves Syria or Lebanon. You're the analyst. Any idea how long the trip would take?"

Shiri thought for a moment. "Shipping from Japan to Israel takes about twenty-one days, so it's a fair guess this will be anywhere between twenty-one and twenty-two days. If your gut is right, the North Korean ship will leave on or around September

18, arriving at a port in Syria or Lebanon around October 12."
Shiri smiled. "Good work, Declan. This partnership is starting to pay off."

Declan looked away. The muscles in his neck tensed up. He cleared his throat. "Th... ah... thanks." The word came out sounding like someone had punched him in the throat.

Shiri tilted her head to the side and raised her eyebrows. "Declan? Are you all right?"

Declan looked down and cleared his throat again. "Yeah, it feels like something is caught in my windpipe." Declan put his hand over his neck as he glanced at Shiri. "Look. It's late. I'll...I'll take you home." He looked down again. "Tomorrow ... tomorrow ... I'll search for answers. It's late. I'll take you home."

The ride to her apartment was quiet. As she stood in front of the door she looked back and watched Declan drive off. *What happened back there? Did I say something wrong?*

Chapter Twenty-Three

WE ARE ENGAGED IN A WAR right now. Some mistakenly call it a spiritual war, but it is that and much more. Both physical and spiritual battles are fought every day. —Awakened Incident Manual, Volume 2, Page 3

September 19, 9:17 a.m., Seattle

Ricki sat at her desk staring at her computer screen, rhythmically rocking. She was wearing the same tattered jeans and pale-blue pullover sweater she had worn yesterday and the day before that.

She glanced over at the window, a new habit she had perfected over the last few days. *Good, I remembered to close the blinds.* She stopped rocking and shook her head. The last thing she wanted to see was CenturyLink Field.

She returned her attention to the computer screen. What was she reading?

Ricki wiped her cold, clammy hands on her sweater and then positioned her fingers over the keyboard. *Now, what command…?*

She pulled her hands back onto her lap, leaned back in her chair, and closed her eyes. She had to get her act together. She needed to get something done before Odette arrived.

At the thought of her friend, her breathing slowed, and her shoulders slumped. Ricki could really use some girl time with her, but it would be even better if Lazarus came back instead.

She glanced up at the clock and did a few mental calculations. In about two hours Odette's plane would land at Sea-Tac, then another hour or so before Ray brought her up here.

At the thought of Ray, she frowned. *Wish he'd let me go with him to the airport.* But Ray was right—it might not be safe for her. Besides, Odette might not be on the plane.

Odette had been scheduled to arrive yesterday but had been delayed because a mindless Level 2 UD had been sighted in the

Washington, DC area. Of course, she had to hunt it down and dust it. Ricki snorted. There was a Level 1 UD here she would like to see Odette dust. UDs ruined everything. She wished she'd never heard of them.

Ricki sat up in her chair, her nostrils flaring. The anger they raised in her seemed to tap into a hidden reserve of energy.

She really should try to get something done. She faced the screen once again and picked up where she had left off with Arioch coming back from the dead.

Arioch looked down. "It gripped my throat and told me it could arrange that for me. You know, seeing Jesus. It said something like 'One less of his followers will improve this world.' Then it...it bit me in the neck." Arioch reached up to feel his throat. "What happened? My neck is fine, but I'm sure it bit me. I could feel the blood flowing down my chest. That is the last thing I remember until I woke up here. Lazarus, what is going on?"

I stepped back. How was I going to explain this to him? Somehow, I knew this would be the first of many times I would have to answer that question. "Like all of us, you died and Jesus brought you back to life."

Arioch's gaze scanned the room. "Jesus is here?"

"No, but he does not have to be present to resurrect someone. Almost everyone in this compound woke up while he was still on the cross."

"Wait a minute. You said I was dead. Dead like you were? For how long? Are you sure?"

"Dead like I was, but only for an hour at most. And yes, I am sure."

Arioch looked down again. "I was dead, and Jesus brought me back to life." Tears flooded his eyes and trailed down his face. "Why? I don't deserve it."

"But that's the point. Jesus has something very specific for you to do for him, for all of us, so he brought you back."

"What could I possibly do that would help him?"

I shrugged. "I know not. I am not even sure what he wants *me* to do..." Then I explained what I had told everyone else in our growing group. Arioch seemed to come to terms with what had happened faster than others. I hoped this whole process got easier if Jesus was going to raise others in the coming years.

I took him around and introduced him to several of our members. I told him we would find space for him in the compound, but he did not want to stay.

"Lazarus, that thing...that thing that bit me... It is still on the loose, isn't it?"

"Yes, it is out there somewhere."

"So what if it does this to someone else? Is there any way to stop it?"

I was afraid of what he planned, especially since Merriam and I had only shared the secret of these beasts with Sapphira and Josias, but I answered truthfully. "It seems when we bite them, they turn to dust."

Arioch's brow tightened. "*Ma*, that is it? They become *dust*. How does that happen?"

"I do not know how it happens; it just does. We found out by accident when one of them grabbed Merriam and would not let go. She did what she had to do—bit it. That is when it turned to dust."

"Could I do that if I find one of these creatures?"

"You could hunt one and bite it, but you have to be careful about all of this. They recognize us like we recognize them. They are not above taking someone hostage and killing them if we do not back off. We already lost one that way. We cannot afford to let it happen again. Our job is to help them..." I rubbed my face. "Let us call them Naturals to keep things straight." (Added note: This is where the term was first used.) "Our job is to help Naturals stay away from situations in which they will be murdered."

Arioch looked worried. "But that is just it. That thing out there will kill them, ah...the Naturals, if we do not stop it. I have to find it and turn it to dust. I think I know who it is...or was."

"You recognized it?"

Arioch nodded. "At the time things moved too fast for me to be sure. Besides, I thought he had died yesterday. Now I can see that face. His name was Vale. He was a Pharisee but could not keep to our rules. We caught him violating several and shunned him. I know where he lives. I must go and stop him."

I considered his request for a few seconds. He was right. "Okay. You can go but be careful and do not let any Natural be harmed. Let me know what happens. When you come back, we will create formal rules for hunting these things."

Arioch returned two days later. He told me the job was done, and Vale was dust. I decided it would be a good idea to record these hunts, so I asked him to write the story of Vale's dusting and give it to me. It was the first entry in the Awakened Incident Manual (Volume 1, Page 3).

Ricki paused from reading for a moment. Could anything in that story help her? She'd have to ask L. She picked up where she left off.

Thirty-eight days after the Resurrection I received word that Jesus wanted me to meet him in Bethany in two days. I had no idea why, but it had been a while since I'd seen him, so I was happy to leave Josias in charge. I arrived a day early.

The next day, Peter found me and escorted me to where Jesus was speaking. Along the way he told me about a meeting the apostles had with Jesus.

When we arrived, Jesus was waiting for me. He made me feel like I was the only one there, but I am sure Peter felt the same way. I do not know how Jesus did it, how he could make everyone feel like they were the sole focus of his attention, but he always did.

He pulled me aside for a few minutes. He told me I was doing a good job. I told him I still didn't know what I was doing in the broad scope of things. He smiled and put his hand on my shoulder. That's when he told me what Peter had already described to me. He said that soon a helper would come, and I should listen very closely to the directions the helper gave me. I still didn't quite understand, but then that was Jesus, and I trusted him enough to know that eventually I would understand. Wasn't that what trust was, after all?

He gave me a big hug, told me he loved me (what a moment that was), and asked me to wait there for a while. He went on to talk to the group that had gathered.

It wasn't long before the most amazing thing happened. I hadn't seen Jesus for a while. I knew he was still here with us because I could always sense his presence when he was nearby (Something I was to later discover was not a property of my relationship with Jesus. Everyone who knew him while he was on earth experienced the same feelings when he was close, even if he was too far away to be seen. I felt what most people felt, a powerful feeling of peace, a sense that all-is-right-with-the-world). The closer I was to him the stronger the feeling. When he was right in front of me I would feel completely enclosed in love. Sometimes it was so strong, I'd have to remind myself to breathe. It has always made me sad that people who didn't believe who he was would never feel this way.

Again, Ricki paused from reading for a moment. Her forehead wrinkled. She closed her eyes to think. *I've felt that once, when was that?* She struggled to remember. There was a strong sense of urgency. For some reason she had to dredge up this memory. *Could the secret I've been looking for be connected to a long-lost memory like this one? It's one of those memories I locked away for the sake of my sanity. Is it safe to expose it now? Lord, tell me what I'm supposed to do.*

When the last word of that single sentence prayer escaped her lips, a bright light filled the room. So bright that she could see it dance on her closed eyelids. She could feel it as if it was coming out of her own skin spreading across her like a warm blanket.

She heard a thud. *What was that?* She resisted opening her eyes to see whatever it was. Then she knew. She had slid out of her office chair and was on her knees in front of the light. *Is that you God?*

Though she refused to open her eyes, she was certain that

deep but gentle voice came from the light. A single word echoed in her mind, *Yes.*

What do you want?

Her mind was flooded with words. Words dripping with truth. Peaceful yet powerful words. *I want you to let that memory pass through. Don't be afraid. I will be with you the whole time.*

She nodded then started a process that had terrified her all her life. She forced her mind to go back to that time. Nothing. She clenched her fists and tried harder as if from sheer force of will she could command the return of the memories. She could feel them gradually inch their way out through the decades of protection she built up to prevent what was happening now. She felt a touch from the light and everything that happened that day flooded her mind. She had rebirthed her past.

The voice spoke again. *My precious daughter, I give you these memories so you can know the truth, so that you can be free of the evil that crossed your path. Don't be afraid. I'll always be with you.*

The light went out. She opened her eyes. Everything was the same. She glanced at the clock. Two minutes had passed. Only two minutes, but it felt like…hours. She grabbed paper and a pen, walked to her couch and laid down. She felt strong enough to expose those memories. She decided to write them down so as to never lose them again.

My mother had just dropped me off at my uncle's house. I didn't say anything. I walked over to the fireplace, sat on the hearth, curled my knees up to my face. He sat beside me. "Ricki, I have a surprise for you in the bedroom."

Usually, I get up and walk to the bed without a word, resigned to my fate, but this time I didn't. I stood up, looked him in the face and said, "No!"

His face turned a bright red. He reached behind me and grabbed the fireplace poker. "You're coming with me or I'll beat any resistance out of you."

At this point, I would give in. I would tell myself that what he wanted from me wasn't as bad as a beating. But I didn't do that because out of the corner of my eye I saw a brilliant light form by the front door. I had no idea what it was, but I sensed it was there to help me. Without saying anything, I turned and walked to the door. I heard him walk behind me. I could visualize the poker raised in his hand. I braced myself for the blow I knew was coming. But it never came.

Instead I heard him scream. A scream of fear not anger. The white light that had been in front of the door now engulfed my uncle. My uncle was struggling to get away, but somehow he was locked in. He fell to the floor, unconscious. I knew the front door was always locked from the inside and he had the only key. I started to bend down to search for it when I heard the door unlatch and open.

I said thanks to whatever it was that helped me that morning. I left his house forever. It took me three hours to walk home in the pouring rain. From that point on, no one talked about those eight years of horror.

After Ricki finished writing down her memory, she sat and stared at the paper. She didn't read it, just stared at it for a while. She took a deep breath and put the paper down.

Jesus was there and He fought for me. Now she was ready to get back into Lazarus's journal.

There must have been around five hundred people there that morning. As might be expected, the crowd broke up into highly fluid groups of two to five or six. And everyone had an opinion about something. It was noisy. Sometimes you couldn't hear what the person in front of you was saying. That's when the first amazing thing happened. Without being told, everyone suddenly stopped talking and turned to face a rock formation on the west side.

Jesus stood on a rock about five feet above us. The story of what happened next depends on who you talk to. That's because everyone to a person claims that Jesus spoke directly to them. I thought Jesus spoke directly to me when he reminded me of how much he loved me. I have no understanding how Jesus could simultaneously address each of our concerns. Of course, I don't understand how Jesus did anything he did. After all, he raised me from the dead.

But that isn't even close to the miracle that came at the end. I missed the beginning of the final miracle because I was wiping tears out of my eyes. What I heard was a cry, "He's flying. He's flying." I looked in the direction of the rock and saw him hovering about five feet off the ground. He stayed there for about a minute or so then he began to float up into the clouds and eventually disappear from sight.

It was a moment of dichotomy for me. It was sad because I sensed this time he was really gone. At the same time, it was awe inspiring. I mean, who floated away in the air like that? I apparently wasn't the only one with conflicting thoughts. By the time Jesus disappeared, the place was bedlam. I must admit, I stood there, frozen in time, unable to move, just staring into the now-empty sky for some glimpse of him. When the spell broke I looked around. Some were on their knees crying out to God, "Father, don't take him away from us and leave us to the mercy of the Romans." Some substituted Pharisees for Romans. Others were shouting, "He's gone to get his angel armies. He'll be back soon." I don't think anyone, myself included, really understood what was going on at that moment. That's as it should be. If we could understand everything he did, he would not be God. Miracles are inherently ambiguous and unintelligible. That's when two men appeared. I recognized them, though no one else seemed to. They told all of us not to worry. Jesus would come back. We were to go about doing what he told us to do. I returned to our compound, but I was in a daze for a while before I resumed my activities.

Note to Ricki

Something else happened at that last meeting with Jesus that I have kept secret until I met you. He told me to keep this journal, to record events as I saw them and as I felt led. He said this journal would contain a secret that even I would not be able to discern until he sent someone to me who would be able to discover the secret and act on it. When I asked him how I would know that person, he told me someone would say in Greek, I agape epikratei opou synchoresi askeitai—"love prevails where forgiveness is practiced."

I kept this in my heart and never put it in the journal I gave to others. I know we have talked about this before, but please do not share this secret with anyone or let anyone see this note. Now we both know that someone Jesus had talked about all those years ago was you.

Ricki wiped away tears. She stopped reading and took a few deep breaths to clear her thoughts. Two thousand years ago, Jesus told Lazarus that he would send her to him. Send her... *Me.* A chill marched slowly up her spine. *Why me? I need a Tootsie Pop.*

She opened the drawer below the computer where she kept her stash and unwrapped one, leaned back in her chair, closed her eyes, and let the wild cherry flavor coat her tongue.

Then a realization hit her like someone had slapped her across her face with an iron glove. She bolted up in the chair. Tears started to flow. *Two thousand years before I was born...before my parents had even met...before my grandparents were born...Jesus knew me. He knew Ricki Spenser.*

She buried her head in her hands. A low mourning wail escaped her lips.

Did He know then what my uncle would do to me?

Chapter Twenty-Four

NATURALS CARRY AN EMPTINESS DEEP INSIDE. It's the part of all of us that we lost when sin entered the world. It is a dark void, a black hole that sucks in all of life. UDs are experts at filling that void with lies that never satisfy. —AIM, Volume 2, Page 71

September 19, 12:47 p.m., Seattle

Ricki stopped reading the journal, folded her arms together on the desktop, and dropped her head on them for a moment's rest. Three hours later, she woke up to the sound of knocking on her office door.

"Ricki, girl, are you in there?"

"Odette!" Ricki stood and ran to the door. She opened it, locked Odette in a bear hug, and started to cry. "Odette, I'm so scared. They...the UDs tried to kill me."

Odette stroked Ricki's hair. "There, there, it's all right. Odette's here now, and nothing is going to happen to you."

Ricki stepped back and wiped her eyes. "I know it wasn't long ago that I visited you, but so much has happened since I got home, and I've missed you...a lot."

Odette laughed and gave Ricki a hug of her own. "Honey, I've heard everything. I'm sorry you've become a target. But I'm not leaving your side until we've—until I've—hunted down those responsible and dusted them all."

Ricki took in a deep breath and steadied herself. "You have no idea how much that comforts me. I have not been entirely...well, a lot's been my fault."

Odette gave her a friendly slap on the back of the head. "I'll hear none of that. No matter what you may or may not have done, nothing in all this is your fault. You never asked to be drawn into a world where power-hungry, undead demons would be chasing you."

Ricki looked down. "Still…"

"Still nothing, girl. It's not your fault. And when we find out why you, of all Naturals, have been targeted, we'll be better able to put a stop to it."

"Maybe they know…" Ricki stopped and sucked in a little air, then coughed. *You've said too much. Get yourself under control.*

"Know what?"

"Ah…I don't know. Maybe they know I'm hiding here. Look, if you don't mind, I don't want to talk about that right now."

"Sure, I understand." Odette's expression said otherwise, but Ricki was thankful she didn't pursue it.

Ricki twisted her hair around her finger. "Have you heard from L? I mean, since he filled you in on what's happening to me? How is he doing? Is he safe?"

Odette smiled. "Oh, he's safe all right." She looked around the sparse office. "Let's get over to your home, pop some popcorn, and talk about things…like L."

11:18 p.m., September 19, Aleppo

Jalal Bashir, Dagger Face, walked into Miraj Barak Quidir's antiquities shop. It was a dimly lit area filled with shelves of Syrian and Iraqi artifacts covered with the dust of history. History that ISIS had planned to destroy or sell. He stopped to admire an ivory statue of a woman pouring water into a basin.

Miraj approached him. "That's a nice piece from 1500 BC. It should easily bring in one-hundred-and-fifty-thousand US dollars."

Jalal nodded. "When did you get it?"

"One of our settlement battalions of the Kata'ib Taswiyya brought it in two days ago. They found it in a church selected for demolition. It will help finance Operation Blood Red." Miraj gestured to the back of the shop. "Now, why don't we go to my office."

His office was a smaller version of the shop. Dark, dusty, and cluttered with boxes of Syrian coins from 500 BC, terra-cotta lamps from 3000 BC, and a few small stone mosaics from 2000 BC. Near the back wall was a desk with a few stamp seals dated as far back as 4000 BC. A small wooden file cabinet stood to the right of the desk with a small stone statue of a cow sitting on top.

Miraj sat at his desk. "What do you have for me? You said it was important."

Jalal set a stack of photos on the desk. "These are from our agent at the Chinese embassy party. Due to an unfortunate accident," Jalal smiled, "he managed to get in as a waiter at the last minute. He was there to keep tabs on Seong-Jin, but he may have stumbled on to something else."

Miraj looked through the pictures as Jalal filled him in on the details.

"Our man thinks a CIA agent is nosing around asking questions about new weapons ISIS might have, and there was discussion of a ship coming in from North Korea. That's him in the picture." Jalal pointed to the tall, dark-haired, and muscular man in the picture in Miraj's hand.

Miraj stared at the photo for a few seconds. "He looks familiar. What put him on to Operation Blood Red, and how much does he really know?"

"Most likely he was alerted by loose lips in our organization, including that Korean at the Chinese embassy. Seong-Jin was seen talking to the naval attaché from Cyprus who then had a secret meeting outside with this CIA agent. As for how much he knows, I have no idea, but we have several agents following him. I think we have to shut them all up and soon, starting with Mr. CIA. Give me the word and he's a dead man."

Miraj smiled. "He's a dead man all right, but not just yet. If you're going to take over my position someday, you need to learn patience. Continue to follow him and identify anyone from our organization or on the outskirts of our organization he may talk to. Kill them. I want death to follow this CIA agent. When we are satisfied the holes are plugged, then we'll kill him. The weapon is already on its way, so we no longer have to grovel to the Koreans. Those infidels will all die anyway when we succeed. Shut Seong-Jin up. Permanently."

"I will see that it is done. It will be difficult because he rarely leaves the embassy, but I'll make sure someone is waiting for him when he does. In the meantime, I will be the agent of death that follows Mr. CIA."

Miraj stood. "I know you will succeed. In less than a month, Israel will be no more, and the world will fear us like never before. Our time is coming."

September 20, 4:12 p.m., Somalia

General Caleb Yaasir, a rank he assumed the day he killed the prior warlord of this band of pirates, stood in the sand outside his headquarters in Northern Somalia. The wind whipped his long black ponytail into his face. In the hot, dry afternoon sun, his large muscular frame cast a dark shadow over the puny man groveling at his feet.

The man cupped his hands and raised them toward Caleb. In almost a whisper, through swollen lips, he repeated over and over, "*Naxariis…naxariis…*"

Caleb had been silent, glaring down at the man. Now he looked over to his lieutenant. "Mercy?" Caleb shook his head. "This Sunni *eey*, this Sunni dog, wants me to give him…"

He paused as he turned his attention back to the man at his feet. He bared his teeth as the last word blasted off his tongue. "Mercy!"

Caleb kicked the man in the gut and watched as he moaned and doubled over landing on his side in a fetal position. "You dare to ask me for mercy! Where was Sunni mercy when they cut my father's head off in front of me? Where was Sunni mercy when they raped and hung my mother? I was only ten. Where was

Sunni mercy when they shot me in the head and left me to die by the bodies of my parents?"

The man rolled his head down into the sand. Caleb kicked him in the leg. "Look at me when I'm talking."

The man let out a whimper and turned to look up at him. Caleb squatted and lowered his head almost to the man's face. "The only mercy I saw that day was from Allah. He let me live but cursed me to always carry this mark as a reminder of Sunni treachery against Shia Muslims." He pointed to the right side of his face that appeared to be frozen in a half grin. Nerve damage caused by the bullet gave him a grotesque look.

No one said anything about it because to mention it, even to stare at it for too long, invited a slow, painful death.

Caleb stood and pointed to his lieutenant. "Did he tell you anything?"

"You were right. He is ISIS."

"I already knew that. How about something of value?"

"Possibly. He said something about a North Korean vessel headed for Lebanon with some sort of special weapon that has the higher-ups in ISIS all excited."

"What kind of weapon?"

"He wasn't sure, except that he detected the words *mass destruction* and *total victory* over and over."

Caleb took a moment to think as he kicked the body of the *eey* in the ribs. The Sunni man moaned. "We have a nuclear device on its way to us, huh? Get a crew together. We need to prepare to acquire that weapon for our own use." Caleb's eyes glazed over at the prospect of becoming the most powerful warlord in all of Somalia.

"Did he mention when we can expect this gift to sail by us and the name of the ship?"

The lieutenant looked down. "No, he didn't say anything else."

"This is a good start. I suggest we send one of our best agents to Mogadishu to get the information we need."

"Sir, what should we do with him?" The lieutenant nodded to the man laying on the floor.

Caleb smiled. "Why we'll do what ISIS did to my brother because he was Shia. Separate his head from his body and throw both parts out for the buzzards to feast on."

Caleb Yaasir curled his right hand into a fist and stared at it. With a nuclear weapon, this fist would rule Somalia.

Chapter Twenty-Five

WHEN WE WORK IN THE POWER and authority of God
- we don't fix we restore
- we don't empower we unleash
- we don't mold we polish
- we don't lead we point.
–Awakened Incident Manual, Volume 2, Page 503

September 20, 6:32 p.m., Tel Aviv

The meeting took place in Ariella's apartment, but L was in charge. He had taken over the major planning for this hunt. It was time to finalize the general plan and parcel out specific tasks. This was a make-sure-everyone-was-on-the-same-page kind of meeting.

L looked at the other three members of the team. He rubbed the back of his neck. It had been stiff and sore when he woke up this morning. This was his first serious UD hunt since WWII. Was he up to the task?

L closed his eyes for a moment. *"Ricki thinks so."* His eyes popped open. Did someone say that? He scanned the room. *Did I think it?*

He rubbed his eyes. He must have thought it. Why did she occupy so much of his time? It was like she had set up residence in his mind.

"L, are you all right?"

He glanced at the group. He tried to shrug off Shiri's question with an unconvincing half smile. "I'm fine. My neck is a little sore that's all. Didn't sleep well last night." He was worried about Ricki after the attempts on her life. He was worried about this hunt. *What did I expect?*

Shiri nodded and sat down.

L remained standing as he started the meeting. "We know Sok Kang Ju's speech will take place sometime in the afternoon of

October 10 and that it is tied in with North Korea's Party Foundation Day celebration. That means we need to be in Pyongyang no later than October 8, but we cannot arrive too early because the longer we are there, the greater our chances of being detected by a UD."

Shiri added, "The fact that it's taking place on Party Foundation Day works to your advantage in that regard. Since Pyongyang will have more than its usual number of visitors, you will not stick out as much as you would on a normal day. And don't forget that a lot of foreign visitors will be there to hear the outcome of the Committee to Reunite Korea.

L nodded. "Right. But still, the timing has to be right. The plan is to fly into Beijing on October 5, fly into Dandong, the Chinese city on the border with North Korea, on October 6. After a two-day layover, we will cross the border on the train for the ride into Pyongyang, which should get us there on the evening of the eighth."

It was Ariella's turn. She stood and moved next to L. "Of course, everything about this hunt changes the moment we get into North Korea. There are probably more UDs per capita there than anywhere else in the world."

Yong Joon raised a tentative hand.

L nodded in his direction. "What's your question, Joon?"

"So you're telling me that I have already interacted with those creatures without knowing it?"

"Good point," Agam interjected. "They are still rare, even in North Korea, but I would guess they love serving as prison guards where they can do anything they want to Naturals. It would be a real thrill to them. So yes, you most likely have."

"What am I to do if I spot one on this..." Joon frowned. "This...hunt?"

"Nothing. Do nothing. If you see it before it sees you, try to get away undetected. Otherwise, you or one of us will have to dust it. That could lead to our team being discovered, which may prompt Kang Ju to cancel his appearance. There is only one target on this hunt; there is only one beast we want to dust, and it's him." L paused to let it sink in for Joon. "Okay, now our work starts. Joon, your role in this will be the most important. You will be our special guide from the Bowibu."

Joon shook at the mention of the Bowibu. "They are soulless animals."

Agam put his hand on Joon's shoulder. "If one of your guards was a UD, then you are more right than you know." Agam looked at L. "Exactly who are these Bowibu?"

"The Bowibu is the Ministry of State Security. They are ruthless, feared, and generally unchallenged. It will help us immensely to have a Bowibu agent as our guide. And thanks to our IT department, Joon will have an impeccable and unimpeachable ID."

L pointed to Ariella. "I'll need you to set up housing, get tickets for our travel, make sure we have passports, etcetera."

"I'm on top of it, Boss."

"Agam, your job is to get our sniper rifle into North Korea."

Agam smiled at L. "Weapons are my specialty, especially when they will dust those creatures…"

In unison both Shiri and Ariella said, "back to hell. We know Agam."

With a puppy dog face, Agam said, "I guess I must say that a lot, huh?"

Shiri nodded. "Yes, you do, but you wouldn't be the Agam we know and love if you didn't."

"All right." L spoke up. "We leave in two weeks so we have a lot to do."

September 20, 8:19 p.m., Tel Aviv

Declan hung up after talking with Shiri. This was going to be more difficult than he'd imagined. His kind of work was never easy, but since meeting Shiri, his world had suddenly gotten so much larger. It was no longer good guys versus bad guys. It was bad guys, demons, good guys, immortal guys, and zombies. *Zombies!* He snorted at that thought. He had no idea where those things fit in.

Five months ago, he had control of his world. He knew where he fit in, but now it was a different story. To top it off, somehow God had reentered his life in a way that made it difficult to ignore Him. *I don't need you, God, and after what you did to Sam, you certainly don't deserve my trust.*

Now Shiri had told him the plan to turn the leader of North Korea into a pile of foul-tasting reddish-brown dust was on for October 10. They needed to locate the vials of a deadly Ebola virus that could destroy Israel and set off a worldwide catastrophe, and it had to be done within a tiny window of time. To disarm ISIS before Sok Kang Ju was dust might lead him to unleash the virus from any stockpiles he may have hidden away. To delay after Sok Kang Ju was dusted could prompt the release of the virus by those transporting it in revenge for the dusting. This dance would require precise timing.

Life never got easier, did it? No matter how many victories you won along the way, the next challenge always seemed to be the most difficult.

He shook his head. If God was trustworthy, this would be a time when Declan would need Him. Maybe he should pray, but he didn't want to waste his breath.

Declan frowned. He hadn't thought about God this much since…well, since God betrayed him. *I've got to stop this.* Thinking about God brought up too many memories. Problem was, he could no longer escape into doubt over His existence.

Unfortunately, what he'd seen these last few months proved it. God exists and his partner in all this actually talked to Jesus two thousand years ago.

He sat down and wiped a tear away as the muscles in his face tightened. *Knowing without a doubt that you exist, God, makes what you did even worse.*

Chapter Twenty-Six

THERE ARE PLENTY OF DEMONS LOOKING for real estate to inhabit, and unfortunately, there are plenty of recently dead Naturals whose lives make them good candidates. — AIM, Volume 2, Page 121

September 21, 2:37 p.m., Tel Aviv

Jalal Bashir followed Declan Walsh down to the old part of Tel Aviv. He got lucky when Declan parked his car and started walking along the street. So he was out for a little stroll in Old Town.

He drove past Declan without looking at him. He turned up a side street and made his way back to where Declan's car was parked. He grabbed a book from his passenger seat. Holding the book, he got out of his car. A few people were on the sidewalk, but no one was paying any attention to him.

Jalal walked toward Declan's parked car, a light-blue Kia Cadenza. When he was at the rear of the car, he dropped the book. In a smooth motion, he bent down, picked up the book, and placed a tracking device under the rear bumper.

Should be a bomb, but that would come later.

He crossed the street. Declan was several blocks ahead, and Jalal followed him to see what he was up to. Maybe he was meeting someone. He tailed Declan along Nahum Goldmann Street past Ha'Shaon Square.

Declan strolled along the boardwalk of the port of Jaffa as if he were an American tourist. He breathed in the fresh salt air, listened to the hungry cries of the gulls, and felt the sun warm his cheeks. It could be classified as a pleasant afternoon if he wasn't on his way to meet Adnan, an underworld character his CI said might have some information on possible ship arrivals.

He paused for a moment to light a cigarette. As much as he wanted to stop smoking, things seemed to go better when he got his nicotine. Today he needed it.

His destination was the Clock Tower past Ha'Shaon Square. He'd parked a good mile away, thinking the walk to Yefet Street might do him some good. The meeting was set for 3:00 p.m., so he had plenty of time. Besides, walking made it easier for him to scope out the area in case more than just Adnan showed up.

Good thing. Within a hundred yards of the tower, a young couple was walking across the street. She had a baby carrier wrapped around her with what looked like the top part of the back of a baby's head peeking out. What caught his eye was that neither parent seemed interested in the child. Both appeared only to be interested in scanning the area ahead of them.

This meeting isn't going to happen. He glanced ahead and noticed a small bench near a patch of grass. *This is not the way it should go, but I might as well watch how this turns out.* He walked up and sat down. *Adnan was a good lead.* His face burned. His lips pinched together. *Could I possibly find another one as good? In time?*

Looking around, he spotted two other clear stakeouts. An old man standing outside the Solan Money exchange about fifty yards ahead, whose attention was directed solely on the tower. On the other side of the street adjacent to the tower, two men sat outside a Lebanese restaurant ostensibly talking, but they periodically glanced at the tower.

Declan bent down to rub his cigarette out on the sidewalk and light another one, while keeping the five individuals in view. While lighting up, a man fitting Adnan's description walked up to the tower. He was tall, rounded face, thin nose, balding, and walked with a slight limp. He nervously scanned the area.

The two men at the restaurant stood and walked over to the tower.

When Adnan saw the two men, panic washed across his face. He turned to his left to run, his limp all but disappearing.

So the limp was a ruse? Not a bad identifying mechanism. He'd have to remember to use that next time.

All five took off after Adnan. The woman with the baby tried to take the baby wrap off while running. It was almost comical to watch her rip at the material until the "baby" fell out at her feet. She had to make an acrobatic leap over what moments earlier had been her child. That was no mother.

Adnan didn't get far before a car raced up and veered onto the sidewalk right in front of him. Adnan stopped to avoid hitting the side of the car just as one of the men from the restaurant came up behind him, followed closely by the woman and the clown that played her husband. With fluid movements they cuffed him, ushered him into the car, closed the door, and sped off.

Most likely Mossad. Declan kicked the trash can to his right. Could this be Shiri's doing? It better not be. This forced them back to square one with less time to work with.

He stood, shook his head, and turned to walk back to his car. He only got a few steps when he heard, "Stop. On your knees. Hands in the air!"

Declan sank to the pavement.

"Good, now lock your hands behind your head."

He complied. Footsteps came up behind him. Someone pulled his arms behind his back and snapped cuffs on them. "Now stand up."

Declan stood and turned to face his captors. It was the "father" of the plastic baby who had been rejoined by his "wife."

"You are under arrest for suspected terrorist activities."

Declan nodded. As calmly as possible, he said, "I'm not a terrorist. My name is Declan Walsh. I'm an American citizen attached to the embassy. I have diplomatic immunity."

"We'll see about that. Right now, you're in our custody, and we are taking you to the station."

"You did what?" Shiri asked. Instead of the embassy, Declan had given the police Shiri's number, and she had rushed over to bail him out.

"I had set up a meeting with an underworld figure who one of my CIs thought might have some connection to this whole plot."

"Without involving me?"

"Hey, I've been doing this since before you were b—" He caught himself. "For a long time. This was a simple information harvest. That's all."

"What's this underworld figure's name? Maybe I know him."

"Adnan is the name I was given. Odds are it's not his real name."

"There are UDs all over this thing. How would you know if this Adnan was a UD? Naturals have disappeared after running across a UD involved in far less than this. Do I have to stay with you twenty-four/seven?"

"Okay, I get it. It's just that partners are…well…problematic with me." He couldn't quite hold back the tension in his voice. "Besides, I'm not used to dealing with zombies."

"Apology accepted, and enough of the zombie thing. They are UDs." The tension eased out of Shiri's shoulders. "And by the way, I've been doing this since before your great-great-great-grandfather was born."

"Point taken." Declan smiled back.

Shiri punched him on the arm. "Hey, we're a team. As a matter of fact, I made a few phone calls before I came here. Not only did I get you released, I got permission for you to question Adnan. And since it is a matter of national security, I'm the only one who can listen in."

"So, he's not a zombie."

Shiri raised her hands and shrugged. "I give up. I saw him. He's not a…a zombie."

Twenty minutes later, Declan walked into an interrogation room where Adnan was already sitting, handcuffed to the table.

"So you're the one who got me locked up. Now you expect

me to talk to you?" Adnan growled, but it was an act. Declan saw his chin tremble.

"First, I didn't get you locked up. You got *me* locked up. Apparently, the police have been following you for over a month. When they heard you were having a meeting that just might involve ISIS, they decided to bring us both in."

"Yet here we are." Adnan's tremble progressed to his hands. "I'm chained to a table; you're free to interrogate me. Did you set me up?"

"I was caught by surprise too." Declan swept his right index finger between himself and Adnan. "This situation—me free, you chained—well, that's because I have friends in high places. And if you're open and honest with me, I may share them with you."

Adnan's hands stopped shaking. He laid them flat on the table and used them to push himself up a little. "It's a deal, but I don't know a whole lot. I have to be out of here in a couple of weeks." His face suddenly turned ashen, as if he had seen a ghost. "I can't stay here. I have to get out soon."

"I'll put in a word for you if you tell me what you know about any shipments from North Korea."

"What do you want to know?"

"The name of the ship, what's on it, when it will arrive, and where it will dock."

Adnan's tremble returned. "Look, I said I don't know much and that's the truth. I want to help you, especially if you can get me out, but..." Adnan shook his head. "I don't know a thing about any shipments."

"That's too bad." Declan stood and turned to leave.

"Wait!" Adnan tried to stand, his whole body shaking. "Wait. I may be able to help you."

Declan turned back. "I'm waiting."

"All I can tell you is that something real big is in the works, and it might involve North Korea. This friend of mine in ISIS told me to get out of Israel by October 10 and plan never to return."

Declan smiled. "That might be useful information."

"Good. Then will you talk to your friends for me? You understand, I need to be out of the country before the tenth."

"I understand. I'll see what I can do for you." Declan headed for the door and walked out.

Shiri was waiting outside. Declan smiled. "He indirectly answered all my questions except the name of the ship."

"What interrogation were *you* at?"

Declan started to count down. "We have a good guess that somewhere within a four-day window the ship must have left North Korea. Now he tells us that something is going down on the tenth. To make that date, the ship must already be at sea, and according to our travel window, the earliest it could get here is the ninth. There are a dozen ports between Syria and Lebanon. The ship will arrive at one of them, but to unload and deliver it to Israel to launch by the tenth, it has to be one of the closer ports. So it's arriving in Lebanon on the ninth. I'd bet everything on it."

"Wow. You missed your calling. You would have made a great analyst."

"We are still missing some puzzle pieces. There are a lot of ships coming and going through Lebanon. We need to find out its name."

Chapter Twenty-Seven

IT'S A SHAME THAT NATURALS CAN'T see in themselves that which is so clear to both our savior and our adversary. Our savior sees their potential for greatness. Our adversary fears their potential for greatness. And Naturals? All too often they reject their potential for greatness. It's a large part of our task to show them their potential for greatness. Awakened Incident Manual, Volume 2, Page 503

September 22, 9:51 a.m., Somalia

General Yaasir loved his vintage WWII jeep. For one thing it was reliable. For another, he loved standing in it while he was driven through villages, imagining he was General Patton after a major victory.

Today he stood as his Jeep rushed through Mareroo to the beach. The warm briny sea air blew across his face leaving a salty taste in his mouth.

He was grinning like the Cheshire cat. Soon he'd be the only Somalian general with his own personal nuclear arsenal. That was more than General Patton had.

He wanted to get to the beachhead ASAP to deal with yet another in a string of hijacking failures. This time by his Captain Cawil Hubane. Caleb glanced down at his watch. He couldn't waste any time taking care of this. *Get it done and get back to planning the raid for the ultimate treasure.*

He tightened his grip on the top of the windshield as the jeep took a sharp right followed by a left onto the beach. A cloud of sand and dust signaled his arrival just in time to greet Captain Hubane.

The captain was almost knee deep in the water, wading in from the small tender used to shuttle people to shore from their primitive attack ship Caleb fondly called *The Black Flag*.

Cawil stopped as soon as he saw Caleb. He stood as the gray-white foam of an ocean wave rushed around his legs on its way out with the tide. He was trembling, and given that the ambient water temperature of the Gulf of Aden was in the mid-eighties, it wasn't from wading onto shore.

Caleb signaled to him to get out of the water. Cawil resumed his walk but at a slower pace, clearly reluctant to approach Caleb.

The captain stopped about five meters from the jeep in which Caleb was still standing, glaring at him over the windshield. "I'm so sorry, General Yaasir. We tried to get on board, but they had especially strong fire hoses. We were taking on a lot of water. If we hadn't turned back, they might have sunk our boarding craft."

There was a silent pause. Finally Caleb spoke. "Help me understand this. Your men had loaded AK-47s, yet you ordered a retreat because they had large squirt guns?"

"It wasn't that way. We were filling with water. Our boats would have sunk."

Caleb drew out another pause to build fear as he stepped out of the jeep and stopped right in Cawil's face. "I received good news from my agent in ISIS in Mogadishu. On the seventh of October, a North Korean ship called *the Blue Mist* will be within twenty-four kilometers of our coast. Do you know what cargo that ship is carrying?"

Cawil looked down while he shook his head. "No, General."

"Of course you don't. It is carrying a nuclear weapon. A weapon that's going to become *my* nuclear weapon."

Cawil nodded. "Yes, General."

"How do you think we're going to pull the theft off if my people are afraid of water guns?"

"But, General, I'm not—"

"Shut up! Here's what I'm going to do. I'm going to teach you not to be afraid of water. I want you to turn around and walk straight into the Gulf. Don't stop until I tell you to."

"But, General, I'm fully clothed."

Caleb shook his head. "Captain, do what I said."

Cawil walked into the water. When it was right above his ankles, Caleb yelled, "Stop!"

Cawil stopped.

"Now turn around and face me."

The captain started to sob. "General, please…"

"Don't worry. I'm not going to hurt you. I need you to help me retrieve my nuclear weapon. Now turn around."

He slowly turned around, his trembling more pronounced.

Caleb smiled. "See, the water didn't hurt you, did it?"

Cawil took a deep breath. "No, my general."

Caleb's smile slowly shifted into a frown. "But this will." Before Cawil could react, Caleb pulled a Glock 19 out of his shoulder holster and fired a single bullet through Cawil's heart.

Cawil's body fell backward and lay in the sand. Bright-red blood seeped into the Gulf as the tide washed over him.

Caleb turned to his two bodyguards. "Leave the body there as a lesson. No one fails me. And let Absame know he's now a captain."

He got in the jeep, and as it turned to leave the beach, Caleb looked back at the body one more time. He smirked. "That had to hurt."

September 22, 10:22 a.m., Tel Aviv

Shiri sat with Declan in a small café on the edge of Tel Aviv. It was a pleasant day: sunny, seventy-nine degrees, slight breeze.

"I hope spending a few hours in jail taught you something, Declan. We are partners. I'm to be included in everything you do on this case."

He shrugged. "I've learned my lesson."

Shiri wasn't done. She sensed sadness buried in Declan's heart. "You said partners are problematic for you. What did you mean?"

He didn't answer. Instead, he gave an almost-imperceptible

wince.

"When you mentioned the problematic issue, you quickly changed the subject to something about zombies." She reached across the small table and grabbed his hand. "Look, if we are going to work together on this, and it's important that we do, we have to talk about what's going on."

She looked him straight in the eye. "Declan, I'm the safest person to talk to you'll ever meet. By nature, I do not judge." Shiri felt Declan's pain. She allowed him to see grace through her eyes. *Jesus, open this man's heart. Let him see you through me.*

He avoided her gaze. "There's nothing to tell. I'm fine."

"You're talking to an Awakened. I know something is wrong." Shiri filled her voice with compassion. "Something that needs to be dealt with. Let's start with, have you ever had a partner?"

He looked up. "Yes, a long time ago. But it was nothing. Let's talk about our mission."

"We are talking about our mission. Was it a man or a woman?"

"A woman."

"What was her name?"

Declan turned his head and stared into the street.

Shiri stroked his hand. "Don't make me guess. What was her name?" *Jesus, I need you here now.*

There was moment's silence, then a sense of peace covered them like a soft blanket. Shiri smiled. *Thanks.*

Declan sucked in a deep, shuddering breath, glanced around as if looking for something, then turned back to Shiri. He bit his lower lip. "Sam...um...Samantha Rhodes."

"So you called her Sam. I like that. How long did you work together?"

"Three years."

"How long has it been since you last worked with her?"

Declan rubbed his eye. "Ten years."

"What happened to break you up?"

He didn't say anything for a long minute. Then he stared straight ahead. "She died. It was...my fault."

Not wanting to break contact, she held his hand while she moved to the seat next to him. *Lord Jesus, heal this man.* With her other hand, she touched his cheek and nudged his head to look at her. "Can you tell me about it?"

"I don't like to talk about it. I haven't for years."

"All the more reason you should talk about it now." Shiri searched his eyes and let him see into her soul. She felt the tension melt out of him. "Don't worry. I'm here. I'll help you through this." She felt the presence of Jesus.

He pulled his hand away to rub the back of his neck. He stared down at his watch. Finally, he looked at Shiri. "It was our last mission together." He stopped to light a cigarette and blow a perfect smoke ring. "We were after a major arms dealer whom we suspected of smuggling nuclear material out of Russia. His name was Solta Barsukov. We traced him from Lebanon to the Czech Republic. It turned out he had a villa outside Prague. We knew he must have documents in his office with information on the location of the material, but the villa was a fortress. We could never get in without tipping him off.

"Then we got a break. We learned he was going to host a large party in one week with more than two hundred guests. He was a ladies' man and..." Declan gulped in air.

Shiri reached out and gently rubbed his hand. "It'll be all right. Go on."

He lit another cigarette. "And Sam was beautiful. We managed to get an invitation for her. I wanted to go with her, but she wouldn't let me. She said it would be easier for her to get close to him alone. I tried to change her mind, but she had a will of steel. On the night of the party, she wore a flowing, light-blue, floor-length gown with her long black hair draped over her shoulders. And she had a smile that could melt your heart. She was stunning.

"As she left, I said, 'Take care of yourself. Don't take any risks.' That was the last thing I ever said to her. I never saw her again. Her body was found a week later in the Vltava River. She had been tortured and shot."

Declan looked down and shook his head. "It was my fault. I should have followed my gut and gone with her."

Shiri started to say something, but Declan held up his hand. "I vowed to kill Solta, but he disappeared. I hunted him for ten months in the Middle East and in Europe. I finally got a break and located him in Bulgaria. He was staying in a safe house in Varna. I staked out the house for a week. Then, in the early morning hours when I was sure he was alone, I broke in. He was in the bedroom, asleep."

Declan sneered. "Did I mention that I hadn't been able to sleep much over those ten months? Anyway, I woke him up and said I was there about Samantha. He remembered her. Do you know what he said? He didn't say anything. He just laughed. He *laughed*. I tapped him once between the eyes and walked out."

Tears glinting in his eyes, Declan looked straight into Shiri's. "I thought I'd feel better, but it didn't help."

Shiri nodded. "Revenge rarely does."

Declan slumped back in his seat and averted his gaze. "I know that now. Anyway, I've never had a partner since...until now." Declan paused for a moment. "She was a believer. She mentioned Jesus from time to time, but I'd shrug her off." He speared her with a glare. "So where was your God when she was being tortured?"

"That's a tough question." Shiri shook her head. "And to be honest, I don't know. I don't completely understand God. If I did, He wouldn't be God. But I trust Him, and I know Sam's death grieved His heart."

Declan shrugged. "I guess I don't know what to believe anymore." He took another drag on his cigarette and blew another perfect smoke ring, regaining his composure. "So that's my deep, dark secret."

"You do know it's not your fault? You offered to help, but she refused it."

He grimaced. "That's an excuse."

Shiri smiled ruefully. "I know, but I had to say it. Because as difficult as it is to believe, excuse or not, it is the truth." She furrowed her brow. "What happened to this guy's body?"

Declan thought for a moment. "That was strange. I don't think anyone found the body. If they did, they disposed of it. I never saw any mention of his death."

"What was his name again?"

"Solta Barsukov."

"And he was an arms dealer out of the Middle East?"

"Yes, and Eastern Europe, why?"

"No reason, just a thought. But you don't have to worry about me. I've already died."

Declan let out a mirthless laugh. "Okay, I won't worry about you. We are a team."

Chapter Twenty-Eight

PAUL WAS RIGHT. WE DON'T BATTLE against flesh and blood. Our battlefield is the mind. Our war begins in that ethereal world where thoughts are born, where beliefs find a home, where emotions are formed. The weapons in that world are not made of wood or steel. The weapons of the enemy, the UnDead, are fear and lies, but our weapons are far more powerful. Our weapons are faith, hope, and love. The strongest of these is love. – Awakened Incident Manual, Volume 2, Page 474

September 22, 5:34 a.m., Seattle

This morning, Odette was on a mission. She had enjoyed the last couple of days with Ricki. They'd talked a lot, especially about L, and watched movies. Ricki had shown her some of the sights of Seattle, always accompanied by at least two other Awakens. She'd even tried to help Ricki with her work.

Ricki showed her the view of CenturyLink Field from her office window and tried to explain American football to her, but as far as Odette was concerned, real football was what the Americans called soccer. But now that she was sure Ricki was okay, she needed to take some time for herself as well as take action.

She was infuriated that Ricki had become a target of the UDs. Motivated not by revenge but by an urge to do something, anything, to protect her new best friend, she decided to go on the offensive. While Ricki was working, she spent her time studying SOAR's intelligence on local UD activity.

The name Lucas Endre had come up. Apparently, he was the head of the UDs in this area. For the most part, SOAR had left him alone because he was, in a word, incompetent. Clearly, he was not behind these attacks, but by the nature of his position, he would know who was. So Odette left Ricki's safe house on a UD hunt, not to dust Lucas, unless she had to, but to discover the real brains behind the operation against her friend.

From SOAR records, she discovered that the UD headquarters was in a run-down building off Pike Place Market in the northwest part of Seattle. She signed out an unmarked SOAR car from the motor pool, a quaint black Volkswagen Bug. SOAR could afford better cars and had many models to choose from, but Odette liked older, unique cars ever since she had ridden in a Motorwagen in 1887 during a brief stay in Germany.

She arrived at Pike Place Market and parked under the Alaskan Way Viaduct. It was early, the sun starting to rise over the city, and most of the market was still closed. She heard the buzz of vendors setting up shop against a background of complaining seagulls looking for their early morning scraps. The strong fish odor hung in the air from yesterday's catch the fishmongers were putting on display. It reminded her of walks by the sea in ancient Israel.

She walked a few blocks, enjoying the stroll next to Puget Sound, until she came upon an old warehouse on the opposite side of the street with several shady-looking offices. One was labeled Agrona Imports/Exports. The place looked deserted. She walked up to the door and knocked.

The direct approach was best.

There was no answer. She tried to peer through the greasy, dusty windows, but it was impossible to see anything.

At least no lights were on. He must not be here yet. SOAR intelligence said Lucas arrived between 7:00 and 8:00 almost every morning, often carrying a case of Dark Horse whiskey.

She checked her watch: 7:14. He should be here soon. Odette went back across the street and sat at an outdoor table in front of a fish and chips restaurant. She didn't have to wait long. At 7:31, Lucas appeared carrying a box with *Dark Horse* written on the side.

He had his back to her as he put down the box and fumbled in his pocket for his keys. She crossed the street and waited a short distance behind him while he opened the door and reached down to pick up the box. As soon as he stepped inside, Odette rushed up and pushed him.

"What the—?" His arms shot out to break his fall to the sound of broken whiskey bottles.

Odette squeezed in and shut the door behind her. "Lucas Endre?"

He gathered himself and pushed to his knees. "Who are you?" He saw the now-wet box that had slid down the hallway when he fell. "Oh no, not my Dark Horse! You're going to be..." He turned to face her and froze.

"Please... Please don't..." He held his hands up in a defensive position.

"I'm not going to dust you."

He relaxed a little. "Thank you."

"Provided you answer my questions honestly."

"Anything. I'll tell you anything you want to know."

"Did you try to kill Dr. Spenser?"

"No. I knew it would cause trouble... I tried to stop him."

"Who?"

"That short Korean guy. Pong or Pak or something Ju. I don't remember. Real scary."

"A UD?"

"Yes...he was a UD... A powerful UD."

"A Korean? Who sent him? Whose orders where you acting under?"

"It was all Sok Kang Ju. I didn't want any part of it."

Odette smiled. "Thank you."

"You're..." Lucas put up his hands again. "Please, you're not going to dust me, are you?"

"Not this time. But if you go after Ricki again, I will come back, and I won't be in a forgiving mood. Do you understand?"

Lucas put his hands down and with a tremble in his voice said, "Yes, ma'am. You can count on me. Dr. Spenser is safe. Even if she walked in here, I wouldn't touch her."

"Make sure that you don't." Odette raised her chin and walked away. "Well, Sok Kang Ju is in for a surprise."

5:17 a.m., September 23. Beirut, Lebanon

The man with one blue eye and one green eye looked up the number and called Dagger Face. "The CIA guy purchased two tickets to Beirut leaving on Royal Jordanian flight 343. They will arrive at 11:25 a.m. on MEA flight 311."

"I bet the second ticket is for that woman who seems to be with him a lot. See if you can find out who she is, and I'll be at the airport in Beirut to follow them. Good work."

The man smiled as he hung up. It was rare for Dagger Face to compliment anyone.

Shiri sat in the stuffed chair across from Declan in the al Mandolino, a cozy café in Beirut. Though the café had outside tables and the day was pleasant, Declan chose to sit inside to wait for his contact. He'd selected an intimate table surrounded by two stuffed chairs and a small couch in the corner. It gave them the privacy his contact required.

Declan looked at his watch.

Shiri reached across and tapped his arm. "It's 1:05. He's only a few minutes late."

Declan nodded as he stared at the entrance.

Ten minutes later, Karim Zahir walked in and sat in the second stuffed chair across from Declan. Tiny drops of sweat dotted his forehead, his hands trembled slightly, and worry etched his face.

Declan introduced him. "Shiri, this is Karim Zahir. He's been very helpful to me over the years. He's the one who set up my initial meeting with Abdul Ba'ith."

Shiri smiled and did her best to project an aura of calm for

Karim's benefit. *At least he's not a UD.* "Karim Zahir, I love your name and how appropriate—'Noble Helper.'"

"My mother told me the meaning later in life. I've never thought of it since and no one else has ever mentioned it."

"I hope you don't mind. I'm somewhat of a connoisseur of the meaning behind names."

Karim nodded. "Names can be interesting."

It was time for Declan to take over. "Karim, we need your help. Something big is brewing, and we need to know about it."

Karim leaned back in the comfortable chair and raised his hands. "I know I've helped you in the past, but I can't anymore. Besides, what little I know I can't tell you."

Shiri reached across the table and took Karim's hand. She spoke in a soft, confident voice. "I know you're scared. Anyone in your situation would be. But something terrible is about to happen, and you can help us stop it."

Karim was silent for a moment, then took a deep breath. "Have either of you ever been in an area when a tsunami hit?"

Both Declan and Shiri shook their heads.

"Right before it hits, everything gets real quiet and the ocean recedes. It's a peaceful time, but it's short lived. Suddenly, a wall of water comes out of nowhere and crushes you. That's what's happening. You might have noticed that things have been quiet in Israel these last few weeks? ISIS has been quiet. It's because we've all been told to get out by October 10. That's when the tsunami will hit, and you don't want to be there when it does. That's all I can tell you. If I were you, I would leave the Middle East as soon as possible." He wiped his forehead and looked around. "Now I have to go before someone sees me here."

Karim stood to leave. Shiri stood with him. "Thank you. You have actually been helpful. I wish you the best."

As soon as Karim was out the door, Shiri and Declan heard a cry. They rushed outside to see Karim lying on the pavement holding his neck with a dagger sticking in it. Blood poured from the wound.

Shiri grabbed her cell phone to call for help. Declan knelt and tried to apply pressure to the wound with little success. He leaned over with his ear just inches from Karim's mouth.

Sirens screamed in the distance. Declan stood. "He's gone. The last thing we need is to be hauled in by the Beirut police. I suggest we scram."

On the flight back to Tel Aviv, Shiri spent most of the time staring out the window. She finally broke the silence. "I hate death."

"No one likes it."

"But that's the thing. Naturals fear death for themselves yet so easily deal it out to others. It breaks my heart to see the enemy win like that." She paused for a moment. "Did Karim tell you something at the end?"

"As a matter of fact, yes, but I don't understand it. As best I could make out, he said over and over again something like 'blow…fist… Blow…fist.'"

"Blow fist? What does that mean?"

Declan shook his head. "I don't know."

Chapter Twenty-Nine

WE ARE NOT HERE TO REMOVE evil from this world. We are here to enhance love in this world. —Awakened Incident Manual, Volume 2, Page 131

September 24, 9:08 p.m., Tel Aviv

L had barely finished preparing the final briefing before his team left Tel Aviv. It was vitally important that everyone be on the same page because they would have only one chance at this dusting.

They sat in Ariella's living room while Shiri shared the events of the last few days. When she was done, L took charge. "So, does 'blow fist' mean anything to anybody?"

Agam said, "If it's the color blue instead of blow it could be blue fist like the Hulk." He smiled.

Shiri slapped the back of his head. "The Hulk's fist is green..." She scanned the room. "And I'm embarrassed that I know that."

Ariella said, "It could be the code name for the attack where the virus is the fist. Maybe instead of a *b* sound it was a *d*. Then it could be something like Divine Fist."

"It was most likely the ramblings of a dying man," Declan said. "But I'll keep working on it."

"Okay, let's get on with the business at hand, and if anyone else comes up with some good ideas..." L smiled at Agam, "you can share them with Declan or Shiri."

L handed out a few papers to the group. "As you can see, we leave in a week on October 2 at 12:50 p.m. We will be traveling under UK passports. Here are the passport names—Larry Walker, Alex Smith, and Angela Jackson. Joon doesn't need a passport since he will be traveling as a North Korean. It's a twelve-hour flight so we'll arrive in Beijing at 4:30 p.m. their time. We have a one-night layover, then leave for Dandong the next morning. I suggest we use that time to brush up on Korean customs. The flight to Dandong is only an hour and a half. We have a two-night layover there. That's the easy part of this hunt. On the afternoon of the sixth, we board a train to Pyongyang. That is only a five-hour ride, getting us into Pyongyang with enough time to scope out the area and find the best vantage point for the dusting, or at least check out Juche Tower to see if it will work.

"Of course, for foreigners to go anywhere in North Korea, it is required to have a DPRK soldier as a guide. This is where Yong Joon comes in."

L faced Joon. "At the train station in Dandong, you will disappear into a restroom and Captain Chin-Hae Hyeon will emerge. For all intents and purposes, you will be a member of the DPRK military."

Joon took a deep breath. "My family suffered at the hands of the military most of my life, but I'd do anything to bring down Sok Kang Ju, so I'm in 100 percent. By the way, I love the irony in the name you chose for me. You do know it means 'virtuous truth.'"

Agam looked up from the itinerary in his hands. "You're right that names have meaning, and I'm glad you like it. That was my idea, and I picked it for exactly that reason. In some small way, we will bring truth into the land of lies."

L turned to Declan and Shiri. "While we're gone, continue to look for the bioweapon, but don't take action until we've dusted Sok Kang Ju, unless it's clear they are going to use it. To keep this thing under control, we must take care of business on October 10. We need to dust Sok Kang Ju and at the same time destroy the virus. Both have to be done in the same short time window."

"Got you." Shiri clapped her hand on Declan's back. "Well, partner, we have our marching orders."

L nodded to Joon. "All right, Joon, you're up."

He stood and cleared his throat. "L asked me to tell you a little about what to expect as you interact with the people of North Korea. First, understand they have grown up in a fog of lies. A fog so thick they can't recognize the truth when they hear it. A fog so pervasive they have breathed it into their bodies becoming part of them, and as a result, they believe the most absurd things, especially about the abilities of their Great Leader. Talking to them can be very frustrating."

L interrupted. "Yes, and don't let it get to you. Remember, these are victims of a great evil. Keep in mind that our goal on this hunt is not to plant truth, but to dust Sok Kang Ju. That being said, look for places where the truth might flourish. We have only one Awakened in the country under deep cover, and I want to send additional Awakens in after our mission is completed. This country needs our help."

L sat down but Joon remained quiet. Finally L said, "Okay, Joon."

"Oh, sorry. I got lost in thought for a moment." Joon dipped his head in a quick nod. "North Korea lives under a very rigid caste system. There are three main classifications and around fifty subclassifications. It's called chulsin-songbun or just songbun. The three classifications are loyal, wavering, and hostile. Songbun dictates everything about a person's life: How far you can go in your education, what jobs are open for you, even how much food you get. As Awakens who are tuned in to suffering, you will be able to feel the toll this takes on the lives of both the wavering and the hostile. They are like tiny drops in a vast sea of sorrow. This is the sea you will be wading into, a sea that will assault your spirit, a sea in which you could easily drown. Watch yourselves out there, okay?"

L stood. "One last issue. While UDs are rare, generally speaking, that is not the case in North Korea. It's likely you will cross paths with a L1 or possibly even a L2 UD. We want to be sure you recognize them before they recognize you. Hence, we will adopt the UD Avoidance mode. Always go out in pairs or more. Constantly scan the environment. Wear dark sunglasses to minimize their ability to recognize what you are through your eyes. No random dustings unless absolutely necessary, because that would alert Sok Kang Ju to our presence. Is everyone clear on that?" L paused for a second. "Anyone have any questions?"

No one spoke up.

They prayed, then L looked each of them in the eye in turn. "This is a challenge unlike any we have ever faced, but we will prevail. On October 10 we *will* save the world."

September 25, 8:03 a.m., Tel Aviv

Declan returned to his apartment after yesterday's meeting with the team and had a peaceful night's sleep. He was pleased to find it clean after the break-in a few days ago. In fact, it was cleaner than it had been in a while. He'd have to give Tom a call and thank him.

He was surprised by a knock on his door. Who could that be? As a precaution he drew his Glock 19. Back against the wall next to the door, he reached over and swung it open with his Glock aimed out.

Shiri held up her hands. "What are you going to do with that thing?"

"Hey. I wasn't expecting anyone. And given the events of the last couple of weeks, you could have been a tango." Declan shrugged and holstered his weapon. "Why are you here anyway? Did I forget a meeting? Or do you have some good news to report?"

"Neither. I want to take you to Prague today. We have an important meeting."

"Why Prague? And who's there who would know anything about this secret ISIS project?"

"It's only slightly related to our project, but it's vital to us as a team. Come on. Pack. We will be back tomorrow. I'll explain everything on the plane."

"All right." Declan picked up a suitcase and set it near the door. "I'm always packed and ready to go. So...Prague, huh?

What time is our flight?"

"It leaves as soon as we get to the airport. We are not flying commercial. I have a SOAR private plane waiting for us."

Jalal sat in the safe house, waiting to hear what Declan, the CIA man, was up to. He was getting a little impatient when the phone finally rang.

It was the man with different colored eyes. "The woman picked him up and took him to the airport. They boarded a private jet. I checked their flight plan—they are headed for Prague."

"Prague? In a CIA jet? What's in Prague or, more to the point, who's in Prague?"

"I don't know."

"Did they schedule a return flight?"

"Yes, tomorrow."

Jalal hung up. He wrinkled his brow. A one-day turnaround. It was definitely a meeting of some sort, but with whom? And what did it have to do with Operation Blood Red? He had to know. Jalal immediately contacted Miraj Barak Qudir and explained the situation.

"Do we have anyone in Prague we can use to find out what they are up to?"

"I'll have to get back to you."

Twenty-five minutes later Miraj called back. "We have a deep-cover cell in Prague. I've activated them with instructions to report to you. You'll hear from a Yusri el-Sylla. As soon as you learn anything, let me know. As far as I know, Operation Blood Red has not leaked to Eastern Europe, but if it has, we may have to change our timetable and forget what those North Koreans want us to do."

Declan and Shiri boarded the plane, a Cessna Citation X. As soon as he stepped in, Declan's mouth fell open. There were four rows. Each row had one overstuffed black leather seat. The interior was white with high-gloss woodwork halfway down the sides. Declan selected the left seat in the first row. Shiri sat across the narrow aisle from him.

Declan surveyed the cabin. "Looks like we'll travel in luxury. Does SOAR have many of these?"

"A few." Shiri shrugged.

"How can they afford them?"

"SOAR has resources. When you can invest, looking decades, even centuries ahead, you can make a lot of money. Besides, we have the best financial minds and money managers who have ever died working for us." Shiri threw him a complacent grin.

Declan grinned back. "And no zombies."

Shiri reached across the aisle and tapped his forearm. "And no zombies. Now cut that out."

"Are you going to tell me what this is all about now?"

Shiri shook her head. "Let's wait until we're in the air."

"So I can't back out?" Declan smirked.

"Yeah, so you can't back out."

Once they reached cruising altitude, Declan said, "All right, no more stalling. What's this all about?"

Shiri looked over at him. "Do you remember when you told me about Sam that I told you I had a thought?"

"Yes, but I didn't think anything of it."

"Well, that name—the name of the arms dealer—Solta Barsukov sounded familiar. When you told me his body was never found, it gave me the idea to check SOAR records on UDs. I found his name. He's no longer dead, and he has a new name."

"What? He's dead all right. I saw him die. I left his brains on that pillow." Declan slumped back in the chair. "You mean he's one of those zombies? He's still out there? Still active?"

"I'm afraid so. Only now he's active as a UD."

Declan looked down. A tear rolled toward his nose. "So I only made matters worse."

Shiri grabbed Declan's hand. "No, you couldn't have known. At the time, you didn't even know about UDs. Besides, we are going on a UD hunt and *you* will dust him."

"Don't you mean you will dust him?"

"No, you will."

"How? You aren't suggesting that I bite him are you? It wouldn't do any good." He paused. "Though the idea does have merit."

Shiri shook her head. "I will give you my gun filled with my bullets, bullets loaded with my blood. The second you shoot him, he will be dust and that will be the end of him for good."

"I get to finish what I started ten years ago." Declan relaxed and sat up straighter. "I'll do it. But do you know where he is?"

"His new name is Josef Gabriel, which is a slap in God's face since it means 'hero of God.' He's anything but. He's still an arms dealer working in Prague. I'm not sure where he is, but I know someone who can help us. Angel Bohdan. We are meeting him as soon as we land. He'll be at the Sedlec Ossuary."

Declan raised an eyebrow and quirked his lips in a crooked smile. "The Bone Church? How appropriate."

Chapter Thirty

THE TRUE POWER OF PRAYER LIES not in the words we say, it is found in the act of faith to speak. It is not measured by how much the world changes but in how much we change. –Awakened Incident Manual, Volume 2, Page 173

1:11 p.m., September 25, Prague

Jumail al-Abdou and Hasana el-Mina arrived at the Vaclav Havel Airport early enough to position themselves to follow the CIA man named Declan Walsh and his female companion when they landed. Hasana held a fax that contained their instructions to follow and kill whoever met with the pair. They were also supplied with a photo of Declan.

They scanned the crowds at the airport's main exit. Jumail saw him first. They watched as their targets got into a rental car.

Declan and Shiri arrived at the Sedlec Ossuary about twenty minutes early after a one-hour drive from Prague. Easy to miss, it was a charnel house with a small chapel and an underground ossuary. It was built on the grounds of the Church of All Saints cemetery. The ossuary contained the bones of sixty thousand people buried there since the 1400s. The bones were arranged as decorations built by Frantisek Rint in 1870.

A large bone chandelier hung from the ceiling in the middle of the ossuary. It contained all the bones of the human body. The coat of arms of the Schwarzenbergs, constructed entirely of bones, was displayed on the left. The largest collection of bones were arranged in the form of bells, which stood in the four corners of the Ossuary.

Declan took in the bone displays as well as the piles of bones lying behind a chicken-wire fence. "Where do we meet this Angel

Bohdan?"

Shiri pointed off to the right. "He said he would be standing by the plaque to the right of the coat of arms."

They walked to the designated place. Not many visitors roamed around the house. An Arab-looking man and woman caught Declan's eye, but they seemed more interested in the displays than Shiri and him.

It wasn't long before they were joined by a small, clean-shaven man with straggly hair and a weather-beaten face. He wore a dirty white shirt with blue jeans and bright-red tennis shoes. The man held out his hand. "Ms. Shiri Liora? I'm Angel Bohdan."

She took his hand. "Hello, Mr. Bohdan. Call me Shiri and this is Declan Walsh."

Declan nodded. You'd think they'd use some sort of code phrase like "the moon rises at midnight" followed by "I don't have change." At least he'd done something like that before.

Shiri got right down to business. "Mr. Bohdan, I understand you might be able to help us. We want to know where the arms dealer Josef Gabriel might be."

Bohdan pursed his lips. "You mean the guy who cheated me on a deal for AK-47s and killed my partner? I've kept tabs on him, but if you want to eliminate him, you might as well give up. I've sent three of my best men after him, and they all disappeared. He's protected by something, but I don't know by whom or what. Whatever it is, it's powerful. He doesn't have a bodyguard. Maybe he's just the luckiest man on earth."

"I appreciate your warning, but we know his vulnerability. We can do this job." Her tone brooked no argument. "We need to know where he is, and by tomorrow, you will never see him again."

Declan flashed a sly grin. "We guarantee it. He will be scattered like the dust in the wind."

Shiri dug her fingernails into Declan's back a little. Declan angled an amused glance back at her.

Bohdan shook his head. "If you want to try, I wish you the best of luck. He resides at a small villa outside Prague. It's on a small man-made lake near Kladno."

"Thank you, Mr. Bohdan. After tomorrow he will no longer be your problem."

Bohdan responded with a curt nod. "I like the way you talk. Glad to be of help." He glanced around and then turned back to Shiri. "Look, Josef Gabriel has spies everywhere. I don't want to be seen leaving here with you, and you don't want that either. So why don't you depart now, and I'll follow you in, say, five minutes?"

Declan nodded. "Sounds like a good plan."

Shiri and Declan left the way they came in.

As soon as they left, the Arab couple walked over to Angel.

The woman standing to his left asked, "Sir, do you have the time?"

Angel frowned, narrowing his eyes. He didn't want to be bothered, but he glanced at his watch, then looked up. "Well...it's..."

A chill went up his spine. The man had a knife. Angel backed up. "What the—?" He stepped back again. This time he hit the wall. His nostrils flared as anger replaced fear. Time slowed. His right hand went up to deflect the knife away from his body.

While the man was off balance, Angel bent down and rushed the woman, his head hitting her chest. She let out a yelp, and he pushed her into a tall pyramid of skulls, knocking them over with a loud crash. One of the skulls rolled across the floor to the foot of a small group of tourists.

For a brief moment they froze, staring down at the eye sockets looking up at them. Someone screamed and they all ran for the exit.

Angel turned to face the man again. The man sliced his knife at Angel, drawing a line of blood across his left arm. Angel jumped back, grabbing his wounded arm. "You don't know who you're dealing with!"

The man only smiled.

Angel heard the clatter of bones as the woman struggled to catch her breath and get up.

The man lunged at him again. This time Angel used both hands to ward him off. Ignoring the pain in his left arm, he grabbed the man's knife hand. He twisted it counterclockwise, stepping to the man's right. Angel pinned the man's arm behind his back.

The attacker let out a guttural roar and dropped the knife.

As Angel bent down to pick up the knife, the woman barreled into his side, pushing him headfirst through the chicken wire and into the pile of thousands of bones. Some of the bones flew up. Others rolled away on the floor as the delicately balanced heap collapsed.

Angel turned over. The man leaped on top of him, holding a thigh bone. The last thing he saw was the bone crashing down on his head.

Jumail got up. He slipped through the fence, stumbling on a bone. Hasana reached out to give him a hand, helping him over the scattered bones on the floor.

"Let's get out of here before the police come." Jumail, covered in bone dust and blood, brushed himself off.

On the way out, Jumail stopped next to the bone chandelier. He reached down, picked up a skull that had rolled across the floor, and threw it up at the intricate structure. He sneered as parts of it fell to the ground. "Blasphemous place."

Once they got to their car, Hasana called Jalal to report in. "They met a man in the Sedlec Ossuary. We listened as well as we could. The man's name was Angel Bohdan. He seemed to be a small-time arms dealer. They wanted to know where to find another arms dealer named Josef Gabriel."

Jalal interrupted. "Josef Gabriel? We've done business with him, but he shouldn't know anything about Operation Blood Red. What did they want?"

"I'm not sure. The best we could tell, they wanted to talk to him."

"Find him first and take him out. I don't want them to get any information, no matter how unreliable it might be."

"We will try."

"You'd better do more than try."

Chapter Thirty-One

THE DIFFERENCE BETWEEN FAITH AND DOUBT is this—when we doubt, we allow the world to shape our thoughts, but when we have faith, we allow our thoughts to shape our world. –Awakened Incident Manual, Volume 2, Page 79

September 25, 8:41 p.m., Prague

Declan and Shiri drove for about three hours to Josef Gabriel's villa where they set up a stakeout to wait until the lights were all out. The villa was small compared to the place he had lived as Solta Barsukov. Declan estimated it at about ten thousand square feet. It was two stories high, and all white, forgoing the more traditional stone-castle look of many of the homes they had passed. A covered porch was held up by thick white columns. There was no gate, no fence, no guards, and only a single car out front.

Declan was a little surprised by what he saw. "He is certainly not concerned about security. The last time I came after him, I had to bypass three guards."

Shiri shrugged. "Now that he's a UD, no Natural can harm him. In fact, he probably enjoys it when a Natural comes after him. He could toy with them like a cat with its mouse. On the other hand, no Awakened can be stopped by either a UD or a Natural."

"But you couldn't kill a Natural who is guarding him."

"Right, but I could let the Natural do his best and then restrain him. The only problem would be if a UD kept a Natural nearby to use as a hostage. Only then would I have to let the UD go."

"Couldn't Solta...er...Josef have a potential hostage in the house with him?"

"He could but I doubt it. It would be more likely if he knew he was a potential target. But I'm sure he feels safe here under our radar. We only have one Awakened in Prague, and she is working with the poor. She is not a hunter and doesn't run in circles where she might encounter Josef."

Two hours into the stakeout, the last light went out. Declan and Shiri decided to wait a couple more hours to be sure Josef was asleep before breaking in.

So, for two hours Declan's eyes remained glued to the mansion.

The slime ball who killed Sam was only a hundred yards away. His body coiled like a compressed spring, every muscle ready to burst into action. He'd killed him once, but Barsukov came back. When Declan exterminated the roach this time, he'd better die or... A frown glided over his face, alarms blaring in his head.

What if Barsukov made them? Was he watching them as intently as he and Shiri were watching him? What if the man could slip out through a hidden exit? Declan had seen two of these creatures turn to dust, but what if it didn't work this time?

He was not used to second-guessing his missions, but then he had never fought demons before. *Get it together, Declan. Trust your partner.*

Then he could finally get justice for Samantha.

Eventually, the time came to act. They got out of the car. A light, western breeze rustled through the trees. The cold air was filled with the sound of crickets as well as the occasional frog. The half-moon shone a dull white about thirty degrees above the horizon in a sky full of stars.

Shiri took Declan's Glock and emptied the magazine. She filled it with fifteen of her silver-tipped bullets and screwed a silencer on the end.

"Silver? Really? So the movies are right about silver bullets?"

Shiri narrowed her eyes as she squinted at Declan. "What are you implying, that we are preparing to hunt werewolves? Is that going to be your replacement for zombies?" With a chuckle, she shook her head. "Declan, Declan, Declan what am I going to do with you? As a matter of fact, silver is as soft as lead, so it easily breaks open in the UD body, releasing the blood. It has other properties that keep the blood stable for a long time. I like to use it, though Ariella usually goes for lead."

Declan's pressed his lips together. "Wait. Before we go in and dust this vermin, I have a question."

"All right, what is it?"

"You said revenge never helps, yet you set this up so I can kill this guy. What gives?"

"Ah, you're listening to me. That's great, but you are not going to kill Josef. He's already dead. He's a UD. You are not his executioner this time; you are his exorcist."

Declan smiled. "Exorcist, huh? Never been called that before." Something about Shiri's touch, about the way she talked to him, gave him confidence. First demon hunt or not, this was going to work.

He looked up at the mansion and sneered. "All right, let's dust that beast."

They crept toward the house across a hundred yards of well-manicured lawn, scanning the area for any guards they might have missed. Arriving at the front door, Shiri quickly picked the lock.

"Impressive," Declan whispered.

Shiri grinned. "I'm pretty good at this. After all, I've developed this skill over the centuries. I've picked complicated locks that don't exist anymore."

Once in, they paused to allow their eyes to adjust. The place was dark and quiet. The ceiling was a good twelve-feet high making the place feel huge. The rug was thick and effectively muffled any sound. They glanced around and found the stairs. As preplanned, Declan led the way with Shiri staying out of sight behind him.

They paused at the top of the stairs and listened. Still no sound. The dim light from the skylight was enough for them to find their way. The hallway to the left had two doors on one side and a single door on the other. It ended with a large mirror. The right hallway ended in double doors.

Declan whispered in Shiri's ear, "I wish he snored. Then we would know what room he is in for sure. But my guess is that double door leads to the master bedroom. Let's give it a try first."

Shiri nodded.

They inched their way down the hall. As soon as Declan reached for the door handle, a phone rang inside the room and seconds later, the lights in the room went on. Declan stood with his back to the wall on the left.

A voice came from behind the door. "What are you doing calling me at this hour?"

After a short delay it was followed by, "I don't care. Handle it yourself."

They heard the phone slam down. At which point Declan pushed open the door and stepped inside. Josef was standing by his bed looking down at the phone on the nightstand. He swung around. "What the...?" As soon as he saw Declan, he smiled. "You look familiar. Who are you and why are you here?"

"I'm Declan Walsh, CIA, and I'm here to fix what I failed to do when I met you ten years ago. When you were Solta Barsukov."

Josef rubbed his chin. "Declan Walsh... Oh yes, you're the one who tried to kill me back then over what I did to your partner. She was...Samantha." He flashed a sardonic smile. "She screamed a lot."

Josef spread his arms. "So you've come to finish it, have you? You have no idea what you're dealing with. Go ahead and give it your best shot." He stood there waiting for the bullet he knew couldn't possibly hurt him.

A voice came from behind Declan. "Josef Gabriel. The truth is you don't know who *you're* dealing with."

"You have a woman hiding behind you? I'll enjoy slowly torturing her after I'm done with you." Josef grinned. "You don't have much luck with female partners, do you?"

Shiri stepped out from behind Declan. Josef's eyes grew wide and his grin morphed into a frown.

Shiri smiled back at him. "I'm sure his luck in partners has changed substantially."

"An Awakened... What's an Awakened doing with a Natural?"

Declan stepped forward. "We're your worst nightmare. We are partners. And to top it off, my Glock is loaded with silver bullets that have her blood in them."

Josef's face went ashen. He held his hands out. "No...no."

Declan fired. Time seemed to slow. It was as if he could see the bullet as it moved across the room, entered Josef's chest creating a fine mist of bright-red blood that sprayed back onto his face, then made its way through Josef and lodged in the wall behind.

Declan gasped. There was no cloud of dust. Josef stood intact. *It...didn't...work!*

Declan watched, for the moment frozen, as Josef looked down at his wound, then stared Declan straight in the eyes. A smile eased onto Josef's face and a hollow cackling echoed through the room.

Shiri yelled, "Take a head shot."

Declan took aim and fired. Josef's arm floated up as if he could catch the bullet. Then he melted into a fine, reddish-brown dust.

Declan looked at the pile of dust, then down at the gun in his hand. He shook his head. *I don't think I'll ever get used to that.* He turned to Shiri. "What happened?"

Her shoulders slumped. "That was my bad. When we're close like this, we almost always aim for the head because sometimes a body shot can go through and through only hitting flesh, so the bullet doesn't break up and release the blood. With a head shot, you're guaranteed to hit bone, breaking up the bullet."

"You might have told me that earlier, don't you think?"

Shiri walked past Declan. "You're right and I'm sorry. But now it's done. It's over."

Declan fought back the tears that wanted to bust out and he nodded. *Sam, it may have taken me a long time, but he's gone.*

Shiri held out her hand. "Partners."

Declan shook it. "Partners."

Sam, I think you'd like her.

Jalal took another call from Jumail and Hasana.

Hasana reported, "We got to Josef Gabriel's house in time to see the CIA man and the woman enter. We couldn't tell if Josef let them in or they broke in. A few minutes later, a light went on in an upstairs room. Twenty minutes later the CIA man and the woman left. The light upstairs was still on. What do you want us to do?"

Jalal sighed. *Idiot.* "Go in and find him. Find out what he may have told the two about Operation Blood Red, then kill him and report back to me immediately." Of course, if Josef told Jumail and Hasana anything about Operation Blood Red, Jalal wanted to know what they discovered, but he'd have to have them killed as well. *What a waste.*

An hour and a half later, Jumail called Jalal. "Sir, we searched the entire house, and no one is there. But Josef's car is still out front. It's like he disappeared into thin air. What would you have us do?"

Jalal took a deep breath. "He obviously escaped somehow, so find him. Don't call me back until you do."

Chapter Thirty-Two

ACCORDING TO THE WORLD, HOPE IS realized only by chance. Those whose hope has become reality are called lucky. Luck and pure chance have become the world's engine of realized dreams. We break this connection between hope and chance when we begin to hope for the things of God. They become reality through faith not luck. –Awakened Incident Manual, Volume 2, Page 351

September 26, 11:15 a.m., Beijing

L felt the need to call Ricki. He wanted to hear her voice, to know she was safe. She answered on the first ring. "Ricki, this is L."

"I know. Remember I have caller ID. Where are you? Are you okay?"

"I called to see if you were all right. I'm in Beijing and the entire team is fine. In a couple of days we'll be in North Korea and not able to contact anyone except on SOAR's satellite phones. Are you keeping yourself safe?"

"Define safe…"

"Not going anywhere without Ray or Odette, for starters."

"Then I'm keeping myself safe."

"Look, I'm sorry I got you into this. You were doing fine on your sabbatical and now you're a target." L wrinkled his brow. Why was he so sorry she was in this mess yet so glad he had the opportunity to know her? And why couldn't he tell her that?

"You didn't get me into anything. God did. I read the note you added to your journal for me, and I have to accept that for reasons I don't understand, God has a job for me. And don't you worry. He won't let anything stop me from getting it done."

"You're right." L smiled. He should be the one encouraging her. *What are you up to, God?*

"Odette's here, do you want to talk to her?"

"No, but thank her for me."

"Okay, she says hi and wants me to tell you that Treebeard is doing fine. We popped a bunch of popcorn, so we'll settle down for a good movie. You take care of yourself."

Ricki sat next to Odette on the couch.

"What job?" Odette asked.

"Job?" Ricki tried to look puzzled as she grabbed a handful of popcorn and stuffed it in her mouth.

"Yeah, what job does God have you doing, like you told L on the phone?"

"Nogho...imtboo..." Ricki spoke through a mouthful of popcorn.

Odette made a fist and tapped her on the arm. "Stop that. What job?"

Ricki swallowed the popcorn and started to twirl a strand of hair around her forefinger. "Just a generic job, you know. He has something for all of us to do."

"Uh-unh." Odette shook her head. "I'm an Awakened. I can tell when you're lying. Now, what job are you doing? Maybe I can help."

Twice Ricki opened her mouth to say something, but she couldn't bring herself to say it.

"Come on, Ricki. I know you're dying to tell me."

Ricki took a deep breath. *She's right, I want to tell her. Maybe she can help me because I don't seem to be getting anywhere.*

"All right, but you have to keep this to yourself. L didn't want it getting out."

Odette nodded. "You have my word, girl."

"I'm searching for patterns in his journal. Patterns that will reveal a hidden message. L thinks I'm the only one who can discover it."

She went on to explain all that happened, including her grandmother's saying. When she was done, she looked Odette in the eyes. "Oh, Odette. What am I going to do? I know L trusts me, but I haven't seen any pattern at all. I'm lost." Ricki tried to slow her breathing to fight back tears, but one escaped and rolled down her cheek. Any attempt to hold back the flood was doomed. Ricki started to cry.

Odette held her for a while, then said, "I understand your tears. I know the pain behind them."

Ricki leaned back and shook her head. "You don't understand. It's not that I have tears that is so painful. It's that I don't have someone to wipe them away that hurts the most."

Odette tilted her head slightly to the left, reached out, and stroked Ricki's hair. "Oh, sweetie, that's exactly what I understand."

September 26, 7:26 a.m., Tel Aviv

Declan and Shiri were about to land in Tel Aviv. Both had slept most of the way home. The seat belt light came on and a SOAR aide woke them to prepare for landing.

Declan looked out the window. He loved watching the early morning sun cast shadows across Tel Aviv. He turned to Shiri. "Well, what next? We still need to locate the ship and the virus. Do you have any ideas? Because I've about run out of tier-one contacts."

Shiri thought about it for a moment. "I have a contact who might have some information. It's a long shot because she worked for Abbud Abbas, even met Abdul Ba'ith once or twice, but never worked for ISIS. Yet I have a feeling she may know something that could help."

"Did Abdul Ba'ith hate ISIS? At least that's what he told me. In fact, he wanted the CIA's help to bring ISIS down."

"I must have slept funny." Shiri squeezed her shoulder. "It's kind of sore. As far as Abdul Ba'ith is concerned, he was lying to you. Remember, before he became a UD he was a leader in ISIS. This go-after-ISIS thing was just a show to confuse us. UDs love to sow confusion and lies."

"All right, let's give this contact of yours a try."

Walking out of the airport to their car, Declan noticed a tall, stocky man with an unusual birthmark on his face. He was clearly trying hard not to be noticed. Declan had seen him before, but where? He shrugged. It'd come to him.

Driving out of the airport, Declan saw the same man in a pale-green car pull out behind them. "I think we have a tail."

"Are you sure? Do you want me to try and lose it?"

"Not sure. You keep on driving and I'll watch."

After about five minutes, Declan's breathing slowed. "False alarm. Whoever it was turned off on a side street." Declan rubbed the back of his neck. "Though he seemed interested in us at the airport. Something was not right about him, and I'm rarely wrong. In fact, he looked familiar to me. I'm sure I've seen him before."

"Apparently he's not following us now."

The rest of the drive was uneventful. In less than an hour, Shiri turned onto a side road with a rather unimposing sign announcing SOAR.

As they drove through the compound's gate, Declan scanned ahead. He saw a vast area of green grass, some of which was being watered at the time by a sprinkler system. To the left several children were playing on swings. To the right was a vegetable garden. Several large white buildings seemed to surround the place, though he couldn't see the other end. One of the buildings looked like a large apartment complex.

As they drove farther in, a great peace descended on him. He took a deep breath. "This is the first time I've actually visited your organization. It's...peaceful. I feel good here. This is quite impressive. What is this place?"

Shiri shrugged. "I guess you could best characterize it as a refugee camp and, for a few, a prison."

"Refugee camp? Where are the broken-down tents? The muddy streets? The water spouts dispensing dirty water? And what do you mean by a prison?"

"For the most part, except for the Awakened staff and administrators, we house Naturals who have crossed paths with an Awakened and it's been determined that they are not safe where they are. We protect them and provide for them. They are free to come and go as they want, but they all choose to stay.

"But some are pure evil who have escaped their country's justice. They are not free to leave but are well cared for. After all, we can neither hurt nor kill a Natural, no matter how evil. We are not in the punishment business, but these people need to be kept out of circulation for the sake of other Naturals."

"Where are we going?"

Shiri pointed ahead. "To the white building."

"They're all white."

Shiri grinned. "To the one on the right, but first I have to stop and run in quickly at the one straight ahead." She reached behind her seat and picked up the bag of dust that had once been Josef Gabriel.

"What are you going to do with that?"

"Oh, we collect the dust and store it at facilities around the world. We call them Dustbins. That building up ahead is the Middle East Dustbin. I'll drop this off and then we can meet my contact."

After Shiri disposed of what remained of Josef Gabriel's dust, they made their way to one of the apartment complexes on the grounds. Declan wiped the sweat off his brow. The building had a large, colorful lobby with the walls in watery shades of blue like a clear, calm ocean pool. The entryway rug was a soft neutral shade of sand, giving the lobby a feeling reminiscent of the seashore. Plants of all shades of green accented the area. Comfortable chairs and couches in vivid shades of orchid were arranged in small groupings all around. Some were occupied by people reading, talking, or simply resting. Light background music only added to the harmonious feeling of the area. Against the far wall hung a sign that read "Life lies on both sides of death."

Declan looked around and smiled. "This place feels...I don't know how to say it. Gentle, safe, restful. I don't even want to smoke."

Shiri nodded. "As an Awakened, I feel those qualities even more. This haven feels isolated from all the hate, anger, and death in the world outside. It's no surprise people don't want to leave."

"I don't want to leave."

Shiri slapped him on the back. "But you have to, Cowboy. We have work to do."

"Cowboy?"

"Isn't that what you Americans say?"

Declan thought a moment. "In some ways I guess I am a cowboy."

"So let's go." Shiri pointed to the stairs. "She'll meet us in her apartment. It's number 323."

They walked up the three flights as Shiri explained to Declan who they were about to meet. They turned left at the top and room 323 was three doors down on the right. Shiri knocked.

A slender woman with straight black hair flowing past her shoulders, a narrow face, and dark skin came to the door. "Shiri. It's great to see you." She gazed past Shiri. "Did Reginia...uh...I mean, did Ariella come?"

"No, but I brought a friend." She turned to Declan. "This is Declan Walsh, my partner." She motioned to the woman. "Declan, this is Damijana. She helped us with our last case in Dubai."

Damijana held out her hand. "Actually I was their last case, or at least part of it. Pleased to meet you, Declan. Come on in."

The room had teal walls and the floor was covered with a tan-colored rug made of the same thick, soft material as in the lobby. The furniture, a couch and two chairs, were tangerine. As they entered, they were greeted by a small black Lab with long, floppy ears. The Lab ignored Shiri and ran up to sniff Declan's pants.

He squatted to pet the dog around the ears. "What's her name?"

"She's Izzy, a black Lab/pit bull mix. She's my kid and such a comfort to me."

Declan stood. "I love dogs. They are the only honest, forgiving creatures on earth."

Damijana looked down at Izzy. "I would have said that five months ago, but I've met a lot of honest, forgiving people here." She gestured to the couch. "Here, come and sit down."

They sat, Damijana taking the chair across from the couch. Izzy curled up on the couch between Shiri and Declan with her head on his lap. Declan smiled.

Shiri turned to Damijana. "How have you been?"

Damijana pulled her hair back from her face. "Better than I ever imagined I could be. I have a home now and people who love me for who I am." She gazed adoringly at her dog. "And I have Izzy. Allah has blessed me. I was a victim—now I'm a survivor. I'm working in the kitchen and enjoying it."

She sat up straight in her chair, her eyes almost dancing in rhythm to her growing smile. "And you'll never guess. I'm going to school...to be a nurse. I want to go back to Dubai and help in the slums."

Shiri smiled back. "That's wonderful news." She sat back on the couch. "This is a business visit. We need your help. I'm afraid we have some questions that might bring up painful memories, and I'm sorry about that, but it is very important."

Damijana rubbed her legs as her smile faded. "I want to help any way I can, but what can I do?"

Declan said, "We want to ask about Abdul Ba'ith's dealings with ISIS."

"I don't know anything. I wasn't that high in the organization."

Shiri nodded. "I understand, but did ISIS ever come up in conversation?"

Damijana thought for a moment. Her eyes watered, and she wiped her hand across her face. "I'm sorry. I don't like to think about that time. But a couple of names came up in reference to the Cesium-137 we got."

Shiri asked, "Do you remember them?"

Damijana covered her mouth with her hands. "Let me think." After a moment she started to rub her legs again. "There was a Jalal Bashir. He was the one who delivered it." She paused as she tapped her finger on her right cheek. "He was a scary man." She shuddered. "He had a birthmark on his face that looked like a dagger. The other name I think was Jalal's boss. Miraj Barak Qudir. That's all I can remember. I'm sorry."

Shiri reached across and set her hand on Damijana's leg. "Don't be sorry. You've actually been quite helpful."

Halfway back to Tel Aviv, Declan's cell phone played "America" by Neil Diamond.

Shiri laughed. "Who's that?"

Declan picked up the phone. "It's my station chief. I'll have to take it." He talked for a moment. He wrinkled his brow, switched off the phone, and turned to Shiri. "Bad news."

Shiri slowed the car. "What is it?"

Declan cleared his throat. "You remember that guy I was arrested with...Adnan?"

Shiri nodded. "Yes."

"It turns out he was murdered in jail shortly after we left him. And there's more. Your contact in Prague, Angel Bohdan? They found his body in the Church of Bones. He'd been beaten to death by a thigh bone. He put up quite a struggle. The place was in shambles. Bones everywhere. And while we were in Prague, Artem was attacked. He is in the hospital, lucky to have survived."

Shiri shook her head. "This can't be a coincidence."

"It's not. Someone has been following us." Declan looked out the back window. "No one is behind us." He paused for a moment. "Pull over."

Shiri drove to the side of the road, stopped the car, and put on the emergency flashers. "What is this about?"

"I'm usually good at catching a tail but apparently not this time. They must have a tracker on the car." Declan got out and searched the car. At the back bumper he knelt and felt the inside corner. He stood and returned to the passenger seat. "Here it is." He dropped a small device on Shiri's lap.

Shiri stared down at it. "Let's get rid of it."

Declan smiled. "No, that would tip them off immediately. I have an idea."

Chapter Thirty-Three

THE ENEMY'S STRATEGY IS ONE OF divide and conquer. Just like the wolf that stalks the sheep who has wondered off from the rest of the pack, he knows that alone we become easy prey. So he wants misunderstandings to go unexplained, words spoken in anger to be louder than all the words of love, and a hurt to become a wound that never heals. We need to stay together.
–Awakened Incident Manual, Volume 2, Page 351

September 26, 7:38 p.m., Tel Aviv

Declan and Shiri arrived at the Azrieli Mall and searched for a car similar to Declan's Cadenza. That was not difficult to do since it was a popular car in Israel.

It only took half an hour to find a light-blue one. It was parked in view of one of the mall's side entrances. Declan got out and placed the tracking device under the back fender.

Declan came back and tapped on the driver's-side window. Shiri rolled it down. "Are we set?"

"Yes. You go and find a discreet place to park." Declan pointed over to the closest mall entrance. "I'll wait over there until this car leaves, then I'll call you. Come and pick me up and we'll follow this car and hopefully see who was tailing us."

As Shiri drove away, Declan walked into the mall. It was enormous. From his vantage point, he could see three floors of shops. The place was full. There was a constant buzz of conversations, and he could smell frying oil and coriander waft in from a nearby falafel stand.

His attention turned to the parking lot outside. He studied the cars that drove by. Nothing seemed too suspicious, but a white Toyota five rows away came by twice, passing obvious parking spots, then disappeared.

About twenty-five minutes later, a woman with two children

walked by Declan. They went for the Cadenza. Declan called Shiri, then watched as the Cadenza drove off. About four minutes later, Shiri drove up and they both saw the suspicious white Toyota leave as well.

Declan jumped into the car. "That white Toyota up ahead is our tail. Follow it."

Shiri stepped on the gas. "Never done this before. This is real spy stuff."

They followed the white Toyota for about twenty minutes, then it pulled off to the side of the road in a small housing development. The other Cadenza, the one from the mall, parked in a driveway three houses ahead. The woman and her two children got out and entered the house.

The driver of the white Toyota also got out of his car and stared at the house. Declan pulled out his binoculars and got a good look at him.

"I know who that is." He handed the binoculars to Shiri.

She took a look. "You're right. He has a dagger-like mark on his cheek. That's Jalal Bashir."

Declan nodded. "It's him all right. Why has ISIS been following us?"

They watched as Jalal got back in the car and drove away. Shiri asked, "Don't you want to pursue him to find out?"

"No, we know who he is. He clearly knows we are on to him, but I'm sure he'll try to follow us again, only this time without the aid of a tracker." Declan focused his attention on the other Cadenza. "I have to get something."

He got out of the car and walked up to the third house. He paused to glance around, then knelt and reached up under the rear bumper. He returned to his car. Before getting in on the passenger side, he threw the tracker on the ground and stomped on it.

"Now that family will not be traced." He got into the car and looked at his watch. "It's getting late. Let's go back to Tel Aviv."

Jalal checked his screen. The CIA man's car was on the move again. He pulled out after the blue Cadenza was back on the street and continued to follow it from a safe, undetectable distance. Eventually it arrived at a house and parked in the driveway.

He gasped. *That's not them. That's a family.* He opened the door and stood, eyes focused on the woman and her two children as they made their way into the house.

The CIA man and his woman must have discovered the tracker.

Jalal got back in his car and sat there, his nostrils flaring, his face burning, his breath quickening.

I've been played a fool by those two. He pounded his fist on the dashboard. *Nobody makes me look like a fool.* He gripped the steering wheel like his fingers were anacondas squeezing the life out of its prey.

He furrowed his brow and narrowed his eyes. Someone had to die for this.

He took another deep breath and glanced over to the driveway. Maybe that woman and her kids. He imagined himself returning to that house and killing the family, taking pictures of the carnage he would unleash and sending them to that CIA man with a note that read: *This is what happens when someone tries to make a fool out of me.*

He continued to sit in the car as his breath settled and his face cooled down. He shook his head. As fun as that would be, it wouldn't be smart. Time to end this cat-and-mouse game. Time to kill the CIA man and his woman.

Jalal drove away imagining the exquisite ways he would torture them to learn what they knew and then kill them in the most painful way possible.

September 27, 9:01 a.m., Tel Aviv

Jalal sat outside the apartment of the woman who seemed to be with the CIA man all the time. He was waiting for a phone call from his man who was on the way to Declan Walsh's apartment.

Jalal's cell phone rang. It was the call he'd been waiting for.

"Any news? Is he there?"

"His car is outside. He must be here. Shall I put another tracker on it?"

"Don't bother. Now that he's on to us, he will check, and I don't want to be sent off following the wrong person again. Stay away but keep an eye on him. Report his movements."

Jalal hung up and looked up to the woman's apartment. It was the one with all the windows. The one with the drapes open all the time. He'd seen her on several occasions staring out the window.

Walsh is going to mess with me? Let's see how he feels when his friend is found dead.

Jalal got out of the car and walked into the building. Minutes later he was standing outside her door. He pulled one of his knives out, holding it ready for the blow. He knocked at the door and stood poised for his retribution. *He won't make a fool out of me and not pay.*

The woman answered the door. With a grin he plunged the knife in her stomach. "This is a message for Declan."

The woman gasped, grabbed the knife, and stumbled backward into the room. Jalal followed and closed the door behind. He was going to watch her die. He would relish seeing the life drain from her eyes.

Only she didn't collapse to the floor. She stood her ground and stared at him.

He looked down at the knife protruding from her stomach. His eyes widened as she pulled out the knife and let it fall to the floor.

There was no blood at the wound, though there was blood on

the knife!

Jalal tried to shuffle backward to flee, but his legs did not cooperate. He managed only a few centimeters. All the while his gaze oscillated like a metronome from the knife on the floor to the strange devil standing no more than three meters in front of him.

"Who...? What...? What kind of devil are you?" Jalal backed up to the door. His hands clammy, his lips trembling, he experienced something he had never faced before—fear. All he could think about was escape. Running from danger. It shamed him. "Who are you?"

With lightning speed, the woman rushed up to him. She turned him around and placed her arm around his neck in a choke hold. He felt the power of her squeeze. Everything went dark.

Shiri dialed Declan's number. He picked up on the first ring.

"What's up?"

"You won't believe this. Jalal Bashir just dropped into our laps."

"You're right. I don't believe it. What's going on?"

"Get over here. You'll see."

Twenty minutes later Declan knocked on Shiri's door. She opened it and, as Declan entered, she pointed to the couch. "There he is. Jalal in all his sinister glory."

Declan stared for a moment. "Is he dead?"

Shiri slapped Declan on the back of the head. "No. I don't kill Naturals." She looked toward the couch. "Even Naturals as evil as he is. He's out cold."

"What happened? How did you find him?"

"He found me." Shiri shrugged. "About an hour ago there was a knock at the door. I answered and he was standing there with a knife. He stabbed me. Then I put him in a sleeper hold."

Declan whistled. "He stabbed you? I bet he was surprised."

"He was." Shiri nodded.

"Okay, what do we do now?"

"I have a couple of Awakens on their way to take him to the facility where you met Damijana. He'll be cared for there. While we wait, I thought we could wake him and ask a few questions. Help me tie him up."

After they secured him, Shiri threw a cup of water in his face. Jalal shook his head, his face ashen, his eyes wide. "What happened? Where am I?" He looked up at her. "You..."

"Jalal, you tried to kill me. You obviously failed."

He gritted his teeth. "*Sheetan*...demon..."

Shiri shook her head. "Actually, closer to an angel."

Jalal's breathing quickened and he started to shake. "I killed you, but you...you wouldn't die."

Declan had been amazed at their luck. Jalal was just the person he needed to talk to. He pointed to Shiri. "Literally, she's impossible to kill, seeing as she already died."

Jalal looked down. Under his breath, he said, "Zombie?"

Declan laughed. "You've seen too many American movies."

Shiri tilted her head. "Let me ask him some questions." Declan nodded and sat across from the couch.

She sat next to Jalal. He tried to slide away without success. Shiri, in her calm, peaceful voice, said. "Jalal, the killing must stop. We will not tolerate any more of that. Do you understand?"

He turned his head away. With a slight pressure, Shiri turned his chin toward her and stared him straight in the eyes. She bared her soul, let her true nature show through. He looked down but didn't turn away.

Shiri gave him a gentle smile. "Jalal, look at me. You may not understand it now, but I'm here to help you. But first I need your help."

Jalal twisted away from her hand. "Never."

Shiri set her hand on his shoulder, and his muscles jerked. "Jalal, look at me." If she was going to break down his barriers, she needed to connect with him. "I don't want to hurt you."

Shiri wished Ariella were here; she was good at this. *Lord, what can I do to get through to this man? Help me.*

She looked at his face. Then she knew what to do. She put her hand over his dagger birthmark. "This has been a curse for you, hasn't it?"

He sat frozen, not moving or saying a word. Shiri felt a warmth fill the room. She smiled. She recognized the calming presence of the Spirit in the room. She glanced over at Declan. He had sunk back into the couch. He felt it.

She returned her attention to Jalal. Like Declan, he had collapsed back into the couch. His forehead wrinkled as he slowly scanned the room. "What are you looking for? Who else is here? I know someone else is in the room."

Shiri looked him straight in the eye for a moment, feeling the power of peace radiate throughout the room. "Jesus."

Jalal rubbed the dagger on his face. "Jesus was a prophet."

Shiri nodded. "Yes, and so much more."

A tear rolled down Jalal's face. "I don't understand…"

Shiri grabbed his hand. "You will someday."

His eyelids drooped.

"Jalal, a lot of innocent people are going to die who don't deserve it, Arabs as well as Jews. We need to know about the plans of ISIS to use the North Korean virus."

His mouth moved but nothing came out. He took a deep breath and opened his eyes. Shiri felt the tension rise in Jalal's body. "No one is innocent."

"Jalal, please."

Jalal shook his head. "I won't…I can't…"

Shiri paused for a moment. He was fighting this. *What can I do?*

Declan spoke up. "He's not going to give us anything. He doesn't understand what is going to happen. He doesn't care."

Shiri smiled. "Thank you, Declan. That's it."

He narrowed his eyes. "What's it? What did I say?"

She bowed her head. *Lord, make him care. Let him feel the weight of thousands of innocent deaths.*

The peaceful warmth slowly drained out of the room, leaving

behind a frigid chill. Jalal shivered as his gaze darted around the room. He started to rock back and forth, and tears streamed down his face. A low, guttural moan emerged from deep in his throat.

He turned his head and threw up on the rug. Still rocking, he repeated over and over, "Make it stop...make it stop."

Shiri eyed Declan who was also crying. "Get some towels from the bathroom."

Declan stood. "What's going on?"

"Get the towels. I'll explain later."

A couple of minutes later, Declan returned with four large towels. Jalal was still rocking, still moaning. He threw three of the towels on the floor over the vomit while Shiri took one and wiped Jalal's face.

"Jalal, I can't make it stop until I know that innocent people will not die. Tell us something easy like, what's the code name of this project."

Jalal looked into Shiri's eyes. "Operation...Operation..." Jalal struggled to keep his mouth closed but in the end he couldn't. "Blood Red."

Shiri smiled. "Thank you. When will the virus arrive?"

"Around October 10."

Shiri nodded again. "Why the tenth?"

Jalal stopped rocking as once again a peaceful warmth filled the room. "Because...that is the day North Korea wanted it used. We had to agree to it before they sent the virus."

"How is it coming in?"

"Boat."

"What is the name of the boat?"

"I don't know. Miraj does."

Shiri glanced at Declan. It was the name Damijana mentioned. "Who is Miraj?"

"Miraj Barak Qudir, my boss. He has all the plan details."

"Where is he based?"

"In Aleppo. In his antiquities shop."

"Which antiquities shop?"

Jalal strained to speak but no words came out.

Shiri put her hand on his leg. "That's all right, Jalal. I know you are tired." She turned to Declan. "We've pushed him enough." She smiled at Jalal. "Thank you, Jalal."

A knock sounded on the door. Declan answered to reveal two men dressed in dark suits, white shirts, and blue ties.

"Can I help you?"

One of the men said, "Shiri asked us to stop by to meet someone."

Shiri glanced over. "Let them in. These are the men we've been waiting for."

They stepped in past Declan. Shiri introduced them to Jalal. "These men are here to help you. You need to go with them."

Jalal nodded.

As soon as the men left, Declan addressed Shiri. "Are you thinking what I'm thinking?"

Shiri smiled. "We need to go visit Miraj in Aleppo."

Declan nodded. "Yes, partner."

Chapter Thirty-Four

FAITH IS NOT BELIEVING THAT GOD will do what you want or even what you ask Him to do. Faith is knowing that God will do what He says he will do. Even more faith is the ability to say to God not my will but yours and really mean it. –Awakened Incident Manual, Volume 2, Page 153

September 28, 5:38 p.m., Dandong

L stared out the plane window as they landed in China. In two days they would enter North Korea. *Will we be ready?* He didn't like being away when Ricki was clearly a target. But they had to do everything they could to remove the threat posed by the virus.

They had to use this two-night layover in Dandong, the result of primitive rail infrastructure, to learn as much as they could about North Korea.

Once they entered the airport, L got Agam's and Ariella's attention. "I need to stretch my legs and I want to talk with Joon about part of our plan. Would you mind picking up our luggage and we'll meet you at the hotel later?"

Agam glanced at Ariella and shrugged. "Sure, Boss. Don't stay out too late."

It was getting dark when L and Joon wandered down to the Yalu River that separated China from North Korea. The river was frozen. Even though he wore a heavy coat, L shivered in the light breeze.

On the other side of the river was the first North Korean city they would travel through. Sinuiju was a city of over three hundred thousand people, yet it looked dark as if it had been abandoned. Only an occasional light could be seen in a window, most likely a kerosene lamp because the light flickered. By contrast, the clouds above L glowed amber and red from the neon lights of Dandong.

L pointed across the river. "Is there even a city there, or is this some kind of blackout against attacks?"

"No, there is not enough electricity, and what little there is belongs to the privileged." His cheeks flushed, Joon dropped his chin to his chest and looked to the ground. "So much for a so-called classless society."

"What was it like?"

Joon turned to L. "What's what like?"

"Growing up over there?"

Joon's shoulders slumped and he drew in a long breath. "For most of my life, I lived in a concentration camp. But..." He pointed across the river. "I was born in Sinuiju and I lived there for twelve years. From what I heard in the camp, we were better off than most. Chinese goods were often smuggled across the river. You could make a lot of money selling them on the black market. My uncle occasionally did that."

Joon paused and stared up at the dark, moonless sky as if lost in memory. "On the North Korean side, possession of a Bible got you executed, or worse—marched off to the horrors of a concentration camp. That's what happened to my family. My father got caught with a Bible, so my parents and all my siblings were sent to the camp."

L laid his hand on Joon's shoulder. "Did you really mean to say it that way? That death was preferable to the camp?"

Tears streamed down Joon's face. "The camps were hell on earth. We worked twelve hours a day. Everyone was starving. The food they gave us was barely enough to support life, if that much. We could be beaten or killed at any moment for any reason. Did I mean it that way? Yes...yes I did."

Joon waved at the river in front of them. "This was a river of freedom and, at the same time, a river of death. It is only ten meters wide and the water in the center only comes up to the waist. An adult could wade across it. Many North Koreans have tried to escape to China across this river. Some succeeded; most died. It was not unusual to see a body float by or someone hanging from the bridge. It is the 'Berlin Wall' of Asia." Joon pointed across the river. "There, people are required to worship a UD, Sok Kang Ju, much like Daniel's three friends had been required to bow to a false god. They even called the three past leaders of the DPRK the 'holy trinity.'"

L wrapped his arm around Joon's shoulders. *Lord, protect your people on that side of the river.*

That night, it hit L that there was far more to this hunt than dusting Sok Kang Ju. Joon's words had opened his heart to the people of North Korea. When he got back to Seattle, he would send more Awakens to this nation.

They arrived a little early at the train station ready to enter North Korea. L approached Joon. "You need to take your suitcase and duck into the nearest restroom so you can come out as Captain Hyeon."

Joon smiled as he grabbed his suitcase and walked away. "I'm on it."

L walked over to Ariella and Agam. "Let's hang loose here. We can't go near the train until we have our North Korean escort. And from this moment on we're British citizens—Larry Walker, Alex Smith, and Angela Jackson."

Soon Joon emerged from the restroom. "How do I look?"

L. scanned him up and down. "I'd say you look different."

Agam stepped up and took Joon's hand. "You must be Captain Hyeon. I'm Alex Smith and my companions are Larry Walker and Angela Jackson of the UK."

Escorted by a North Korea soldier, they were directed to the cars near the end of the train. These were the cars for foreign visitors, effectively isolating them from contact with the North Korean passengers at the front of the train. The car looked brand new. Inside they found a row of six private sleeping rooms that could accommodate four people each. Their room was the one at the end. Their beds, which were unnecessary for the five-hour trip, were arranged in bunk-bed style, two to a side. The top bed on each side was folded up so they could sit comfortably.

They settled back for a hopefully uneventful journey that began almost immediately by crossing the bridge into Sinuiju. Ariella looked out the window as they entered North Korea, then she looked back at Dandong. They had left a colorful, alive city and entered a drab, black-and-white land. "It's like *The Wizard of Oz* running backward."

Day 17, September 28, 5:42 p.m., Sinuiju

Bong Jun-Ho had died in the sixteenth century at the age of thirty-one. It was 1636, to be exact, during the second Manchu invasion of Korea. Nine years before his death, he'd fought in the first Manchu invasion and developed a sense of purpose. He fought for Korea, for his country, for his honor. He fought for glory and the pride of victory. But after he'd been reanimated, all that changed. Now there was no honor, no glory, no country. Now he fought to kill Naturals. Even better, he enjoyed the battlefield because he loved watching Naturals kill each other. Something they did very well.

Korea had been a great place to live since it experienced invasion after invasion. He had all the war he wanted. But that time had long passed. The last few decades had been a disappointment. Sure, the DPRK talked an aggressive line, and Jun-Ho loved the hate that fueled everything, but where were the wars? What happened to the mass killings, the conflicts over ideas? He missed the things that made this new life pleasurable.

Hence, the reason he went to work at the Sinuiju Concentration Camp on the North Korean border with China. It was a beautiful place for Jun-Ho. A place where he could watch Naturals slowly starve to death. A place where twenty people were stuffed into a cell made for ten. A place where hope evaporated as quickly as a small puddle under a desert sun.

The cries and screams of Naturals were the soundtrack of life, the music of his existence. There he could freely kill or torment Naturals. But as with the battlefield, he loved sitting back and watching those who were created in the image of God torture each other.

That's how he came to meet Woojin Gunwoo, the most sadistic guard at the camp and his first real friend in centuries. Sure, he was a Natural, but his hatred of others was off the charts.

But now, as Jun-Ho reported for duty, he received word that his friend had died several hours earlier, possibly of a heart attack. In fact, his body was already in a body bag and ready to be loaded on the train to Pyongyang, which stopped at Chongju where his family lived.

He would have made a great UnVeiled. Oh, the fun they could have had together. That thought brought another to mind. He left his post to rush to the train station in nearby Sinuiju. *I hope I'm not too late.*

Jun-Ho arrived at the train station to find the train about to leave. The stationmaster told him the body was already locked in the storage car. He had to act soon; he couldn't delay his plan. It was already approaching the deadline, so he bought a ticket. Even though he was not a foreigner, because of his status at the camp he was given a sleeping room in the first of the two cars near the end of the train. As he boarded, he noted the train had six coach cars right behind the engine, followed by the dining car, the two sleeping cars for foreigners, and at the end of the train the baggage car.

Once in his room, he decided to wait for half an hour to ensure everyone had settled down and then make his way back to the baggage car. He was not authorized for what he was about to do, but he wasn't worried. Kang Ju would love the outcome. He relaxed and dreamed of a world without Naturals.

Chapter Thirty-Five

PERHAPS FAITH REALLY IS TRUSTING THAT something meaningful lies beneath the surface of the senseless, that purpose exists in the randomness of life, that joy is independent of your circumstances, that you should move toward what your heart desires more than run from what you fear, and that what you believe is ultimately real. –Awakened Incident Manual, Volume 2, Page 703

September 28, 6:01 p.m., Sinuiju, North Korea

The train whistle blew three high-pitched warnings and set off, creaking slowly toward the east as it gained speed. Ariella's car lazily rocked from side to side like a ship swaying on a gentle sea. The rhythmic clanking of the tracks spoke to her, reminding her of the days when a train was the only means of long-distance travel.

Her thoughts drifted off to a train trip she had taken with her mother and brother in 1891 from Magdeburg to Kiel. She rubbed a tear from her eye. She hadn't thought about her family for decades. She loved them. Her childhood had been filled with fond memories, yet those memories had been filed away in the recesses of her mind.

She ran her hand through her hair. Her mother and father had died of illness within a year of each other. Her brother had died somewhere on the Western Front during the waning days of WWI. Her memories of them were all that kept them alive in this new world. A twinge of guilt fluttered through her body as her lower lip quivered. Such was the curse of immortality in a world of death.

From across the aisle, L tapped her knee. In a quiet voice he asked, "Are you all right?"

Ariella said nothing, only nodded.

She laid her head back and looked out the window as the train climbed a steep, pine-covered mountain. Her thoughts strayed to the beauty of this country that stood in stark contrast to the dark evil that covered it. She once again filed away the memories of long ago, of loves lost, of a yesteryear only she could carry.

Jun-Ho's walk to the back of the train was uneventful. He had his guard uniform on. That, combined with the aura of a UV, guaranteed no one would challenge him. The baggage car was locked with a flimsy-looking padlock. Not one for finesse, he didn't bother to pick the lock. Instead, he grabbed it, gave it a firm twist, and pulled it off, then dropped the broken lock on the floor.

His friend's body was easy to find. He was laid out in a body bag on a cart near the front of the car. Jun-Ho unzipped the bag and examined Gunwoo. He checked his watch: 6:33. Since Gunwoo had died just before 11:00 a.m., he was pushing eight hours dead. Reanimation success dropped off significantly after five hours, and relatively inexperienced UVs like Jun-Ho were never supposed to perform the ritual eight hours after death, but he had a confidence in his abilities. *I rarely fail at anything. Besides I've seen this done many times. It never looked difficult.*

Jun-Ho had to find a way to get the body to his room unobserved. There he would be able to set up the right conditions to possibly reanimate his friend as well as provide a fresh piece of real estate for a waiting demon. He rummaged through the baggage car to find something large enough to hold Gunwoo's body. Luckily, Gunwoo was no more than five-foot-two and 114 pounds. His arms were as thin as pipe cleaners. His viciousness had most likely been compensation for his weak-looking stature. Killing prisoners affirmed his manhood.

It didn't take long to find a small trunk that would be perfect. He smashed the lock and dumped the contents on the floor. He glanced around and smiled. Looked like a windstorm blew through here. Someone was going to be upset.

Jun-Ho forced the body into a fetal position and tried to place it in the trunk. It barely fit, but that was all he needed. He stepped back and admired at his handiwork.

There might be some small cuts in his legs. But when he was reanimated, those would heal immediately, and he'd only be a little sore. Jun-Ho closed the trunk, found a small handcart, and left for his room.

He got to his sleeping car undisturbed and, as far as he could tell, unseen. Both sleeping cars were quiet. He pulled down one of the beds and laid the body out. He was ready to start the process.

There were no magic words to recite for the reanimation process, no powders to sprinkle, no dances to perform. All he had to do was find a comfortable position, concentrate on the body, and call out to his gods. It either worked or it didn't. Most of the time it didn't, but he was convinced he had both the strength and the will to get this done. He lit a few candles and placed them around the room. Not because they had any power, but because they helped him set the mood and focus his mind.

For twenty-three minutes, Jun-Ho alternately sat and walked about. He cried out to the exalted one. He would stand and stare at the body concentrating all his will on raising the body until drops of sweat formed on his forehead. As he was about to accept failure, Gunwoo's body jerked. His mouth opened, his body arched, as he gulped down a big helping of oxygen.

Jun-Ho bent over the body, placing his ear near Gunwoo's mouth. He definitely felt the air of light breathing. He jolted back when Gunwoo opened his eyes.

"Welcome back to the world. I guess now you're going to learn my little secret."

Gunwoo didn't respond. Instead, his gaze darted around the room.

Jun-Ho tapped Gunwoo on the shoulder. "Hey, look over here. I'm sure you have a lot of questions."

Jun-Ho remembered the shock of his own reanimation. It had taken him a moment or two to become aware of what had happened. He tapped Gunwoo again, this time on the cheek.

"Wake up, buddy."

Gunwoo bit Jun-Ho's wrist. He yanked his arm back, "Hey, that hurt! Why did you do that?"

Gunwoo sat up and growled. Jun-Ho stepped back. He'd failed. It saddened him. *Oh no, Gunwoo is a Type 2. It didn't work. That's what I get for performing an unauthorized reanimation. Now what am I going to do with it?*

It stood, looked around with blank eyes, and limped to the door, the left foot bruised from where Jun-Ho had twisted. It wouldn't heal because Type 2s didn't heal like Type 1s.

Jun-Ho watched it walk into the hallway. *Well, it's not my problem now.*

Most Type 2s were docile and eventually ran into an Awakened who would dust them, but that was unlikely in North Korea. In all these centuries, he had never seen an Awakened. He shrugged. What were the odds it would run into an Awakened? It wasn't like there were Awakens next door. Gunwoo was destined to wander or simply squat somewhere, never to move again.

Jun-Ho decided to sit down and listen for the screams from the dining car. If this was an aggressive one, there might even be some deaths. He smiled. Lots of deaths. Maybe this wouldn't be such a wasted effort.

Agam relaxed, leaning up against the cabinet wall. The team was discussing their plans and Agam jerked. What was that? He slowed his breathing to listen. There it was again. Agam stood straight. "Shh, did anyone else hear that?"

"Hear what?" Joon asked.

Agam held out his hand. "There it goes again. There was a growl followed by some kind of banging noise. It's either coming from a room near us or the hallway. I'll see what the problem is."

Agam stepped into the hallway in time to see the back of a man stumbling toward the dining car. "Sir, do you need help?"

It glanced back, snarled, and continued limping its way to the next car. Agam saw the reason for its limp. He sucked in a deep breath and turned to the others in the room. "It's an L2!"

Joon looked at the other two and bit his lip. "What's an L2?"

L answered. "That was a UD, what we call an L2 or Level 2. It's someone who died and was reanimated by Satan. But something went wrong, and it is a mindless beast."

Agam added, "It looked like a fresh one, which means there is a UD on this train. And when it realizes the L2 has disappeared, it will know there's at least one Awakened on board. If it gets away, our cover is blown."

L shook his head. "Agam, go after that L2 and dust it before it can do any damage. Joon, you go with him. He'll need both your authority and your translation. While you're doing that, Ariella and I will go the other way to search for the UD. If we haven't found him by the time you come back, we will plan a formal UD hunt on this train."

Agam and Joon ran down the aisle, the rocking of the train throwing them from side to side. Screams sliced through the dining car as they entered in time to see the L2 move on to the next passenger car. Four diners were huddled in a corner, shaking and crying. One was bleeding from her arm. She was quiet. Her eyes dull. She stared straight at the two of them.

Agam ran up and examined the wound. "Joon, tell her she'll be all right. Then go get L and Ariella. Tell them this one is a biter."

Joon nodded and yelled something in Korean in a voice that confirmed the authority of his uniform to the wounded woman and the other three terrified passengers.

Agam asked, "What else did you tell them?"

"I told them that that thing escaped from the nearby concentration camp, and I am going to hunt him down and kill him. They should not tell anyone, or they will be in trouble with the Bowibu, the Ministry of State Security."

"Good thinking. Now get the other two while I try to find our L2."

Chapter Thirty-Six

WE KNOW THAT THE CLOSER WE are to the glory of the Lord, the more we can bring light into this world. –Awakened Incident Manual, Volume 2, Page 703

L and Ariella moved to the second sleeping car. There were six rooms down the hallway. They tried the first two doors. Empty. As they approached the third room, they heard sounds. L opened the door and found three people sitting in the cabin. Two were clearly European and the third wore the uniform of the KPA, the Korean People's Army. As far as L could tell he was a lieutenant.

The lieutenant glared at L through cold, hard green eyes, his face reddening. In perfect English he said, "What are you doing? And where is your escort?"

L bowed his head. "I am so sorry. We were looking for our friend. He left the room to go to the bathroom ten minutes ago and has not returned. We were afraid he got lost or maybe fell off the train."

"This is a train. The bathrooms are at the front of each car. How could he get lost? I'll ask you one more time, where is your escort? When I find him, I'll put him up on charges for allowing you to wander around the train alone."

L started to say something when Joon ran up. L smiled in relief and faced the lieutenant. "Lieutenant, here is our escort, Captain Chin-Had Hyeon of the Bowibu."

At the mention of the Bowibu, the lieutenant blanched. He snapped to attention and delivered the North Korean salute. His mouth started to move but nothing came out. Eventually he managed to sputter, "Captain Hyeon...do...can...can I do something to help?" He looked down. "I am at your disposal."

Joon returned the salute. With a scowl he said, "No, Lieutenant, but I ask that you no longer delay my guests."

The lieutenant stepped back and with another salute shouted, "Yes, sir!"

Joon whispered in L's ear. As L and Ariella ran off, Joon's eyes narrowed. "Carry on, Lieutenant." He left as the officer stepped into the hall and yelled another, "Yes, sir!"

While Joon ran back to the sleeping car, Agam opened the door to the connecting space between the dining car and the first passenger coach. The Level 2 was standing ahead of him, glaring out the small window in the side exit. It snarled at Agam and, as if sensing the danger, moved into the passenger coach.

At that moment, one of the men from the dining car grabbed Agam's arm and pulled him back in with a strength fueled by fear-induced adrenaline. Through trembling lips in broken English "*Abeg*. Don't...left."

Agam had to pry the man's hand loose, then he jumped into the space where moments earlier the Level 2 had been. Screams echoed through the car up ahead.

He pushed through into the next car. The car reeked of day-old sweat and oil. Stuffing poked out of the tattered seats. The dirt-streaked windows allowed little light in. Unlike the dining car, this car was full. There were thirty rows of seats, four seats to a row, two seats on each side, with a narrow aisle running up the center.

The Level 2 limped up the aisle. It let out a low, guttural growl like that of a rabid dog.

People were standing on the seats, scrunched as close to the outside wall as they could get. Some were crying. Some were screaming. Several were in the aisle, trying to run ahead of the Level 2 into the next car.

Panic could be heard above the rhythmic rattle of the train as it raced down the tracks. In one motion, the Level 2 reached to the right and pulled a terrified man into the aisle. The man fell backward.

Instantly the Level 2 was on its knees gnawing at the man's hand. The victim's eyes were closed, but his screams told Agam he was still alive.

Agam yelled, "Stay calm. Don't move. You will be taken care of."

Someone in that car must have been able to understand English because Agam heard a woman speaking in Korean as Joon ran in with L and Ariella close behind. Agam's words, as translated by the woman, seemed to quiet some of the louder passengers. All eyes were wide in horror and fixed on the man and the Level 2 on the floor in the center of the car. No one seemed to notice a member of the Bowidu was in the car.

Joon tapped Agam on the shoulder. "She told the passengers what you said." As the train made a left turn, the sound of its whistle reignited the screams. The car tilted to the left, causing a few of the passengers and the luggage to fall into their seats. Several pieces of luggage bounced into the aisle, blocking Agam's access to the Level 2.

Agam caught Ariella's attention, and spoke in a low voice to prevent the English-speaking woman from hearing. "I saw a power switch right past the doorway in the back. Go and switch it off long enough so I can dust this thing." Ariella nodded and ran back.

Agam moved up, grabbed the Level 2's face, and pulled the man's hand out of its mouth. "Now!" he yelled to Ariella. The car went dark.

Moments later Agam yelled, "Done." The lights came on.

Cradling his hand, Agam walked back to L. "The idiot L2 bit me." He shrugged. "At least it saved me from having to bite it."

L turned to Ariella. "See what you can do about that man's hand." He tapped Joon on the shoulder. "And Joon, tell them it's over. You've captured that thing, and it will be executed. Tell them not to speak of this ever."

He nodded and once again spoke with authority in Korean, warning them of repercussions from the Bowibu if anyone shared these events, even with their family. At the mention of the word *Bowibu*, several passengers trembled.

Ariella tore a strip off the bottom of her shirt and used it to stop the bleeding and wrap the man's hand. She helped him up to his seat and reported back to L. "He'll lose a couple of fingers, but the hand should be okay. He's very pale, his skin is clammy, and he's sweating a lot. I'm afraid he's going into shock. He needs a doctor as soon as possible."

L nodded. "Joon, go through the rest of the train and see if you can find a doctor. If you can, bring him back to work on this man. Look for the UD as well."

Jun-Ho sat back, enjoying the gentle rocking of the train. He'd heard a few distant screams. Some people ran by his room, and once he thought he heard the word 'biter' yelled down the hallway. Good old Woojin Gunwoo. Even in death, he could frighten Naturals.

Things seemed to have quieted down, so Jun-Ho decided to walk up the train to inspect the damage his little escapade had inflicted. Upon entering the dining car, he was rewarded with the sight of four Naturals huddled near his end of the car, obviously terrified. One woman was holding her arm, which was still seeping blood.

Too bad a Level 2's bite wasn't poisonous, then they would be worth something.

He walked up to the group. "What's going on?"

A man dressed in wide, dark-gray trousers and a dark-gray shirt with a pin of the North Korean flag above the left-hand shirt pocket shivered. "A madman burst through here and attacked my wife. He bit her arm." He pointed to the next car. "Then an American chased it into the next car. We don't know what to do." He looked at Jun-Ho with pleading eyes. "What should we do? Is it safe?"

He gave them a frosty glare, but inside he was dancing.

Gunwoo had certainly been entertaining tonight. "I don't know. Stay here and…"

The door leading to the next car opened, and three men and a woman stepped inside. Jun-Ho had never seen an Awakened before, but he recognized one as soon as he gazed into the eyes of the first man through the door.

He froze for a split second, then grabbed the woman with the wounded arm standing next to him and a knife off the dining table and held it to her throat. In perfect English he sneered, "Back away or I will kill this Natural."

The team stood motionless facing the UD with the female hostage. L's first thought was, at least they didn't have to hunt the UD. It found them. His second was, they had to save the woman.

He held up his hand. "All right, don't hurt her, and we will back off."

L motioned for everyone to step back. As they did, he noticed something in the woman's face. She tightened her fist, set her jaw, and stared straight into L's eyes. Worried she might do something rash, L shook his head and mouthed *no*.

Too late. In three fluid motions, the woman kicked back and up with her right leg into the UD's groin, swung her right elbow into its gut, and bit the arm that had been wrapped around her head.

The UD let out a low-pitched shriek, bent over, dropped the knife, and let go of the woman. She, her husband, and the two remaining diners scrambled over the tables toward L and his team. The UD recovered and, with a murderous glower, ran back toward the sleeping car.

L smiled at the woman's bravery. "Joon, stay with them and make sure they get safely to the next car. Agam and Ariella, let's dust that thing."

As soon as they passed through the doorway at the rear, they heard the *whoosh* of the door at the far end. L said to Ariella,

"Search the rooms in this car. Agam, come with me."

L and Agam ran into the next sleeping car, then froze, listening for any sound. Everything was quiet. L motioned to Agam to search the first compartment while he tried the second. Nothing. He opened the door to the third and ran into the lieutenant and his party again.

The lieutenant stood, his face turning as pale as it did before. "Is everything all right? Does the captain need my help?"

L shook his head. "No. Did anyone come in here, or did you hear anyone come by?"

The lieutenant licked his lips before he spoke. "No one but you, though we did hear someone run by, followed by the sound of the door to the baggage car opening."

"Thanks."

Agam had joined L. As the two of them ran toward the baggage car, the lieutenant stuck his head out and yelled, "Be sure to tell the captain how helpful I have been."

When they entered the baggage car, the overhead lights would not turn on. The area smelled of mold, and the only sound was the clanking of the wheels against the tracks. Stacks of luggage scattered throughout the car cast faint shadows from the little light sneaking through the only two windows in the car. It gave the enclosure an eerie atmosphere, especially knowing a UD was hidden somewhere.

They scanned the area. L whispered to Agam, "It could be hiding anywhere. There is not a lot of room to maneuver in here so stick close to me." Agam nodded.

They began to weave their way through the piles of luggage, looking for any sign of the UD. Suddenly the train whistle blew three times, and the train slowed as it made a turn to the right. The car tilted and luggage slid toward the left wall. Agam fell back as a stack of luggage dropped on him.

Then the faint light extinguished as the train ran through a tunnel. L tried to listen for movement in the dark when he was hit by a cart and pinned against the side wall. Something ran by him, and the door back to the cars opened.

L shoved the cart and raced to the exit. The UD was struggling to open the outside door. L leaped toward it just as the door opened and the UD fell forward.

L managed to grab a tenuous hold on the UD's right foot, leaving the rest of its body hanging out the door of the train moving at more than sixty kilometers an hour. The force of the wind against the UD kept it parallel to the ground. L strained to hold on.

He tried to yell over the sounds of both the train and the wind across the now-open door. "Agam, help me hold him. We can't afford to lose him."

L's grip was slowly slipping off.

Just when it seemed he couldn't hold on anymore, Agam grabbed the UD's leg above the ankle. They both pulled it toward them. When he got close enough, L lunged forward and bit the UD on the ankle, leaving nothing more than dust scattered by the wind across North Korea.

L stood, spitting dust out of his mouth. "Where's a gun when you need one?"

Ariella joined them and helped Agam close and seal the door. The three of them walked back to their compartment to wait for Joon. Ariella took a deep breath. "I hope our primary mission is not as exciting as this impromptu hunt."

Chapter Thirty-Seven

SOMETIMES THINGS HAPPEN IN OUR LIVES that defy explanation. No matter how hard we try, we can't make any sense out of the things God puts in our path. Yet if we remain faithful and patient, God often puts all the pieces together and reveals his purpose. He truly works in mysterious ways." —Awakened Incident Manual, Volume 2, Page 311

Day 17, September 28, 6:41 a.m., Seattle

Ricki was enjoying her time with Odette. After being kidnapped, shot at, and chased through CenturyLink Field by an UnDead assassin, she was ready for a break. This morning she sat in the sun room of the safe house in the middle of one of Seattle's famous rainstorms.

She lay back, her eyes half closed, her fingers laced behind her head, and watched the gentle splashes of rainwater roll down the glass roof as the wind rustled through the trees. The smell of the morning's bacon still lingered in the air. Her breath was deep and cleansing, her mind floating. For the first time since that morning Wade Hall knocked on her door an eternity ago, she felt...hope...free.

At the same time, a few pangs of guilt snuck into her mind. For the last week, she hadn't looked into the journal, hadn't thought about the secret buried there. A secret that might change the world.

Instead she and Odette had gone shopping at the Westlake Center, walked through Pioneer Square, had dinner at the Space Needle, strolled along Puget Sound at Alki Beach. She'd even introduced Odette to Mary, and the three of them had a great time in Tacoma. It warmed her heart to see her two best friends in the world hit it off so well.

In the evenings, they watched movies and talked about

men—really about L, about Lazarus. She preferred to use his full name but never around him. She loved hearing stories about him, and Odette had centuries of those. Though she had to admit, picturing him in a suit of armor made her laugh.

Today they would go back to work. She and Odette were going to SOAR—Odette to conduct business and Ricki to get back to the journal. Maybe this time wasn't wasted. Maybe this time allowed her mind to rest and sharpen. Maybe this time she would find the secret.

A few hours later, Ricki sat in her office and pulled up the journal. She stared at the screen, fingers poised over the keyboard, frozen in place as part of her resisted returning to Lazarus' world. As the internal battle slowed, she interlaced her fingers and stretched her arms out. *Ricki, get yourself together. They need you here. Lazarus needs you here.* She sat up straight and clicked the journal file.

It'd been so long she had to take a moment to remind herself where she had left off. She shook her head to try to loosen things up. She smiled. That's right. Jesus had ascended into heaven and Lazarus was back in the compound.

After I returned to the compound, it didn't take long for me to be surrounded by people with questions. Lots of people. Lots of questions. All about Jesus.

"Did you see Jesus?"

"Did he really leave?"

"When is he coming back?"

And the question I'm always asked, "What are we to do now?"

I decided to call a general meeting for that evening so I could tell everyone at one time what little I actually knew, and we could all talk about it together.

I met with Josias, Sapphira, and Ari to go over what I should say and, as leaders in the camp, to equip them to answer questions as well. By the time we got to the meeting room, it was already full. And noisy.

I walked up to the front and turned to face all those who had gathered. "Good evening, everyone!" My voice carried over the crowd, quieting them.

After giving them a moment to settle, I started. "As most of you know, I just returned from seeing Jesus, and the most astonishing thing happened. I saw him rise and disappear into the clouds."

Someone stood and yelled, "So I was right. He left us...again."

Someone else jumped up. "Yah, but this time he didn't die. He left voluntarily."

I held up my hands. "All right, let me finish." Things quieted down for a moment. "We were all told that he is coming back again."

A voice in the crowd yelled, "When?" to a chorus of, "Yes, when?"

Josias, who had been sitting next to me, stood and waved his hands. "Let Lazarus finish. Then you can ask all the questions you want." He nodded at me and sat back down.

They quieted again and I continued. "Josias is right. If you'll let me finish and then ask questions, this will go much smoother." I pointed in the general direction of the first 'when' question. "I don't know when. He didn't say. But until he does, Jesus said he will send someone in his place." I went on to describe what Peter and the other disciples had told me as well as other details of that remarkable experience. Then I opened it to questions.

We had a lively discussion that lasted into the early morning hours. Eventually, I had to call a stop and tell everyone to seek their rest.

While Josias and Sapphira talked with a few of the stragglers, Ar came over. "You never answered the question: What are we specifically supposed to do?"

I nodded. She was right. I only wish I had a good answer. "I don't know. Jesus gave us a general idea. I hope we will know more when the Holy Spirit comes. Peter and the others went back to Jerusalem to wait." I shrugged. "I suppose that is what we all should to do as well. John said they would let me know if he learned anything. In the meantime, we need to get better organized so we will be ready when the time comes."

Ricki turned away from the computer screen and looked out the window to organize her thoughts. It was still raining, and the wind had picked up. She could feel the slight sway in the building. Maybe the secret came from the Holy Spirit. Maybe she'd run across it now.

September 28, 10:15 p.m., Chongju, South Korea

The team sat in their compartment while the train sat on the tracks. Shortly after the UD had become dust, scattered all over the North Korean landscape, someone on board had ordered the train stopped.

L leaned back in his seat. If this turned into a major incident, they could be held here for hours or even days. Still, he couldn't blame them. After all, there were two injured passengers on board, a missing body, and a crazed man running loose who vanished. On top of all that, a camp guard had taken a passenger hostage, threatened to kill her, and then, apparently, jumped off the train.

L had to smile. He shook his head. *So much for a covert entrance.* The only way to top this would be to carry neon signs announcing their entry. Only it wasn't funny. If they were discovered or delayed long enough, the mission would have failed. L frowned. And millions of people would die. Was this going to be Berlin for him, only this time escalated to the level of a global catastrophe?

Agam glanced at his watch. "What's keeping Joon?"

Joon had exercised his authority as Captain Hyeon to accompany train security as they questioned the passengers.

Ariella patted Agam's left leg. "Don't worry. He'll get here as fast as he can. My guess is that should be soon."

Ariella was right. A few minutes later, Joon walked in. "What happened?" Agam was on top of this.

Joon sat next to L. "The good news is that the memory of most of the passengers faded away. Most likely the result of the orders from the Bowibu captain." Joon smiled. "The bad news is that the hostage remembered everything. She told them some Americans had saved her. This did not sit well with the security personnel because in North Korea, Americans are bloodthirsty, degenerate pigs. If Americans were on board, the obvious conclusion would be that they were behind all this. Case closed. When it appeared that you three were going to be the focus of the investigation, I protested and showed them your papers. I told them you were British not Americans. That seemed to appease them a bit, but since you were the only ones roaming the train at the time of the incident, they are still suspicious. I think we will face more fallout over this."

L nodded. "I agree. I don't think we've heard the last of this, but we need to remain focused on our mission."

By the time security had released the train, it was running several hours late. L felt the train jerk a couple of times, then it started to pick up speed on the way to its next stop, Chongju. L looked at his watch. Their little adventure was going to cost them precious time in Pyongyang.

Chapter Thirty-Eight

THE DESERT OF THE SOUL IS that dark, quiet, foreboding place inside us where secrets lie buried, the chains that bind us find anchor and despair makes its home. It is a place in which it is easy to get lost. It is also the place where Jesus goes to find us and when he does hope overwhelms despair, chains are broken, secrets are washed clean and what was once a desert blooms with beauty.
—Awakened Incident Manual, Volume 2, Page 166

Lieutenant Sung-Hoon Myeong was tired. It was only an hour into his late-night shift at the Chongju police department, and already he wanted to go home. After twenty-seven years as a police officer, the glamour had worn off. He had seen terrible things, he had done terrible things, and sometimes he had prevented terrible things. In the end none of it made any difference.

He would never say it aloud—he'd be shot if he did—but there were times when he doubted the justice of the Great Leader. Feelings like that had to be kept hidden deep down. In North Korea, it was best to wear a permanent mask. At least it was dark and quiet tonight, exactly the way he liked it. He was leaning back in his seat with his legs up on the desk when the call came in.

He sat up and rubbed his hands over his face. This was a peaceful city. Who could be calling at this time of night?

The call instructed him to meet the Pyongyang train as soon as it entered the station. He had been called out to the train station in snow and -7 degrees Celsius weather over a missing body, a missing camp guard, a missing crazy man, and two wounded passengers. Myeong cracked his knuckles. The camp guard had most likely defected as soon as the train left Dandong. As for the missing body, a check back at the station in Sinuiju would probably discover it stored in a room because some *babo* forgot to put it on the train. The only thing that made this case interesting was a crazy man biting two passengers, and train security should have taken care of that. In other words, this was most likely going to be a big waste of time.

He slammed the door behind him as he marched out. "I'm too old for this!"

The Chongju train station was, like almost every building in the city, a small, drab, gray cement structure. The only thing that distinguished it was a sign that was in disrepair announcing the Chongju Train Station and a long neon light in the lobby area. It and the police station were always the last to lose power during the frequent city-wide blackouts. The lobby had the obligatory picture of Sok Kung Ju, actually two of them. Several worn wooden benches and a ticket booth with peeling red paint. The neon light flickered and cast eerie dancing shadows as it swung in the light breeze that penetrated the building.

Especially macabre was the way the constantly shifting shadows at night made Sok Kung Ju's smile on the nearest photo flicker between uncomfortable and just plain sinister. But no one would ever say anything about that.

When Myeong arrived at the station, four strangers were sitting on one of the wooden benches in the lobby. His sergeant was standing near enough to keep an eye on them, but not close enough to carry on a conversation. Everyone looked unhappy.

One of the strangers wore the uniform of a DPRK captain, complete with one of those silly caps that looked like he was wearing a partially inflated balloon. Myeong sighed. But who was he to criticize their Great Leader's uniform design?

The captain stood and approached him. "I must firmly protest this treatment of my very important guests."

"And who are you?"

"I am Captain Hyeon Chin-Hae of the Ministry of State Security, and I have Larry Walker, Alex Smith, and Angela Jackson with me. They are citizens of the UK who have come to celebrate Party Foundation Day with us. They should be allowed back on the train before it leaves this station."

Myeong bowed slightly. He was too tired, too old, and too smart to allow the Bowidu to complicate things. "Captain Hyeon, I am sympathetic with your problem, but we have a missing body, a missing person, and—"

The sergeant stepped up and whispered into Myeong's ear, requiring his immediate attention. "Captain Hyeon, my sergeant would like to talk to me. Would you excuse us for a moment?"

"Certainly not. He can speak in front of me."

"As you wish." Myeong nodded to the sergeant. "What do you want to tell me?"

"There's more going on than we had been told. For instance, the missing camp guard was on the train and even took a hostage before disappearing."

So much for defecting. "Go on."

"And the cart carrying the body as well as the body bag were in the baggage car. Someone took the body out while the train was moving, and the luggage compartment was a mess."

So much for a simple case. Myeong pointed over to Captain Hyeon's three guests. "Why are they here?"

The sergeant avoided looking at Captain Hyeon. "They were the only ones seen walking around during the time all this happened."

I don't need this. "I see." Myeong turned to Captain Hyeon. "From what my sergeant says, this case is more complicated than I thought. I'm more than happy to turn it over to the Ministry of State Security. You can call your investigators in, and I'll go back to my warm police station."

Captain Hyeon did not arrogantly jump on his offer. Instead, his brow wrinkled, and he glanced back at his guests. He was a strange Bowibu.

After a short pause, Captain Hyeon turned back to him. "Lieutenant, I don't have time for this. I'm under orders to get these three guests to Pyongyang in time for the ceremony. This should be a simple case. I'll cooperate, but you need to resolve it now."

"Thank you. Then tell me. Your group was in the compartment next to the missing camp guard. Did you hear anything? Did any of you leave your compartment to go anywhere on the train?"

"No, we didn't hear anything." Captain Hyeon paused and covered his mouth with his hand for a second. "Oh, wait. I remember we did hear someone rather clumsily walk down the passageway right before the commotion started. As for my guests, I can tell you that all three of them were in my sight at all times. They had nothing to do with any of this."

He's lying. Why would a captain of the Bowibu lie to a lieutenant of the local police?

"I'm not doubting you, Captain, but since you gave me this case, there are procedures I am required to follow. Your little group either did something or witnessed something. I need all of you to come down to the station for a short while. I'll check their documents, ask a few questions, and then you'll all be on your way."

The captain looked back at his guests again. Mr. Walker nodded almost imperceptibly. Captain Hyeon turned back to face Myeong. "Okay, but make this fast."

"I guarantee it will go as fast as I can make it." Myeong flashed a glance at Mr. Walker. What was that all about?

When they got to the police station, Joon, as Captain Hyeon, was escorted to the lieutenant's office. L, Agam, and Ariella were ushered to a holding cell. L took one look at the cell and smiled. Every few decades he ended up in jail. This one was a milestone since it was the tenth country where he'd been a guest of the authorities. There were no windows, only three walls of bare cement and one wall of bars. It was gray and cold, with the overpowering smell of mold and urine. They sat on the floor with their backs to the cement wall.

Agam pushed to his feet and walked to the bars. "I can't see them. What is Joon doing? It's been over an hour." He turned back around. "There is no good outcome to any of this. We are losing valuable time. We may get there before the ceremony but not have time to find a good sniper's spot. Or worse, we may not get there until the ceremony is over. Maybe Sok Kang Ju will hear about this and guess we are Awakens and go into hiding. Or worse, release the virus." He shook his head. "I have a bad feeling about all of this."

"It's been closer to two hours, but who's counting," L said. "I trust Joon can get us out of this. He has several things going in his favor. One, he's an Awakened, and Naturals find what Awakens say to be persuasive, even though they aren't conscious of it. Two, he's a captain in the Bowibu, at least that's what the police think, and North Korean society fears authority even if they don't respect it. We stand a good chance of getting out of this in time to complete the mission."

Agam sat back down next to L. "You said several things were in his favor. What's the third one?"

L smiled. "God."

Thirty minutes later, Joon stood outside the bars with a big smile. Ariella asked, "What happened?"

"There's another train leaving in thirty-five minutes. We'll be on it."

Lieutenant Sung-Hoon walked in with the keys. "I assume the Captain told you…"

L stood to meet him. "Yes, yes, he did."

"I'm sorry I detained you. You can pick up your documents on the desk as you leave. If you wait outside, my sergeant will bring around the car and drive you to the train station."

The group huddled outside near the door. L asked, "What happened back there?"

"It's the strangest thing," Joon said. "He scanned all our

documents and emailed them somewhere. Then he asked me what happened on the train. Of course, I couldn't tell him the truth, so I told him the next best thing."

"Which was?" Agam asked.

L interrupted. "In case anyone asks, you need to commit Joon's version to memory. I'm sure you already know that the first sign that we are hiding something is different stories."

"Got it." Agam nodded.

"We were in our stateroom when we heard a commotion down the hall. I looked out and saw a suspicious man stumbling down the hall toward the dining car. Not wanting to leave you three alone, I brought you with me. We got to the dining car after he had bitten a passenger and moved on. We followed him to the next car. I grabbed him just as the lights went out. He managed to get away and disappeared. I assume he may have jumped off the train. On our way back to our compartment, we found the camp guard in the dining car. He took a hostage, but when the hostage broke free, he ran back to the sleeping car. He must have jumped off the train as well. I went back toward the baggage car to investigate and discovered the door to the outside was open. I closed it." Joon rubbed the back of his neck. "I told him that's all I know."

"Good job." Ariella patted his shoulder. "Did you say anything else?"

"I suggested either the crazy man or the camp guard or both must have dumped the body and searched the baggage car for something."

"Evidently he bought that, so what took so long?" Ariella asked.

"I don't think he bought it, at least not at first. He asked me my story, shuffled through the papers, wrote some stuff down, and about thirty minutes later he asked me again. The last time he asked me, he left the room for a while. When he came back, his phone rang. I think he was being reprimanded. His face turned red, and all he said was 'yes sir, no sir.' When he hung up, he told me to tell you he was cutting us free."

Ariella asked, "What was that phone call all about?"

L's brow creased with worry.

"I have no idea, but it must have been about us. Are we being set up?"

Day 17, September 28, 11:48 p.m., Pyongyang

Renaud sat at his makeshift desk in his temporary housing during the reunification talks. The small housing was merely adequate, but hardly something befitting his elite status as both the lead French negotiator but more so as the leader of the UVs. Someone came in every day not to clean the drab, dirty yellow room, but to wipe down Sok Kang Ju's picture to make sure no dust or dirt of any kind settled on it.

He stood, moved to the window, and looked out over Pyongyang. Its population was approaching four million. The city had been destroyed during the Korean War but had been entirely rebuilt since then, making it the most modern city in North Korea. It was a city with wide tree-lined streets and many, many monuments. It was a city only the privileged were allowed to live in.

Renaud sighed as he surveyed the view. On one level he liked what Kang Ju had done with this nation. He'd buried the country under such a mountain of lies that now, no matter how absurd, people believed them. It was so complete that there wasn't even the tiniest fissure that would allow any truth to seep in. He'd really done a marvelous job. Renaud would love to keep him around, if only he didn't believe his own press. But none of that justified a refusal to obey his orders.

A few minutes later, Park Kye walked in. "Remember when you told me to leave specific instructions that if anything involving an unexplained, sudden disappearance occurred, it should immediately be reported directly to you?"

"Yes, I remember. Does this mean you have something for me?"

Park Kye set three passport pictures on the desk in front of Renaud. "Recognize anyone?"

All it took was a glance. "Well, I'll be... this Larry Walker is Lazarus. Where did you get these? Does that mean he's in country?"

"It does." Park Kye smiled. "These were forwarded to me by a Lieutenant Sung-Hoon in the Chongju police department. It seems they are, along with a Captain Hyeon, implicated in the disappearance of a body and a prison guard."

"Do we know who the guard is?"

"Yes, one of ours, a UV. And we can't get hold of him. We think this Larry Walker...ah, Lazarus, must have dusted him."

"Where are they now?"

"Lieutenant Sung-Hoon is holding them."

"Contact this lieutenant and get them released immediately. We don't want their mission delayed. I want them followed. Give strict instructions that no one is to interfere with them in the slightest, under penalty of immediate execution."

"It will be done." Park Kye left the office.

It was just like that line in that movie called *Field of* something 'If you build it, they will come.' *Thank you, Lazarus, for making everything fall into place.*

Chapter Thirty-Nine

JESUS WAS INCLUSIVE. HE LEFT NO one out. To him, everyone had worth. He was just as likely to be at a poor man's home as he was to be in the home of a Pharisee. That is how we are to live.
—Awakened Incident Manual, Volume 2, Page 97

September 29, 6:00 a.m., Pyongyang

The team arrived in Pyongyang early in the morning. The sun was coming up, the sky was clear, and it was fourteen degrees Celsius outside. The taxi ride to the Koryo Hotel was short and uneventful, which was a nice break.

Agam looked up at the imposing twin towers. "Wow, this must be forty stories high."

"Actually, it's forty-three." Joon was back as travel guide.

"It's the only building we've seen in North Korea so far that doesn't look like it's ready to fall apart." Agam smiled. "And lucky us. It's where we are going to stay."

They exited the taxi and collected their luggage. Standing on the street corner in front of their hotel, they quietly surveyed the surrounding buildings and streets.

Agam ran his hand over his hair. "Does this feel eerie to anyone else?"

Ariella glanced down the street to her right. "I feel it too. There is almost no one out. No cars and maybe a couple of people walking away from us. With the exception of our hotel, the rest of the buildings are a dull gray. All we need is a few newspapers blowing down the road to complete the illusion that we arrived after the apocalypse."

L nodded. "This is a cold, drab, ominous country." He reached down and picked up his suitcase. "Before we go in, I want to make sure everyone is aware of our living arrangements. We have three rooms reserved. One for Ariella, one for Agam and myself, and one for Joon."

Agam patted Joon on the back. "How come we have to share a room and Joon gets one all to himself. Hardly seems fair."

Ariella laughed. "What Bowibu captain would stay in a room with the likes of you two?"

They checked in without incident. The rooms were small but adequate and likely bugged, so mission planning had to be done outside and away from people. They agreed to rest, then meet outside to talk about their plans.

Three hours later, they gathered outside the hotel entrance. They were not allowed to leave the hotel property without Captain Hyeon, but with him they were free to roam. Since the hotel was located in the downtown area, they decided to take a walk to see the sights.

It was a perfect day for a stroll through the old city. A light breeze blew, and the sun shone through thin clouds. But as Awakens, they were especially sensitive to the pain of an entire people. The oppressive air was heavy with mistrust, thick with fear. They walked in silence.

Eventually, L spoke up. "It's September 29. We have eleven days to prepare. We have to select a sniper site. The Tower sounds like the best place, but we won't know for sure until we see it. We have to check out other possible locations as well. It will be a tough shot for Ariella since Kung Ju will be surrounded by Naturals. She'll only have one chance to get it right. If she fails, a Natural could be killed, or worse, Kung Ju could unleash the plague on mankind and millions will die."

Ariella tried to smile. "No pressure on me, is there?"

Agam nudged her in the arm with his bent elbow. "We have the utmost confidence in you. You can do this. You're the best in the world."

She shrugged and scratched her nose.

L continued. "Once we settle on a site, we have to visit it several times to build familiarity and estimate possible wind conditions or anything else that might affect the shot. We also have to work up possible entrance and egress routes. There's no room for error."

L looked at Agam. "The rifle will be ready?"

Agam nodded. "It will be delivered October 6."

"Good. We have to be ready for everything and anything by October 10. That is the day the world will change one way or the other."

Day 18, September 29, 10:21 a.m., Damascus, Syria

Declan and Shiri arrived in Damascus without incident. Declan had hoped to fly directly into Aleppo, but all flights into the city had been canceled due to recent activity by ISIS, government forces, and the opposition paramilitary forces. They faced a long drive along what was considered to be the world's most dangerous road, the Salamiyah- Ithriya-Khanasser Road. In peace time it was only a five-hour drive, but now, because of delays at military checkpoints and long detours, bypassing portions of the highway closed due to military activity, it could take up to nine hours.

When they got to the Jeep, Declan checked the hidden weapons cache. As he expected, he found two Beretta M9s, an M16A3, the same assault rifle the SEALs used, four M84 stun grenades, and three M8 smoke grenades along with extra ammunition.

Shiri watched as he checked each item. "That's quite an arsenal for a visit to an antiquities shop."

"Better to have more than you need than not enough. We will be entering a hot war zone. The road we are on is contested by the Syrian Army, ISIS, the Ahrar al-Sham and other rebel groups, and in some places even the Kurds. Not to mention air strikes by the US, UK, France, and Russia. Even the Gulf nations like the Saudis and the UAE are bombing Syria. That's a lot for us to dodge."

She sighed. "You know I can't use the rifle or the pistols to kill a Natural, and they won't work on a UD, making them useless for me." She paused and wiped the sweat off her forehead. "However, I understand this war-torn world, and though it deeply saddens me, I know why you have them. I will not interfere with your use of them, but I hope that doesn't happen."

Declan nodded. "So do I. But you can use the smoke grenades—they are nonlethal weapons."

"Sure, and I can bluff my way with one of the pistols. Now as to driving, I think the more experienced driver should take the first shift."

"And how long have you been driving?" Declan grinned.

"Decades before you were born, partner."

"Then I think this is a job that should be left to the younger, fresher member of the team."

Shiri shook her head. "Okay, you win this round. But no smoking in the car."

They ran into the first checkpoint less than half an hour outside of Damascus. The guard looked like he was only nineteen and not the least bit interested in his job. He glanced at their papers and waved them on.

As they drove through the checkpoint, Shiri glanced back. "Well, this should be a piece of cake."

Declan shrugged. "It never is."

The desert was flat and rocky with scattered shrubs and the occasional burned-out tank or truck. About three hours into the trip, they passed a downed helicopter that was still smoldering in the hot desert sun. They went through three more checkpoints as easily as the first. Once they saw aircraft fly over, and about ten minutes later they heard bombs exploding in the distance.

An hour outside of Aleppo, they were stopped at yet another checkpoint. There was a small shelter beside the road with a makeshift bar that stretched across the road. Ten men manned the station.

As they drove up, Declan tapped Shiri's arm. "Those guys don't look like the Syrian Army. I think they are rebels. Be careful."

A man with a weather-beaten face and a scraggly beard walked up to the Jeep. He was missing his left arm but carried a pistol in his right hand. Two men with AK-47s stood in the road about a dozen feet ahead of them.

Standing on the passenger side, the one-armed man asked Shiri for their papers. She got them out of the glove compartment and handed them over. He put his pistol in its holster and took them. He barely looked at them and then threw them in the Jeep.

With a sneer he stepped back. "Get out of the car."

Shiri glanced at Declan then turned to the guard. "What seems to be the problem?"

He put his only hand on the butt of his pistol. "Get *out* of the car."

The two men with AK-47s walked up as Shiri and Declan did what they were told. The one-armed man pointed to the two other guards and said something in Arabic. They strapped their AK-47s over their shoulders and opened the doors to the Jeep.

Declan whispered to Shiri, "He told them to search the Jeep."

Shiri nodded her understanding. "I know. I've been speaking Arabic for almost two thousand years."

Declan shrugged. "Yeah, I forgot. If they find the weapons, we'd better be prepared to take them down."

Suddenly the high-pitched whistle of a mortar shell rang out, followed by an explosion about a mile ahead of them. He grabbed Shiri and pushed her to the ground, covering her body with his own. The guards turned and ran to the checkpoint.

Another mortar shell fell just short of the roadblock. One of the guards went down as a large plume of dust and smoke blew over the road. Eight of the guards were on the ground, firing their AKs to the south.

Declan pulled Shiri up, and they ran to the Jeep. He started it and threw it in reverse, skidding all over the road and throwing up dust. Another mortar shell fell right where the Jeep had been moments earlier.

He was still speeding in reverse when the one-armed man walked through the smoke of the last shell with his pistol raised. He aimed it at the Jeep and fired. The first bullet missed, but the second round crashed through the windshield between them, narrowly missing Declan. Another mortar shell fell about ten meters behind the one-armed man, sending him to the ground.

Declan backed up for about a half mile before he stopped and raised a brow at Shiri. "Piece of cake huh?"

Shiri smiled. "Hey, we survived. What was that all about?"

"I was right. Those guards were most likely rebels. It could have been ISIS or the Syrian Army wanting to take control of this segment of the road. They targeted us with 60mm mortar shells that have a blast radius of twenty-five meters. Luckily they weren't 81mm or we'd be toast."

"What's the plan now?"

Declan pointed to the right. "The attack came from the north. We should leave the road here and head around to the south, giving them a wide berth."

"Okay, partner. At least they never got a chance to find our weapons." Shiri paused and hit Declan on the shoulder. "Oh, the next time bombs start falling, let *me* cover *you*."

September 29, 9:46 a.m., Seattle

Ricki and Odette had stayed up late last night. They didn't stop talking until three in the morning, so Ricki felt like sleeping in and going to SOAR later in the day. Besides, she wanted to have a serious talk with Odette before moving on in the journal.

Odette had made her favorite Middle Eastern breakfast for them: fool, hummus, falafel, and pita bread. She had heard of falafel, fried vegetarian patties, and, of course, hummus. But fool?

Ricki peered at the plate Odette put in front of her. "Okay, what's fool?"

Odette sat down. "As a dip, it's mashed cooked fava beans

with a drizzle of olive oil and lemon juice. Try it. It's good."

Odette was right. It was good. Ricki quickly ate everything on her plate and asked for more. As soon as Odette sat down again after refilling Ricki's plate, Ricki looked at her. "I have a question about your past. I know we haven't talked about it much. I sort of assumed you didn't want to. Was I right?"

"Not at all. I don't often have other Awakens ask about it, but it's certainly not off-limits. What do you want to know?"

Ricki let out a sigh. "That's a relief. There's so much I want to know, but right now, I'm about to read what Lazarus wrote about the coming of the Holy Spirit. Somehow, I feel like that's significant for me, so I wanted to hear about it from you as well."

Odette nodded. She didn't say anything as she stood and walked to the living room window. For a moment she stared out at the gray Seattle morning.

Ricki sidled up beside her. "I'm sorry. Did I say the wrong thing?"

Odette turned, her eyes clouded with tears. "Oh no, girl." She smiled. "You asked exactly the right thing. It brings back amazing memories. Give me a moment to soak them in."

In a few moments, Odette faced Ricki again. "Look around this room. I mean, really look."

Ricki scanned the room. The walls were a pale warm peach. The couch and chairs were a light teal. The white stone fireplace had a small gas fire burning. The coffee table in front of the couch was white and sitting on it was a lovely vase with canary yellow flowers. "It's nice."

"How does it make you feel?"

She thought for a moment. "It's inviting, warm, safe."

Odette nodded. "Now look outside."

The sky was cloudy with a light drizzle. The dim, scattered light made the usually bright-green grass seem dull. The raindrops on the window obscured and distorted many of the colors of the nearby homes.

Ricki returned her attention to Odette. "Okay, what does that have to do with what you and Lazarus experienced that day?"

Odette smiled. "Honey, it has everything to do with the Holy Spirit. Check outside again. This is a dull, dreary day. On other days there could be a cold storm raging. Still other days could be bright and warm. They change from good to bad. Now look inside. No matter what is happening outside, the inside is always inviting, warm, and safe. Jesus inside of you makes you like this room. He brings you peace no matter what may be occurring around you. Of course there's a lot more to it than that, but that is Jesus 101."

Ricki nodded. "How was it for you on the day the Holy Spirit first came?"

"I wasn't in the upper room that morning, but I certainly heard about it. My indwelling happened later. In my case, there were no tongues of fire. I didn't start speaking a foreign language. But I grew to feel warm and safe inside. I knew something very significant had happened, but at the time, I wasn't sure what it was."

Ricki stared out the window, thinking over what Odette had said. Then, without looking at Odette, she asked, "Do I have the Holy Spirit?"

Odette smiled and hugged her. "That's a question only you can answer. Let me ask you this. Have you accepted Jesus as your Savior?"

"I did...or I think I did...once." Tearing up, she put her head on Odette's shoulder, thankful for her friend's hug. "But I walked away. I was hurt. Where was Jesus when my uncle was repeatedly raping me?" She withdrew and paced a few steps away, panic swelling inside. She needed to run, to scream, but her muscles froze. *Why, God? Why didn't you protect me?*

Once she regained her composure, she faced Odette. "I guess I lost my belief, but after all I've seen, all I've been through, how could I not believe now?"

Odette put her arm around Ricki's shoulder. "If you're not sure you can always ask again. Accepting Jesus is how it all starts.

But if you're not sure you have the Holy Spirit, you can always ask for Him."

Ricki hugged herself and nodded. They both stood silent, looking at the rain outside. Ricki's mouth moved but no sound came out.

Eventually, she looked up at Odette. "I asked, but I don't feel different."

Odette smiled. "You will, girl, you will."

Chapter Forty

RESTING IN GOD CAN ACTUALLY BE a lot of work. But it feels so good you want to do it forever. —Awakened Incident Manual, Volume 2, Page 131

September 30, 9:16 a.m., Pyongyang

Outside the Koryo Hotel, L hailed a taxi. They didn't have to wait long for one to pull up. The four of them squeezed into a taxi with Joon sitting in front. The driver shifted as close to his door as he could. Joon was in full uniform, and the driver was clearly uncomfortable sitting by a member of the Bowibu.

Kim Il-Sung Square turned out to be only 2.5 km from their hotel. It was a six-minute ride. When they were dropped off, Joon said something to the driver and then nodded after the driver responded.

Agam tapped Joon on the shoulder. "What was that about?"

Joon pointed back in the direction of the hotel. "I asked him if it was always this fast to get here from the hotel. He said almost always except that on October 10 it might take as long as an hour because of the crowds gathered here."

L smiled. "Good thinking, Joon. You'll make an agent yet."

They made their way to the square, which was fairly empty given the morning hour. As they walked out to the middle, Agam waved an arm. "This is one of the largest open areas in a city I've ever seen. No wonder they're holding the Party Foundation Day here."

"Actually," Joon said, "I think I mentioned it's the thirty-seventh largest square in the world."

"You did, but being here puts that in a different light."

Ariella, who had been scanning the area, said, "So, you've been here before, Joon?"

He shook his head. "I've never been to Pyongyang before. But every child is taught about the wonders of the city."

"Then you really could be our guide, couldn't you?" L asked.

"I hadn't thought of it. I guess I sort of assume everyone learned what I learned as a child."

Agam laughed and patted Joon on the back. "Nothing could be further from the truth, especially for us. Not only did we spend our childhoods in different countries, we spent them in different centuries."

Joon chuckled. "I don't know if I'll ever get used to thinking that way."

"You will," Agam said.

Ariella looked at the ground. "What are those painted dots?" She scanned more of the square. "They're everywhere."

Joon followed her gaze. "I've heard about this but never imagined what it would be like. When they have events here that require soldiers in formation, they all stand in perfect lines. To accomplish that, each soldier stands on one of those dots."

Ariella smiled. "What else can you tell us about Kim Il-Sung Square?"

"Not a whole lot." Joon shrugged. "It opened in August 1954 and can accommodate more than a hundred-thousand people."

Agam whistled. "That's a lot of people in one space, even a large space like this. It must be a security headache, which may or may not work in our favor."

Joon shook his head. "Don't forget, we're in North Korea where every other person is either an informer or believes in the almost godlike stature of Sok Kang Ju, or most likely both. Otherwise they are in a camp, dead, or soon to be dead. Security is not as big an issue here as it might be in a society with even a little freedom."

L nodded. "But given that the results of the peace talks will be announced, I suspect a lot of foreign dignitaries will be here, more than ever before in North Korea. They will all bring their own security problems with them. Though you are right it will be nothing like say, South Korea, would experience."

Agam tapped Ariella on the shoulder to get her attention, which had been directed to the surrounding area. "Any good options for a nest?"

"The square is ringed by several large, austere-looking buildings." Arielle pointed to the largest building at the other end of the square. "Joon, what's that building?"

"That's the Grand People's Study House. It's a library." Joon pointed at other buildings around the square. "There's the Korean Art Gallery, the Ministry of Foreign Trade, the Workers' Party of Korea Headquarters, and some other government buildings."

L turned to Ariella. "Any of these look like good locations?"

"Of course there are the obvious ones—any third story or above window from the buildings on the left or right of the square, but those are government buildings so I assume they will be cleared or at least closely monitored."

"Any not so obvious ones?" L asked.

"Kind of. That building in the northeast corner with those Korean characters on standing boards has a flat roof. It would be the ideal place for a nest in terms of both protection and distance, but that means it will most certainly be cleared and security placed on it."

"That leaves us with...what?" L rubbed his forehead. "All right, there are some possibilities here but they're not ideal." L turned around and pointed. "That tower across the river, Joon, is that the one we talked about?"

"Yes. That's the Juche Tower."

"We need to visit it next. It has perfect line of sight, but it would still be a difficult shot because it must be five hundred to seven-hundred yards from the target. That may work in our favor because I'm sure they will empty it. Though they may only use a few guards during the ceremony."

The team finished exploring the square and moved across the river to scope out Juche Tower. On their way over, L took in a deep breath. *We may pull this off after all.*

Joon really took to his tour guide role. "This tower is 560 feet tall. It's the second largest tower of its type in the world. It was constructed to commemorate Kim Il-Sung's seventieth birthday. The bronze statue at the base represents three types of workers: the intellectual, the laborer, and the peasant. An elevator takes you to the top, giving you the best 360-degree view of Pyongyang you can find anywhere. How's that for your new guide?"

Agam laughed. "You did great."

They went into the ticket office and paid their five-euro fee for the ride up. On the elevator to the top, they were careful not to talk about their mission.

Ariella and L walked around to the west side facing Kim Il-Sung Square while Agam and Joon scanned the city from the east side. Ariella held her hands up to her eyes like she was holding an imaginary pair of binoculars. "I can see the whole square from here. That's good. Next time we come, I'll have to bring binoculars. I understand there is a pair on its way with the gun."

L nodded. Once back down and in a safe area to talk, he asked for Ariella's recommendation.

"This is the best place for the nest, especially if the wind is as good as it is today. It will be a tough shot based on the distance, but everything else looks good. I can do it from here."

L nodded and smiled. "So, everyone agrees? We set up the sniper's nest on top of the Tower?"

He scanned the group. Everyone nodded yes.

"All right. We need to visit here as much as possible so we learn the schedule of the security guards and check it out under different weather conditions. I want Ariella to know this place like the back of her hand." He turned to Joon. "Since this is a manually operated elevator with Korean labeling, I need you to watch the operator and learn how he handles things. We will need you to work the elevator on the tenth."

Joon nodded. "Never done that before, but it doesn't look difficult."

"Great. Now let's get back to the hotel, and remember not a word of our plans while in the hotel. Our rooms are probably bugged. We have to be ready to go without a hitch on October 10."

September 30, 6:55 a.m., Aleppo

Declan and Shiri finally made it back to the Salamiyah-Ithriya-Khanasser Road about ten kilometers outside of Aleppo. Their detour from the last checkpoint turned a two-hour drive into almost a twenty-four-hour drive. Of course, their speed was slower over rough desert terrain, but they also had to swing around two rebel patrols. The only good thing was that Hayyan had packed water and food in the Jeep.

Once back on the right track, they began to encounter civilization, which meant bombed craters and rubble-lined roads. They had one more checkpoint before they could drive into the city proper. This time they encountered the Syrian Army.

As they drove through the checkpoint without a problem, Shiri slapped the dashboard. "See, what did I tell you? A piece of cake."

"If you call driving all day and all night through the Syrian Desert a piece of cake, then you're right."

At the entrance to Aleppo, the road became a divided highway. Traffic was light and the city was eerily quiet. They were greeted by a colorless gray stone and brick desert. All around them were bombed-out and collapsing buildings surrounded by piles of rubble. It looked like a ghost town that had been abandoned decades ago. The streets were empty except for the odd stray cat or malnourished dog. Occasionally they passed a random anomaly, an intact building, standing like a lighthouse in the middle of a raging storm, alone and unapproachable.

They drove by a burned-out tank sitting in the median of the divided highway. Side streets were sometimes blocked by cars covered in layers of dust. The whole scene was surreal and in a strange way cinematic.

Declan slowed the Jeep and came to a stop near one of the

hollow, bombed buildings. The wind whistled through it as though it were a musical instrument for a giant.

"Why did you stop?"

Declan pointed to a rusted gray sign near a building that read *Hospital*. "Even the hospital wasn't safe. I guess war hasn't changed a lot over the centuries."

Shiri sighed. "Sadly, no."

They rode in quiet for a while. The scene didn't change. Shiri's shoulders drooped. She shook her head and in a flat, monotone voice said, "So much death."

As they wove their way through the city, they finally came upon a section that was relatively untouched, and people walked the streets, Eventually, they drove up to a hotel, intact, except for random rubble in front.

Declan stepped out of the car and stretched. He patted his jacket to dislodge layers of desert dust. "As soon as I get to my room, I'm taking a shower."

Shiri wiped the dust from her eyes. "Me, too. Then we can get something to eat and plan how to find the antiquities shop tomorrow."

Chapter Forty-One

JUSTICE RESTORES US FROM THE MISDEEDS of others. Mercy redeems us from our own misdeeds. We all want justice, but we all need mercy far more. —Awakened Incident Manual, Volume 2, Page 234

October 1, 12:37 p.m., Pyongyang

Park Kye sat in Renaud's temporary office waiting for Chavvah to come on Skype. Renaud was trying his best to get Skype up and running. He was working at the keyboard mumbling to himself. Eventually he leaned back and, with a broad gesture, hit the Return key. Chavvah appeared on the screen.

Renaud leaned forward near his computer. "You have to hand it to Naturals. They do come up with creative means of linking together. Sometimes when I have a few moments free, I roam social media and love reading all the hate comments between Naturals who don't know the first thing about each other. It's a thing of beauty. Not only can they hate their neighbor, they can hate a stranger halfway around the world and tell them that over and over again."

"I agree," Chavvah said. "God gave them the gift of creativity, and they use it to find better ways to spread hate. I just don't understand why He doesn't finish the job He started with Noah."

"If He won't, we will. That's why I called. You remember Park Kye here." Renaud gestured to him over his shoulder.

"Sure, hello, Monsieur Sok."

Park Kye nodded in the direction of the computer.

"Park Kye has information on Lazarus and his team. I want him to share it with both of us, and I'm interested in your insights." Renaud turned to Park Kye. "Tell us what you know."

"We followed them to their hotel. Their rooms are bugged,

but as we expected, they are too careful to talk about their true purpose here. After a short rest, they went to Kim Il-Sung Square—"

Renaud interrupted. "That's where the announcement will be made on the tenth and where Sok Kang Ju will appear."

"Yes," Park Kye said. "They spent a lot of time walking around the square. The woman especially seemed to be scanning the surrounding buildings."

"That, according to our records, would be Ariella," Renaud added. "She's their best sniper." He focused on Chavvah, and his face heated. "You might remember, she was the one who dusted Abdul Ba'ith in that fiasco you got us into a few months ago."

Chavvah remained silent but she had a defiant look about her.

Renaud smiled. "The fact that she is part of the team means they are serious about dusting Kang Ju, just as I planned. It's almost as if I'm running SOAR too. Go on…"

"After they left the square, they crossed the bridge and headed to Juche Tower. After spending some time visiting the observation deck, they returned to the hotel."

Renaud slapped the top of his desk. "I knew it. That's where they will take the shot. It's the best place for someone of her talents. What kind of security is planned for the Tower?"

Park Kye checked his notes. "Minimal. The Tower will be emptied and locked. There might be three or four guards on the grounds. It is far enough away across the Taedong River to be considered a very difficult shot for anyone to make."

"For any Natural to make," Renaud said. "But this is an Awakened with almost three-hundred years of training. She can do it."

"I hope you're right. If she misses, my father stays in power."

Renaud laughed and turned to address Chavvah. "The boy here wants to rule. I love it." He slapped Park Kye on the back. "I'm right. I trust Lazarus's judgment. He wouldn't pursue this if he wasn't sure he could dust Kang Ju. If she misses the shot, she will most likely hit a Natural and Lazarus would not risk that. Not after that mess in Berlin. Trust me, by this time on the tenth, your father will be dust."

"What do you see happening then?" Renaud asked Chavvah.

Chavvah was quiet for a moment. "It's going to happen, no doubt, but there is something else going on. I feel it, but can't put my finger on it. I must advise you, Renaud, not to attend. I fear you will die."

"Nonsense. I have to be there. This is my moment. This is where the world will take notice of me. My ascension begins on that day. Nothing will keep me away from there. Besides, I'm still a Natural, and there is no way Lazarus will target me. He doesn't even know the importance of October 10. It's the first day of the end of the world."

Chavvah pushed her blonde hair back. "Still, something is not right."

"*Merci* for your assurance, but this will happen the way I want it to happen." Renaud closed Skype.

Park Kye's eyebrows drew together. "How did she know to warn you? Did you tell her about my father's plans to kill you?"

"*Non*, her fears are unwarranted. A lot of other people have plans for October 10, and they are all going to be disappointed. I'm in charge here."

October 1, 9:03 a.m., Aleppo

Declan and Shiri met in the hotel lobby, such as it was. The building was intact, but it had not totally escaped the conflict. The ceiling was cracked, paint was peeling off the walls, and dust was everywhere. It was as drab and gray inside as the city was outside.

Declan stifled a yawn. "How did you sleep?"

"Apparently better than you. Certainly better than a night racing across the desert in a Jeep. Are you all right?"

"Fine. I was up a little while trying to find our antiquities shop. Did you know there are fifty-two antiquities shops in the city? They are more plentiful than Starbucks."

"No, but I'm not surprised. This is an ancient city. There must be a lot of archaeological sites in and around this place."

"We need to find Miraj Barak Qudir's, a shop that is somehow connected to ISIS. This could be a difficult task if it weren't for—"

"Don't tell me you have a contact here in Aleppo." Shiri huffed.

"How did you know?"

"You have contacts all over the Middle East. I wouldn't be surprised if you had some in Mecca."

"I may, but I'm not saying. At any rate, I set up a meeting for ten tonight in the Citadel."

"Couldn't we meet earlier?"

"Aamir will only meet with us after dark. He sells antiquities to various buyers around here. He's been known to sell a fake one or two to overseas collectors and occasionally something to ISIS."

"Why a meeting? Couldn't he just tell you?"

"He doesn't do business that way. Of course, he wants to be paid. Ten thousand US dollars, to be exact."

"But we don't have any US dollars."

Declan signaled her to move over to a corner of the lobby by a small, dusty window. Once there, he glanced around. The lobby was empty, except for a clerk sitting behind a desk reading a newspaper. With his back to the clerk, Declan pulled a small velvet bag out of his pocket and poured a few diamonds into his palm. As he rolled them around, they sparkled in the dim light from the window. "I have these."

Shiri's mouth opened. "Where did you get those?"

He smiled. "I don't suppose you ever saw the *Maverick* series on TV?"

"No, what's that?"

"He was an old west gambler who always had a thousand-dollar bill pinned inside his jacket for emergencies. I always carry twenty, small half-carat diamonds in the hem of my pants for emergencies. Diamonds are better currency than anything else, especially in this area. Each of these is worth about seven hundred dollars, so fifteen of them should satisfy Aamir."

"Questionable contacts, hidden diamonds—why you're a regular James Bond, aren't you?"

He nodded. "My childhood hero."

"What's on the agenda until ten tonight?"

Declan shrugged. "I thought we might get familiar with the city, and who knows? Maybe we'll get lucky and stumble on the shop on our own and save ourselves a few diamonds."

October 1, 7:51 p.m., Aleppo

Declan and Shiri spent the day exploring the city. They drove to various shops, stopping in one occasionally to wander along the dusty shelves, looking at what each had to offer. About a third of the shops they drove to were either bombed out or closed. Several shopkeepers tried to sell them obvious fakes. In another, the owner stared at them the whole time, making it clear they were not welcome.

At one point as they left a shop and got into the Jeep, Shiri asked, "Exactly what are we looking for?"

Declan shook his head. "I'm not sure. Just something different about the shop, something that says ISIS."

Their next and last stop until going to meet Declan's contact was the Souk of Aleppo. Once a large, thriving market filled with stores, it had burned down in 2012. Now they found only a few partially rebuilt shops, one of which specialized in antiquities called Khan Antiquities.

They had to step over a pile of fresh rubble to get into the shop. It was a typical antiquities store with a glass case opposite the door and low shelves on the sides. But unlike the others, it had a number of impressive items on its shelves, mostly small pieces. There were a lot of stamp and cylinder seals, small statues suitable for a desk or tabletop, oil lamps, and fragments of larger statues.

Two men in the store were talking to the owner. One, with a thick beard that made his face inscrutable, turned to look at them. Shiri and Declan ignored him as they looked over the shelves. They stopped to admire a bust of someone who must have been important.

"Do you recognize this person?" Declan grinned.

Shiri discreetly pinched his arm. "No. It's not anyone I know. That's like me asking you 'do you know Susan Doe. She's from the US too.'"

"All right." Declan rubbed his arm as if it really hurt. "Then tell me about all these stamp seals. Every shop has been full of them."

Shiri smiled. "Back in my day, everyone important had a personal seal they would stamp in wax on important documents. Usually they were destroyed when a person died, but sometimes they were overlooked or lost. Hence, all the seals you see here today."

"Interesting." Declan glanced at his watch. "I see nothing unusual here, and it's time to leave for our meeting."

Chapter Forty-Two

WE DON'T STRUGGLE AGAINST CHANCE. WE are not striving for that elusive moment of luck. We are in the hands of God, not only can nothing take us out of there, it is a peaceful place to be.
–Awakened Incident Manual, Volume 2, Page 186

Day 20, October 1, 8:39 p.m., Aleppo

They hadn't driven far when Declan tapped Shiri on the shoulder. "Did you notice we picked up a tail?"

"No."

"That guy in the shop, the one with the beard. He followed us out. Now he's in the car behind us."

Shiri glanced back. "What do you think he wants? Has he made us?"

"I don't think so. But we need to lose him before we meet Aamir."

"Can you do it?"

"Watch me."

They drove onto the divided highway that led out of Aleppo. The Rio followed them. Declan aimed for a large, overturned, rusted tanker truck sitting in the median up ahead. He sped up. "Hold on tight."

The Rio kept up with them. As soon as they passed the tanker, Declan turned onto the median. The curb was high, and they were bounced up out of their seats. He turned so the tanker was between them and the Rio and stopped. They heard a crash as the Rio tried to negotiate the high curb and instead, the undercarriage of the car scraped the cement, bringing it to a halt.

Declan's Jeep jolted forward, went around the tanker, and bounced back onto the road. They raced past the now-stuck Rio. The driver was pounding his fists on the steering wheel.

The Aleppo Citadel was in Old Town perched on a hill, rising fifty meters above the city. Declan had read it was considered to be one of the oldest and largest castles in the world, dating as far back as 3000 BC. It had survived the Greeks, Byzantines, Egyptians, Romans, and the Muslims, but not this war, not the bombs dropped from the air or set off on the ground. Part of the wall had been reduced to rubble. Debris littered the moat. Several of the rooftops inside the walls had large gaps in them.

It used to be the most visited site in Aleppo. During much of the war it was occupied by the Syrian Army, which had since withdrawn. Today it sat empty, a hollow shell of its former glory.

Declan parked near the castle and unloaded the car. He took his Beretta M9 and a M16A3. They both took flashlights.

Shiri looked at Declan. "Do you really need all that armament?"

"I hope not, but I'd rather have it and not need it than need it and not have it. Besides, I can't survive a gunshot like you can. And I'm not ready to check out." He handed her an M84 stun grenade and a M8 white smoke grenade. "Here, put these on your belt."

To get in the Citadel, they walked up and across the bridge over the moat, dodging rocks and moss. They passed through a door engraved with snakes into the Royal Hall.

Shiri's flashlight couldn't find the other end of the hall. "This is a big place. Where are we supposed to meet Aamir?"

"At the base of the South Tower. I'm not sure how to get there, but I guess we should walk to the end of this hall and see what's on the other side." Declan glanced at his watch. "It's 8:31 so we're a little early."

Shiri was quiet for a second. She scratched her cheek, then grabbed his arm. "Declan, I know where it is."

"How?"

She shrugged. "I was here for a month a long time ago. I

didn't tell you because I wasn't sure if I would remember much, but now that we're here it's coming back."

"How long ago?"

She bit her lower lip. "It was in...AD 124. I was leading a team to dust a particularly nasty UD. It was a difficult hunt."

"*Now* you tell me."

She shrugged. "I told you I didn't think I would remember the layout, but now I do. Follow me and I'll get us to the South Tower."

As soon as he got out of his crumpled car, Suhail called for help. While waiting for his ride, one of his friends called him.

"Suhail, I drove by the Citadel and saw two people get out of a Jeep and walk in."

"Could you see their faces?"

"It was too dark."

"But they got out of a Jeep?"

"Yes, a Jeep."

Boiling with fury, Suhail ground his teeth together. "All right, that could be the American and his woman. Stay there in case they come out. If they do, follow them. I'm waiting for my ride. When it comes, we will meet you there, and I want the honor of killing that infidel."

Declan and Shiri reached the base of the South Tower a little early. Fifteen minutes later, his contact arrived.

"Aamir." Declan shook hands, then kissed him on both cheeks. "It's so good to see you again."

Aamir returned the greeting. "It's been far too long, my friend."

Declan tilted his head toward Shiri. "This is my partner, Shiri Liora."

Aamir nodded in Shiri's direction. "What can I do for you?"

"You can tell us where we can find an antiquities shop owned by Miraj Barak Qudir."

Aamir shook his head. "Oh, my friend, when you gave me that name on the phone, I did some checking. You do not want to get involved with that man. He is dangerous, very dangerous. I do not think even you are a match for him."

"I appreciate your concern, but this Miraj will never know we have been there. I just need the address for his shop."

Aamir shrugged. "It's your risk, but don't say I didn't warn you. You have the price?"

Declan took a small black bag out of his pocket and poured fifteen diamonds into Aamir's hand. Aamir examined them under the light from his flashlight. "Excellent. They are your usual high quality. Here is the address you want." Aamir handed Declan a piece of paper.

As soon as Declan put it in his pocket, he heard a sharp crack followed by a piece of the tower stone flying past his ear. All three hit the ground and turned off their flashlights. By the dim light of the moon, Declan made out four shadows creeping across the courtyard about seventy yards ahead.

A sound in Arabic echoed off the walls of the Citadel. "I told you not to fire until we were closer."

Declan whispered to the other two as he pulled out his Beretta M9. "They are spread out enough that all our escape routes are blocked, and there's no cover here. Aamir, are you armed?"

Before Aamir could answer, Shiri stood and pulled the door to the South Tower open. She whispered, "Stay down and get in here."

Declan and Aamir crouched down and entered the tower. Shiri stepped in and closed the heavy wooden door and pushed the metal latch shut. Almost immediately they heard gunfire and bullets striking the wood and stone of the Tower.

They turned on their flashlights. Aamir scanned the room.

"Okay, we are safe for the moment, but we're also trapped. That door is the only way out, and sooner or later those guys will break it down."

Shiri pointed to the steps on the right leading down. "We are going to the basement. There is a secret passageway leading out of the Citadel."

Aamir shook his head. "That's a myth. There is no passageway."

Declan tapped Aamir on the shoulder. "If Shiri says there's a passageway, there is a passageway. Now get going." There was a loud *crack* and the door moved. "That will not hold long."

Aamir was the first one down followed by Declan. Shiri held back until he and Amir were down the first flight of steps.

Shiri spoke just above a whisper. "I'm going to leave them a little surprise."

They were down the second flight of steps when they all heard a grenade go off behind them. They continued running farther down into the depths below the South Tower as Declan turned to Shiri. "I hope that was you."

Shiri nodded. "It was. I threw in an M8 smoke grenade. When they break in, which will be soon, I want the room full of smoke. My guess is they'll assume we went up, thinking nothing is down here, but I want to keep them confused for as long as possible."

At the end of the third flight they were in the basement. It was rectangular shaped about twenty by thirty feet and full of debris in the form of bricks, stone, and wood as well as the dust of centuries. Declan looked around. "Where is the entrance to this secret passageway?"

Shiri walked around the room. "When I was last here—to hide from a group of angry Muslims—all this rubble wasn't in the room." She stopped at the wall underneath the stairway. Stone and rocks had built up in front of it. "Help me move this stuff."

While moving the debris, Aamir asked Declan, "Who is she? What did she mean by it was clean when she was last here? This place looks like it hasn't been used for centuries."

286 | Richard Spillman

Declan lifted what was easily a fifty-pound piece of stone and moved it to the other side. "Trust her. She knows what she's doing."

"You didn't answer my questions." Aamir slid some wood across the floor.

Suddenly a coughing sound came from above, followed by footsteps. Declan paused. "We've got to get this done soon."

When the wall area was clear, Shiri ran her hands along it.

Declan followed Shiri with the light from his flashlight. "I can't see any seams."

Shiri nodded. "There never were any. Ancient craftsmanship." She stopped in the middle and pushed. A part of the wall started to move. It complained with a squeak. As she continued to push, it started to move easily and quieted down.

When it was wide open, Declan shone a light in. The floor seemed to move as cockroaches scattered, making clicking noises as if thousands of little pins were striking the stone floor. He raised his hand to brush away a cobweb and stepped in. Aamir followed. Shiri was last. She turned around and pushed the door closed, then found a piece of wood to jam into the opening mechanism.

When it was safely closed, she stepped ahead of the two men. "Follow me, boys."

"Where does this come out?" Aamir waved toward the dark area ahead.

Shiri shrugged. "I'm not sure anymore, but it's got to be better than the alternative."

They walked in the tunnel for about twenty minutes, waving aside the cobwebs that hung from the ceiling and being careful to avoid the fragments of the wall that littered the floor. Occasionally they heard a *crunch* when someone stepped on something that moments earlier had been alive.

They eventually came to a solid wall, a dead end. Shiri ran her light around and illuminated the same opening mechanism as the other end had. A rope hung just above where a doorknob might be found. It was long enough so two men could pull on it at once. "All right, guys. It's your turn to pull this open."

Declan looked at it. "Shiri, we don't know what's on the other side. Why don't you stand against the wall ready to throw in your M84 stun grenade if necessary?"

Shiri took position while the Declan and Aamir pulled. The door moved slightly. They felt something roll against it. They pulled again, harder this time, and the door sprung open. They jumped back as more rubble fell into the tunnel.

Aamir peeked in. It was dark. Not tunnel dark but nighttime dark. "I think this opens into the old Palace of Justice."

The three of them scrambled over the remains of part of the palace into the night air. They stopped to breathe in freedom. Declan turned to Shiri. "Thanks, Shiri." He patted Aamir on the back. "I guess this is where we part company, old friend."

Aamir nodded and took off to the south. Declan pointed north. "Our Jeep should be up there somewhere."

He was right. It was close and they jumped in it. Declan looked up at the night sky. "Tomorrow we visit Miraj Barak Qudir's shop."

Suhail and his three men were coughing. They came out of the South Tower where they could breathe. White smoke still lingered in the Tower.

Suhail shook his head. "Where did they go?"

One of his friends spoke up. "I don't know. We searched the tower from top to bottom, and there's no sign of them. Maybe they only wanted us to think they had gone in and slipped around us in the dark."

Suhail shrugged. "I'm going to find that white demon and he will experience a slow death."

As they walked back to their cars, Suhail grumbled, "If they weren't in there, then who locked the door and set off the grenade? Miraj needs to know about this."

Chapter Forty-Three

THE PRESCRIPTION FOR LIFE IS QUITE SIMPLE. Love God and love those around you. What's so difficult about that? How did we come to a place where we live as if there is no God to love and it's best to hate anyone who is different? We have to be the voice of life in this wilderness. —Awakened Incident Manual, Volume 2, Page 310

October 2, 8:12 a.m., Pyongyang

"I understand that Kim Il-lung is dead, is that correct?" Sok Kang Ju asked.

Park Pong Ju answered with a head bow. "Yes, Great Leader, and I might add it was a very painful death."

"Excellent. Then nothing stands between me and absolute power. That weasel of a Natural, Renaud, will be dead in only ten days." Kang Ju broke out with a satisfied smile. *I'm only days away from my final victory.* "South Korea will be blamed. And after a couple of weeks of 'investigation,' our attack with our new weapon on South Korea will be launched. Within months our army can march in unopposed, and Korea will be united under my rule. From there we can move forward and rid this world of the plague of humankind."

"Great Leader, what you describe is the dream of every UV. I'm honored that you have chosen me to fire the first shot."

Kang Ju looked at the clock on his office wall. "It's 8:15. Get the South Korean army uniform and your rifle. Be at the building in the northeast corner of the square at precisely 10:30 on the tenth. I have called all the building guards to a meeting at 10:15 so the building will be unguarded until 11:00. Once in the building, put on the South Korean uniform and make your way to the roof. I will instruct the guards not to return there as it will be patrolled by a helicopter. Take your position. At 1:30, I will move close to

Renaud. That is when you'll take the shot. I want him to die in my arms. I want to watch the life drain from his eyes. Are you clear on everything?"

"My general, it will be done as you have ordered."

"It's somewhat ironic that WWI, the Great War, began over the assassination of Archduke Ferdinand, and it led to a lot of heartwarming suffering. Now I will start the world's final war by the assassination of Renaud Christian Yount."

Kang Ju smiled and looked down at his hands. "It appears that I have determined the ultimate destiny of Naturals. It will be entertaining. Very entertaining." And God would have to sit back and watch them prove Him wrong.

His eyes twinkled as he thought of something amusing. "I still remember the day God created man. I had no trouble with it until He started fawning over them like they were somehow better than us. Then I found out that He had planted His image in them—in mankind! Outrageous! Now I will be the one that will make Him sorry."

Day 21, October 2, 8:51 a.m., Aleppo

As Declan drove through the city to find Miraj Barak Qudir's antiquities shop and stake it out, he used the opportunity to look at Shiri. *Maybe this God-thing isn't so bad after all.*

He was surprised to find it less than thirty minutes from their hotel in a district of Aleppo that had escaped much of the conflict.

Shiri's eyes widened as they drove through the area. "This doesn't look like a war zone at all."

Declan pointed up ahead. "There's part of the reason why. There's a school up there so the US and other forces would avoid bombing this area."

He drove one block past the school and pointed again. "And there's the other reason. Our mysterious antiquities shop is not only close to the school, but if, as we suspect, it's the site of major

ISIS activity, then ISIS would keep the area protected on the ground."

They came up to the shop. Shiri nodded at it. "Should we go in and check it out like the other shops?"

Declan shook his head. "No, as much as I would like to get a peek inside, after last night we might be made."

Shiri scanned up ahead. "That building over there across the street. It has a flat roof. If we could get up there, we could watch the shop without exposure."

Declan looked in the direction she was pointing. "You're right. Why don't you get out here and find your way up while I park the Jeep a few blocks ahead?"

Shiri grabbed her duffel bag and left the Jeep. When she got in the building, she saw the stairs at the back. Before long she was on the rooftop. Ten minutes later Declan joined her. She broke out the binoculars and they settled down to watch the shop.

The sun beat down on the tar that covered the roof. Declan took the first watch, allowing Shiri to sit in the shade by the small structure jutting up from the roof enclosing the door leading back down. Declan wiped the sweat off his forehead as he surveyed the area. The road below was dusty and the soft breeze, which was their saving grace on that roof, blew the dust around in gentle swirls.

Shortly after they got situated, Declan saw a grandfatherly man with a thick silvery beard and leading a bulldog, unlock the shop door and walk in. Declan turned to glance back at Shiri. "That's probably Miraj Barak Qudir."

She nodded and continued fanning herself.

Around noon Declan motioned to Shiri. She moved back out in the sun next to Declan. It was her turn to take the watch. Declan cleared his throat, dry from sitting so long in the desert sun. "Well, I'll be." He pointed down to the shop door. "You'll never guess who I saw enter the shop."

Shiri glanced over the roof edge. "That man with the beard who followed us last night?"

Declan dropped his shoulders. "How did you know?"

"He's the only person in Aleppo who you've seen and would be concerned about. Also, it was a good guess."

Fifteen minutes later two other men entered the shop. One of them stopped at the door, turned, and scanned the street. His gaze froze at the building that was Declan and Shiri's observation post as if he sensed he was being watched. Declan ducked for a few seconds, then peered back at the door. No one was there.

Miraj sat at his desk, studying the papers in front of him and petting Adaral standing off to his right. He looked up when the bell over the door clanged. It was a tall man with long black braids.

"Suhail." Miraj waved him in.

Suhail entered Miraj's office, stood in front of the desk, and cleared his throat. Miraj waved him toward a chair. Suhail sat down and waited.

After shuffling a few papers around, Miraj looked up and stared at Suhail for a moment. *Suhail is a nothing but a troubled hot head. I wonder what he did now?*

Miraj asked, "What are you doing here? What do you want?"

"There's a resourceful American with a Middle Eastern woman in town."

Miraj nodded. *I suppose he has a body he wants me to dispose of.* Suhail had a burning hated of Americans fueled by an all-consuming need for revenge. He blamed them for the bombing raid last year that killed his wife and two-year-old daughter. "So? We still get the occasional American here in spite of the war."

Suhail shook his head. "No. This one's different—arrogant—capable. Snooping around. I tried to kill him last night. I had him cornered in the South Tower of the Citadel, and he disappeared on me. Just like that, he was gone. And weren't you looking for a CIA agent and a woman in Tel Aviv?"

"Jalal has that under control. He's following them right now.

If they came here, he would have told me."

"Where is Jalal now?"

Miraj rubbed his chin. "I don't know. He hasn't reported in for...four days. But that's not unusual. I'll reach out to him and see if he knows anything."

"And what shall I do about the American?"

Miraj waved at Suhail dismissively. "Do what you want. Don't bother me about it. Now leave. I have work to do." Suhail started to leave but Miraj stopped him. "And don't leave by the front door. I don't want others to connect me to you."

Suhail bowed his head and left.

Nothing happened over the next three hours of the stakeout. A few minutes after Shiri took the next watch, she signaled Declan, who was resting. "Didn't you say you saw that man from last night enter the shop?"

"Yes." He checked his watch. "About three hours or so ago."

"Did you ever see him leave?"

"No, did you?"

"No, but I just saw him enter again."

Declan reached out for the binoculars. "Let me see."

"Okay, but he's already gone in." Shiri handed them to Declan.

He surveyed the building. "There must be another exit somewhere."

"Remember last night when you downloaded the plans for that building? There was no other exit. This front door is the only way in or out."

"There has to be one."

Six quiet, hot, dry hours later as the sun was going down, Shiri handed the binoculars to Declan. "Does that seem like the same man you saw open the shop this morning?"

Declan took a look as the man locked the door and turned to leave with his dog. "That's him. My guess is that's Miraj Barak

Qudir."

The lights in the shop were out and apparently it was empty, but Shiri and Declan waited another three hours to make sure.

Declan checked his watch. "Midnight. It's dark enough and we've waited long enough. Time to move."

Shiri smiled. "I'm ready."

They gathered up everything and made their way downstairs and across the street to the shop. As expected, they found the front door locked. They saw Miraj lock it, but they had to try anyway.

"I've got this." She pulled out a small tool set and within a minute or so the lock clicked open. She put her hand on the doorknob. "Let's hope there is no alarm."

There was an alarm.

Declan rushed in and up to the blinking panel on the wall. "Okay, we have ninety seconds before it goes off. You keep time." He snapped the panel off and examined the wires in the wall. "Good. I'm very familiar with this one. Ordinarily I'd just cut these wires…"

"Sixty seconds left."

"But that would announce our presence in the morning. I'll have to short it out."

"Forty-five seconds left."

Declan studied the back, then pulled a wire with alligator clips on each end out of his pocket.

"Fifteen seconds."

Declan clipped the wire on the back panel and the low-level beeping stopped. "There. It's reset." He removed the wire he'd attached and replaced the panel cover. "Now lock the door. I don't want the shop to appear different in case someone walks by."

Shiri locked the door and took in a deep breath. She pulled night-vision goggles out of her duffel bag. They both put them on and scanned the shop. It was quiet. Quiet as a tomb. A tomb already filled with images of gods long forgotten.

They made their way around the shelves and behind the glass

counter to the back room. It was stocked with more artifacts in no particular order. At the far end was a door. They walked over and opened it to what clearly was Miraj's office.

More artifacts littered the room. The desk across from them was covered with papers. To its right was a dirty gray file cabinet. The bottom drawer had a combination lock built into it.

Shiri pointed down to the dial. "I was hoping if there was a lock, it would be something I could pick."

Declan nodded. "I have an old CIA trick." He pulled out his cell phone. "First, I need a picture of the top of the cabinet."

Shiri took the picture. "Why?"

"You'll see. Now we have to clear everything off the top."

They took the various small artifacts and the few papers off the cabinet.

"Now help me move it around so we have access to the back."

It squeaked a little as they started to move it. Declan held up his hand. "We have to do this slowly."

They got it around. Shiri asked, "Now what?"

Declan pulled a small battery-powered drill out of the duffel. "Now we drill three holes."

"Won't that announce our presence?"

"How many times do you look behind a file cabinet? It will be a long time before anyone runs across this little modification, and they will probably think it was always that way."

The process took only a few minutes. Declan returned the drill to the duffel bag and pulled out a thin fiber-optic cable and a long, stiff wire with a hook on the end. "I'll put the cable in one hole to give me light. The wire goes in the other hole. And I'll look through the third hole."

"What will that accomplish?"

"The latch on these things is easy to move, so I'll move it down a bit and we'll be in."

He put the tube and the wire in, took off his night-vision goggles, and placed his right eye up against the third hole. He twisted the wire several times. It made a faint clicking sound. On the fourth try, there was a louder click and the file door moved forward a fraction. "Got it."

As Declan stood, they both heard the front door open.

Chapter Forty-Four

PERHAPS WHEN BAD THINGS HAPPEN IN your life and you begin to question the love of God, it is important to remember that real love is not measured by the number of gifts you shower onto someone rather it is measured by the sacrifices you make on behalf of that someone. –Awakened Incident Manual, Volume 2, Page 611

October 3, 7:02 a.m., Pyongyang

L did not sleep much during the night. The team had spent the last couple of days making their way to the Juche Tower at different times through different routes to gauge how long it should take. They'd visited the top of the tower to assess wind conditions and to allow Ariella time to get used to the distance and time for all of them to observe the guards' schedules. It was going smoothly, but still something nagged at him.

This morning they were going to repeat the process. He shrugged. Maybe he'd figure it out today.

The team gathered outside the hotel, and L laid out another variation of the route to test. "In case traffic is crazy, we'll take a cab partway there and walk the rest. I want to know the best path to take and the time involved."

They'd ridden a little over halfway to the Tower when L asked Joon to tell the taxi driver to pull over. They got out and started walking. A few clouds floated overhead, carried on a light breeze, but the sky was basically blue. The temperature was pleasant, and the air was sweet, mainly due to the early morning rain.

About fifteen minutes into the walk, Agam lined up next to L. "Did you notice the couple that pulled up about three car lengths behind us?"

"Yes, I did."

"They seem to be following us."

L nodded. "This is day three of our reconnaissance, and every day I've felt uneasy, like we were being followed, but it's never the same people twice."

"We can't stop them. It's their country. But I'll watch them today."

"Thanks." It'd been so easy up until now. Maybe too easy. Who was watching them? What did they know? Would they stop them before they could finish their mission?

October 3, 12:28 a.m., Aleppo

The alarm went off again. Shiri signed to Declan to drop, but he already had. They listened, prepared to spring up at any immediate threat.

Two men entered Miraj's shop. She peeked up and whispered to Declan, "One of them was the leader during our little incident last night."

The one Shiri identified pointed to the alarm illuminated in the sparse moonlight through the shop's window. "Ghaith, punch in the code to turn that racket off."

The other man stood in front of it for a moment. "Ah, what's the code again?"

The leader clenched his jaw. "Hit 3-3-5-7-0-1, then hit Off." The alarm stopped its noise. "Let's get downstairs. We're already late."

Ghaith walked behind the glass counter to join the leader. "Why did Miraj get us out this late at night?"

"Something about Jalal disappearing. Now open the door."

Ghaith bent down, fiddled with something on the floor, then pulled up a trapdoor that led to a long stairway down. "Okay, it's open." His attention focused on the hallway to Miraj's office. "Ah...Suhail? His office door is open."

He shrugged. "Sometimes he leaves it open. Let's get going."

The two disappeared down the stairs. The trapdoor closed behind them.

Shiri took a deep breath and slowly exhaled. She signaled to Declan to remain quiet for a moment longer in case someone else came in or the trapdoor opened again. He nodded.

After what seemed an eternity, Declan whispered, "I think it's okay to get back to work."

Shiri nodded and whispered back, "We now know what happened to those men who entered but never left the shop. There must be an exit out of the basement."

Declan looked down at the file cabinet. He smiled. "I almost forgot. We're in."

Shiri squatted and rummaged through the files. "Here it is: Operation Blood Red. Do you have something I can put in here to mark the file's location?"

Declan glanced around and picked up a paper from the desk. "Use this."

Shiri inserted the paper in the file drawer and handed the file to Declan. "We don't have time to read it. Take the pictures and we'll look at it back in the hotel room."

Declan opened the file on the desk. It contained twenty-five numbered pages. He carefully photographed each one, making sure they went back into the file in the same order he pulled them out. He handed it back to Shiri. "Done."

She put the file back, closed the drawer, and turned the combination dial. As carefully as they could, they moved the cabinet back into position. Then they put everything back on top of the file cabinet as it appeared in the picture they had taken earlier.

Declan took a quick look around to make sure they didn't leave anything that might make someone suspicious.

They made their way out of the shop and to the Jeep. Back at the hotel in Declan's room, they reviewed the photos. Shiri pointed to the entry. "There it is. The name of the ship is *Blue Mist. Blow Fist* was *Blue Mist.* We were so close. And it's landing in Tyre, one of the closest ports to the Israeli border."

Declan laughed. "How did I get *Blow Fist* out of *Blue Mist*?" He grabbed Shiri's hand and looked her in the eyes. "We've done it. We've saved the world."

Shiri stared back, lost in his deep-blue eyes. She smiled. "We still have to return and stop this on October 10...partner."

October 3, 2:01 p.m., Damascus

Declan and Shiri arrived in Damascus after another long trip across the Syrian Desert. Things must have quieted down in the ongoing war across Syria since they only had to pass through three uneventful checkpoints.

At the airport, Hayyan met them to retrieve the Jeep and the weapons. He rubbed his neck. "Where have you been?"

Declan shrugged. "In Aleppo, of course. Why?"

Hayyan shook his head. "Bob Hoskins has been trying to get a hold of you for two days. He wants you in Tel Aviv. Now."

"My phone has been off. Besides, he doesn't have any authority over me."

"He does now." Hayyan swallowed. "The Tel Aviv chief was called back to Langley. Bob is the acting chief of the mission."

"All right. I'll call him and see what he wants."

While waiting for their flight to Tel Aviv, Declan tried to reach Bob. His secretary said he was out of the office so Declan left a message. Half an hour later, Declan's phone rang. "Walsh here."

"I've been trying to reach you for days. Why haven't you returned my calls?"

Declan grimaced. "I was on a mission in Syria, Bob. I went dark."

"Syria? What kind of mission? I'm the mission chief now, and I need to know where you are and what you're up to at all times. I want you in my office tomorrow morning. No excuses. Am I clear?"

"Clear, Bob. I'll be there. In fact, I'm waiting for a plane right now."

Bob hung up. Declan turned to Shiri. "Looks like I'm in the hot seat."

"What's going on?"

"You remember Bob Hoskins. You met him at the party at the Chinese embassy."

"Yes. You had some kind of problem with him."

"Sure did. Now he's the acting CIA mission chief, and he wants to see me first thing tomorrow morning. He's always hated the fact that I was allowed and even encouraged to go off on my own. I'm sure he wants to reel me in, which puts our work in jeopardy."

Shiri smiled. "I got this. I'll call L's assistant. Matthew has contacts at the highest levels of government. I'll get you officially assigned to us for the time being."

"That may be difficult. The CIA gives a lot of weight to the mission chiefs."

Shiri's grin widened. "Not a problem. I guess you can say we are good at miracles."

October 5, 1:42 p.m., Tel Aviv

"You officially work for me now." Shiri smiled as they sat down for lunch at one of Declan's favorite restaurants in Tel Aviv.

"I'm impressed. SOAR must have connections at the highest levels."

"We do, but remember, we are the good guys."

Declan fiddled with the position of the silverware. "You know…the whole age and already-dying things aside, you're the most extraordinary partner I've ever worked with."

Shiri laughed. "That's a lot to put aside, but I understand what you're saying. And I've worked with a lot of partners over the years, but you are by far the most talented."

Declan shrugged. "Thanks. I guess what I'm getting at is, I hope we can work together again after this is done."

She nodded. "I feel the same way, and I'm sure SOAR can use your skills."

"And…this whole Jesus thing. I've thought about it. After all I've seen, how could I not believe? Yesterday I even picked up a Bible for the first time since I was a child." He moved his silverware again. "Of course, there are still things I don't understand…"

Shiri's eyes watered. She reached across the table and took Declan's hand. "I know, and I'm here anytime to answer questions, but I won't push you where you don't want to go."

He nodded and took a deep breath. "We need to start planning how we'll stop that shipment without releasing the virus. We only have five days before it arrives."

Shiri's face softened. "To start with, we can expect at least one UD traveling with the virus and only a few Naturals involved in delivering it because they don't want to call attention to themselves. I can handle the UDs, but I'll need you to deal with the Naturals."

"I can bring a couple of others into this operation to make sure we can handle any situation. What we need now is to scope out the area where it will be unloaded."

"Then it's off to Lebanon." Shiri stood. "Could I have a hug before we head out?"

Declan's face turned a little red. "Sure."

Chapter Forty-Five

THE FULLNESS OF FAITH REACHES FURTHER than the desires of the doubtful. For one can move mountains while the other languishes in the land. –Awakened Incident Manual, Volume 2, Page 283

October 6, 10:36 a.m., Pyongyang

Ariella and Joon left to retrieve the sniper rifle that had been smuggled in through other channels.

Joon was quiet most of the way until they got out of the taxi. Ariella tapped him on the shoulder. "Penny for your thoughts?"

Joon's eyebrows lowered and his nose wrinkled. "What?"

Ariella laughed. "That's a saying in America. I picked it up from L. It means will you share what is making you so quiet."

"Oh, for a moment I wondered... I don't know what I wondered." He shrugged. "I was looking at the people we passed and realizing they are locked up in a prison of the mind far worse than the camp I was in. A lie confines you in a box and clouds your reason. The truth sets you free to see things as they really are."

"That's profound. Jesus said the same thing. 'The truth will set you free.'"

They walked another two blocks toward the post office on Moranbong Street. Ariella saw it first and pointed up ahead. "There it is. L said we'd make contact in the main lobby. An Awakened will be there with an oversized brown briefcase."

"And what if there is more than one person with a brown briefcase?"

Ariella smiled. "He will be the only Awakened. Just like you can always recognize a UD, you can always recognize an Awakened. You'll get used to this soon."

Joon rubbed his forehead. "I don't know. This is all so new."

They entered the post office lobby. It was small and drab. The walls were a light gray, and the floor consisted of dirty tiles that might have been white at one time. A few wooden chairs were scattered about. And, of course, the large portrait of Sok Kung Ju was front and center on the wall.

To their left about nine meters away, a small man, wearing a thin black coat, was hunched over with an oversized brown briefcase at his feet. Ariella pointed in his direction. "Does he stand out to you?"

Joon looked over. "Yes. He somehow looks familiar though I've never seen him before."

Ariella nodded. "You see the heaven in him. It's exactly like the heaven in you."

The man saw them. He walked away to a bench and sat at the end, putting the briefcase against the wall beside him. After a few moments he stood and walked away, leaving the briefcase.

Ariella tapped Joon's shoulder. "It's our turn now. Walk over to the bench, sit where he did, wait a few moments, then come back here with the briefcase."

Joon followed Ariella's instruction, and soon they walked out of the post office and back to the hotel with the sniper rifle in the briefcase.

October 7, 6:11 a.m., Somalia

General Caleb Yaasir rose early that morning to prepare for the biggest pirate assault he had ever attempted. He held nothing back because the prize was worth more than anything he had gone for in his life—a real nuclear weapon. His means to absolute power.

They had arrived about a mile off their target, the *Blue Mist*, right as the sun rose over the blue-green waters of the Gulf of Aden. Conditions were almost perfect for a morning assault. There was a slight breeze. The seas were calm. It was raining, but that shouldn't create any problems. They had attacked ships in far worse conditions.

Standing outside on the upper deck of his Russian-built trawler, Caleb took a deep breath as he drank in the cool salt air. He listened to cries of gulls as they circled overhead. The rain bathed his face as if anointing him for his new status. *It's a good day to become the most powerful warlord in Somalia.*

A small white butterfly fluttered around his face, then settled on the deck to slowly fan its wings. Where did that came from? He ground it into the deck with his right foot.

Now it was time to transform his life. He turned and walked into the bridge, grabbed the mic for the loudspeaker, and turned it up to full volume.

"Attention...attention...Captain of the *Blue Mist*. This is General Caleb Yaasir of the *Black Flag*. You are carrying illegal cargo that belongs to me. Hand over the nuclear weapon and you will be free to go. If you don't, you will be boarded, we will take the weapon, and we will kill every one of you. You have half an hour to decide."

He gave the signal to launch two skiffs, each with four men armed with AK-47s and RPGs, keeping one skiff in reserve for him and his bodyguard once the issue was settled.

He almost hoped they would choose to fight. Then this day would become a day of legends. *Ah...even if they give in, I may kill them all anyway.* It would make for a great story. People would fear him.

Gyeong Kwang woke up to pounding on his cabin door.

"Mr. Gyeong...wake up! We're being attacked. Wake up!"

He leaped out of bed with Yong Ki doing the same. "Okay. I'm coming." He opened the door to find the captain in a state of panic.

"Mr. Gyeong." The captain bowed. "Oh, and Mr. Yong." He bowed again. "We are under attack by pirates. They are demanding a nuclear weapon. Your special cargo isn't a nuclear weapon, is it?"

"Of course not."

"Then why do they want a nuclear weapon from us?"

"Because they're insane or they've mistaken us for another ship."

"They've given us half an hour." The captain checked his watch. "We have twenty-two minutes left to give them the weapon or they will board us and kill us all."

"I'll come up and talk to them on the radio." Kwang slipped into his clothes.

"We don't have radio contact. He's using his ship's loudspeaker."

"Okay, I'll talk to him on our loudspeaker."

The three of them rushed up to the bridge where the captain gave Kwang the microphone. "He says his name is General Caleb Yaasir of the *Black Flag*."

Kwang nodded and took the mic. "General Yaasir of the *Black Flag*, this is Gyeong Kwang of the Democratic People's Republic of Korea. You are mistaken. We do not have a nuclear weapon on board. It would be a violation of a dozen or more international laws to carry one. I repeat, we do not have a nuclear weapon on board."

The response didn't take long. "Mr. Gyeong, very reliable sources tell me that you do, in fact, have a WMD. It belongs to me, and I intend to claim it. You have sixteen minutes left to hand it over peacefully, or you will be boarded, killed, and I will take it anyway. Which will it be?"

Kwang put down the mic. That explained it. Someone in ISIS who didn't have much information talked, and this idiot assumed only nuclear weapons were WMDs. He was not getting their bioweapon. *The fool...* He was in for a surprise if he boarded them.

Kwang turned to the captain. "Since we can't meet their demand, he will board us in fifteen minutes. I want you and the entire crew to go down to the engine room. Lock every door down there and wait until I give the all clear. Under no circumstances are you or anyone else to leave that room without my permission. Is that clear?"

"Yes, sir. But what will you do?"

"Don't worry about me. I can take care of myself. I will negotiate with this idiot in the only language he apparently knows. Now get to it."

While the captain made a general announcement on the ship's intercom, Kwang pulled Mr. Yong aside. "I want you to get an AK-47 and go to our cabin. Lock yourself in and jam the door as best you can. If anyone breaks in, kill them. If there are too many, shoot into our package. No one is getting it today. I'll get you when this is all over. Do you understand?"

"Yes, sir."

"Good. No matter what you hear, do not leave the cabin until I tell you to."

Yong Ki bowed and ran to get the gun.

Within minutes, Kwang was alone on the bridge. He smiled. Looked like he was going to get his wish after all. *I get to kill Naturals on this trip. This is going to be fun.* He left the bridge to prepare for the attack.

Chapter Forty-Six

HOW MUCH FAITH DOES IT TAKE to raise the dead? Only as much as is required to try. –Awakened Incident Manual, Volume 2, Page 83

Armed with a M16 assault rifle, his Ruger P semiautomatic pistol, and KA-BAR fixed blade, Kwang returned to the bridge deck. He smiled as the two skiffs in the water threw grappling hooks up to the midship railing followed by two long, thin metal ladders. He could smell death and it was sweet.

He allowed the eight pirates to reach the deck. They were all armed, seven with AK-47s and one, with hair so thick on his face you could only see his eyes, was carrying an RPG. *I'll call him Gorilla Face.* He had to be the first to die because the RPG could do some significant damage to the ship. Kwang couldn't allow that.

Gorilla Face was standing in the open looking around, most likely for a target. Kwang took aim and tapped him once in the temple. He crumpled to the ground, dropping the RPG. The other seven looked up to the bridge. Six of them sprayed the area with gunfire while the other reached down for the RPG lying in a small puddle from the light rain. Critical mistake. Kwang tapped him twice, once in the left shoulder, causing him to pull back from the RPG, and once in the head to finish him off.

The remaining six scattered among the containers, which meant Kwang would have to go down and hunt them. That was fine with him. It made this all the more fun. It had been a long time, too long, since he'd hunted Naturals.

He left the bridge. Halfway down to the main deck, he saw one of the pirates climbing up the center crane. He shot out his legs and the man fell to the deck. That left five.

When Kwang got down to the main deck, his first task was to get rid of the RPG. When he reached the two bodies, he pushed Gorilla Face aside, grabbed the RPG, and threw it overboard. He turned to find two pirates standing in front of him, pointing their AK-47s directly at him.

They smiled as Kwang put down his M16 and slowly reached for his knife. Once it was in his hand, the man on his right said something, then fired two shots in Kwang's chest, pushing him back. Kwang looked down as his wounds healed immediately.

Kwang looked back up at the pirates with a grin, rain dripping down his forehead. "That hurt. And that's going to cost you."

The one who fired shivered and raised his eyebrows, his forehead wrinkling. He glanced down at his gun. In that split second, Kwang thrust his knife into the man's heart and swung him around so the body was between him and the other pirate. That pirate panicked and fired in full auto mode, hitting his already-dead friend more than a dozen times.

Kwang threw the limp and tattered body at the pirate. It knocked him to the ground. It only took one shot to finish him. Now there were three.

Out of the corner of his eye, Kwang caught sight of one of those three running toward the boats. When he was only nine meters away from Kwang, he threw his knife. It imbedded in the fleeing pirate's neck. He crumpled to the deck, his hand grabbing at his throat only half a meter from the ladder down to the boat.

Kwang smiled. Now there were two. For his plan to work, he only needed one alive.

A nearby door clanged shut. The man wouldn't be safe inside. That meant one was still on deck, hiding among the containers. Kwang hunted the one outside first.

This was a small cargo ship. It had fifty-three containers laid out on the deck in a single layer spaced one meter apart. He climbed the nearest container to get a good view of this new hunting ground. It was difficult to run between them without hitting the sides, especially when the ship rocked from the motion of the sea. The rain had also picked up, making the deck slippery.

Kwang stood on top, scanning the field and listening for the sound of a rifle hitting the corrugated steel wall of a container. All was quiet except for the sound of rain pounding down on the metal containers.

Kwang yelled, "You're going to die just like your friends."

The wind had started to pick up. A storm was approaching. The ship rolled as a wave hit it. Then Kwang heard it. The clang of metal against metal. It was coming from his right two containers over. With the agility of a mountain goat, he leaped across the gap to the next container, paused, then leaped again toward the source of the sound.

Pistol ready, he glanced over the side. Nothing. He stood and listened again. Another sound, this time straight ahead. He leaped across to the next container and ran to the end. He steadied himself as the ship rolled again. He detected the sound of a body slipping on the deck. When he glanced over the side of the container through the sheets of falling rain, he saw a blurry figure lying on his back, an AK-47 pointed up.

Kwang was immediately hit in the shoulder. The force of the shot pushed him sideways. Another roll of the ship spun him over the edge and down to the deck not far from the pirate. Kwang landed with a *thud*. The sound of the rain echoed down this little one-meter-wide metal canyon like Thor pounding his hammer on raw steel.

The pirate smiled and struggled to stand, but he slipped and dropped his AK-47. As he floundered for his rifle in the growing stream of rainwater, Kwang stood and laughed. He walked over and grabbed the terrified pirate by the throat, then raised him in the air as if offering him to his god. He slowly strangled the life out of him and dropped the body to the deck. Now there was one.

Kwang ran back to the door that the remaining pirate had opened. There were a lot of hiding places, and a search could take time. Time Kwang did not have. He had to find this man quickly if his scheme was going to work.

He opened the door, and to his relief, wet footprints led up the nearby stairs. *Good. His going up will make this easier.* Kwang followed the footprints. They turned to the left, then after only a few steps disappeared. He looked down the passageway and smiled. This passage ended at the galley.

Kwang crept down to the galley door, listening for any sound of movement. "Come out and I'll show you mercy."

He put his ear to the door. Quiet. He stood for a moment to prepare, then shoved open the door. He was immediately shot in the chest. Kwang fell backward into the doorway.

Good thing I'm already dead or I'd be dead now.

He stayed down as the pirate inched his way to his body. When he got close, Kwang could see a smile form on the pirate's face. When the pirate bent over to move his body out of the doorway, Kwang struck. He grabbed the pirate's throat and threw him to the side.

Kwang stood and grinned at the pirate. "You missed."

The pirate's face sank. He trembled all over. Kwang helped the pirate up, then kicked him in his left knee, breaking it. The pirate let out a howl.

Kwang pulled out his pistol. "If you want to live, you are going up to the bridge with me and call your general. You will tell him that all but one of the crew is dead. The one left alive will lead only the general to the weapon. We will be waiting on the bridge. Do you understand?"

Through clenched teeth, the pirate said, "No, you'll have to kill me."

"That can be arranged, but I assure you it will be quite painful." He kicked the man in his injured leg.

The man cried out. "Okay...okay."

As soon as the general was notified, Kwang disposed of the pirate and prepared for the General Yaasir's visit by dumping all the remaining bodies overboard. Kwang returned to the bridge to await the general's arrival.

That was fun. I wish they'd sent more.

In less than a half hour, the general and his bodyguard arrived. As instructed, they headed for the bridge, only to find Kwang sitting alone in the captain's chair.

The bodyguard immediately pulled his Glock 19 and pointed it at Kwang.

"Put that away. It won't do you any good." Kwang smiled.

The general held his hand out in front of the bodyguard. "Where are my men?"

"Well, General, I'm afraid they are all dead."

The general shrugged. "Too bad, but there are more where they came from. Of course, I still expect you to hand over the nuclear weapon or"—he tilted his head to his bodyguard—"he'll shoot you and I'll find it myself."

"I'm afraid I can't do that."

The general shrugged again. "Suit yourself." He stepped away from the bodyguard. "Kill him."

The bodyguard smiled and fired two shots into Kwang center mass, pushing him into his chair for a moment.

Kwang stood. "Those 9mm bullets hurt a lot." He drew his Ruger P. "But I bet this .45 caliber round will hurt you even more." He tapped the bodyguard twice in the chest. The bodyguard fell to the ground, his face frozen in a grimace.

General Yaasir stared at his now-dead bodyguard and then up at Kwang. He shook as he started backing up. "Who are you? What are you? What do you want?"

"First, you idiot—there never was a nuclear device. Oh sure, we have a WMD on board, but it's a bioweapon. If you had taken it, you would have killed yourself and most of Somalia. Don't get me wrong, I wouldn't mind that, but you would also have interfered with our plans for the Middle East, and that I couldn't allow."

"What'll happen to me?" The general tensed.

"Good question. I've thought about that. I should let you live and continue to terrorize the seas. After all, you are the kind of person that would embarrass God to say you were created in His image. But then I had second thoughts. You would also make a great candidate for joining us."

"I'd love to join you. What do I have to do?"

"That's just it. First, you have to die." Kwang raised his gun and shot the general between the eyes.

Kwang threw the bodyguard's body over the side where he had disposed of the others. He walked back to the bridge and stood over the general's body. He'd make a great piece of real estate, and it shouldn't take long to bring him back. He was fresh and he was evil.

Kwang knelt and put his right hand over the general's heart and concentrated. Within five minutes, which had to be some kind of record, the general gulped in air. He looked around and sat up slowly. He felt his forehead, then tried, unsuccessfully, to speak.

Kwang put his hand on the general's shoulder. "Welcome back. How do you feel?"

General Yaasir stared Kwang in the eyes with a who-are-you kind of expression. Then recognition gradually emerged. "You...you shot me."

"Yes."

"I was dead?"

"Yes."

"But I'm not anymore?"

"Yes."

"What is going on? How did this happen?"

Kwang wiped his hands. "You'll understand more in a few moments. There is a voice inside you trying to get your attention. If you want to stay alive, listen to it. Do what it says. Eventually it will be like it's not there at all. It will protect you."

The general sat there in a daze for about ten minutes. Then understanding slowly flowed into his eyes. The general stood. "I'm ready." He looked different. A deep darkness pervaded the general's eyes.

"I know. There is a lot to tell you, but for the moment follow my lead and that of the voice inside you. You'll adjust. You'll be okay."

Kwang took the general with him as he gave the all clear to the crew and to Yong Ki. He explained that General Yaasir had switched sides and was now a valuable and trustworthy asset.

Kwang told the captain, "We are behind schedule. We need to start moving and pick up the pace as much as we can."

Kwang put his arm around the general's shoulder. "The rain has stopped, General. Let's go out on deck and enjoy this fresh sea air." This diversion had been an unexpected but welcome break from routine, but October 10 would be far better.

Chapter Forty-Six

IF ONLY WE COULD BE ONE tenth as patient with each other as God is with us, what would the world be like? –Awakened Incident Manual, Volume 2, Page 83

October 9, 3:48 a.m., Seattle

Ricki and Odette met Matthew in the communications room. He was there with Bobby.

Ricki smiled. "So they got you up at this hour to join us?"

Bobby nodded. "Several days ago, Matthew briefed me on everything that's been going on."

Matthew interrupted. "L thought he might be helpful if any messages with a new code came out of North Korea."

"Yes." Bobby nodded. "I asked if I could join in when things all come together." He scanned the room then turned to face Ricki with a smile. "The last time I was in here we saved the world. Looks like we have to do it again."

Ricki shrugged. "I guess we do. I'd swear we were living in a novel, but no one could make this up. Another case where truth is stranger than fiction." Ricki paused. "Oh, I'm sorry, Bobby. This is Odette from Washington DC. Odette this is Bobby. He broke the code that allowed us to identify Abdul B'aith in time."

After a quick exchange of pleasantries, Odette turned to Matthew and raised her brows. "So, Matthew, what's going on?"

"L and Shiri need to coordinate their efforts, but he can't get a signal through to the Middle East from Pyongyang. He can, however, link directly with us via satellite as can Shiri. So we are functioning as the go-between."

They sat down. Ricki looked up at the big screen. It was off. She turned to Matthew. "No visuals?"

"I'm afraid not. All we can get is audio."

Ricki hunched back in her seat and sighed. She was hoping

she could see L.

October 9, 8:52 p.m., Tyre

The *Blue Mist* docked an hour later. Kwang stood in the control room, his eyes on the main entrance to the port. Yong Ki and Caleb Yaasir were beside him. The captain was down on the deck supervising the preparation for unloading that afternoon.

Ki asked, "When are we moving the package?"

Kwang looked over at him. *I think I'll kill him as soon as we release the virus.* "As soon as the truck gets here, but I don't expect it for another six hours. Then we'll take it to the border where it'll be picked up."

Kwang smiled. "Our Glorious Leader wants it passed over while he's speaking at 1:00 p.m. his time. That will be..." He looked at his watch. "That will be 7:00 a.m. our time. So we are still on schedule."

Kwang looked at General Caleb. This one needed to be prepared. Maybe Kwang would let him kill Ki. It would be good practice for him. He put his hand on Ki's shoulder. "Why don't you go back to our room and watch the package. Caleb and I need to talk."

As soon as Ki left, Kwang sat down with Caleb. "I know it's only been a couple of days since your rebirth and it can take several weeks for most new UnVeilers to get used to their situation, but we have something going on here you will definitely want to participate in."

Caleb nodded as he stared off into space. Kwang grabbed him by the shoulders and shook him. "You need to listen to the voice in your head. It will help you."

Caleb glanced down. Suddenly his whole body shivered like he had recently come out of a deep freeze. He looked back up at Kwang. "I'm...I'm...okay." Caleb took a deep breath, paused a moment, then stood. "That feels better. Now what is this project?"

Kwang smiled. "You're going to like this. Tomorrow we will make history."

Shiri and Declan stood on the roof of a small two-story office building right inside the northern port of Tyre. It was a clear moonless night, the stars dotting the sky like flickering fireflies frozen in space.

Shiri put down the night-vision binoculars and turned to Declan. "I've seen very little activity on the *Blue Mist* since it docked two hours ago. Certainly no sign of a UD. Now it's your turn to watch. My eyes get tired easily looking through those things." She gestured to the binoculars. "Even though I recover almost as soon as I stop using them, I find that pale-green background is strange."

Declan picked them up. "It does take a little getting used to. I'll watch the next hour. I'll let you know when anything happens. Or if we make contact with Lazarus."

Shiri nodded. "Most likely a small truck will come to pick up the virus." She glanced at her watch. "In a few hours it will be October 10."

October 10, 11:17 a.m., Pyongyang

A traffic jam in Pyongyang, or anywhere in North Korea, was an unheard-of event unless it involved military vehicles. L thought leaving the hotel at ten o'clock would get them to Juche Tower in plenty of time, especially since the ceremony did not start until one. Yet it was almost eleven thirty, and they were sitting stalled in the taxi.

L tapped Joon on the shoulder, "Ask the driver how far it would be to walk to the Tower from here."

Joon nodded and asked. The driver gave a short three-syllable answer. "He says maybe half an hour, no more than an hour."

"All right, team." L shrugged. "We're walking from here."

The four of them exited the taxi. Ariella held on to her briefcase like it was full of diamonds. They started to walk toward the Tower. As they crossed the bridge to get to the Tower side of the river, Agam looked back and noticed the growing crowd near Kim Il-Sung Square. "Wow, they really turn out for their rallies."

Joon followed his gaze. "You're right, but for many of them it's mandatory or someone will get suspicious."

It took them forty minutes to finally arrive at the grounds of Juche Tower. As they approached it, L saw only a few people at the foot of the steps, and their attention was directed across the river at crowd in the square. Only one soldier guarded the Tower's front door, and his attention was also directed on the square.

L slid a subtle nod toward the Tower. "That guard is a UD."

Agam took a quick peek as the team moved out of sight behind a concrete retaining wall. "You're right. Why only one?"

Ariella said, "As long as there are no Awakens expected, they only need one."

"We're lucky he didn't see us first," Agam shook his head, "or he would have set off an alarm."

"So, what do we do? Clearly we have to dust him, but I can't pull out my rifle and shoot him. We're out in the open. A Natural would be sure to call the police." Ariella was rightly concerned.

L thought for a moment. "I've got an idea. Joon, being in North Korea it's not likely that this UD has ever seen an Awakened. He still would recognize what you are, but it would take him a little longer. Besides, being in uniform, you look like you belong here. If you wear your sunglasses, keep your hat down, you should be able to get close enough to dust him before he notices."

"All right, but I don't have a gun with those special bullets, so how am I supposed to dust him?" Joon grimaced. "Oh, please, don't say I have to bite him. That's disgusting."

Agam laughed. "I agree, but you get used to it." He rocked

back on his heels, his lips curling in a smug grin. "Then again maybe you don't have to do that. I've got an idea. Give me your knife."

Joon pulled his military knife out of his belt and handed it to Agam. Agam took it and slid it across his palm, drawing blood. The wound healed before Agam could pass the knife to Joon. "The knife has my blood on it so it will do the trick. The slightest nick from that knife will dust the UD back to hell."

Joon took the knife and put it into the sheath in his belt. He put on his dark glasses, pulled his hat down, and looked up to the Tower door where the UD stood. He couldn't bring himself to take the first step. *He looks so human.*

Ariella put her hand on his shoulder and whispered, "My first dusting was difficult too. It looks human especially to a newly Awakened, but trust me, it's not. The human part of it is melting away. It comes from the depths of hell, and you're just sending it back."

Joon nodded and took his first step and his second and his third. It seemed to take forever, but in less than a minute he passed by the UD on the way to the door. Maybe it would let them walk in.

When he tried the door it was locked. Joon shrugged. *Guess I should have expected that.* The UD faced Joon. "Sir, the Tower is closed until after the ceremony."

Like a veil had been lifted from his eyes, Joon saw the thing standing in front of him for what it really was. He sucked in a breath. Evil so thick he could taste it. Joon struggled not to show his dismay. "That's okay. I'll wait."

It shrugged and turned to watch what was happening across the river. Joon drew his knife and took two steps toward the guard. It must have sensed his presence because it turned around and froze for a brief second.

Joon raised the knife to cut its neck, but the guard grabbed his wrist with enormous strength. Then it said, in Joon's father's distinctive voice, "You don't want to do this, son."

Joon froze and tears rose in his eyes. It released its grip, stood back, and laughed at him in his mother's voice. Then it snarled at him. "You don't deserve that Carpenter."

In a frenzy Joon swung the knife at its neck. The tip just barely scratched the skin, but it was enough. The UD dissolved into a pile of reddish-brown dust. Joon stood there and stared at the UDs remains. "You're right; I don't deserve Him."

The rest of the team joined him. L collected the dust while Agam picked the lock, then they entered and Agam jammed the door behind them. "That's so no one can come up and surprise us."

During the elevator's ascent, Ariella asked, "Joon, are you okay? It's difficult to dust a UD so soon after waking."

Joon stared off into space for a moment, then looked directly at her. "It knew my parents…"

"What?"

"It used the voices of both my mother and my father. How could it do that?"

L said, "I've heard of strange things like that. Apparently some UDs have special powers. Like the one you dusted, some can imitate voices from your past. Some know your deepest secrets. Some know your greatest fears. It happens but it's rare, and I have no explanation for it. That was not your mother or your father. It was nothing more than a cheap lie. UDs are expert liars."

Chapter Forty-Eight

SOMETIMES THINGS HAPPEN IN OUR LIVES that defy explanation. No matter how hard we try, we can't make any sense out of the things God puts in our path. Yet if we remain faithful and patient, God often puts all the pieces together and reveals His purpose. He truly works in mysterious ways. —Awakened Incident Manual, Volume 2, Page 171

October 10, 11:43 a.m., Pyongyang

In a matter of hours, we will either have saved the lives of millions or sealed their fate.

L watched Ariella set up her sniper gear on the observation deck. He closed his eyes and prayed. After a few minutes, he opened his eyes. *Now let's get this done.*

L and Agam circled the viewing deck, looking out at the city. L said, "It's amazing that even in a city like this, one covered by a thick blanket of lies, one ruled by evil, there is still beauty to be found. I think it's a testimony to God's image in man that the beauty of creation may become corrupted but never totally eliminated."

When L got back to where Ariella was setting up, he pulled out the satellite phone and called SOAR headquarters. "Matthew. Can you hear me?"

"Yes. Ricki and Odette are with me as well."

"Hi, guys. Glad you can follow what happens. Matthew, do you have contact with Declan and Shiri?"

"Not yet, but we should soon."

"All right, I'll keep this line open on speaker."

Ariella announced that she was ready. L checked his watch. It was just after noon. The ceremony started in an hour. No telling when Sok Kang Ju would appear, but probably at the beginning. Agam scanned the square with binoculars while they settled in to wait for their opportunity to strike.

L went over the plan with Ariella. "We can't dust him while he's speaking because everyone will be focused on him. It would be difficult to explain why and how he turned to dust, and it would be on film. We want to wait until someone else is speaking and he steps back, then everyone's attention will be on the new speaker. Agreed?"

Ariella nodded. "Yes, but I will get him in my sights while he's speaking, then I'll follow him when he steps down and fire when it's the right moment."

October 10, 12:55 p.m., Pyongyang

The entire Awakened team from Seattle, Tyre, and Pyongyang waited, watching the clock for the ceremony to start, for the fate of the world to be decided. L, Joon, Ariella, and Agam fixed their eyes on the empty podium across the river in Kim Il-Sung Square, waiting for someone to step up and start this event.

In Seattle, Matthew had finally made contact with Shiri. "Everyone needs to have their earbuds and portable mics on, and I'll keep this link active. Shiri, how's it going on your end?"

"We're watching the ship. There's movement on the main deck, but no one has left and no truck has come so we're in waiting mode."

L chimed in. "So are we."

The square itself was jammed. L estimated at least ninety-five-thousand-plus people. He glanced at his watch. It was 1:07 and still the podium was empty.

Agam approached L. "What's going on? That podium should be full by now."

L shook his head. "I don't know what the delay is."

Matthew spoke up. "L, I was checking the news feed. It seems there is a last-minute issue that came up. Both parties of the delegation are talking about it now."

"Thanks, Matthew. Keep us posted if you hear anything else."

Ariella stood and backed away from the edge. She swung her arms in small circles as she breathed in through her nose and out through her mouth. "I need to keep loose."

L checked his watch. *It's late. What is going on?*

Agam saw it first. He pointed down to the podium area. "See that? Someone is walking up to the mic."

Joon looked in Agam's direction. "Yeah, but it's only one person. Shouldn't there be a lot more?"

All four of them watched as a lone man marched up to the microphone. He spoke in Korean, but a large screen above him translated it into French and English. Testing...testing." He tapped the mic. It was working. "I'm sorry for the slight delay. The ceremony will start in about ten minutes."

True to the speaker's words, at 1:26 p.m., the dignitaries filed onto the speaker's platform. The man who had spoken earlier issued a general thank-you for coming and asked everyone to stand for the North Korean national anthem. Even though L and the team were across the river and near the top of the Tower, they had no problem hearing the program because of the powerful speakers they were using.

Once the anthem was finished, they introduced the VIPs, beginning with their target Sok Kang Ju. He was followed by a high-ranking South Korean official, then by the name that shook L to the core—the head of the French delegation, Renaud Christian Yount.

Using his binoculars, L stared at the man who used his cane to stand as the introduction was made. French...Renaud...was this a coincidence? L studied his eyes, his bearing, every detail of his face. This man was not a UD. Through and through he was a Natural.

He'd seen this man before. When he was in Paris. When he was looking for the Renaud that was the UD leader. The day he was along the banks of the Seine near the French Foreign Ministry building, L had seen this very man with his cane. The man that had made him nervous.

How could this man L had been hunting lead the UDs—he was a Natural.

Ariella got into position as Kang Ju walked up to the podium. She had plenty of time to make sure he was solidly in her sights. Now that she had a chest shot, she held her position, ready to follow him as he stepped down.

Kang Ju started his speech. All of them except Joon read the translation off the screen. "In three minutes, at precisely 1:50, I am going to announce the purpose of this historic ceremony, the likes of which has never been seen before. At that same moment, the president of South Korea will make the identical statement to his people, and the president of France will announce this astounding news to the European Union and to the world.

"While we wait for the right time, I want to praise the man most responsible for this moment: Renaud Christian Yount of the French Foreign Ministry. He is a man of great wisdom, he is a man of peace and understanding, and he is the only person in the world who could have brought about this reunification. Together we will count down to the announcement."

Kang Ju turned to look up at the giant count-down screen that now had a 10 showing. He pumped his hand as he spoke each number. "9...8...7...6...5...4...3...2...1."

He quickly turned back to face the crowd as the final number appeared on the screen. "As of this moment, the Korean war is over. The cease-fire that has been in place for all this time is over. One year from today, the two parts of Korea will reunite as a single nation, one people..."

Suddenly Agam grabbed L. "Look over to the top of that building. The one that Ariella saw as a potential sniper's nest."

L swung his attention to the building in the northeast corner of the square. There was a South Korean soldier crouched down with a rifle pointed at the speaker's platform. The man cocked his head in L's direction.

L saw his eyes. "It's a UD!"

Ariella took a look. "What's a South Korean UD doing in a sniper stance?"

"There can be only one reason." L frowned. "He plans to kill a Natural. One of the Naturals on the podium."

"But who?" Joon asked.

"It doesn't make any difference. We have to stop him." L turned to Ariella. "Kang Ju is going to finish and step down any moment now. We have to dust the sniper first, then immediately turn your sights back on Kang Ju."

Ariella looked at the venue for a moment. She took a deep breath and exhaled. "I can try, but if Kang Ju is behind that sniper, then he may see it dusted and immediately take cover. We may lose our chance to dust him. Or, even if he doesn't notice, there's a chance I may not get back to him in time to take another shot. Our mission is on the line."

L nodded. "It's a risk we have to take. You don't want the deaths of more Naturals on your conscience." L shook his head. *Not like what I've gone through after Berlin.*

Declan spoke up. "Shiri and I talked about this a couple of days ago. The greater good would be to ignore the evil that is about to take place, even though you have a strong chance of stopping it now, in order to improve your chance of stopping something even worse down the line. Am I right?"

Both L and Shiri spoke at the same time. "Yes." L finished the thought. "You are right."

Everyone could hear wisdom in Declan's voice. "Then our responsibility is to face and defeat the evil in front of us and trust God to handle the coming evil."

Matthew's voice cut in, "Both Declan and L are right. Besides, this UD may be planning to take out most of the officials on the stand. They represent a number of countries. We could be averting a massacre that could lead to WWIII."

Chapter Forty-Nine

SOMETIMES WE MAY FEEL LIKE A tiny soap bubble adrift in the wind, so fragile that a single touch will cause us to burst, yet that same soap bubble shines with the iridescent colors of the rainbow, is filled by the breath of the creator, and is safe in his hands.
–Awakened Incident Manual, Volume 2, Page 814

October 10, 4:12 a.m., Tyre

Declan and Shiri had found where the *Blue Mist* was to dock. In the hours before it arrived, Declan had raised a small team among his most trusted colleagues to help with the operation. Everyone was in place. Declan and Shiri took the lead, positioned on top of a small hill in the boat yard. From that point, Declan watched the *Blue Mist* while Shiri kept an eye the front gate. He shifted his feet. "I hate the waiting most of all. I feel far more useful in the middle of the action."

Shiri sharpened the focus of her binoculars even more. "You get your wish. A small blue truck with a canvas cover just came through the front gate. Anything at your end?"

"This may be it. Someone came onto the main deck holding a box. Followed by two men."

Shiri maintained surveillance on the truck as it moved into the port and drove up to the side of the *Blue Mist*. "This is it!" She looked at the main deck and froze. "Declan, those two men following the box—they're both UDs. I didn't think there would be two."

"Can you handle both?"

"I can, but as soon as I dust one, the other may try to run or worse, take a Natural hostage."

Declan shrugged. "We have no choice. Too much is at stake. I'll notify the rest of the team to block the port exit. As soon as they load the weapon in the truck, we need to get down there."

Shiri took another look at the UDs. One was definitely Korean. The other looked more African. A representative from ISIS? Then the African turned its head and stared up in her direction. She ducked. "Declan, get down. One of the UDs might have seen me."

October 10, 4:17 a.m., Tyre

Yong Ki stood by the gangplank ready to take the box to the truck. Gyeong Kwang and General Yaasir stood behind him talking.

"You're still new to this." Kwang leaned in so no one else could hear. "Follow my lead and listen to that little voice and you will be fine. Remember, you are more than a general now. You are an UnVeiler, and you are about to witness the single most monumental disaster since the Black Plague was unleashed."

The general smiled and nodded. "It takes a little getting used to." He squinted and stared off in the distance, transfixed.

He continued to stare until Kwang tapped him on the shoulder. "What are you looking at?"

"I don't know. For a moment I thought I saw a flash of sunlight off of glass."

Kwang followed his gaze. "Nothing's there." He glanced at his watch. "Let's get going."

The three of them headed down the gangplank to the truck.

Ariella focused on the target with the sniper rifle. She brought the UD into her crosshairs, paused a moment to sense the movement of air and to relax, then gently squeezed the trigger. There was a slight *whoosh* as the silencer did its job. She kept her eye on the target, ready to double tap if necessary. It wasn't. All four watched as the South Korean sniper dissolved into dust that floated off on the wind, leaving the rifle in its firing position.

Whatever Natural was its target would live for another day.

She turned her focus once again on the main target, but Sok Kang Ju had finished his speech and stepped down to be replaced by Renaud. She scanned to the right through her scope to pick up Kang Ju standing behind a Natural.

She had lost her opportunity.

October 10, 1:32 p.m., Pyongyang

What a great acting job. I was able to get those words out and without choking once. Kang Ju smiled as he passed Renaud. That weak loser had only minutes to live. He'd die, South Korea would be blamed, Kang Ju would be justified in unleashing his weapon, and Korea would be united, only not in the way Renaud thought.

Kang Ju did not even bother to listen to what Renaud had to say. Instead he walked into the crowd of Naturals and engaged in a whispered conversation, waiting to hear the crack of gunfire that would announce the end of the "Great Negotiator."

Kang Ju checked his watch. *What's taking Pak Pong so long?* He glanced up to the building where Pak Pong was stationed, but he was too far into the crowd on the speaker's platform to see anything. He bit his lip. What was going on? When this was over, he would make Pak Pong pay for the delay.

Renaud's speech was almost done. Kang Suk checked his watch again. He smiled, nodded, then excused himself and walked a few steps toward the front. He looked up at the building where Pak Pong's sniper's nest was located. He still couldn't see anything, so he leaned out over the railing. He could barely make out the gun, but only because he knew it was there.

Why…? He looked down at his chest and noticed a tiny red dot. He stared up at the Juche Tower. "Oh…"

"You got him!" L yelled.

Ariella set down the rifle and stood with a big smile. "He's had that coming for a long time."

Agam clapped. "The wicked witch is dead."

Ariella put her hand on his shoulder. "Don't you mean wicked warlock?"

Agam returned her smile. "Whatever."

The four packed up their gear and descended to the Tower lobby. Nobody paid any attention to them when they arrived at the hotel.

Chapter Fifty

GOD DIDN'T SPARE JESUS FROM UNDESERVED suffering. He spared us from deserved death. –Awakened Incident Manual, Volume 2, Page 113

October 10, 8:17 a.m., Tyre

Shiri peeked over the roof's edge. The Natural was carrying the box down to the truck, followed by the two UDs.

Declan turned to Shiri. "What happened?"

"I don't know. It seemed like one of the UDs was staring up at us."

Declan peeked over the edge of the roof. "They appear to be moving down to the truck now. We need to get down and beat them to the gate."

He radioed to the two cars containing his team right outside the gate. "It's the blue truck with the canvas cover. It will be heading for the gate any moment now, then you'll have..." Declan looked at Shiri. She held up both hands all the fingers extended. He nodded. "You'll have ten minutes before it arrives. Set up a roadblock outside the gate. The drivers stay in both cars, ready to pursue if they break through."

Shiri signaled Declan. "The Korean UD just got in the cab of the truck with the driver, who I assume is a Natural. The other UD and the Natural with the box got into the back. They will leave any second now. We have to get down there."

Declan and Shiri got to the port road when the blue truck was ahead of them and about a hundred yards from the main gate. The roadblock had been set. Declan sped up to get closer to the truck before it was stopped by his men. The truck momentarily slowed down, then sped up.

Shiri yelled, "They're going to crash through!"

Declan radioed ahead. "They want to play chicken with the

virus. Let them win. Get your cars out of its way and be ready to follow behind us."

The truck ran through the gate and turned right onto the main road, heading to the Lebanon/Israel border. Declan took the turn twenty yards behind the truck. The other two vehicles followed behind him.

Declan fought to stay in control of the car. "They're heading to the border. It will take less than thirty minutes to get there, but they can't get through. It's closed."

"I know. But before the border, there is an old farm road to the right that leads up a hill..."

"Are you sure? Have you been there?"

Shiri rolled her eyes at Declan. He bit his lower lip and his face reddened. "Oh...yeah. I forgot."

"Anyway, that hill is the highest point this side of the border. It's not far from Nahariya on the Israel side. If they have some way to get it in the air with this northern wind, it could blow over that city. There are almost sixty thousand people who could be infected. It might even reach as far as Haifa."

Declan nodded and radioed back to the other cars. "We don't want to push them into doing something stupid. We have to catch them when they stop to set up their delivery system. Stay back for now."

Shiri stretched out her hands onto the dashboard. "If we don't stop this, Nahariya and maybe even Haifa could be ghost towns in a week."

Matthew had an idea. He contacted SOAR's communications department. "Could we get real-time satellite images of the Lebanon/Israel border near Nahariya on our main screen down here?"

"Let me check."

Matthew stayed on the line for a minute or so when the

communications tech returned. "Yes, sir, it will be up in about five minutes."

"Great. Focus on the road out of Tyre."

He hung up and returned to the connection with Declan and Shiri. "In a few minutes we will have a high-res visual of your area. I'll let you know what we see."

Shiri answered. "Great idea. Look for the highest point on the border to the right of the road."

Odette turned to Ricki with her hand hiding her mouth from Matthew's view. "Finally, we'll have something to look at. I hate talking to a blank screen."

Because Declan slowed down, the blue truck increased the gap to about 150 yards. After fifteen minutes of struggling to remain close but not too close, he informed Matthew. "Can you see us? We are losing contact with the blue truck. Let us know if it turns off. Shiri, do you see it?"

She grabbed her binoculars and shook her head. "No. Matthew can you see what happened?"

"Yes, it turned off on a small dirt road about two hundred yards ahead where the road curves."

Shiri poked Declan's arm. "You heard that? I was right. Once you turn on that road, it's only five or ten minutes to the top." She reached into the glove compartment and pulled out a Browning Hi-Power 9mm pistol. She checked the magazine. It contained thirteen silver bullets each with a drop of her blood.

Just as the road curved, she pointed up ahead. "There it is. They're ahead of us, but it will take some time to set up something to get the virus high enough to catch the wind. We need to be ready to bail as soon as we get there."

Declan nodded. "Matthew, where are they now?"

"They stopped at the top. Two men got out of the back, one out of the passenger side."

"All right, we will be over the crest of the hill in a minute.

We'll have them in sight then." Shiri turned to Declan. "Of course, they will see us as well." She smiled. "It's almost time to make history, partner."

Kwang jumped out of the passenger side of the truck, already yelling as he walked around to the back. "How did they know we would be here?" He balled his hands into fists. "Who leaked information? Someone is going to die a painful death." His face burned and he glared at Ki. "Get those rockets out and set up. Now!"

Ki jumped out and turned around to pick up the partially assembled hobby rockets.

Kwang signaled to the general. "As soon as he sets the rockets up, bring him the virus." He turned at the sound of a car engine racing up the hill. He kicked the back wheel of the truck. "They found us. Now they will die."

He ran up to the driver's side and pulled the driver out. "Get your rifle!" While the driver fumbled around in the back of the cab to get his AK-47, Kwang ran around to the passenger side and pulled out his rifle.

Ki started to fetch his weapon, but Kwang bared his teeth. "No! Get back to those rockets. I'll take care of the intruders."

Kwang paused and took a deep breath as he walked out into the road. This wasn't so bad. It would be like the old days. Just. Like. War. He smiled as he stood in the open between the truck and the cars making their way up the hill.

He raised his AK. *Bring it on.*

Chapter Fifty-One

TIME IS A MEASURE OF THE point something begins and the point it ends. As a result time is no longer relevant in eternity because once you enter eternity everything begins and nothing ends.
–Awakened Incident Manual, Volume 2, Page 392

October 10, 9:12 a.m., Tyre

As soon as the car crested the hill, Shiri saw the Korean UD standing with an AK-47 pointed right at Declan. Shiri pointed to the gunman and Declan nodded.

He made a tight turn so the passenger side of the car faced the threat. Then he slammed on the brakes, bringing the car to a halt. He opened his door and leapt into a combat roll onto the ground, his Glock 19 aimed at the blue truck as he came up.

At the same time, Shiri opened her door and stepped out. She couldn't help but admire the smooth way in which they performed that maneuver. Declan was right. They needed to keep this partnership going. She locked eyes with the Korean UD.

Its grin morphed into an ugly frown as its face paled. *"Awakened."*

Shiri took aim and fired. The Korean UD dissolved into dust as the AK-47 fell to the ground. The other UD standing over the open box of the virus panicked at the sight of the dusting. He jumped into the back of the truck, hiding behind the tailgate.

The truck driver tried to get in the truck, but one of Declan's men tapped him in the head. The Korean, the one who was a Natural, reached down to pull his sidearm when Declan tapped him twice—once in his hand, forcing the gun to fly off and the other in his left knee cap, dropping him.

Shiri ran over and high-fived Declan. "The virus is ours." She grinned. "And thank you for not killing that Natural. We'll take him and see what we can do. We are quite the team."

He nodded. "We sure are. No one is going to break us up after this."

Shiri gave him a big hug. "Why don't you scoop up the virus while I search the area for any stray UDs?"

"Sounds like a plan."

Shiri watched him walk toward the virus. She'd never met a man quite like him. She smiled and headed off to her right. She had taken only a few steps when a chill skittered through her.

She turned to see a hand reach out from the back of the truck and toss out a live grenade. It hit the ground and rolled to within a half a meter of the open virus container.

Time seemed to slow. Shiri glanced over at Declan. He was frozen in place, looking at the grenade about thirteen meters ahead. His muscles tensed and she knew what he was going to do.

She sucked in a deep breath and then yelled, "*STOP!*" The word took forever to fill the hilltop, then seemed to echo in her mind as it died down.

Declan did what she feared most. His eyes focused straight ahead as if his universe contained only the grenade and him. He took one step. Then another. And another. His adrenaline-fueled muscles propelled him to his target.

Shiri started to run. To catch him. To stop him. To save him. She was too late. She stopped.

Declan extended his arms. He leaped like Superman preparing to fly.

His body landed on top of the grenade. His body lifted under the force of the explosion. His vest contained almost all the shrapnel.

"*No!*" Shiri ran up to him. She turned him over onto his back. He was still alive but barely. She cradled his head in her arms. "Declan, why?" Tears streamed down her cheeks.

He coughed up blood. In almost a whisper he said, "If I didn't, the vials would have broken and released the virus. Millions would have died." He coughed up more blood. His hand moved to her cheek. "It will be okay. I gave... my life... for...

others." More blood flowed out of his mouth. He smiled. "Like Jesus did…didn't I?"

Shiri stroked his hair away from his forehead. "Yes, sweetie, just like Jesus did."

Declan closed his eyes. Shiri took him in her arms and rocked. "Just like Jesus."

She stopped and wiped the tears out of her eyes. "You're going to really like Jesus."

She sat silent for a moment listening for the Spirit's direction to pray over Declan that he might be raised. She heard nothing. She took a deep breath and looked up, "Jesus, take care of him."

She stood and walked over to the UD in the truck who had thrown the grenade. She felt an anger begin to rage within her. *I'm going to enjoy biting this one.*

The truck bed was empty. She glanced around. No sign of the UD.

One of Declan's men walked up beside her. She was covered in Declan's blood. Shiri wiped her eyes. "What happened to the one in the truck?"

"As soon as you ran over to Declan, he jumped out and ran the other way. I swear I hit him at least three times before he disappeared down the hill, but it was the darndest thing. It didn't stop him."

Shiri nodded. She would hunt it down later. Now she wanted to stay with Declan and see that he was taken care of while the virus was transported back to SOAR.

3:46 p.m., October 10, Pyongyang

Park Kye walked into Renaud's temporary office. "So, my father's plans to take control failed and yours succeeded."

"Chavvah assured me that would be the outcome. I must admit, she is getting stronger and just in time. But I fear not everything succeeded. I expected to hear from ISIS by now that the virus has been launched, but they are quiet. If I don't hear soon, I'll initiate my backup plan."

"What's next for me?" Park Kye sat down.

"You will do everything in your power to make this reunification work. I will return to France in a couple of days to receive my rewards. Within a year, I will be in a position that will make it safe for you to take control of the reunified Korea and reestablish the kind of state you are used to."

"And what about Lazarus and his team?"

"His usefulness is over. Now all he can do is cause trouble. Frankly, the fewer Awakens in this country, the better. We can't kill them. The best we can do is get them out of the country as quickly as possible. Keep all UVs out of his path, we don't want any encounters that will be difficult to explain. Besides, my time to confront L isn't here yet, but it's coming. I want you to make sure his exit is smooth and uneventful."

October 11, 5:10 p.m., Sinuiju

L and the team had gotten up early to catch the train back to China. Ariella, Joon, and Agam were in fine form after such a successful mission. However, L left plagued with questions. Who was this relatively obscure Renaud who was now on the world's stage? All the evidence suggested that Sok Kang Ju wanted to kill him. Right before the sniper was dusted, Kang Ju looked up where the sniper was supposed to be as if he expected something that hadn't happened, and it was while Renaud was speaking. Why? Could a Natural like Renaud really be the leader of the UDs? By ordering Ariella to dust the sniper, L had saved Renaud's life. Was that a mistake?

As the train stopped in Sinuiju on its way to Dandong, L continued to worry that it had all been too easy. Sok Kang Ju was pure evil and had to be dusted, but L expected more opposition. What about that other UD? Before dusting the sniper, they took his picture and sent it on to Seattle. Maybe counterintelligence could identify him and that would answer at least some of these questions.

While lost in thought, Joon came up to him. "I've reached a decision."

Startled, L jumped a little. "What decision is that?"

"I don't belong in Seattle. I belong here."

"What do you mean?"

"God raised me to help you on this mission. It's done. You don't need me anymore, but the people in the camps throughout North Korea do."

"But as reunification progresses, they will be released."

"Some, perhaps, but my guess is that most will be killed to cover up the crimes of this state. I can save some of them." Determination glowed in Joon's eyes. "Look, this is my home. I really believe God wants me here. And didn't you say you needed more Awakens in North Korea? The reunification only makes that more necessary. Start with me."

L thought about it for a moment. Joon made a good case. "Okay, but is there anything we can do to help right now?"

"If you could create fake orders sending me, or rather Captain Hyeon Chin-Hae to serve at the nearby concentration camp, that would be a good start."

"As soon as I cross the border it will be done. I'll also notify one of the Awakens we have working in North Korea. She'll get in touch with you."

Joon hugged L. "Will you tell the others good-bye for me? I need to exit the train before it leaves the station."

L nodded and watched as Yong Joon walked off into Sinuiju. *He's going to have some stories to tell.*

Chapter Fifty-Two

FOR EVERY MYSTERY THERE IS A miracle and for every miracle there is a mystery. For the mystery of God's love there is the miracle of the resurrection. For the miracle of our salvation there is the mystery of Christ's sacrifice. –Awakened Incident Manual, Volume 2, Page 415

October 12, 12:43 p.m., Pyongyang

Renaud entered Sok Park Kye's new office. "I like what you've done with this place."

Park Kye smiled. "I have a number of ideas, but I had to start by getting rid of that ridiculous picture of my father."

"It's a good start. Now you need to work hard on making this reunification go smoothly. My rise to power depends on it."

"I'm not my father. I'm committed to our ultimate goals. One way or another, we'll rid this planet of the human plague."

"Good. We are close. I talked with the president of France today. He offered me France's rotation as president of the council of the European Union. It starts in a couple of weeks. He says there is some interest among the member nations to make my appointment permanent. There's even talk of a Nobel Peace Prize for me. At any rate, I stopped by to tell you I'm returning to Paris in the morning. My ascension has begun."

October 14, 3:41 p.m., Seattle

L stood outside Ricki's office. He took a deep breath. *She is the best part of coming home. I wonder how she feels about me?*

He knocked on the door frame to the partially open door. Ricki looked up. "L!" She leaped out of her chair and ran to him, giving him a big hug. "It's so good to see you. Odette and I watched the news. We heard how successful you were in North Korea. Have you been following the news about your hunt?"

"No, what are they saying?"

"There are all sorts of strange stories floating around. Some said that with the reunification, his work on earth was done, and he was summoned to heaven. Some, who saw him disappear out of the corner of their eyes, said his speech was insincere, that he didn't want reunification. Much like Lot's wife, he was turned into a pile of dust. Most believed he was tired of politics and retired in secret to someplace in China."

L gave a half smile. "And I guess we are the only ones who know the truth." L looked into her eyes for a moment. "It's great to see you too. I missed you and I was so worried about you."

"I've learned my lesson. I'm not going to do anything foolish. Besides, you're back. I feel safer already."

L nodded. "That's good to hear. Ah, could we sit down? We need to talk."

Ricki twirled a lock of her hair around a finger. "I'm not in trouble, am I?"

"Oh...not at all. I just want to talk about your progress and see if you have any questions, or if there is anything I can do to make your search through my journal easier."

"I'm still stymied I can't find a pattern in anything yet. At times, I think this may be a fruitless effort."

"It's not. I know a pattern is there and you will find it because Jesus said so. I'm only concerned because I think I've done something terribly wrong, and it means we have less time than I hoped for."

"You dusted a vile target you've been after for a long time. How could that be wrong?"

"You're right, but when I was in North Korea, I ran across Renaud Yount."

"Oh, the French negotiator? He did an amazing job. Because of him the world is more peaceful today than it was last week."

"Well...I think he might be the Renaud I went to Paris to

find."

"You mean he's a UD?"

"That's just it, he's a Natural. But because of what he did in North Korea, he is now on the world's stage in a big way. He's moving up and quickly. I have a bad feeling about it. I may have helped him gain power."

"And that's a bad thing? The world needs people like him making decisions rather than the scum you dusted."

L looked down. "I know...but it's his name... Did you know that Renaud means 'counsel'? I can't help but think he chose it to mimic 'Wonderful Counselor,' one of the names of Jesus."

"So it's his name that bothers you?"

"Yes, names have meaning."

Ricki's face glazed over. She turned to stare out the window. "His name..." Suddenly, she cupped her face in her hands. "Yes, that could be it."

"Ricki, what are you talking about?"

She wore a puzzled expression as she turned to L. "I think I may have an idea. It's crazy, but it may work. Could you give me a couple of days to think it through? If it looks promising, then I could use your help."

"What is it?"

Ricki raised her hand, palm out. "No, it's a long shot. I don't want to get your hopes up or disappoint you. Let me flesh it out first. If it looks like it will work, I'll call you immediately. Deal?"

L stood. "Deal."

It didn't take Ricki two days to find the answer. It only took her two hours. She sat at her desk, staring at the solution she had been struggling to find these last few months. Only she wasn't happy at all.

She focused her eyes on the words on her computer screen, and all she could do was say, "No. O God, please no. Not this. Please, God, not this..."

Note from the Author

This is the second book in the Lazarus Chronicles trilogy. In the author notes at the end of *The Awakened*, the first book, I describe the unique way I was led to write this story. The encounter with ISIS that I write about in that note was such a life changing experience for me that it bears repeating here especially if you missed it in book one.

It was my work with the Kingdom is Near Ministries in 2014 that lead me to write *The Awakened*. That year I took a team with me to work at our school in the Philippines on the island of Mindanao. We were scheduled to teach at a jungle church on the southern tip of the island. Several days before we arrived, I received word that the pastor of that church had been kidnapped by a group flying the ISIS flag. If ISIS had waited less than a week, my team would have been kidnapped as well.

In an amazing story of God's intervention and protection, the pastor escaped and was picked up by our representative at the school. When we arrived, we provided funds to hide the pastor and his family (he had a wife and eight children, one of which was only three months old). While in the hands of ISIS, they took his cell phone which gave them the number of our school. They sent us death threats (to behead us in the standard ISIS form) because we were harboring the pastor and his family that had been targeted by ISIS.

That led me to want to write something about man's capability for acts of great evil as well as acts of amazing sacrifice. This is the theme of *The Awakened*. As you read it, you'll see the struggle within the characters as they try to deal with this dichotomy throughout the events in the story. I also wanted to write something that makes Jesus real - something that clearly points to him as the one who has already provided a way out of this conflict.

I also want to note that the bone church, site of a major conflict in the story, actually exists as described. The fight that led to many of the bones being scattered was, of course, fiction. Though I have never had the opportunity to visit the site, I'm told by many who have that it is a place for solemn contemplation. I would hope that no one would take the fictional encounter in this story as something to be done in such a sacred place.

I love to connect with readers—please check out the following sites to connect with me. If you enjoyed my book, I'd love if you'd leave a review on Amazon, ChristianBook.com, Goodreads, your blog or FaceBook, or tell your friends about it. Reviews help authors so much!

Web page: www.spillmanrichard.com

Author FB: Bit.ly/spillmanauthor

BookBub: spillmrj

Goodreads: Richard Spillman

Instagram: @spillman_author

Amazon author page: www.amazon.com/author/richardspillman

Book Discussion Questions

1 What character from THE ASCENSION do you like or admire the most? What features of his-her personality, attitudes or behavior attract you? What does this character make you think about? Feel? Want to do or not do?

2 What themes do you see in this novel? Do you see any of these themes playing out in the world today? In your life?

3 Each of L's team members serves God on earth in some way. Each of these characters struggle to one extent or another while carrying out their service. In what ways are you serving God now? Are you avoiding doing this service in any area of your life? What difficulties have you had while carrying out your service? How have you benefited from your work for God?

4 One underlying theme in this book is loss. L lost his family and friends, his way of life, his world. Joon lost his freedom and his family. How do the characters handle their losses? What gives them the strength to keep going? What losses have you experienced? How did these losses affect you and the people around you? What can you do to recover from or lessen the power of these losses?

5 The Awakened seek to help people on earth on many levels from the international to the interpersonal. What characters and situations demonstrate this breadth of work? Do you see God operating like this in the world today? Where? How? Do you think He is personally involved in your life? In what ways and with what effects?

6 How is Jesus depicted in this movel? What are some of his purposes? Strengths? Has your picture of Christ changed as a result of reading this novel? If so, in what ways?

7 The primary weapon of UDS is lies. People who believe in their lies are led to do things we know are wrong and harmful to others. What are some examples in this book? Where have you seen lies put forth as truth in the world today? How have they influenced your life? What lies have caused you to believe, feel, or behave in ways that are harmful to yourself and others? How can you learn to identify lies around you? Where do you search for truth?

8 Despite the work of the UDs, the Awakened live in a strong sense of hope for the future. What is their hope based on? Is it realistic? When you think about the world today, are you hopeful? Why or why not? Do you find any reason for hope in your personal life? Why or why not?

Now, A Sneak Peek at Book Three

The Atonement

Chapter One

August 6, 1945 Hiroshima 4:21 am, Report of Hayate Kazuki, Awakened Incident Manual, Pg. 791

I woke with a start. I lay in bed with my eyes open, my breathing shallow. My body was stiff as if I was paralyzed. *What happened?*

As I struggled to regain control of my breathing, I listened intently for any sound that might have woken me. I slowly sat up. The room was dark, the only source of light was the slight glow of the moon through the paper walls. I stood and tried to shake the fog of confusion out of my head.

Something was terribly wrong, but I couldn't pin down what it was. The last time I'd felt like this was seven months ago when I was murdered. I walked over to a small window. *Has it been seven months already?* I stared out the window, not really seeing anything of the scene outside. Instead, I was looking inside myself trying to make sense of the fear that was growing in my gut like a balloon inflating with every breath inside my stomach.

I'd awakened with this same feeling of dread last February. I'd shaken it off then went on with my day as if nothing was wrong. And I was right–until I walked home that night having forgotten all about the creepy feeling that had awakened me that morning. That is, until I crossed the path of a drunken sailor who had spent the day at a nearby bar blaming all Japanese Christians for Japan's recent string of costly military failures.

Someone must have pointed me out as one of those Christian traders. I shook my head. But before I knew it, someone or something had ambushed me from the side, pushing me into a nearby dark alley. A shiver ran up my spine as the memory of those dirty hands around my thoart played out in my mind. At first, I struggled to free myself from the ever-tightening grip. But near the end I struggled to gulp oxygen, a gulp of anything, really, to fill my empty lungs. Nothing came until everything went blank. There was no bright light, no darkness, no fire, no feeling of peace, no Jesus. Just—nothing.

I must have lain in that cursed alley for hours. But the truth is I really don't know how long I was there. After all, I was dead, stone cold dead. Then I was suddenly awake. Awake and feeling good, better than I had ever felt while I was alive.

I heard a voice that sounded distorted, almost like it was coming from a distance. It also had a slight echo, as if it was on the other end of a long tube. It was difficult to understand, but I think it was "wake up...wake up." I opened my eyes. Everything was kind of blurry, but it looked like I was in a small church. At least, the wall across from me was decorated with a cross and several pictures.

I squinted to try and force my eyes to focus. It didn't help. But I could make some things out. I appeared to be lying on a table. There was a man standing next to me. To my right was a raised platform with a few chairs. To my left there were three rows of about eight chairs. The wall behind those chairs had two windows covered in a thick layer of dust that filtered out most of the outdoor light. The place was a little dark and had a musty smell. Two men were sitting in the back row, staring at me. My attention turned to the man who was asking me to wake up. He was blurry as well, but as best I could tell, he was a short, somewhat over-weight, Japanese man. His hair was long, down to his shoulders and he had what appeared to be, a well-groomed beard.

I waved my hand in front of my face. "I'm awake...I'm awake."

"Welcome back. How's your vision?"

I blinked my eyes several times–apparently the right thing to do. "Fine, maybe even a little better than fine."

"Excellent. Well, then there's no reason for you to continue to lie down like that," The man put his hand behind my right shoulder and helped me sit up. "Now, how do you feel?"

I mentally scanned my body. Everything felt great. "Strong and at peace."

The man smiled and grabbed my hand for a gentle shake. "That's what I love to hear. I'm Ayumu Chiyo. I'm the one who brought you here. You were in bad shape, since you were dead and all. Anyway, I'm glad to meet you and your name is..."

"Hayate Kazuki."

Chiyo pumped his right fist through the air. "I knew it. I knew it."

I put my hands up in front of my chest. "You knew what?" I scanned the little church. "And where am I? What's all this stuff about me being dead?" I paused and shook my head. "Exactly what happened to me?"

Chiyo put his hand on my shoulder. "Let's start with that first question. Your first name, Kazuki, means 'one hope' which I interpret to mean that you were sent to us by our 'one hope,' Jesus Christ. Just as my last name, Ayumu means 'walking dream.' I have visions from time to time. Visions that I call my walking dreams. And I had one of those walking dreams two days ago. In it, I saw you lying dead in that alley. I stood over you as a voice said, "take him home and pray over him. He is a gift from the world's one hope." He spread his arms and with a big smile he said, "and see, everything happened exactly as I dreamed it."

He paused as if waiting for applause. I watched as his face went from joy to sadness. "I'm sorry, Kazuki. Sometimes I get carried away when I see God at work. You have a ton of questions. I will give you answers, because you have stepped into a new world, the real world, where there are powerful forces at work. Forces that hide in the shadows."

With that, Ayumu took me on a week-long journey. He told me about the Awakends, Normals, and UDs. He explained the role of Awakens in this world. A role which had become mine as well.

And that is how I came to be here today, standing outside my apartment in Hiroshima at 6:42 on the morning of August 6, 1945, feeling like something was very wrong. The last time I felt like this was the day I died, but as an Awakened, I can't die again. Does this mean someone else, maybe someone I know is going to die today?

People were up and the city was starting to stir. I decided to walk to the Industrial Products Display Hall near the center of the city. I didn't know what I was looking for, I guess something out of the ordinary.

Taking my time, I'm only half way there when the air raid alert goes off. I look up but see only one plane in the air. That can't be serious. It's probably mapping potential targets for a later attack. I check my watch. It's 8:15. I watch the plane drop a single bomb. *Nothing to worry about. If it were a serious attack it woud come in waves of American bombers dropping hundereds of bombs.*

I'm following the path of the plane over the city when I notice that everything is quiet. The entire city seemed to be blanketed with silence. I looked for the bomb the plane dropped. Before I can find it in the distance, there is a flash of light so intense that it burns into my eyes. The air was unbearably hot. I'm thrown at least fifty feet backwards into the crumbling wall of an office building. I lose conscienceness for at least a minute or two. When I wake up, I can feel my body repairing itself. I look around and the city I knew was gone. Almost nothing was left standing. Now I know why I felt uneasy this morning. I see death all around me. I feel death on my skin. I smell death. I hear the sounds of death.

I sat there for at least an hour, afraid to move. Afraid of what I will see. Lost in my thoughts, footsteps coming from the center of the city pulled me back. I stood and looked in the direction of the sound and, sure enough, a large man was walking toward me.

At first, I felt hopeful. *Someone survived.* But as he got close enough for me to see his eyes, they were dark wells of pure evil, I knew it was a UD. It was only the second UD I'd seen since I died and returned, but there was no mistaking it.

As it got closer, I could see the large smile. It stopped and spoke. "Hayate Kazuki I presume. I was wondering when we'd meet."

It knew my name! I stared at it, but I refused to talk to the vile creature.

"So, I'll get the silent treatment. That's all right, I'll go ahead and gloat anyway." It paused, looked back at the city, and took a deep breath. "Look at what mankind has accomplished here today. It surprises me. I didn't think they had it in them but, at least today, I think they've outdone me." It turned back to look at me with a grin. "Not really, but I have to admit, they've come close."

I showed no emotion. I continued to stare at it with a blank face.

"Well, you're not very fun, and I have more of the city to explore so I'll be on my way."

It started to walk away but stopped after a few steps and turned back to face me. "By the way, we are going to win. We have mankind on our side now."

I waited until it was out of sight. I sat down in the rubble, buried my head in my hands, and cried.

Made in the USA
Middletown, DE
01 July 2022